Prodigal Child

Prodigal Child

A Novel by
E. David Moulton

www.**MoominBooks**.com

Cover design by Curtis Killorn
First printing 2003

ISBN 0-9726693-4-5
LCCN 2002116283

ATTENTION CORPORATIONS, UNIVERSITIES, COLLEGES, AND PROFESSIONAL ORGANIZATIONS: Quantity discounts are available on bulk purchases of this book for educational, gift purposes, or as premiums for increasing magazine subscriptions or renewals. Special books or book excerpts can also be created to fit specific needs. For information, please contact Moomin Books, PO Box 81084, Charleston, SC 29416-1084; ph. 843-225-8885; www.MoominBooks.com.

Chapter 1

I LOOKED ACROSS AT THE young man sitting opposite; I decided I didn't like him. This troubled me. I saw myself as a decent person and it was my philosophy in life to be nonjudgmental. And here I didn't like someone I had met not five minutes ago when he knocked on the door of my hotel room.

I had spoken to him on the phone several times and we had set up the appointment, but this seemed a different person. I pictured him older, only to find he was in his mid-twenties. How can someone who has lived so little be objective about my life? Twelve, thirteen years ago as he was reaching puberty I had already had three successful careers and was considering another.

He opened a backpack and took out a tape recorder. What is it with this generation and their backpacks? Doesn't anyone carry a briefcase anymore? Here I was, being judgmental again; maybe here in New York City it's safer to have your personal belongings strapped to your back.

My guest sat the tape recorder in the center of the table and looked across at me. "I like to tape my interviews rather than take notes." He quickly added, "We can turn it off and take a break at any time—just let me know."

Maybe he sensed my uneasiness. It was not so much I didn't like him, I just didn't want to be doing this. A few years ago when I was an unknown songwriter I'd have given my left nut for an interview with *Rolling Stone* magazine, but now it was happening I didn't want to do it. To turn it down didn't make sense either. I was angry with myself for feeling this way.

My album had gone platinum, and I was getting air play nationwide. I was on a roll and it was obviously a good career move to do this interview. So what was the problem? I didn't know, just a gut feeling that I didn't need to put my life out there for the whole world to read about.

The young man pushed the record button and spoke. "Kevin Robinson, interviewing Eddie Conner for *Rolling Stone* magazine, New York City, July 16, 1994."

He leaned back in his chair and started the interview with, "Do you mind telling me how old you are?"

His question struck a nerve like a dentist drill hitting the bottom of a cavity.

"Jesus, what is this fucking preoccupation journalists have with people's age. Is this the most important thing about me, that it's the first thing you ask me? Let me ask how old are you? Twenty-five, twenty-six? Shit, I've got clothes in my closet older than you."

There was no reply; he sat there wide-eyed in stunned silence at my outburst. He reached over and turned off the tape recorder. I got up and walked to the window.

We were on the sixth floor overlooking Central Park. I looked at the people below enjoying this beautiful summer day and wished I were there with them. I knew I either had to end this interview right now or get my shit together and go through with it. I walked back to the table and sat down. It was Kevin who spoke first.

"I'm sorry, Mr. Conner. I meant no disrespect. I usually ask that question first just to get the ball rolling."

"You mean the stone rolling." I tried to inject a little humor to diffuse the situation, because now I was embarrassed. My effort either went completely over his head or he was afraid to laugh, so I continued. "No, I'm sorry, Kevin. It's just the whole age thing is a touchy subject with me; I quit celebrating birthdays a long time ago. I find to be constantly talking about one's age is to keep it in mind. That's how people become old by constantly thinking about it. Can we start again?"

Kevin smiled uneasily, reached over, and pressed the record button. Before he could speak I added, "I won't tell you exactly how old I am, but I will tell you this. I'm from that same fucked-up generation that gave you the Beatles and the Rolling Stones. I'm about the same age as those guys." Actually I was two or three years older than most of those guys, but I wasn't about to admit it here.

"But I'm younger than Willie Nelson," I added.

"Well, shit, everyone's younger than Willie." Kevin had relaxed some since my outburst. "So, Mr. Conner—"

"Call me Eddie, please."

"Eddie, here you are seemingly an overnight success and, by your own admission, from the sixties generation. I can't believe it's taken you this long to get where you are today. What's the story behind that?"

"I had some success in the music scene in London around the late 1950s and early 1960s before bands like the Stones even started. Maybe my timing was off, but instead of sticking with it I dropped out to pursue other things. By 1963 and 1964 when I see all these bands making it I felt I had missed the boat, so to speak. Years later I realized it's never too late and reentered the music scene."

Kevin commented, "But the Beatles and the Stones were only the first wave of the British Invasion. There were others that followed—like The Who and Led Zeppelin. You could have come back in at any time."

"Yes, in retrospect I could have done just that but who knew back then, we all thought it wouldn't last. If you watch those old interviews from the sixties with Paul McCartney and the other Beatles for example, none of them could imagine performing rock-n-roll at forty years old and beyond."

"So what happened? Why did you drop out from the music scene?"

"I didn't apply myself. I didn't take the music seriously at that time."

I was lying. I took the music very seriously but from 1960 to 1964 when my career should have been developing I was behind bars as a guest in one of Her Majesty's prisons in England. But I wasn't about to reveal that here for publication in *Rolling Stone*. I knew this was why I didn't want to do this interview. I had to lie, or at least gloss over the truth. I had agonized over this. Should I come clean and reveal my past?

Merle Haggard revealed he had been in prison as a young guy in his teens and twenties and it probably even helped his career, it certainly didn't harm it. With me it was different. I was a Brit, an alien with a Green Card, and to reveal a criminal past at this time might have repercussions that I would not want. Merle got a pardon from the Governor of California. The only way the Queen would utter the word "pardon" would be on burping after cucumber sandwiches at a Buckingham Palace Garden Party.

Kevin continued. "So when did you get back into music?"

"I started to write songs again in the eighties, but did nothing with them until friends encouraged me to start performing my own stuff. This started me thinking that I didn't fail because I had no talent, I just never applied it, and if there ever was any talent in me then it was still there. By the eighties, rock musicians like the Stones and singer-songwriters had gotten older, and all those other bands were still around so it was okay for someone like myself to be performing. Not that it mattered, this was what I wanted to do."

Kevin nodded. "So you were around the music scene in London when the Stones got their start? Did you know any of those guys?"

"No I was from Stepney, a working-class neighborhood in the East End of London. The Stones got their start in Richmond, which was an upper-class neighborhood in West London. And I had quit the music scene by 1961, when the Stones were only just starting."

Kevin asked, "Did the music you were doing in the East End of London differ from what bands like the Stones were doing in West London?"

"Yes, very much so. In England in the mid-fifties there was still somewhat of a class system in effect. Working-class kids generally didn't hang out with middle-class kids, and vice versa. When rock-n-roll burst on the scene in 1956 with Bill Hayley and the Comets and Elvis, it was like a breath of fresh air to us working-class kids. It was raw, it was primitive, and you could dance to it. The middle-class kids who considered themselves more sophisticated were into modern jazz and while some of them probably listened to rock-n-roll, if you were middle class, to admit you liked rock was not considered cool. I've read where Keith Richards was snubbed by some of his peers early on because he liked Chuck Berry."

"So when did this change?"

"Not until the Beatles. They were a rock-n-roll band pure and simple, and they were so good they couldn't be ignored. John Lennon was working class, so all of a sudden it was okay to be working class. But before that—around 1958—the middle-class kids had switched their allegiance from modern jazz to traditional jazz, New Orleans, and Dixieland style. Music that had been popular in America in the 1920s and 1930s. Like rock-n-roll, it was raw, primitive, and you could dance to it. An offshoot of this was that some middle-class kids got interested in the blues and were influenced by people like Robert Johnson and Muddy Waters."

"Who were your influences?"

"Elvis, of course. Gene Vincent, Little Richard, and Chuck Berry, who themselves had been influenced by Robert Johnson and Muddy Waters so we all ended up at the same place. The Rolling Stones started out as a blues band and became a rock band. I was into rock-n-roll as early as 1957 when there were few British rock bands."

Kevin nodded his understanding. "Earlier you referred to your generation as that 'fucked-up generation.' Why do you say this, and was your generation any more fucked up than the generations that followed?"

"Probably not, but we were fucked up for different reasons, mainly because our childhood was spent during World War II. It affected our parents so it affected us. I believe the reason all the great music that emerged from the UK in the sixties was because we spent our childhood during the war years."

"Why do you say that?"

"When you fuck with a child's mind, they often turn inward and use their imagination to escape. This imagination becomes creativity. The child may become a great artist or he may become a criminal. I see a thin line between the criminal, the insane mind, and the creative mind. Criminal activity can be creative, albeit negative creativity."

"Were you abused as a child?"

"Yes."

"By whom?"

"My father, but not just him, the British school system did its share also. They didn't call it abuse then; it was called corporal punishment. But legal or not the effect was the same. "

I was being pushed into revealing things I didn't even discuss with those closest to me, let alone a complete stranger, and a young stranger at that. I was feeling very uncomfortable. "I'd rather stay away from all the negative stuff. Can we talk about the music?"

Kevin nodded. "Of course. You had a number-one hit in Britain first, which got you noticed in the U.S. Tell me about that."

"Yes, I'd lived in the U.S. since the seventies and always wanted go back and tour England. It was like a healing thing."

"In what way?" Kevin asked.

Immediately I knew I had said the wrong thing. The truth was for years I had felt somewhat bitter toward my own country. Not the people, but the establishment. I felt I had been robbed of my chance of success in the early sixties, and not entirely through my own fault.

"Can we take a break?" I asked. "I need to take a leak."

Kevin stopped the tape. I went inside the bathroom and closed the door. I stood leaning on the vanity top, my arms spread. Head down, staring into the empty bowl, I talked to myself under my breath. "Damn, how can I make this story interesting and not tell the truth?"

That was the key—I had to make it interesting. The truth was interesting but I didn't want to reveal it. I looked up and studied my face in the mirror. This was like trying to peek at a snake in a pool cue case. "Fuck it. If the snake gets out there's not much I can do but hope the bastard doesn't turn around and bite me."

I didn't need to take a leak but I flushed the toilet for effect and returned to the table. "Now where were we?"

Kevin rewound the tape and the words "It was like a healing thing" came back to haunt me.

"That was not a good choice of words. What I meant to say was it was good to perform to the home crowd. I had had a little taste of the glory in the early sixties and wanted to relive that. An old friend in London had a recording studio and I went back there to record an independent album. To promote it we played around the London pubs and clubs.

"I was fortunate enough to get some press coverage, you know, 'exiled Brit comes home' type of thing and the name of our band Prodigal Child played right into that angle. Before I knew it the BBC wanted to do a TV special. After that the band took off and we went on a nationwide tour. A song called "When I Hear My Little Girl Cry," which I wrote about my daughter, went to number one."

I paused briefly, then Kevin and I spoke at the same time. He apologized and said, "Go on."

"I was just going to say that in England they don't have the country charts and so on, that are predominately made up of what adults are listening to. They basically have one top ten chart and you sometimes get this strange phenomenon called 'the Mom and Pop factor.' The British top ten reflects mostly what the kids are listening to, but sometimes you can get a song like mine, and the older generation will buy it and send it to number one. That's pretty much what happed here. The British top ten is published in the U.S. so people started to ask 'Who is this guy?' And the rest is history, as they say."

The interview went on into the late afternoon, and we mostly talked about the years from the 1980s on, which suited me. I had managed to peek at the snake without letting it out.

Chapter 2

I LOOKED AT THE BEDSIDE clock. 5 A.M.; I was wide awake. I'd had a restless night after the *Rolling Stone* interview the previous afternoon; so much of the past had been dragged up. Most of the night had been spent going over my life like old television reruns.

I thought about my father and how I swore so many times while he was alive that I would never cry over his passing. How a year ago when I got a phone call from my sister telling me that he had died, crying was the first thing I did. I forgave him his transgressions long ago, not that he ever asked for or expected forgiveness from me. Forgiveness is often more for the benefit of those sinned against than for the sinner.

I was too young to remember him before World War II and wondered during the night, what if he had been killed in the war? My mother no doubt would have told me wonderful stories about him, I would have photos of this handsome man, and he would have been my hero for the rest of my life. Would it have been any easier to mourn the loss of a father than to mourn what I never had? The father he could have been but wasn't?

My mother was a widow in her late thirties with a teenage son when she married my father. My father was Irish and much younger at twenty-five. He was unusual in that he was a Protestant from the south of Ireland, which is predominately Catholic.

He joined the British Army when he was eighteen and went to India, a British colony at that time. On his release from the army he was somewhat of an outcast in his own country. Being Protestant and ex–British Army, he immigrated to England. He became a stevedore, a laborer who loaded and unloaded ships in the docks in the East End of London.

Because my father had been a regular in the British Army, he was one of the first to go when the war started in 1939. He had told my mother,

"It's just a scare, I'll be home in a couple of weeks." That's got to go down as the understatement of the century. My mother was carrying my sister at the time and she was born three months after he left, so he never saw her as a baby.

He was part of Montgomery's 8th Army that fought Rommel's German army through North Africa. My sister Elizabeth was almost five years old when he returned. He came home briefly, then was a part of the Normandy Invasion in 1944 and didn't come back until the war ended the following year. He went through all this with not so much as a scratch. When so many others died, is it surprising I should wonder "what if"?

Eventually I came to the conclusion, that as bad as things had been at times, I wouldn't change a damn thing. We are all a product of what we've been through. I have seen sons of successful fathers who were more screwed up than I ever was.

I looked over at the clock again, now it was 5:15 A.M. It had rained during the night and the temperature had cooled a little. I had got up earlier, turned off the air conditioning, and opened the windows. I lay watching the window drapes blow in the wind, listening to the street noises below.

Garbage men were emptying dumpsters in the alleyway between the buildings. I could hear boom, boom, boom, as the mechanical arm lifted the dumpster and beat it against the top of the truck to shake loose every last bit of garbage. My mind went back to another time when I was only three years old.

Lying in my bed in my home in London, England, listening to German bombs drop in the distance, boom, boom, boom, when suddenly without warning a bomb fell in the next street behind us. There was a tremendous explosion and every window in back of the house was blown in.

My room was in the front of the house. The blast blew open the bedroom door and it slammed against my bed, which was right alongside the door. The next thing I remember was my mother snatching me up in her arms along with my sister, who was a baby about a year old at the time.

She rushed into the back bedroom where my stepbrother Alan had been blown out of bed and hit by flying glass. Although cut and bleeding he was conscious, so my mother took my sister and me all the way down to the cellar beneath the house. It was a coal cellar and as dark and dirty a place I'd ever been. My mother lit a candle, sat me on a cardboard box, and laid my baby sister across my lap.

"Hold on to Elizabeth and don't move. I have to get Alan."

I was terrified and would have followed her but the cardboard box had collapsed. My butt was stuck and with a baby lying across my lap I couldn't move.

I can't remember if I was crying, but my little sister was screaming. There would be a silence that seemed like an eternity while she replenished her lungs with air, then out would come this piercing scream and her little body went ramrod stiff and shook with the vibrato of her screaming.

I could hear my mother calling out as she came back down the cellar steps dragging a mattress. "We're coming, We're coming."

She dropped the mattress on the floor. Alan was with her, carrying blankets and pillows. Fortunately his wounds were not serious. My mother took Alan's pajama jacket and tore it into strips for makeshift bandages.

We spent the night huddled together listening to the bombs exploding around us. Luckily no more fell as close as the one that had sent us scurrying for cover like frightened rabbits in this cold, dark, damp hole in the ground.

It is unusual to have distinct memories as early as three years old, but I guess that particular night was so traumatic, they are as clear to me today as the events of a week ago.

A few days after the incident my stepbrother Alan joined the Royal Air Force. He was only sixteen at the time but like so many others, lied about his age and said he was eighteen. He told my mother he couldn't stand by and let the Germans drop bombs on us; he had to help stop them.

I have no other memories from that period of my life. It was soon after this incident my mother took us out of London to live with her sister Joyce in the countryside of rural southern England. It was in this somewhat idyllic setting most of my childhood memories were formed.

Aunt Joyce had one son, my cousin Roy, who was seven years older than me. Her husband Bert was in the Navy so he was away in the war the same as my father. We lived together in cramped conditions until my mother was able to rent a small cottage in the same village.

This was one of four tiny cottages joined together in a row, built at 90 degrees to the road with a single gate to serve all four houses. Ours was the second cottage. The front door, which was the only door to the outside, opened directly into a small living room that must have been about ten feet by ten feet.

A cast iron coal range served for both cooking and heating for the whole house. Behind the living room was an even smaller room, which we called the scullery. In the corner to the right was a pantry, and in the opposite left-hand corner was a steep narrow staircase leading to two equally small bedrooms above.

There was no electricity or running water in the house. Lighting was by oil lamp and candles; water was drawn in a bucket from a communal well at the roadside behind the house. On the end of the four houses were four coal sheds, and next to that four outhouses with bucket toilets.

There was a large garden divided into four plots, one for each house. Almost everyone grew vegetables; this was wartime and food was scarce but my mother made provision for a little patch of grass where I could play. There was also an apple tree with a swing suspended from a branch.

Next door to us in the first house lived Mr. and Mrs. Holmes and their daughter Lena. Mr. Holmes never spoke; my mother told me that he was "shell shocked" from World War I. Today we would say he suffered from battle fatigue or post-traumatic stress syndrome.

Our neighbors on the other side, in number three, were an elderly couple named Mr. and Mrs. Campbell. They had two cats, and it was old Mr. Campbell who taught me how to tell the time when I was young, before I started school.

In the last house, number four, lived the Flynn family, a widow with three young daughters, the eldest being my age. Mr. Flynn had been killed in the first year of the war.

And so it was in those early childhood memories, there was this thing called a war going on. I never really understood it, but felt its implications. I had a father, my mother told me so, but didn't know what it was like to have a father.

Soldiers were everywhere, training and playing at war games. We would find and collect spent brass rifle and machine gun shells along with the clips that originally held them together, then join them back together and wear them across our chest Mexican bandit style.

I was with a friend one hot summer day on the lawn outside his house. We heard gunfire from an airplane overhead. Looking up we saw a plane towing a target, rather like an advertising banner. A single Spitfire was diving in and shooting at this target. We watched, fascinated, when suddenly huge brass cannon shells started falling all around us. They bounced on the lawn at our feet, much larger than the rifle shells we usually found. They probably would have killed us instantly had they hit us on the head. With no sense of danger, we scrambled and fought with each other to be the first to gather these trophies.

They were still hot from firing and as quick as we picked them up, they burned our fingers and we dropped them. We started kicking them like some crazy football game until we eventually called a truce and decided to share the shell casings. I think we ended up with about three each.

Going to church on Sunday with my mother, I was exposed to wounded soldiers who had returned home from the war. They often wore a distinct light blue hospital uniform. Seeing one horribly disfigured man I remember asking, "Mummy, what's wrong with that man's face?"

She told me a German sniper had shot him. The shot had hit him from a high angle almost directly above him. The bullet entered his left eye, went diagonally through his face, and took out most of his lower jaw on the right side.

At one time it was feared poisonous gas might be used against us, so everyone was issued a gas mask. Someone came to our house one day to instruct us on how to use them. I was still quite young so I got what was called a Mickey Mouse mask. It was bright red and had a rubber tube-like nose at the front that made a farting noise when I breathed out.

My sister was still a baby and had a device where her whole upper body was placed inside and tied around her middle. There was a Plexiglass window in the top, and a hand pump on the side with which my mother had to pump air.

The whole thing was like some weird game to me. Looking like aliens from another planet, my mother with her mask on, pumping away at this black rubber tube with the muffled screams of my baby sister coming from inside, and me making little farting noises in the corner. Thank God we never had to use them for real.

The closest we ever came to being under attack was when a single German plane came over in daylight and dropped a bomb on a town about five miles from where we lived. He was aiming to take out the main railway line from Bristol in the west, to London. He completely missed the railway station and hit the school next to it. Luckily it was Saturday and the building was empty.

He was chased by the British Air Force and dropped the rest of his bombs harmlessly in open fields. The plane was eventually shot down and crashed in the hills nearby. The German pilot bailed out and was taken prisoner. My cousin Roy, who was about thirteen years old at the time, went with some of his friends to look at the wreck of this plane and came home with pieces of it as souvenirs.

Those early years were generally very happy for me in spite of a war. The best times were when Alan came home on leave. He would take me fishing and show me how to make model airplanes. He was a fighter pilot and quite a hero. He would tell me stories of enemy planes he had shot down.

One Christmas he took me to the woods, where he climbed a large pine tree and cut the top off. We brought it home and decorated it.

I started school at age five, going with Lena Holmes, the girl next door. Those first two years at school were great; my first teacher was Miss Thornton. She was a kind and loving elderly lady with gray hair, which she wore in a bun. She made learning fun.

After two years with Miss Thornton I moved up to the next class in the little two-room school. For two years I had no idea what horrors went on in that next room. My new teacher was Miss Jones, and unlike the kind and loving Miss Thornton, she was cruel and sadistic. I got the impression that she hated kids, especially boys. She kept an official school cane in her desk. These canes were thin bamboo sticks and were furnished to schools along with books, pencils, and other supplies.

Never in my years at school did I see a teacher use the cane as much as Miss Jones. One time she hit a kid so hard she broke the cane and immediately went back to her house, which adjoined the school, and got another. She told us, "I have a cupboard full of these."

She would single out me and three other boys for punishment anytime it suited her. If she left the room and the class was unruly when she returned, the four of us would have to go to the front of the classroom for two or three strokes of the cane across the palm of our hands, whether we had done wrong or not.

At first I would cry when I got the cane, but in time I became immune to it. I told myself it was only pain, and I could take it. I would stand with my arm straight, palms up, look her defiantly in the eye and not even wince, which of course pissed her off even more.

I would deliberately misbehave and give Miss Jones a hard time just to get back at her. My attitude was, if I was being punished for no reason, I might as well do something.

It was about this time that my whole world started to fall apart. I came home from school one day to find my mother crying. She showed me a telegram she had received saying Alan's plane had been shot down over the English Channel and he was missing, presumed dead. We cried together, then I became angry and said., "No, he's not dead, he's coming home."

But the days became weeks, and the weeks turned into months and Alan did not come home.

Chapter 3

IT WAS 1944, THE YEAR after my brother died, the year my father came home briefly. But before that there was the arrival of the American army prior to the invasion of France that year. The way those men, some of whom were still only boys themselves, treated us English kids was great. This is probably where my affinity with the United States began.

My first encounter with the U.S. Army was coming home from school one day with two of my friends. We were passed by truckload after truckload of American soldiers in convoy. It seemed there were hundreds of trucks one after the other without a break. They were traveling in the same direction as we were and in the two-mile walk from school there was not a break.

As each canvas top truck came by we saw smiling faces, men waving and calling out to us. My friend Freddie Brooks who was a year older than me and seemed to have more knowledge of current events, told me when I met an American I had to say, "Got any gum chum?" And they would give me chewing gum.

I had never tasted chewing gum before.

"You only chew it." Freddie told me "Don't swallow it or it will clog up your bum and you won't be able to shit."

"What do you do with it if you can't swallow it?" I asked.

"Well, you chew it all day long, and when you go to bed you stick it on the bedpost so you can chew it again the next day."

It sounded wonderful to me and I couldn't wait to try chewing gum.

More trucks came by, this time the smiling faces were black. I had never seen a black man before.

"The white soldiers don't like the black soldiers," Freddie told me.

"Why not?"

"I don't know, they just don't."

"Well, I like them," I said, returning their waves.

When I arrived home I had a dilemma. How could I cross the road to my home, with all these trucks coming by? There were no breaks. Freddie and my other friend were okay, they lived on the opposite side to me. When I got to my house I could see my mother standing at the garden gate. She called across to me between the trucks roaring by, "Don't cross yet!"

I saw her step carefully out onto the narrow road and hold up her hand. Just then a jeep came by with white-helmeted military police on board. They saw my mother and held up their hands to stop the convoy.

"Come across now!" my mother called and I ran to her.

The policeman tipped his white helmet to acknowledge my mother's thank you, and the convoy moved on.

"Mummy, Mummy, I saw some black men. Freddie told me the white soldiers don't like the black soldiers. Why is that, Mummy?"

"I don't know," my mother answered.

"But aren't they all here to fight the Germans?" I said. "You would think if they're all on the same side they would like each other."

"You would think so," my mother said in agreement.

In the days that followed I thought a lot about the black soldiers. When Freddie Brooks came to me that weekend and said he knew where the American camp was, I said, "Let's go see the black men."

The camp was in the next village about three miles away; Freddie and I walked there. When we arrived we squeezed through a gap in the hedgerow and came across rows of wooden huts with corrugated tin roofs. I walked in through the open door of one hut; inside were rows of double bunk beds. A young fair-haired man greeted me.

"Hey kid, what are you doing here?" he asked.

"I've come to see the black men"

"There are no black men here. Why would you want to see a black man?"

"Because I've never seen one up close."

The young man laughed and called further down the hut to another man, "Hey, there's a kid here who has never seen a black man."

"Well, damn, I guess he's lucky. I've seen too many in my life."

As he spoke he walked down the hut toward me and pointed to another young man seated alone under a tree some yards from the hut. "There's the nearest thing you'll find to a black man around here. He's an Indian, his name is Running Horse."

I looked at the young man under the tree, he was dark skinned and had close-cropped black hair. I walked over to where he was sitting, "Hello, is your name Running Horse?"

The young man looked up and smiled. "Yep, that's what they call me."

"That's a funny name."

"You think so?"

"Oh, I meant funny peculiar, not funny ha ha."

The young man laughed. "So, kid, what's your name?"

"My name is Eddie. My real name is Edward, but everyone calls me Eddie."

"Well, hi, Eddie, I'm very pleased to meet you." He reached out and shook my hand.

"That man over there said you were an Indian. Is that right, a real Indian like in cowboys and Indians?"

He laughed again. "Yes, Eddie I'm an Navajo Indian or Native American, and yes like cowboys and Indians but around here there's way more cowboys than Indians."

I looked around. "I don't see any cowboys"

"Oh, they are here, they're just not wearing their hats, but they're here."

Running Horse was carving a piece of wood with the most beautiful knife I had ever seen. It had a deer antler handle and a large blade about six inches long.

"Can I see your knife?" I asked.

It was a lock-back knife and he pushed in the lever and folded the blade before handing it to me. It felt heavy in my hand.

"How do you open it?" I asked.

"It's very, very sharp, so it's best you don't open it."

"Where did you get it?"

"This knife is very special; my father made it."

"My father's in the war," I said as I handed back the knife. "What are you making?"

Running Horse held up the piece of wood he was carving. "What does it look like?"

"It looks like a bird with its wings open."

"That's exactly what it is; it's an eagle."

"What will you do with the eagle when it's finished?"

"Maybe I'll sell it to a cowboy." We both laughed.

I suddenly remembered I still hadn't seen any black men. "Where are the black soldiers?" I asked.

"They're not at our camp; they have their own camp."

"I heard the white soldiers don't like the black soldiers, is that true?"

"Some of them don't."

"Why not?"

"Well, Eddie, how can I explain it so you will understand? My father told me a story when I was about your age.

"A man was out hunting one day when he saw a dark figure approaching in the distance. It was too far off to see if it was a man or a wild beast. Maybe it was a bear, so he was afraid. Then as the figure came closer he saw it was a man, but he was still afraid because he didn't know if it was a friend or an enemy. Then when the man got closer he saw it was his brother.

"So, Eddie, maybe the white man is not close enough to see the black man as he really is, that's why he doesn't like him."

I didn't fully understand the meaning but the story was good and would stay with me.

"Say, Eddie, I like to go fishing, is there anywhere around here I could catch fish?"

"Yes, I know a place; my brother used to take me. I'll show you where it is. Do you have a fishing rod?"

"No, but I could make one."

"You can borrow my brother's fishing rod."

"Would your brother mind?"

"My brother is dead; he was killed in the war." I felt a lump come to my throat as I realized this was the first time I had said the words "my brother is dead." I had finally accepted that he was not coming home.

Running Horse reached out and touched my shoulder. "I'm so sorry, Eddie."

"That's all right," I said, fighting back the tears. "Do you still want to go fishing?"

"I would love to, but we have to clear it with your mother first."

"We can go now. We have to go past my house to get to the river, so we can pick up the fishing rod and ask my mother at the same time."

"Okay. It's Saturday, so I'm free today. I have to tell my sergeant where I'm going, but that won't take a moment."

My new friend walked to the hut I was in earlier and came out seconds later. "Let's go catch some fish. You lead the way."

I ran ahead, out through the same gap in the hedgerow I had used when I entered the camp and on to the narrow country road on the other side. "This way," I called back as Running Horse strode out and was soon by my side. We had gone about a mile when I suddenly remembered

Freddie Brooks. We had separated the moment we arrived at the camp. I stopped.

"I forgot my friend Freddie."

"Do we need to go back?"

I thought for a moment. "Nah, he knows his way home."

We covered the three miles to my house in very short time; I opened the garden gate and ran ahead into the house. Running Horse waited outside.

My mother was ironing at the kitchen table.

"Mummy, Mummy, Freddie and me went to the American camp. We didn't see any black men but I met an Indian, you know like cowboys and Indians, his name is Running Horse and we want to go fishing. Can we please, please, Mummy?"

My mother stopped ironing, her eyes open big and wide. "Now slow down, and tell me that one more time. You did what?"

I grabbed my mother by the hand and dragged her to the door. "Mummy, this is Running Horse."

There was silence for a moment as my mother stared at the young man standing before her in his army uniform. "Good morning, ma'am, your son offered to show me where I could catch fish, and I said we must clear it with you first."

More silence, then my mother stammered, "Yes, why don't you come in for a moment and have a cup of tea?"

In any situation where the English are not sure what to do they offer you a cup of tea. And so it was, we found ourselves inside the house. My mother quickly cleared the ironing from the table, and we sat down. As always there was a large iron kettle of water permanently simmering on the coal stove, so tea was quickly made and homemade cake was brought out too.

"So you want to go fishing. Well, I suppose that's all right. Actually Eddie hasn't been fishing since his brother was—" My mother's voice trailed off.

"Eddie told me about your other son. I'm very sorry, ma'am."

"Thank you. Might I ask how old are you?"

"I'm twenty, ma'am. I'll be twenty-one at the end of this year."

"Alan would have been twenty this year." She paused shaking her head. "My God you're all so very young."

I looked up and could see her eyes were beginning to fill with tears, as she must have been comparing this young soldier with Alan. I got up from my chair and stood beside her to give her a hug. I hated to see her cry. She hugged me back and reached out to hold the hand of my new friend.

"Why don't you boys finish up your tea and cake, and go fishing? Otherwise the day will be over," she said as she got up and left the room.

Chapter 4

THE YOUNG NAVAJO INDIAN BECAME a good friend to me, that spring of 1944. There was a beautiful spot near my home where the river ran through woodland, and we went fishing there on numerous occasions. We would catch good size rainbow trout. Running Horse would show me how to turn over rocks and find worms for bait, or he would cut open rotting wood with his large folding knife and find larvae.

Sometimes he would bring bread with him and we would light a fire and cook the fish on a wooden spit. He taught me to thank the fish for feeding us and to never take more than we needed. The small fish he would always let go and talk to them, saying something like, "On your way, little one; we will meet again one day."

When we turned over rocks to find worms, he would explain to me the importance of putting the rock back as we had found it so the worms would still have a place to live. We always cleared a large area around our cooking fire, so there was no danger of the fire spreading. After, we made sure the fire was out and everything put back as we found it.

He made me aware of nature in a way I had never thought about before. Fishing had always been fun, but now it was an adventure. Running Horse was like a big brother to me. I don't think I realized it at the time, maybe he became a replacement for my brother Alan. Any excuse I could find, I would go see him.

One day I was playing at home with some toy lead soldiers. I came across a horse that originally had a rider. I had left it lying on the floor and my mother accidentally stepped on it and broke the rider off the horse's back. The horse still had the rider's legs either side of its body, the rest of the rider was missing above the horse's back. I looked at it; it was a running horse.

I put the horse in my coat pocket and headed over to the American camp. I found Running Horse sitting alone as he invariably was under the same tree some fifty yards from his hut, where he had been that first day I met him. He looked up and smiled as I approached. "Hi, Eddie, what are you up to?"

"I have something for you." I said holding out my hand with my fingers still clutched tightly around the lead horse to delay the moment of surprise.

"What is it?"

I opened my hand. "It's a running horse."

"Well I'll be—so it is. Is this for me?"

There is no pleasure greater as a child than to give someone you care for a gift and have them show appreciation. Even though we realize as an adult that the appreciation was probably exaggerated to suit the occasion.

"Thank you, Eddie, that's one of the nicest gifts I've ever had."

I pointed out the ex-rider's legs still attached to the sides of the horse, fearful that he might be disappointed should he discover them later.

"The horse had a rider at one time, but the rider got broken off. See, there's his legs."

"I can see that. That's okay; that makes it even more special. I'm going to keep this with me always." He put the lead horse in his shirt pocket. "Thank you again, Eddie."

"Why do you always sit here alone under this tree?" I asked. "Don't you have any friends?"

"Yes, I have friends, but I don't always care to do the same things they do. Let me tell you, Eddie, you can be alone without being lonely. This tree is my friend."

"You can't talk to a tree."

"Sure you can; it can't talk back but it knows you're talking to it. This tree is a living thing and although it has no brain like you and I, it has consciousness, it is conscious of you and me sitting under it, and is conscious of the birds and the squirrels that sit in its branches."

Just then a crow landed close by. "There's another of my friends. I swear that's the same old black crow that used to visit me back home. So, Eddie, always remember you are not alone just because there are no other people around."

Running Horse was still working on the eagle he was carving from a piece of wood; it was almost finished.

"I wish I could make something like that; would you show me how?"

"I do not need to show you how; the Spirit will show you if you just let it."

"Where is the Spirit?"

"It's in here, it's in you too." Running Horse first put his hand on his chest and then pointed to my chest. "You can't see the Spirit but it's in us, it's in the animals. See that bird's nest in the tree over there?" He pointed to a tree some two hundred yards away. It was early spring and the tree was still without leaves. High in its branches was a bird's nest from the year before.

"A bird built that nest, but how did it learn to build a nest? Another bird didn't teach it. No, the Spirit showed the bird how. That same Spirit will show you how. When you want to make something or draw a picture, don't think with your head but let the Spirit inside you guide your hand. The Native American calls this Hand Magic."

I listened intently to Running Horse. "So, did the bird build the nest or was it the Spirit?" I asked.

"The Spirit is the source of all creation. Sometimes it creates through a bird, sometimes through us." Running Horse stood and brushed the seat of his pants. "Hey, you hungry, Eddie? Let's go over to the mess hut and find us a sandwich."

The mess hut was a short distance away. From the outside it looked like all the other huts but inside it consisted of a large dining hall, with a kitchen at the far end. There was a center aisle with rows of plain wooden tables with bench seating on both sides. A few small groups of men were scattered throughout the large room. Someone called out as we walked back toward the kitchen.

"Hey, Running Horse, who's your buddy?"

We took a detour over to man who had spoken; he was dressed in a white cook's apron and was seated with two other men.

"Carlos, this is my friend Eddie. Eddie, this is Carlos."

Carlos reached out and shook my hand,

"Glad to know you, Eddie." He was dark-skinned with black hair very much like Running Horse's.

"Are you an American Indian too?" I asked. Carlos laughed.

"No. Running Horse is the only Indian around here. Me paleface." The whole group laughed.

"Well you don't look like a cowboy."

"No, I'm not a cowboy either."

He turned to the man seated next to him. "Now Chuck here, he's a cowboy, he's from Texas."

"Is that right? Do you have a horse?"

"Yes, but they wouldn't let me bring it with me."

There was more laughter from the group. The third man spoke. "Say, Eddie, do you have an older sister?"

"No, he doesn't have an older sister." It was Running Horse who spoke this time. "Hey Carlos, can you make us a sandwich?"

"Sure, what will it be?"

"How about ham and Swiss on rye? What would you like, Eddie?"

"Can I have a cheese sandwich?"

"A cheese sandwich? We can do better than that. Make it two ham and Swiss."

"Coming right up," Carlos said as he left the table and disappeared into the kitchen. Running Horse pulled the lead horse from his shirt pocket.

"Look what Eddie gave me. It's a running horse." He handed it to Chuck.

"It used to have a rider but he got broken off," I explained. Chuck handed back the horse.

"So now we'll have to call you Running Horse with Broken Rider. Hey, that sound's pretty good; it's got a kind of poetic charm.

"You wouldn't know poetic charm if it jumped up and bit your ass," Running Horse said as he put the lead horse back in his shirt pocket.

Carlos came back with the sandwiches; they were the best I'd ever tasted. While we were eating Carlos went back in the kitchen and came out with a cardboard box full of food. There was canned ham, canned fruit, butter, and sugar.

"Here, Eddie, take this home to your mother. I know your food is rationed; maybe this will help out."

I thanked him for the box of food and the sandwich and we said our goodbyes. Running Horse took the box from me.

"Here I'd better walk you home and carry this for you."

We arrived at my home and I invited Running Horse inside. He set the box of food on the table. My mother came out from the back scullery to greet us.

"Mummy, we have some food that Carlos gave us."

Running Horse explained about his friend Carlos who worked in the kitchen. My mother looked inside the box, picking out the cans of fruit.

"Thank you, I'm most grateful, this will really help out. Why don't you come to dinner next Sunday? Bring Carlos if you wish."

"Thank you, ma'am, I'd like that very much. I'll have to see if Carlos and I can get off."

But that Sunday dinner never came to be, because the following week my father came home after being away for four years and eight months.

It was a rainy day, so I was playing indoors with wooden building blocks. I had the whole kitchen table covered with a large castle I was building for my lead soldiers. My mother was sitting in an armchair with my sister, who was four years old now, reading her a book.

Suddenly the door burst open and in came this rough, dirty, unshaven man in army uniform and dumped the many kit bags he was carrying on the table, scattering wooden blocks and lead soldiers everywhere. My mother jumped to her feet, sat my sister in the armchair, and rushed to his arms.

My sister started crying, obviously scared. I just stood there with my mouth open. I instinctively knew this was my father but didn't know what to make of the situation. What I can remember is, he was complaining.

After being away from home for almost five years, was he happy? No. He was pissing and moaning about something or other, which I came to learn was pretty typical of the man. I don't know what the problem was—maybe we were supposed to meet him at the train station. It appeared he had written a letter that my mother had not received, and she had no idea he was coming home. Eventually he stopped complaining and his homecoming turned into a somewhat joyous occasion.

The next few weeks were confusing for me. I never knew how I was supposed to act toward my father. He rarely spoke to me and we never did anything together. He only ate and slept at home; the rest of the time he was at the local pub, drinking.

Weekdays I was at school, so he was in bed when I left. I would see him briefly when I got home before he went to the pub for the evening. Soon I learned it was best to not go home straight from school. I would go play with my friends, or go over to the American camp. My mother had told me not to bring Running Horse home.

"Your father won't understand," she had said, and was she ever right about that.

I tried to tell him one day about my special friend. I missed going fishing, and I had really been looking forward to Running Horse coming to dinner before my father came home. My father called my mother into the room.

"What the hell is this boy talking about? Something about a running horse."

My mother tried to explain. "Eddie has this friend over at the American army camp, he's a Native American named Running Horse. They go fishing together. He's the same age Alan would have been."

"Well, I don't like the sound of this, " my father said.

"Maybe if I brought him over here so you could meet him…" I looked up at my mother standing behind my father; she was shaking her head. The message was clear. Stay quiet, let it be. She knew he was a bigot. I had not grasped that concept yet.

The following Sunday my mother, my sister, and I had just got back from church. My father had been drinking at the local pub as usual and had gotten home early. He was waiting for us. He was very drunk and very angry. As we walked into the house he slapped my mother hard across the face.

"There's talk in the village that you've had a black man 'round here. Is that true, you got yourself a nigger lover?" He slapped her again.

My sister was crying and clinging to my mother's legs. My mother bent down to pick her up. "That's not true. We told you about Eddie's friend. For God's sake, he just a boy, twenty years old."

"You didn't tell me he was black."

"He's not black, he's a Native American."

I rushed to my father. "Daddy, stop."

He picked me up bodily and threw me against the wall. "Get away from me. You'd protect your mother by pretending he's your friend."

"But he is my friend!" I ran from the house. I had to go over to the American camp and get Running Horse. I felt that if my father saw him everything would be all right. I ran all the way there and found him.

"You have to come with me. My father is hitting my mother because he thinks you're her friend. I told him you're my friend, but he won't believe me."

"Well, I don't know about that—if your mother and father are fighting, I really shouldn't get involved."

"But please, you must."

Running Horse looked at my face. I had a large bruise on the side of my face where my father had thrown me against the wall. "Did he do that?" I nodded.

"Okay. I'll see if I can help."

In the time it had taken me to get to the camp and for us to get back, things had calmed down a little. There was no sound coming from the house as I walked in. "Daddy, I brought Running Horse."

That was all I was able to get from my mouth before my father leapt from his chair. Pushing me aside he rushed out through the front door and punched Running Horse square on the jaw, knocking him over backward. He pulled the dazed young man to his feet and began beating him unmercifully.

Running Horse tried to defend himself but the twenty-year-old was no match for my father, a thirty-four-year-old hardened war veteran. What I couldn't understand was that my father had a dark complexion and black hair, and after being in North Africa was deeply suntanned. He was the same color as Running Horse and yet he was calling him a black man.

The neighbors came out to see what the commotion was about. I rushed in and tried to drag my father from my friend, my mother tried to protect me and was slapped again. It was Mr. Holmes, the World War I veteran who I had never heard speak before, who stepped in to stop the melee.

Mr. Holmes was a big man, and he spoke softly as he pulled my father from the battered and bleeding Running Horse. "Now, Ted, that's enough."

"But this young bastard has been screwing my wife."

"Ted, that's not true. This young man is Eddie's friend, I've seen them go fishing together. Don't forget Eddie lost his brother, that's hard for a boy."

"Well, his brother was no good either," my father retorted.

Anger flashed across Mr. Holmes' face. His huge hand clamped my father's face like a vise as he slammed his head against the house. "Your son was a hero who died for his country; don't you ever say he was no good." He released the grip.

"He was her son, not mine," was all my father could say as he stumbled back into the house.

My mother turned to Running Horse. "I'm so sorry, I don't know what to say."

"It's not your fault, ma'am."

Mr. Holmes stepped up again. "I'll take care of him. Come with me, son." I started to go with them.

My mother stopped me. "Eddie, you come with me."

In the house that night all was quiet. My father knew he was wrong but he was not the kind of man to admit it or to ever say he was sorry. He told me, "You're not to go to that American camp again, do you hear?"

"Yes." I was smart enough not to argue with him. I did, however, disobey him and went a few days later after school. I had to see if Running Horse was all right. I found him, he was pretty badly cut and bruised.

Before I could speak he said, "Eddie, don't say anything, it's not your fault, it's no one's fault—not even your father's. It's this damn war. Try to understand what your father has been through."

"But my father says I can't see you again." I started to cry. Running Horse put his arm around my shoulder.

"I know, but you must do as he tells you, he is your father and pretty soon I'm going to be leaving here anyway. We have to go fight a war. Just remember what I told you about never being alone, you don't need other people. You don't even need me, you always have yourself, be your own best friend."

His words were of little comfort as I walked slowly home that evening or in the weeks that followed as I tried to figure out what was happening.

I came home from school one day and I could see my mother had been crying. "Your father's gone; he had to go back to the war."

The words meant only one thing to me: I could see Running Horse. I ran from the house. I could hear my mother calling me to come back but there was no stopping me.

I ran all the way to the American camp and through the gap in the hedgerow. The first place I looked was under the tree where Running Horse always sat. He was not there. I ran to his hut. It was empty. The whole camp was empty. It was the first week of June 1944. The invasion had started.

Chapter 5

WARTIME BROUGHT MANY SUDDEN, dramatic changes into everyone's life. I never knew what it was like to have a father, then suddenly I had a father, and just as quickly my father was gone again.

There were American soldiers everywhere and army vehicles on the road—large trucks, jeeps, and even tanks. They appeared one day as if out of nowhere. We became used to them being around, then almost overnight they were gone.

I had lost my brother Alan and it hurt terribly; then I found a surrogate brother in the form of a young Native American and now he was gone. The hurt was there but not as bad as the time Alan died. I knew I would never see Running Horse again, just as I would never see Alan again, but I was over the loss more quickly this time.

Was I getting used to these sudden changes? Was I becoming immune to the hurt or was it that Running Horse had instilled in me that it was all right to be alone? That my happiness did not have to depend on others.

I was beginning to realize it was other people who caused most of the pain in my life. My teacher Miss Jones, my father, and even my friend Freddie Brooks, who was older and bigger than me and could be a bully at times.

The weeks passed and soon it was summer and there was the long break from school. I would go fishing alone and would go though all the things I had done with Running Horse. Find bait, catch a fish, light a fire, and cook the fish—even thank the fish for feeding me as he had done. It was like my special friend was still with me; I felt his spirit was there, in the trees, in the animals and birds around me.

I had a favorite tree I would climb to the top of and look out over the canopy of this large woodland area. Up there I was in a different world. I imagined I could walk out on the treetops like it was some rich green landscape. This was my own private kingdom where I ruled and other people were not allowed. If I sat still and quiet, birds and squirrels would come close to me, and I would remember what Running Horse had told me about the tree being conscious of myself and the birds and squirrels on its branches. This tree was my friend, as was the whole woodland. They didn't cause pain, like people. Here I felt nothing but contentment and pleasure.

One rainy day I was indoors drawing a picture, and I remembered what Running Horse had told me about the Spirit of Creativity. I tried not to concentrate too much on what I was doing, but to let the Spirit guide my hand. I drew a picture of Running Horse and myself sitting under the tree at the American camp. I showed my mother.

"Eddie, that is remarkable," she said. "You have so much talent. I can see that is Running Horse."

It would soon be time to go back to school and I couldn't wait to show off the picture I had drawn. My first day back I showed the picture to Miss Jones.

"You little liar," she said with disdain. "You did not draw this picture. An adult drew it." She tore up my picture and threw it in the trash. Reality hit like it had fallen from the sky and landed on my head. But maybe she was right—I did not draw the picture. Spirit had drawn the picture through me and maybe I was wrong to take credit.

Time passed and before I knew it we were into winter. Winter brought different things to do. Snowmen and sleds to build. Leather boots would get soaked and then freeze, as did hand-knitted woolen gloves. Rubber boots kept your feet dry but were poor insulation against the cold. I would stay out in the snow and play until my fingers and toes were so cold that I could stand it no more and I would have to go home. Thawing out in front of the fire was a painful process if it was done too quickly.

The year ended and the war was drawing to a close. I was aware of this because my mother showed me the newspaper each day and explained what was going on. There were maps of Europe with arrows showing the advancement of the Allied forces, and with Russia pushing from the east it was clear the days were numbered for Hitler and his army.

One sunny spring day in May 1945 I came home from school and my mother greeted me at the door. "It's over, the war is over," she sad. "The Germans have surrendered."

Just as I never fully understood the war, I didn't fully understand what it meant for the war to be over.

"Your father will be home soon, this time for good."

I could see my mother was happy, so that made me happy, and in spite of the bad experiences the last time my father was home, I was still excited at the prospect of seeing him again.

With the war over, one of the first things we did was to go visit my grandmother, who lived on the south coast of England near Folkstone. There had been travel restrictions during the war, so my mother had not seen her mother in over five years. I was too young to remember my grandmother before the war and she had never seen my sister as she was born after the war started.

We traveled by train to London, and then on to the south coast. It was my first trip on a train. This was the steam engine era, so for a young boy it was pretty exiting. I had seen trains from a distance, but to be standing on the station platform when this huge iron and steel monster come roaring in with whistle blowing and smoke and steam billowing everywhere was both exiting and intimidating.

Up until this time the farthest I had traveled was the occasional bus trip into a nearby town to shop, but now I was seeing places I had never seen before. When the trip started we traveled through open country with farms and animals in the fields, much like where I lived. Then we would come to a town and the train would pull into a station and there was the sound of carriage doors being opened and slamming shut again. People getting off and hurrying to their destination, other people hurrying to get on. As we approached London the fields and open country gave way to more and more houses and buildings.

"This is London," my mother told me. "This is where we lived before the war."

We reached an elevated section of track and I looked out over the endless, random patchwork of rooftops.

"It's big." I said. "Which house was ours?"

My mother smiled. "We lived a long way from here. This is the West London; we lived in the East End of London, near the River Thames. Your father worked on the docks, loading and unloading the big ships that came in there."

"Will Daddy work there again when he comes home?"

"Maybe. That will be up to him."

"So we might live in London again?"

"We'll have to wait and see. Let's get Daddy home first."

The prospect of living in the big city seemed exiting and I smiled to myself as I kept my nose to the carriage window.

On arrival at the terminal station in London we took a short bus ride to another station where we boarded a train for the south coast. We arrived at my grandmother's house that evening.

My grandmother seemed like an older version of my mother, there was a strong family resemblance. She had gray hair, worn in a bun at the back of her head. She hugged first my mother and then my sister and me. Tears were steaming down her face.

"Why are you crying, Grandma?" I asked

"I'm so pleased to see you. My what a big boy you are! You were still a baby when I saw you last, you probably don't even remember me." She hugged me so hard I thought my bones would break, but it felt good. I didn't remember her, but I felt that family bond that made it as if I had always known her.

The little house she lived in was about the same size and layout as our cottage. Just two rooms downstairs and two bedrooms above. The only difference was her stairs led straight up from the front door, with the living room to the right. There was also plumbing, gas for cooking, and electric light—unlike our rural cottage, which had none of these.

After eating we went to bed, tired after the long and exciting day. I had my own little bed in the back bedroom, and my mother and sister shared a big bed in the same room.

The following morning it was a clear, sunny day and after breakfast my mother said, "Let's go look at the sea."

I had never seen the sea and as for all children there is something magical about seeing the ocean for the first time—even though this was technically the English Channel and not the ocean. We took the short walk up the street outside my grandmother's house, which led directly to the seafront. We could not go on the beach because it was still mined as a wartime defense and was blocked by barbed wire entanglements. This was only weeks after the war had ended, but just to see such a large expanse of water and the waves breaking on the shore was still a thrill for me.

We walked along the seafront and I could see some of the buildings were damaged. My mother explained that during the war the Germans had some big guns that could fire shells across the English Channel. Several of the seafront hotels had been hit, and decoy buildings, which were nothing more than a plywood front painted to look like a hotel, had replaced them. The real hotel buildings were painted camouflage.

My mother pointed out the white cliffs on the horizon. "That's France you can see over there, a little over twenty-five miles away. This little strip of water between France and us was all that stopped us from being invaded. That and our Air Force and the bravery of pilots like your brother Alan."

Her voice cracked and I could tell she was crying. I realized as she did that Alan was somewhere out there in the English Channel. This was his final resting place, he had never been found.

"Don't cry, Mummy," I said giving her a hug.

"Don't cry, Mummy," my little sister echoed although I'm sure she had no idea what was going on.

The visit with my grandmother was a short one, and in a few days, we were on the train headed back. We arrived in London and instead of going straight to the other train station, my mother said, "I want to take you to where we used to live."

We went down some steps to the underground station. She told me, "During the war when the bombing was going on, the people slept down here at night."

"I remember the bombing," I said.

"Oh, I'm sure you don't, you were only three years old."

We emerged from the underground having reached our destination and walked a short distance to an area that had been completely destroyed by bomb damage. The streets and sidewalks had been swept clean and the bricks and mortar that were once houses pushed back into piles of rubble. My mother stopped.

"This is where we lived." She hesitated, then moved a few yards down the street. "No wait, this is where the house was. It was the third house from the corner, see here are the covers to the coal cellars, one, two, three from the corner."

She pointed to the round cast iron manhole covers in the sidewalk. "This is where they used to empty the coal into the cellar."

"That's where we went when the bombing was going on," I said.

A look of astonishment came over my mother's face. "My God, you do remember."

"Yes, you sat me on a cardboard box and put Elizabeth on my lap while you went back upstairs to get Alan. I told you I remembered."

"That's amazing, you were only three and a half years old, I didn't think you could possibly remember. I'm sorry I doubted you"

"I don't remember," my sister said. She was five now and becoming very observant of everything going on.

I looked around at the flattened houses. "If we come back to London, where will we live?"

"We will have to rent another house.."

I looked around at the rubble as we walked away. "It's a good thing we moved." My mother agreed.

Chapter 6

MY FATHER'S RETURN FROM THE war in Europe was déja vu. I was playing indoors, just as I had been when he returned home the previous year. Suddenly the door burst open and in came my father, dumping all his kit bags on the kitchen table. I had no idea he was coming home; if my mother knew, she hadn't told me.

One always has a picture in their mind of a soldier in uniform being of somewhat immaculate appearance. Neatly pressed uniform, polished boots, and so forth, but in wartime anything goes. A soldier on the front line is not going to be put on a charge for having dirty boots or a button missing. My father looked as if he hadn't washed for at least a week. He was unshaven, his steel helmet had a large dent in it, and he was wearing a ragged and torn leather sheepskin jacket he said he took from a dead German.

"The winter was damn cold over there, so I reckoned I needed it more than him," was his comment.

My father soon fell back into his routine of lying in bed until late morning and then leaving the house to go to the pub. When my father awoke, he wanted a cup of tea. Weekends or at any time I was off school, my mother sent me upstairs with his morning tea and the newspaper or anything else that he needed.

When my father was home there was a stench of urine and stale to-bacco smoke in the bedroom. Because there was no indoor plumbing, there was a white enamel bucket in the bedroom. The sight and smell of that bucket full of urine with cigarette butts floating in it is a revolting memory for me to this day, and probably the reason why I never took up smoking in an era when everyone smoked.

He would always wait until it was filled almost to the top, then he would tell me to take it and empty it. Urine would splash onto my feet and on the stairs as I carried it down.

I wanted to be closer to my father and I tried. One weekend a few weeks after he came home, it was afternoon and he had been drinking as usual. He was sitting in the armchair and my sister was sitting on his knee. They were looking at a book together. My sister got down and left the room and I decided to take her place. I sat on his knee and he was smoking a cigarette.

"Do you want to see smoke come out of my eyes?" he asked. I nodded, anxious as all young boys are to see a new trick.

"Put your hand on my stomach here and watch my eyes."

He took a drag on his cigarette and I sat there with my left hand on his stomach and looked straight into his eyes, waiting for the smoke to appear. He stubbed his cigarette out on the back of my hand. I let out a scream of pain and jumped from his knee. I started to cry.

"Don't you cry, you sissy," he said. "And don't you ever sit on my knee again. Little girls sit on their father's knee, not little boys—unless they are sissies."

My mother rushed into the room. "What happened?"

"Daddy burned me with his cigarette."

"It was an accident." My father said like it was no big deal.

"It wasn't an accident, he did it on purpose."

My father half stood raising his hand, threatening to backhand me across the face.

"Go play outside, and leave your father alone," was my mother's response.

I ran from the house and down to the end of the garden. I sat on my swing under the apple tree, nursing the burn on my hand. I blew on it to try to cool it, I told myself it was only pain, just as I did when Miss Jones gave me the cane at school, but this was different. If I rubbed my hands together after getting the cane the hurt went away, but this was a burn. It hurt like hell and I couldn't even bear to touch it.

I got up from the swing and decided to walk to the river. Maybe I would just keep walking and never come back. I hated my father. He had hurt me, not just physically but by telling me I was a sissy for sitting on his knee. How was I supposed to know I shouldn't sit on his knee? He could have told me.

I picked a big green dock leaf from the hedgerow and put it on my burn; it felt cool and soothing. I decided I would stay out until evening when my father would be gone to the pub. I got to the river and lay on the bank with my hand in the cold water, there was no pain as long as I kept my hand there. I thought about what had happened and my mother's words "leave your father alone." That was probably good advice. I decided to distance myself from my father as much as I could both physically and mentally.

I could see the sun was setting so it was probably all right to go home now. When I arrived my mother asked to see my hand and put some ointment and a bandage on it.

"What happened?" she asked.

I explained about how my father said he could make smoke come out of his eyes.

"I'm sure he didn't mean to burn you."

I didn't argue with my mother. I was beginning to learn that when it came to my father she was in denial most of the time.

Later that year we moved back to London. My father had been offered his old job back working on the docks. There was a shortage of housing because of the bombing, but dockworkers were given priority.

Moving day came and our furniture was loaded into a large van. My father rode with the van and my mother, sister, and I traveled by train. I was glad my father was not traveling with us; I didn't want anything to spoil the fun of a train ride.

Our new home was a Victorian terrace house, typical of the working-class homes built in London and other large cities in England. The houses were a single room wide, built in a row, covering the entire length of the street. A front door opened into a room about twelve feet square, with another room the same size behind it. Between the two rooms were stairs up to two bedrooms and in this house was a third attic bedroom above that. This was to be my room.

Behind the two main rooms was a tiny kitchen about six feet by eight feet. A back door opened into a small yard with a brick floor and a toilet outside attached to the kitchen. This was a flush toilet, and along with this and gas and electricity in the house, was luxury compared with what we had been used to, even though there was still no bathroom and we had to bathe in the kitchen.

The house next to us was a reverse mirror image of ours, kitchen and toilets back to back. This was repeated the length of the street. The small outside yard ended with a wooden fence and a gate leading to a common walkway. On the other side of the walkway were houses that faced the next street. Between every sixth house was a tunnel leading to the center walkway and allowing access to the rear of the houses. Two stone steps led from the street up to the front door. Beneath the front room was a coal cellar, with a manhole cover in the sidewalk and coal chute into the cellar. This with a few variations is the basic layout for every small terrace house in Britain.

My new school was big, with hundreds of pupils; it was less than a mile away from where I lived so it was an easy walk each day. We had many different teachers, not like the tiny rural school where I had to deal with Miss Jones every day; I did not miss that. Some teachers were strict disciplinarians but others were more lenient. There was still corporal punishment but this was dealt out by the headmaster. Girls were caned on the hands, but we boys had to bend over and have our backsides tanned. Generally we had to do something pretty bad to be sent to the headmaster, unlike Miss Jones who would bring out the cane at the slightest whim or provocation.

Dealing with the other kids at school was tough at first; I was physically small and prone to be the victim of bullying. There were two distinct groups of kids, those who stayed in London during the war and those like me who evacuated to the country. I was fortunate in that my mother had moved to the country with me; some kids went to foster homes and had to deal with the double whammy of adjusting to their home life and school.

The kids who had stayed in London were tough, street smart, and knew their way around. They were full of confidence because of this, unlike us evacuees who were like fish out of water. Almost overnight we found ourselves transported from the relative tranquility of rural living into the hustle and bustle of the big city. We had picked up the local accent of wherever we had been so we talked differently and were open to ridicule.

I found one new friend in a kid named George, who stayed in London throughout the war. His house had been bombed and he had been trapped under rubble while the house burned. The right side of his face was burned and badly scarred, he had no hair on that side of his head, and most his ear was missing, as was his right eyebrow. The other kids picked on him because of this.

He was a tough kid. One day, he was in a fight with another kid who was always picking on me, so I jumped in to help him just for the hell of it. The result was, we were all sent to the headmaster and received six strokes of the cane across our backsides. After that George and I spent a lot of time together on evenings and weekends. He really knew his way around the neighborhood and soon I knew my way around and found myself accepted by the local kids. George and I formed a friendship that would last many years.

If I was gaining acceptance in the neighborhood, my father was not. He was still drinking heavily and after a few beers became obnoxious and opinionated. If anyone disagreed with his opinion, fists would start flying. He sometimes took on as many as six men, got a whipping, and then bragged that it took six men to beat him.

My father was a boxer and had a few professional fights before the war. There was a boxing gym near where we lived. My father hung out there and made a little extra money as a sparring partner. I think he dreamed of making it as a pro fighter again, but it was not going to happen because of his age and heavy drinking.

George and I often stopped by the gym; it was a cool place to hang out and the trainers and fighters knew me because of my father. I also scored points with my father because he thought I was interested in boxing and whenever I was in his favor he was not slapping me around. However, this ploy backfired on me one day when my father came home with boxing gloves saying he was going to teach me to box.

The boxing lessons would become a ritual that I hated. We would put the gloves on; my father would get down on his knees and poke at me with the tips of his gloved fingers teaching me how to defend myself. He would torment me. I would put up my hands to protect my face and he would flick me alongside the ear; if I protected my ears he would poke my nose. All the time taunting me, "Look at you, you're wide open."

My mother would be saying, "Now don't get too rough."

He encouraged me to hit him as hard as I could, and in time I would get mad enough that I would catch him with a punch that hurt. Then he would get mad and flatten me. He would either knock me across the room, crashing into the furniture, or he'd punch me in the chest so hard it felt like my heart had stopped and I would go out like a light. The next thing I remembered I would be in a chair with my mother giving me a drink of water, saying, "I told you not to get too rough, you'll hurt the boy."

My father would say something like, "He's okay. He's as tough as nails, just like the old man."

The outcome of these so-called boxing lessons was that I had no interest in real boxing but got into more fights at school. The one thing that deters anyone from fighting is the fear of getting hurt, but no one in my school could hit me as hard as my old man. I found that if I backed down from a fight the bullying would increase, but if I stood up for my-self eventually they would leave me alone.

One thing was certain, if I got in a fight with some kid at school and his parents came to my house they had to deal with my father, and of course he would take my side and be so proud of me. I didn't love my old man, at times I hated him, but I always wanted acceptance from him.

My new school had a choir that sang every morning at assembly and other school functions. The music teacher's name was Sam Fletcher; he was a kind, easygoing man and we all liked him. Any new kids in the school had to learn a piece of music and sing it solo in front of the class. As a result I was asked to join the choir. This meant staying behind after school for extra practice. Anything that got me out of the house and away from my old man was fine by me.

Mr. Fletcher called me aside one evening after choir practice and told me, "Eddie, you have a truly beautiful voice. You are always in tune and your sense of timing is excellent."

I should have thanked him but this was the first time anyone at school had ever given me credit for anything; all I usually got was criticism. I didn't know what to say. Mr. Fletcher continued, "Tell me, Eddie, are you Church of England?"

I nodded. "Yes, why?"

"I am choirmaster at St. Clement's Church and I would like you to join our choir there."

"I'll have to ask my mother, but I'm sure it will be all right."

When I got home I told my mother what Mr. Fletcher had said. She was delighted. "Oh, that's wonderful. I've been thinking about going to church again and St. Clement's is such a beautiful church."

My father, who was shaving in the kitchen, could hear what we were saying came to the door with shaving soap on his face.

"You need to check out this choirmaster, some of them are—" He finished his sentence with a little Donald Duck noise and motioned with his fingers toward his butt crack.

"Oh, don't be silly, he's Eddie's teacher."

"Never you mind, you check him out."

My father went back to his shaving.

Nothing more was said and I joined the St. Clement's choir. There were about forty members in the choir made up of men and boys from nine to thirteen years old. The different parts with different melodies that we would all sing and how they blended together in harmony fasci-nated me. Soon I was also singing solo parts and I loved to hear the sound of my own voice echoing around this big stone building accompanied by a huge pipe organ.

My mother attended church and was always telling me how proud of me she was, which pleased me. I wanted my father to come hear me but he never did. I guess church time always coincided with opening time at the local pub.

Chapter 7

GEORGE'S FATHER FRANK WAS A bookie; in other words, he took bets on horses, which was illegal in 1946. He carried out his business on the streets; pub landlords would not tolerate him taking bets on their premises as they could lose their license if he was caught. The same was true if he took bets from his home as he could be evicted. He had to hang out in the same area each day so his clients could find him, but this also made it easy for the police to find him. George and I would act as lookouts. I stood on one corner, George stood on the next corner down the street, and his father operated somewhere in between. Police patrols were on foot so we would easily spot them coming with their tall helmets. If we saw one approaching we would run ahead to where Frank was and say, "Look up, it's Old Bill."

Old Bill was universal slang for the police. Some policemen could be bribed and we got to know who they were. On more than one occasion I saw George's dad hand a police officer his notebook where there would be a five-pound note between the pages. The policeman would slide it out, hand back the book, and walk on. With several bookies on his beat, this particular policeman had a steady extra income.

The regular clients got to know George and me, and would ask, "Where's Frank?" We would tell where he could be found or sometimes the client would hand us the betting slip and we would run it to him. Regular clients had credit with George's father, as he did with the bigger bookmakers. Sometimes if he took a large bet he would have to lay it off or cover the bet, and George or myself would run over to this place we knew well, a little office over a barber's shop.

"Now take this over to Big Arthur and make sure Old Bill's not around when you go in," I was always warned as I was handed the slip of paper.

This office was the ideal setup for an illicit gambling operation. There was a folding iron gate that was open during the day and a passageway led to an upstairs office. To the right at the bottom of the stairs was a glass door into the barber's shop. Anyone observing from the street would not know if people going in were going upstairs or into the barber's shop. Not that Big Arthur took bets from just anyone; he was only interested in large money bets and only dealt with people he knew.

At the top of the stairs was a door that was always locked. On the door was a sign that said something like "Apex Import & Export." Because this was the East End near the docks, there were a lot of import and export companies. I never knew if this was just a front for the gambling operation or if it was a legitimate business and the bookmaking was a sideline.

I would knock on the door and a voice would call out, "Who is it?" A little peephole about three inches square would slide open.

"It's me, Eddie."

"Eddie, how the hell are you?" The door would open.

"Come in. How's yer dad?" I had told Big Arthur many times Frank was not my father but he never remembered, so I would just say, "He's fine."

Big Arthur was aptly named; he was six feet six inches tall and weighed about three hundred pounds. Not the kind of man you would want to owe money or mess with in any way. He always wore a dark suit, his long dark hair was combed straight back cut square just above his collar, and he wore glasses with heavy black frames. To me he was like a kind and lovable uncle; he would always give me a chocolate bar whenever I went to his office. This was such a luxury because sugar and candy were still rationed and remained so for about three years after the war had ended. There was always a black market supply of any rationed commodity, and no doubt this was the source of the chocolate bars.

George and I loved to run. We got plenty of exercise working for George's dad, but other times we were together we chased or raced each other, rarely walking anywhere. We were both about the same height but George was slightly heavier than I was. He was not fat but more solidly built. I could usually outrun George but he was stronger than me if it came to lifting or carrying anything.

On Saturdays or school holidays if we were not working for Frank we would take the underground train to one of the big London parks. We would usually buy the cheapest ticket that would officially only take us to the next station but would stay on the train beyond that stop. When it was time to get off and go through the gate with a ticket man, we would get up close behind someone. As the person in front handed in his ticket I would dart around him to the right and when the ticket man tried to grab me George would slip by on his left. We would run as fast as we could up the steps and out of the station. George got caught once when someone grabbed him; I crept back and watched from a distance to see what was happening. George was crying and saying he'd lost his ticket, and some kind lady paid his fair and gave him money for the return trip. The scars on George's face would often evoke sympathy from strangers.

One time in the park I suggested we climb a tree.

"I don't think we're supposed to climb trees," George said.

"Well who's going to stop us?" I asked as I climbed on the back of a park bench to gain height to reach the first branch. I swiftly climbed to the top with George following close behind me. It felt good; I hadn't climbed a tree since leaving the country over a year before. For George this was a new experience.

We were up there for about five minutes when we heard a loud voice say, "Hey, you kids come down from there." We looked down; it was a park warden in his blue uniform.

"You know you're not supposed to climb the trees."

"See, I told you so," said George.

"Why not?" I asked.

"Because you'll damage the tree."

"I won't hurt the tree; trees are my friend."

"You come on down." George had already climbed down so I followed him.

"Stay out of the trees and keep to the path; if you don't you'll have to leave the park," the park warden warned us.

George turned to me as we walked away. "What did you mean 'the tree is your friend'?"

"Trees are a living thing and they know when you are climbing them."

"Who told you that."

"A friend I once had. He was an American Indian; his name was Running Horse."

"Was he Big Chief Running Horse?"

"No, that was his name."

"What a load of bollocks." This was George's way of implying that I was full of shit. He laughed and took off running. I chased after him and was just about to catch him when he reached out, grabbed hold of a lamppost, and swung around to go back the way we came. By the time I had stopped and turned George had gained some ten or fifteen yards on me. I chased him down again and we ran past the park warden.

"Hey, you kids, I'm warning you!" he called out after us.

George and I remained good friends but I never mentioned Running Horse or the things he had told me again. George had never lived in the country and experienced nature as I had. This was the city and a whole different world. Although I sometimes missed living in a rural area, the city offered a lot of excitement and there was always something to do.

George's scarred face was something I became used to, but strangers on the street often stared at him. He would overcompensate for this by clowning around. If a child was staring he would go up close and try to scare them. If it was an adult he would sometimes turn around and follow them walking like he was some deformed hunchback or chimpanzee. He would often go quite a distance before the people realized he was following them; when they did they were embarrassed and didn't know what to do. George would just stand there making monkey noises, then turn and walk away quite normally with no sign of deformity.

He did this one day with a group of six kids about our age; we were out of our neighborhood so we did not know them. The biggest kid in the group spoke to me.

"Hey, what's wrong with the monkey's boat race?" He was referring to George's face.

I looked him straight in the eye. "Nothing compared with what your face will look like if you don't leave off."

He took a step forward. "Oh, and who's gonna do that?"

I replied with a hard punch to his face and took off running. This was a ploy to break up the group. I ran around a corner and stopped, as the kid came around the corner I hit him in the face again. The combination of my punch and him running into it knocked him on his back. I knelt on his chest and punched him three or four times hard in the face.

I ran back to George who was wrestling with one kid on the ground, another was trying to pull him off. I punched this kid hard a couple of times and the next thing I knew I was being attacked from all sides as the other kids joined in, and the first and biggest kid had come back into the fray.

Suddenly I felt myself being lifted bodily by my coat collar and a loud voice said, "Hey, pack it in."

A large policeman was holding my collar with his left hand; my feet were barely touching the ground. In his right hand was the collar of my original adversary, he was holding us apart at arm's length. George had picked himself up and there were now only two kids from the original six; the others must have taken off when the policeman arrived.

"What's this all about?"

No one answered. The policeman was still holding my collar but had relaxed some. I was now standing on my own feet.

"I know you," he addressed the big kid first and then turned to me. "But where are you from?"

"Stepney," I replied.

"Well, you get on back to Stepney and don't come over here unless you can behave yourself." He shook me hard; my feet were off the ground again. "Understand?"

"Yes." He released his grip.

"Get on home then." George and I walked on as the policeman continued talking to the others.

George turned to me and asked, "Are you crazy, why did you start that? We could have got a right kicking."

I laughed. "Good thing Old Bill showed when he did."

The truth was I was beginning to enjoy fighting, and I was beginning to take on my father's perverted sense of values. There was no honor in picking on someone who was smaller or weaker but if you took on someone bigger or started a fight when outnumbered, you were left with some sense of achievement even if you took a beating. To the juvenile mind the excitement was in reliving the experience afterwards. Getting bigger and bigger with each telling.

When I got home I did just that, giving my father a blow-by-blow account of the event. My father laughed and ruffled my hair. "Good boy. You're like your old man; you don't take crap from nobody."

My mother spoke up. "I wish you wouldn't encourage the boy to fight—just look at his face."

"Eddie has to stand up for himself or people will walk all over him."

My father ruffled my hair again and hugged my head to his side in a rare display of affection.

Chapter 8

MY VALUES IN LIFE BECAME somewhat of a paradox over the next few years. I continued to sing in the choir at St. Clement's Church, which was something I really enjoyed, and I went to church twice on most Sundays. There was holy communion in the morning and an evening service—the choir sang for both services. There was also choir practice and other services during the week. With all this exposure to church and with my mother's encouragement I was developing some sound Christian beliefs; for example, I would not dream of stealing anything.

Not paying the underground fare was in fact stealing but to me that was cheating, not stealing. Stealing was taking money or property, which I wouldn't do, even though some of the kids I hung out with, including George, were not beyond stealing given the opportunity. I never judged or condemned George or the others; I just would not participate.

At the same time the fighting continued and Mr. Fletcher and the vicar of St. Clement's were always censuring me for showing up in church with cuts and bruises on my face although they didn't know it was sometimes my father who caused the injuries. The boxing lessons continued at home and I would take out my anger and frustrations with my father by hitting him as hard as I could knowing this would lead to my being hit even harder in return. Most times it was the only way to end the torment.

The same feelings were brought out if I were tormented by a school bully older and bigger than I was. I would lash out even though I knew it meant getting hurt. This was also true if a teacher tormented me mentally. There was plenty of that in the British school system—sarcasm, ridicule, and put-downs. I would take only so much before I would say, "Fuck you. I'll take my punishment and be damned." My philosophy in life became, "Love thy neighbor, be kind to your fellow man, and don't hurt anyone unless they ask for it."

In 1948 I turned eleven years old and had to move on to another school. This was an even bigger school with more than a thousand students and was the last I would attend until I left at age fifteen. George and I had birthdays that were only a few weeks apart so he came to the new school as well. We had a bus trip of about five miles each day on public transport and were supplied with a free bus pass.

The new school had a running track and a swimming pool. George was a very strong swimmer and was soon on the swimming and diving team. I was on the athletics team running the quarter mile and half mile. I had not been at the new school many weeks when the music teacher called me aside.

"Eddie, I see at your last school you did very well in music."

"Yes, sir, I was in the choir there and I'm also in the St. Clement's church choir. Mr. Fletcher, my last music teacher, is choirmaster there."

"Yes, I know Mr. Fletcher. Would you like to join our choir here?"

"Thank you, sir, I'd like that very much."

Once again I was in the school choir. We led singing at morning assembly and gave concerts around Christmastime. I enjoyed singing, especially when I could sing solo, which was quite often. The choir was made up of between sixty and eighty boys and girls ages eleven to fifteen. There was also a school orchestra that performed with us.

At my new school I was an average student, except for art, athletics, and music. I excelled in those areas. My new music teacher was Mr. Abbott, who the kids nicknamed "Bud" after the famous comedian. We got along well and he was one of the few teachers who encouraged and praised me. I had been at this school for about a year when Mr. Abbott asked to talk to me one day after class.

"Eddie, how would you like to audition for the St. Paul's Cathedral Choir?"

"I dunno, I never thought about it."

"The boys who are in the choir are mostly from the big public schools, but now the other local schools in the area are being invited to submit students for audition."

The so-called public schools in England are expensive, private schools where only the children of the privileged and wealthy can afford to attend. Mr. Abbott continued, "This would be a tremendous honor and opportunity as it could lead to a music scholarship with one of the universities.

"You are the first student I have told about this but before I submit your name I must talk to you about your constant fighting. If I submit your name you must promise me that there will be no fighting with the other boys in the choir; they will not tolerate anything like that. You deserve a chance to audition; you have the best voice in this school. But if you are expelled for fighting or any other trouble, you are depriving someone else a place in the choir. Can you promise that you will not let me down?"

"Why—er—yes," I stammered. My mind was spinning at the thought of singing in this huge cathedral.

"I've never been in a fight in the St. Clement's choir. I don't have a problem if people leave me alone. I don't go looking for fights."

"I know, Eddie. You don't have to look for trouble, it finds you. This is the problem; you have to learn to back down once in a while, not go lashing out at the slightest provocation. Do you understand that?"

"Yes, I understand, and thank you, Mr. Abbott."

"Now don't breathe a word of this to anyone yet. I intend to announce it at assembly tomorrow morning."

"Can I tell my mother?"

"Yes, you can tell your mother, just don't tell anyone in the school."

I rushed straight home after school.

"Oh, that's wonderful!" she said when I told her and she hugged me to her. "I'm so proud of you. Imagine, my son singing in St. Paul's Cathedral!"

"Wait, Mum, I have to pass the audition first."

"I know. You'll pass, I have faith in you."

The next morning Mr. Abbott announced to the school that four students from our school would be auditioning for the St. Paul's Choir. There would be three other boys and myself. For the next three weeks we rehearsed our audition pieces. I chose to sing "Jesu, Joy of Man's Desiring" by Bach, which was a challenging piece. It had an instrumental theme that ran in between and behind the vocal lines and it was imperative that I came in at the precise moment each time. Mr. Fletcher at St. Clement's Church also gave me extra coaching and practice time and allowed me to sing the piece at Sunday evening service the week before my audition as a kind of dress rehearsal.

Mr. Fletcher also took me to St. Paul's, as I had never been inside. During World War II bombing had leveled the whole area around the cathedral but St. Paul's suffered no serious damage. By 1949 most of the area had been cleared and some reconstruction started. To see this magnificent building standing high above the desolation around it was an awesome sight. The inside was even more impressive. The size of the building was overwhelming. Mr. Fletcher took me around and as we went explained some of the history. As we left he paused outside.

"Now, Eddie, please don't get into a fight just before the audition. To go in there with a black eye or a fat lip would not give a good impression, and don't be calling your interviewer 'guvner,' refer to them as sir or madam."

"Okay, guvner."

Mr. Fletcher gave me a playful slap on the back of my head.

The day of the audition came and Mr. Abbott drove the three others and myself from my school to a venue, which was not the cathedral but a building close by. Inside we went up some stairs to a large hallway on the first floor. The building was very impressive, with polished wood floors and marble pillars. Huge oil paintings hung on the walls between the marble pillars, and massive oak doors at least ten feet high led into the rooms off the hallway.

"Blimey, how big are the geezers that go through them doors?" I commented. "You could get an eight foot Bobby wiv his helmet through there."

The other kids in my group giggled.

"Keep it down, and you behave yourself, Eddie." Mr. Abbott said sternly.

I was relaxed and enjoying the occasion, which was as well because after about an hour wait it was my turn to go in. Mr. Abbott led me through the big oak doors into a long narrow room. There were about eight large windows across the back wall and directly in front of these were ten very serious-looking people seated at a long table.

I remember looking at them, thinking, "God they must all be a hundred years old." The only hint of a smile came from a lady third from the left. I stood on a rug in the center of the room facing a man in the center of the table who would do most of the talking. Mr. Abbott took his place at a piano to my right. The man in the center spoke.

"Edward Conner." It seemed strange to be addressed as Edward.

"I see you have chosen 'Jesu, Joy of Man's Desiring' to sing here today. Why did you choose this particular piece?"

"Well, sir, Bach is one of my favorite composers, and I like the way the music goes fast and the singing goes slow over the top of the music." That over-simplified the rhythmic structure of this piece, but I did detect a few smiles on the otherwise stern faces. The questions continued.

"Edward, why would you like to sing in the St. Paul's Choir?"

"I'm in the St. Clement's Church Choir and I like it when I get to sing solo. I love to hear my voice in a really big building and as St. Paul's is so big you could get St. Clement's inside with room to spare, I wonder what my voice would sound like in a building that big."

They continued with questions about my school and where I lived, then the lady third from the left spoke. "Edward, what does your father do?"

"Do you mean for work, or when he gets home?"

The lady's smile became a chuckle. "I mean his work."

I was relieved because his main hobby was drinking and beating his wife and kids and I didn't quite know how to express that eloquently.

"He's a stevedore, madam, he works in the docks."

"Are you ready to perform your piece?" It was the man in the center who spoke.

"Yes, sir."

I opened my music book and looked over at Mr. Abbott, who gave me a smile and then turned to start playing. I looked down at the music following the notes and waiting to start singing. When the time came I lifted my head and looked straight at the man in front of me and sang out as clear as I could. The first line ended and I looked down again at the book, following the music and concentrating on my breathing. My voice sounded good in this large room and I finished the piece without any flaws in my performance. It felt good.

There was a silence when I finished that seemed like an eternity, then the man in the center spoke with no sign of emotion.

"Thank you, Edward, you may leave now." I thanked him and looked across at the lady third from left. She was smiling. I returned the smile and left the room. Mr. Abbott stayed behind briefly to speak with the panel before joining me in the hallway.

"Good job, Eddie, excellent. I wish I could say the same for your interview before the singing. But I think your voice and your performance will carry it for you."

One week after the audition, Mr. Abbott stood before my school's morning assembly: "I have an announcement to make. Eddie Conner has been accepted as a member of the St. Paul's Cathedral Choir. We are all very proud of him, as he is the first student from this school to be accepted into such a prestigious choir." I was the only one from our school to be accepted.

Mr. Abbott called me to the front of the stage and the whole school applauded. I was embarrassed as I had never been the center of attention like this before, but I quite liked it. Mr. Clarke, the headmaster, got up and shook my hand and congratulated me, which seemed strange because the only contact I had had with him before was when he was tanning my backside with a cane as punishment for fighting or some other misdeed.

Later that day Mr. Abbott took me into the headmaster's office and Mr. Clarke reiterated what Mr. Abbott had told me before the audition. "Eddie, you are a good student for the most part, but you always seem to have this problem of fighting with the other boys."

"I only get into fights when someone picks on me; I don't start it."

"I know, Eddie, there is a lot of bullying goes on here and I intend to put a stop to that. But when you get to St. Paul's Cathedral Choir you will be representing this school and you will be amongst a different class of boys. They may accept you or they may not, but you must learn to turn the other cheek, as the Good Book says. Can you see that, Eddie?"

"Yes, sir, I have already promised Mr. Abbott I will not get into fights at St. Paul's."

Later Mr. Abbott told me St. Paul's Choir had practice twice a week. "I will take you there the first time so that you know where to go, but after that you will have to make your own way. There is a bus you can catch."

I couldn't wait to get home and tell my mother but before I did I stopped off at my old school to tell Mr. Fletcher, after all it was he who first encouraged me to sing.

"Congratulations, Eddie, I knew you would make it. I'm going to miss you at St. Clement's though."

"You mean I can't sing at St. Clement's?"

"How can you? The Cathedral will want you on Sundays. You can't be in both places at the same time."

I hadn't thought too much about that. "Well, I'm not so sure about that, I like singing in your choir."

"Eddie, this is a wonderful opportunity and you can come back and sing at St. Clement's anytime you are free."

I thanked Mr. Fletcher and rushed home to tell my mother. She was in the kitchen preparing the evening meal; my father was in the armchair reading the paper.

"Mum, I was accepted by the St. Paul's Choir. I'm going to first practice tomorrow evening."

My mother hugged me and came from the kitchen to talk to my father.

"Did you hear that, Ted? Eddie's going to sing in St. Paul's Cathedral."

My father looked up from his paper. "Nobody asked me if this was all right, how much is this going to cost us?"

"It's not going to cost us anything, it's a great honor."

My father went back to his paper and said nothing more until later in the week when my picture appeared in the local paper with an article about my acceptance into the St. Paul's Choir. He suddenly came home all excited and said, "Hey, the boy must really be able to sing."

"I've been telling you that for years, but you would never come to church to hear him," my mother said with some measure of frustration in her voice.

Chapter 9

MR. ABBOTT DROPPED ME OFF for my first St. Paul's choir practice and showed me where to catch the bus home. I had no problem with this; I was twelve years old and knew my way around the city pretty well.

This first session we did little singing but got to know the other new choir members and were fitted with our choir robes. We wore a bright red robe called a cassock, which went down to our ankles. Over this was worn a type of white shirt called a surplice. It came just below the waist with wide three-quarter sleeves and was trimmed with lace. Around our neck was a stiff starched collar, with half-inch pleats rather like a lampshade. This collar stood straight out around our neck and under the chin. I remember thinking that I hoped none of the other kids at my school would see me.

Most of the other kids in the choir were upper-class kids with wealthy parents. I met one kid that first night there named James. He spoke impeccable BBC English and insisted on calling me Edward, as did most of the people there. He referred to his parents as Mater and Pater. James seemed friendly enough and was full of confidence, which I liked. My East End cockney accent seemed to amuse him but that was okay because his precise English amused me.

The Tuesday evening practice was in the same building where the auditions were held. Thursday evening practice was in the cathedral with the huge pipe organ in accompaniment. The newcomers to the choir would have to practice for a month before joining the choir for Sunday Services. We not only had to practice singing, but we also had to learn how to line up before each service and had to take our seats in an exact formation. It was almost like a military drill.

I came to recognize three of the people who had been on the audition panel. There was the musical director Mr. Penson, the organist and dean of St. Paul's; somehow they didn't seem so old now.

With all this choir activity I was seeing less of George outside of school. He was heavily involved with the school swimming team and his swimming practice was on different nights from my choir practice. We saw each other at school each day and remained close friends.

James was my friend at choir practice but we didn't meet outside of the choir activities; he was from a different world and we both knew it. I met his mother one day as she came to pick him up in the Jaguar. I could almost see her cringe as James introduced us. The other kids would mock my cockney accent and most of it was lighthearted and I didn't mind it, but one kid, called Nigel, took it a step further and made remarks about my personal hygiene.

I resented this deeply. I came from a poor neighborhood and we didn't have the luxury of a bathroom but my mother made sure I was clean and gave me a clean shirt for every practice, even though she had to wash our clothes by hand. My clothes were worn and sometimes patched, but they were clean.

Nigel was a big kid a year older than I was and about five feet eight inches tall. I was only a little over five feet at that time. I pulled him aside one night after choir practice and told him. "Nigel, I eat kids like you for breakfast so do yourself a favor and leave it out."

I remembered my promise to Mr. Abbott and hoped that Nigel would back off.

Christmas came and there were extra carol services and I was asked to sing a brief solo of "Away in a Manger." I had been in the choir for over six months now and this was the opportunity I had been waiting for.

The carol service was in one of the smaller chapels off to the side, not in the main body of the cathedral, and the choir was reduced in size but it was a start. After that Mr. Penson gave me other small solo parts to sing. Then one day just before Easter he said, "Edward, I remember for your audition you did 'Jesu, Joy of Man's Desiring' and you did it so beautifully I would like you to do it again solo for the Easter evening service."

"Thank you, Mr. Penson. This is what I've always wanted."

"Yes, I remember you said so at your audition. The simple and down-to-earth way you expressed your ambitions impressed me."

The next two weeks I practiced the piece with the choir and the organ. Nigel started to give me problems again. "How come you're old Penson's favorite?"

"Maybe it's because I can sing. Did you ever think of that?" I had made up my mind I was not going to let Nigel spoil this for me.

Easter evening I was getting ready for the big service, my mother was getting ready to go also; this was our big night. I had to get there early; my mother was to follow on later. My father came into the room with the boxing gloves. "Come on, son, let's have a couple of rounds."

"No, Dad, I have to get to St. Paul's. I'm singing solo tonight."

"Put the gloves on, Eddie." My father put one glove on and started poking at me.

"Dad leave it out, I'll be late."

My mother came down from upstairs. "Ted, for God's sake leave the boy alone. He has to go."

My father gave me a hard jab to the chest, knocking me over. I picked myself up and finished getting ready. I rushed down the street and around the corner to see the bus pulling away from the bus stop.

"Damn my ol' man and his fucking boxing lessons," I mumbled to myself as I walked slowly to the bus stop and waited for the next bus. The buses were infrequent on Sundays and I had to wait half an hour for the next bus. After about twenty minutes my mother arrived surprised to see me still there.

"Eddie, you missed the bus."

"Yeah, an' it's all Dad's fault. Now I'm gonna be late."

"I know, Eddie, your father is the way he is. We can't do anything about it."

The bus finally came and when we got to our destination I had to run ahead to the cathedral. The choir was already starting to line up in the vestry. Mr. Penson saw me come in.

"Where have you been, Edward, you know how important tonight is."

How could I explain it was my father's fault without delaying myself even more? I said nothing. One of the men in the choir helped me with my cassock, surplice, and collar. I took my place in the lineup just as the organ was about to play the music to start our walk out to take our seats. Nigel was standing behind me. "Where have you been, Edward, digging the dirt out from behind your ears?"

"Leave it out, Nigel." I was already pretty upset and didn't need this.

"Oh look, there's a lice." He picked at the back of my head pulling a small clump of hair. I snapped. I turned and punched him hard on the nose. He fell over backward. It was not so much the force of my punch that knocked him over but more likely that he stepped back and caught his heel in the hem of his cassock. Nigel, being a big kid, knocked over the boy behind him and the two of them knocked over the next boy, they were falling like dominoes.

Pandemonium broke out. The choir members at the front had just started to walk out, stopped, and turned to see what the commotion was. Nigel was lying on top of two other boys and trying to get up. The dean rushed down from the back and pulled Nigel to his feet. He stood there, blood pouring from his nose and running down the folds of his starched collar like rain off a tin roof, dripping down the front of his white surplice.

"Pull this boy out." The dean motioned for Nigel to be led away. "And pull this boy out." He grabbed my arm.

Mr. Penson intervened. "You can't pull Edward out, he's singing the solo tonight."

The dean hesitated, then reluctantly said, "All right but I'll deal with this later."

In the meantime the music had started and the organist must have been wondering why we had not appeared. We started our walk out to take our seats. The music ended before we were all seated and the organist had to improvise a longer ending.

My anger spent, I felt remarkably calm. I knew I was in deep trouble, but this was my time, the night I would sing solo in St. Paul's Cathedral. I gathered my thoughts together and concentrated on the task ahead. When the time came I did just as I had done during my audition, I concentrated on the music from the organ, looked straight ahead, took my cue from Mr. Penson, and sang out as I had never sung before.

After the service back in the vestry, the dean came to me. "See me in my office at ten tomorrow morning."

I took off my cassock and surplice and went to find my mother. She was so happy I did not have the heart to tell her what had happened.

"Eddie, that was so beautiful. I am so proud of you."

An old gentleman overheard our conversation. "Excuse me. Is this the boy who sang 'Jesu, Joy of Man's Desiring'?"

My mother swelled with pride. "Yes, this is my son, Eddie."

The old gentleman shook both our hands and turned to me. "Son, you have the most beautiful voice I have ever heard from a boy. Your singing brought me to tears."

I thanked him and my mother and I left.

The following morning I went to the dean's office. The week after Easter was a holiday so there was no school. Mr. Penson was there with him. I stood in front of the Dean's large oak desk.

"Tell me, Edward, what happened last night?"

I explained how Nigel had been riding me, and had pulled my hair. "My God, that's no reason to punch a boy on the nose."

I couldn't explain that it had been my father that had upset me first, and Nigel's jibes were the last straw.

"Never in all my years at St. Paul's have I seen such a thing. You realize I can't allow you to continue to be a member of the choir."

Mr. Penson spoke up. "Dean, I beg you please reconsider, maybe a suspension. There was some provocation from the other boy."

The dean stood firm. "No. I can't allow young hooligans from the East End streets to behave this way in my Cathedral."

Mr. Penson spoke. "I have to abide by your ruling, dean." Then he turned toward me. "Edward, the way you performed that piece last night was truly beautiful, you have the voice of an angel."

"Yes, a devil with the voice of an angel" were the dean's last words.

I caught the bus back home and broke the news to my mother.

"Eddie, what is wrong with you? Why do you do these things?"

"It was Dad's fault, he put me in a bad mood to start with, and then when Nigel started in I just smacked him one. I wasn't thinking."

"That's your problem, Eddie, you don't think. You have to learn to control your temper." I needed sympathy, not a lecture. "I'm going out," I told her. I left the house, slamming the front door as I went.

I wandered down the street, my head down, kicking at the paving stones. I was confused and frustrated. I had my father on one hand telling me to always stand up for myself, and my mother and just about everyone else telling me to control my temper. I hated my father, I knew he was an idiot so why should I pay attention to what he said, especially when everyone else was telling me different?

However, I did not feel sorry for what I had done. I was sorry I had lost my place in the choir, but giving Nigel a knuckle sandwich felt good. I relived the moment. I could picture Nigel lying on top of the two other kids trying to get up and I smiled to myself. I looked up; a kid I knew from school was coming toward me.

"Hey, Daisy. Seen George?" His last name was Day but we called him Daisy.

"Yeah, he's up the road wiv 'is ol' man." He indicated with his thumb over his shoulder back the way he had come. I found George and told him what had happened the night before.

"This kid Nigel, he just wouldn't leave it alone, so in the end I've gone pop right on 'is hooter." The word "pop" was always accompanied by a gesture of a clenched fist going back ready to strike. "He went over backwards, took two other kids wiv 'im, an' he's lying there claret all down the front of 'is lace frock. So the upshot of all this is, I got slung out of the choir."

"That's all right, Eddie, you didn't belong up there wiv all them bleedin' toffee-nosed gits anyway," George said trying to console me.

"Old Bud Abbott ain't gonna be too happy about it."

"Fuck it. Don't worry about him."

I did worry about it though; I had let Mr. Abbott down. I had given him my word and I had not kept it.

George spoke up again. "I have to hang around here, keep an eye out for my ol' man. Do you wanna go on the next corner an' keep an eye out there? Later we can get some fish an' chips." I walked up the street and saw George's father Frank.

"Hello, Eddie, long time no see. Did you see George?"

"Yes, I'm going up the next corner to look out for Old Bill."

"That's the ticket. Good boy." This was like old times again. I was feeling better.

The following week back at school, I talked to Mr. Abbott. He had already heard what had happened.

"All I can say, Mr. Abbott, is I'm sorry. I know I let you down, but I really did try."

"I'm not going to lecture you, Eddie, you've hurt yourself more than you have hurt me."

I never went back to the school choir again, I just stayed away. I thought it best and Mr. Abbott never asked me to come back.

A few weeks later I talked to Mr. Fletcher and he asked me to come back to the St. Clement's Choir, which I did. I remained there for another year and then my voice started to break. I could no longer sing those boy soprano parts and so I eventually left.

Chapter 10

IT WAS 1951 AND GEORGE and I were now 14 years old and in our last year at school. Fifteen was the normal age to leave school in the United Kingdom at that time. After I left St. Clement's Choir we pretty much fell back into our old routine. We helped George's dad, and just generally hung out together, sometimes just the two of us, sometimes with a bunch of other kids from our neighborhood.

We were both physically active: George was still on the school swimming team and I was on the athletics team. I swam with George and he would train with me when I ran.

George still did a lot of clowning around when he was out. I think this was his way of coping with his deformity. From his left profile he was a good-looking young boy, but from his right side he looked like something from a horror movie. If we passed by a crowd of people, in line outside a theater, for example, he would find an empty paper cup and beg for money.

He would go into his deformed hunchback routine twisting his body into a grotesque form. Dragging one leg and with one arm appearing bent and paralyzed and the other thrusting out the paper cup, he would work his way slowly down the line of people. He would twist his head to one side and keep the bad side of his face thrust forward for effect, and if people didn't put money in his cup he would stop and make whining and grunting noises as if he were a deaf-mute. The people would become so embarrassed and uncomfortable that they would give him something just to have him move on.

We—his friends—would watch from the other side of the street. When he got to the end of the line he would put the money in his pocket and the paper cup in the nearest trash can. He would then jump high into the air kicking his heels together, run across the road dodging between cars to join us on the other side, and continue down the road in a normal manner.

In time George became pretty well known for this act and those in the crowd that knew him would go along with it and give him money, just for the entertainment of seeing him work those who didn't know. The crowd would sometimes give a big cheer at the end when he took off running. He often made enough money to buy us all lunch or take us to the movies, or "the pictures," as we called it. But making money was not the purpose of George's antics; he just loved to be the center of attention, and the bigger the crowd the more he liked it.

Another trick he did was to jump off one of the London bridges into the River Thames. This started out as a way to cool off on a hot summer's day, but he took it a step further when he jumped off the bridge inside a large sack. I wasn't with him the first time he did it but got to hear about it the next day at school.

"Hey, George. What's this I hear about you jumping in the river in a sack?"

"Oh, you should have been there, it was a giggle."

"Are you bleedin' nuts? You could have drowned."

"No, here's what we did. I got this big ol' sack, big enough to get inside, and put it up on the bridge parapet. Then I jump up and stand inside the sack and pull it up 'round me neck. I stand there a few minutes and a crowd gathers, then without saying a word, I pull the sack over me head an' I jump in the river."

"How did you get out of the sack?" I asked.

"I didn't tie it or anything, I just held it closed from the inside. Once I hit the water I got me arms out and then kicked the sack off me legs as I'm swimming. But here's the best part, I jumped off the bridge on the downstream side, and when I get in the river I swim under water against the current and come up under the bridge where no one can see me. Everyone expects me to pop up downstream 'cos that's the way the river is flowing."

"So then what happened?" I asked.

"I waited about three or four minutes then I dive down under water and come up a short distance downstream an' wave to the crowd. You should have heard them cheer. They thought I'd been under water all that time.

Roger, another kid we hung out with, spoke up. "I was with George. Some of the people were getting real worried. One geezer was ready to jump in but I told him it was okay 'cos George could stay under water for twenty minutes. I said his mother was a pearl diver."

Roger had a quick wit and could always be relied on to fabricate an amazing story to suit any occasion.

The following Saturday was a hot summer day. George came to see me after breakfast. I could tell right away he was all pumped up and had something planned. We left the house; George was carrying a small bag.

"What you got in the bag?" I asked.

He opened up the bag and showed me a large empty sack, a towel, and a length of rope tied with knots about every twelve inches. "I wanna do the old jump in the river in a sack trick," he explained.

"Roger can't come this time, and I need someone to hold my clothes and to help me out of the river after. That's what the rope is for."

I guess I agreed by default because I went along. When George got one of these ideas, he was going to do it whether I would agree or not, and one thing was certain—it would be an adventure. We caught the underground train to the Waterloo Bridge.

That year there was a Festival of Britain Exhibition on the South Bank of the Thames, and Waterloo Bridge was the closest bridge to the site, so it was packed with pedestrians. We walked out on the bridge, not to the center but about the second arch of the bridge. We were on the downstream side. George sat the bag down.

"Now here's what we do. See that barge down there? That's where you go and wait for me after I jump in." He pointed to a barge tied up to the bank about four hundred yards downstream to our left. "When I get in the water I'll swim back to come up under the bridge and wait about four or five minutes; this will give you time to get down there. Wave to me when you're there. Tie the rope to the railing just the other side of the barge."

George stripped off his shirt, shorts, and shoes; he was wearing swim trunks under his clothes. I pulled the sack from the bag and put George's clothes in its place. He positioned the opened sack on the bridge parapet, jumped up and stood inside pulling the sack around him. A small crowd gathered and George addressed them.

"Ladies and gentlemen, you are about to witness an amazing feat as I jump into the River Thames and attempt to make a daring escape under water." He turned to me. "Eddie, go across the road and make sure that nothing is coming down the river, I don't want to land on a boat coming under the bridge. Give me the thumbs-up if it's okay."

I walked across the road and looked over the bridge. The river was clear, I turned and gave George the thumbs-up sign. I saw him pull the sack up over his head and jump backward off the bridge. People on my side of the road also saw him jump and ran across to join the crowd looking over the parapet.

I started to walk off the bridge toward the North Bank; there were people lined up from about the center of the bridge to the embankment all looking over into the river. Suddenly I saw the tall dark figure of a policeman walking toward me; he too crossed the road to see what everyone was looking at.

"Oh shit," I mumbled under my breath as I hurried off the bridge. I did not turn right to go downriver where George had said, but instead turned left and looked around the upstream side of the bridge. I called out to George who I knew was waiting out of sight behind the first arch of the bridge.

"George! George!" No sign of him. I put my fingers in my mouth and gave a short sharp whistle. George's head appeared from behind the stonework of the bridge. I beckoned frantically.

"Come here." He pointed downriver.

"No, come here." I beckoned even more frantically. I was afraid to shout too loud for fear of attracting attention to myself. George swam toward me.

"What's up?" he asked as he got closer.

"It's Old Bill."

"Where?"

"On the bridge." I tied the knotted rope to the railing and George climbed the twelve feet or so from the water to the street.

"Come on," I said. "Don't run or we'll attract attention, just walk fast."

We walked quickly along the river embankment; George dried himself with the towel as we walked and put on his shirt. When we were some distance from the bridge we stopped and George put the towel around him, removed his swim trunks and put on his shoes and shorts. We looked back and could see crowds of people looking over the bridge and lined up along the riverbank near the bridge.

"Let's go back," George said.

"What, are you nuts?"

"No, come on, no one will know it's us. Let's see what's going on back there."

We walked back and over the bridge, the crowd was so big by now we had to walk to the far side of the bridge before we could find a place to look over.

"What's going on?" George asked someone.

"A young boy jumped in the river."

"Was he drowned?"

"We think so; he never came up."

George nudged me with his elbow, smiled and gave me a wink. He was loving every minute of it.

We stood and watched and saw two river police boats arrive and anchor by the second arch of the bridge where George had jumped in. We watched as police divers in wetsuits dove repeatedly into the river. After a while they moved some fifty yards downstream and repeated the search. We must have watched them for about an hour and they were still there when we left.

Later that afternoon we were passing a newsstand and George stopped. "Hey, look at this." He bought an evening paper. On the front page was the headline, "Boy jumps off Waterloo Bridge. Feared drowned."

"Wait 'til I tell the others at school about this."

That turned out to be our downfall. He told the story at school on Monday and on Tuesday George and I were called out of class and taken to the headmaster's office. When we got there, two very big policemen, one in uniform and one in plain clothes, were waiting for us. They questioned us about the bridge-jumping incident and at first we denied it. It appeared that some kid at school had told his parents ,who in turn had called the police.

In the end we 'fessed up. George was pretty easy to describe with his scars and his right ear missing—not too many kids fit that description. So with eyewitness reports and others naming names, we were caught "bang to rights," as we would say—in others words "busted."

We were taken to the local police station in a police car and lectured on the gravity of what we had done and told of the amount of time and money that had been wasted. They gave us lunch at the police station and kept us there all day. Some of the policemen were serious and others thought it was a huge joke. I learned that day a policeman's sense of humor can vary tremendously and is usually dependent on how much work or trouble your actions have caused him personally.

At the end of the afternoon we were told we would not be charged with anything and were let off with a warning. We were driven home in a police car and the policeman told my mother what we had done. After he had left my mother continued the lecture I had been hearing all day. "Eddie, whatever possessed you and George to do such a stupid thing?"

"Well, it would have been all right if that Bobby hadn't come along when he did. George would have popped up and swam down the river as we planned an' none of this would have happened. We only did it for a giggle."

"Some giggle. George could have drowned."

"George is not going to drown, he swims like a bleedin' fish."

"Don't you use that kind of language. I don't know what your father's going to say."

My old man came home and treated the whole thing as big joke. "Boys will be boys" was all he had to say when my mother told him. That was the thing about my father, you could never predict how he would react to anything I did. For some little thing he would beat the living tar out of me, and then for something like this when I would expect punishment he would let it go. One reason I guess was that my dad was no fan of the police; he had been arrested several times for fighting and being drunk and disorderly. He had often spent a night in the police cells. So my doing something to piss off the local constabulary was all right by him.

George's father, what with him being an illegal bookmaker, had much the same reaction, but both of his parents were concerned for George's safety so he had to promise there would be no more jumping off bridges. All in all we came out of the whole incident pretty well. There was a follow-up article in the London papers; the headline read "Police question boys on river drowning hoax." Our names were not mentioned because of our age, but the other kids in school knew it was us and for a while we were treated like little celebrities.

Chapter 11

IT WAS A FEW MONTHS before my fifteenth birthday when my father asked, "What are you going to do when you leave school?"

"I dunno. What about the work you do?"

"You don't want to do that, son, it's a back-breaking job and there's no future in it. No, learn a trade, that's my advice."

My old man was not one to give out too much good advice but this was sound. He continued, "Someone I work with has a boy who is apprentice with Anderson's, the crane builders; they build and maintain all the cranes on the docks. You should think about something like that."

The idea appealed to me and so I applied and was granted an interview with Harold Anderson & Son, Crane Builders. This was an established company that had a large factory near the docks and was within walking distance of my home. On the day of the interview I put on my best suit, polished my shoes, and wore a clean shirt and tie. I had my school report in a large brown envelope and a letter of recommendation from Mr. Fletcher at St. Clement's Church. Although I no longer sang in the choir, I did still occasionally go to church with my mother on Sundays.

I walked up to the imposing front office. There was a large sign on the front of the building, and brass plates engraved with the company name and the words "Head Office" on either side of a huge doorway. Stone steps led up to the double doors that opened into a hallway with a marble floor. On the wall was a large oil painting of Harold Anderson, founder of the company. Judging by the clothes the old gentleman was wearing, and the silk top hat and white gloves he was holding, the painting was from the late 1800s or the early 1900s and the bewhiskered old gent was probably long gone and now it was "& Son" who was in charge.

I was led along a maze of passageways to a door marked "Personnel Office." My interviewer was a pleasant man who seemed to like me. My school report showed grades that were above average and the letter of recommendation, together with the fact that I had been a member of the local church choir, I think clinched it for me. I was provisionally accepted as an engineering apprentice.

The five-year apprenticeship would start on my sixteenth birthday and end when I was twenty-one. My first year would be a probationary period during which I would go to technical school one day and one evening a week, and if I did well in that first year, I would become an apprentice and eventually a skilled engineer.

A month or so later I finished school and the following Monday left for work for the first time, carrying my lunch in a tin box. There were three other new apprentices starting the same time as me, one I recognized from my school. We were issued with a dark blue boiler suit, or coveralls, and safety boots with steel toe caps. The first morning we were taken on a tour of the factory and watched a film on safety in the workplace.

At first I was given menial tasks to do, like sweeping the floor or cleaning machine parts, but soon graduated into more interesting things. I learned how to dismantle and assemble pieces of machinery. I also learned how to cut steel with an oxyacetylene torch and to weld with an electric arc welder. Eventually I got to go out with one of the maintenance men and work on the dockside cranes. We would load our tools onto a handcart and walk the short distance to the docks where big ships from all over the world were being loaded and unloaded. I learned the workings of the big cranes and the periodic adjustments and safety inspections needed. This work involved climbing all over these giant structures, which I didn't mind; it kind of reminded me of climbing trees as a kid.

The men I worked with were always giving the new apprentices a hard time and generally playing tricks on us until we would eventually catch on. We were all issued our own toolbox and hand tools, but some specialist tools were kept in a central tool store and issued as needed. The apprentices would often be sent to pick up tools and soon after I started work a coworker named Stan said to me, "Hey, Eddie, go to the tool store and ask for a long weight."

I was too naive to notice the twinkle in eye as he sent me on this errand. I got to the store and said, "Stan sent me here for a long weight."

"Okay," the store man said. "Stand over there." He disappeared behind the tool shelves and reappeared minutes later and carried on attending to other business, ignoring me completely. Some five minutes went by and another man asked me what I needed. I repeated my request.

"I'm here for a long weight." He then did exactly as the first man had done.

Another ten minutes went by and I asked again. "I need a long weight."

"How long?"

"I don't know. Stan didn't tell me."

"Well, you'd better stand there a little longer then."

Then it dawned on me I was not there for a long weight but a long *wait*. I walked back and Stan and the others were all smiling.

"Did you get a long wait, Eddie?"

"Yes I did," I replied embarrassed that I had fallen for such a dumb trick.

"Well where is it?" Stan asked.

"I left it there." Everyone around me laughed.

That evening I hung around and waited until everybody left. Stan had left his safety boots under his workbench and worn his own shoes home. The leather on the toes of the boots was worn away exposing the steel toe caps. Kneeling and crawling on the floor while working on machinery caused this. I found a short piece of steel chain and welded the first link to the steel toe caps, joining the pair of boots together. I doused the weld in cold water so as not to burn the leather, then I welded the other end of the chain to a short piece of a heavy steel beam.

The next morning Stan tried to pick up his boots.

"What's that on yer boots, Stan?" one of the other men asked.

"Looks like a long weight to me," I said.

"You young bastard..." Stan grabbed me and playfully put his arm around my neck in a headlock. He was laughing as he did so and released me after ruffling my hair.

The whole shop stood around and watched, laughing as Stan put the chain in a vise and cut his boots free with a hacksaw. The shop foreman came over to see what was going on.

"When you children have finished playing, there is work to be done," he said trying not to smile then turned and walked away shaking his head.

At home the boxing lessons evolved into stand-up, knock-down fights. That is me standing up to my old man and him eventually knocking me down. It started one day soon after I had started work; my father brought out the boxing gloves and told me to put them on. I refused, and he tormented me in the usual way until I lashed out with my bare fists. He hit back hard with punches to the body and face, knocking me down. He never asked me to put the boxing gloves on again.

By now I was as tall as my father, although he was heavier and stronger than me and could always beat me in a fight. I would never back down until he knocked me down; he was going to hit me anyway so I would at least try to get a few good punches in myself. I will admit I often stayed down after being knocked down and pretended I was hurt more than I was. I was not stupid, this was not real boxing so why take more of a beating than was necessary?

I found that if I put up a fight, he would respect me for it, and he would be my pal afterwards for a few days. The same was true if I got into a fight outside of home and showed up with cuts and bruises on my face. I would be his hero and he would leave me alone.

The other reason I would get into it with the old man is that he would slap my mother around. I had witnessed him doing this for years but now I wouldn't allow it anymore. I would jump in and throw a few punches myself and he would turn his attention to me, but at least he would not hit my mother. My father would go out drinking most evenings and when he arrived home late at night he would demand food and a cup of tea. If my mother stayed up and waited for him to come home, they would often get into an argument and he would start slapping her around. So I would offer to wait up for him and my mother would go to bed.

I would make him tea and a sandwich, and as much as I hated talking to him when he was drunk, I would often humor him to avoid a fight. I only had to talk about some fight he had been in and we were off on a game of reminiscing. My old man made good money working on the docks. It was a union job, and he worked a lot of overtime. He was generous when it came to money and if he was in a good mood he would give me a five- or even a ten-pound note, which was quite a bit in those days. My old man gave out cash in place of affection and I took it. I didn't make much as an apprentice.

My father was from the old-fashioned school of fighting, born out of his boxing background. "Always fight fair," he would say. "Only use your fists. Never kick a man, especially when he's down. People will respect you for it."

I soon found out that on the streets there is no referee enforcing the Marquis of Queensberry rules of boxing. A head butt ("putting the nut" on someone as we called it) or a "swift kick in the bollocks" is what you would get if you tried to stand there and fight with your fists. The so-

called "fair fight" I reserved for my father; on the streets it was "Do whatever you have to, to end it quick before it's done to you."

We never carried weapons, knives, or anything like that. The police in
England could stop and search you at any time and often did, so to have
a knife you could go to jail. Big Arthur the bookmaker once told me,
"Never carry a knife, Eddie. Old Bill will nick you and no one will respect
you for it. If people know that you can "march on"—fight—"they'll leave
you alone, and if someone pulls a knife on you, you can usually find
something to defend yourself with. A chair is a better defense than another knife."

I respected Big Arthur; he had spent years on these East End streets
and knew all there was to know about surviving. This was a balance between not letting others walk all over you, but at the same time not getting
yourself killed or seriously hurt. The other trick was stay on the right side
of the law and stay out of jail.

Another piece of advice he gave me was, "Don't go looking for trouble;
treat others with respect especially if you don't know who they are. There
are harmless-looking people around here that would kill you as soon as
look at you."

I was still hanging out with George, Roger, and Daisy and a few others from my old school. We had remained friends and met mostly on the
weekends. We would often go to a local place called Steve's Café , which
was a hangout for young kids. It had a jukebox that played the big 78
rpm records. I became interested in popular music; this was the early
1950s and the artists we were listening to were Frankie Lane, Johnny Ray,
and Hank Williams. It was the tail end of the big band era and bands like
Count Basie and Duke Ellington were still popular.

I was exposed to a wide variety of music in those early days. Saturday
evenings we would often catch a bus or the underground up to the West
End and go to a jazz club where the smaller jazz groups that were becoming popular would perform. These would be trios, quartets, or quintets
that were replacing the Big Bands.

Many of the young people that hung out at these West End nightspots
were middle class and into high fashion and we soon followed suit. We
were the first generation of teenagers after World War II and we wanted
to be heard and noticed. There was no one selling fashionable clothes
for teenagers at that time; we had to create our own. Men's clothes in the
late forties and early fifties were wide. Wide pant legs about two feet
around, wide jacket lapels, and wide ties. We would seek out a bespoke
(that is, custom) tailor and have a suit made in a style that befit us. Our

suits were fashioned after a style that was popular in the early 1900s: narrow trousers with sixteen-inch pant legs and high button jackets with narrow lapels and a narrow tie. Because this was known as the Edwardian style after King Edward VII, we were nicknamed "Teddy boys."

There were an abundance of Jewish tailors in the East End; their main business was outfitting customers from the financial district not far from us. These suits would cost about a hundred pounds, which was more than a month's wages for the average working man. The only way we could afford this was because these tailors would extend us credit, and I could swing it with the subsidies I was getting from my old man.

When we would dress up in our high-fashion suits and go "up West" to a jazz club we couldn't be distinguished from the middle-class kids. That is until we opened our mouths, then the cockney accent was a dead giveaway. But that was okay, we were proud of where we were from and it gave us a confidence the other kids admired. So much so that some of the middle-class boys would try to talk like us. It was the old "If you can't beat 'em, join 'em" strategy.

If the middle-class boys admired us, the middle-class girls loved us. We couldn't go wrong. Many of them had led somewhat sheltered lives and had never been exposed to the working class, so we were a little mysterious, maybe even a little dangerous. Even George with his horribly disfigured face was a huge hit with these middle-class girls; they heaped sympathy upon him and smothered him with love and affection.

I had always been protective of George ever since we were kids, although George was quite capable of looking after himself. He was short, powerfully built, and as strong as a horse. In a fight he would wrestle rather than punch. One night I saw him grab an opponent by the crotch of his pants. "Balls an' all" was the way George later described it. With his other hand on the man's coat collar, lifted him high into the air and body-slammed him across a table full of drinks and beer glasses. The noise was tremendous, clearing the room and ending the fight right then and there. We walked out, leaving this one person nursing his aching balls, with friends picking broken glass from his back, and no doubt reflecting on the wisdom of his remarks about George's face.

George was getting more and more into thievery. He would sometimes tell me little bits of information of things he had done, but we both respected the other's different view on the subject and didn't let it get in the way of our friendship. I didn't feel my earlier church choir activities leading to a belief in God necessarily made me any more righteous or better than he was. But the way I saw it there was a definite commandment saying, "Thou shalt not steal." Fighting was different. There was no commandment saying, "Thou shalt not punch someone's lights out."

I was walking home alone one cold, foggy November evening. It was one of those "pea soup" London fogs that we still had in the 1950s before pollution controls eased the situation. The busses had stopped running; in fact all motor vehicle traffic had stopped. Visibility was down to less than six feet and it was impossible to see beyond the hood of a car.

As I passed by a butcher's shop I saw someone standing in the doorway. The shop was closed and the lights were out. I almost walked by when I saw it was George.

"Hey, George, what's going on?" He immediately shushed me and was mumbling incoherently. He was acting very strange.

"Are you coming home?" I asked.

I heard a noise above us and stepped out of the doorway to look up. George grabbed me and pulled me back as a huge cast iron safe came crashing down on the sidewalk; it was pushed out of an upstairs window. On impact the brittle metal shattered into a hundred pieces. I remember paper and money everywhere and almost immediately saw the figure of a London Bobby loom out of the fog. I heard George yell out, "It's Old Bill!"

I took off running up the street back the way I had just come. I didn't know if the policeman was chasing me or where George was, but I remember thinking that at any moment I would run into a lamppost or another pedestrian. It was almost like running with my eyes closed. I finally stopped running and walked out into the street, crossed over to the other side, and stood still to listen. I heard nothing; it didn't appear the policeman had followed. I took a detour away from the area and finally arrived home.

The next day I found George still pumped up from the night before. "Can you believe it? That cozzer caught me bang to rights. I mean he had hold of me and then he says 'On yer way' and let me go. Did you see all that money? There must have been two or three thousand quid there."

"Damn, you were lucky. What the hell were you doing there?" I asked.

"I was supposed to be the lookout. Some use being a lookout when you can't see yer bleedin' hand in front of yer face. All the others got out through the back, the same way they got in."

That afternoon the London evening papers ran the story of the robbery. The headline read, "Safe thieves under the cover of fog, net five thousand pounds." George read the story in disbelief.

"I wondered why that bleedin' cozzer let me go. He took the money. The bastard."

It was true; the East End Police at that time were more crooked than some of the people they put away. I had seen a lot of money on the ground, so where did it go? There was only one conclusion.

Chapter 12

IT WAS OVER A YEAR since the butcher shop robbery. George asked me one day, "Do you remember Bobby Johnson at school?"

"Bobby the Bully? Yeah, I'll never forget that bastard. Why?"

"I saw him the other day. He joined the police force—he's a cozzer."

"Bobby's a bobby? I don't believe it. I can't wait to see him in his helmet. I'll take the piss out of him."

Bobby Johnson was two years older than me and a big kid—even at school he was almost six feet tall. I had suffered many a beating from this bully but I would never back down and I had managed to hurt him a few times. Eventually he left me alone and picked on easier prey. I had not seen him since he left school.

A few days later I was out with a few friends walking down the Mile End Road, when George nudged me. "Hey up, here comes Bobby Johnson."

Sure enough a baby-face young policeman was walking toward us. We stopped and watched as he approached. I was the first to speak.

"Hello, Bobby," I said putting a strong emphasis on the name "Bobby."

"Don't call me that, Conner." I was surprised he remembered my name.

"Why not? It's yer name." I hesitated, then added, "Now it's yer occupation."

The others in the group laughed.

"You can call me Constable Johnson."

"Okay *Cunt*-stable."

"I'm warning you, Conner." He stepped forward, his face becoming bright red.

"That's Mr. Conner to you. Listen Cunt-stable Johnson, I wasn't afraid of you at school and if you want to come down here one evening without that bleedin' uniform, I'll show you I'm not afraid of you now."

George grabbed me by the arm and pulled me away. "C'mon, Eddie, leave it out. He's not worth it."

I was dragged away and reluctantly walked on down the street with the others. Seeing Bobby Johnson again had brought back all the memories of the beatings I had suffered. I was seething inside.

"I know I could give him a kicking now, as big as he is. If he just wasn't wearing that uniform."

"I know you could, Eddie," said George. "But that's it. He's the Filth now, Old Bill. You can't beat Old Bill. Just stay out of his way."

I agreed and we all had a laugh at our meeting with Constable Johnson. It was Roger who suggested that in the Middle Ages they used to cut off "pricks," stretch them on the rack until they were six feet long, and put them on the street as policemen.

"That's why they designed the helmet that way," he added. "It's traditional. Looks like the head of a big prick."

It wasn't many weeks after this incident that Roger and George were caught breaking into a warehouse near the docks, and they were both sentenced to Borstal Training. Borstal was like a reform school and was supposed to help the young offender mend his ways. Some saw it as an apprenticeship for prison later on.

George was sent to Yorkshire in the north of England, and Roger went to the west somewhere near Wales. There was a void in my life after George left; we had been through so much together since we were kids. I wrote to him a few times, but he was only allowed to write one letter a week, and he sent that to his mum and dad. I would see George's dad quite often and he told me George was doing okay and had sent his regards. He was too far away for me to visit; even his parents didn't get to see him that often. The journey by train from London to Yorkshire took almost a whole day.

The only one left from the old crowd was Daisy. He was an okay kid and I liked him but he couldn't fight his way out of a paper bag and would run at the slightest hint of trouble. In the weeks and months that followed George and Roger's departure, I hung out less with the boys. It wasn't the same anymore. I spent quite a bit of time alone or I dated girls. Sometimes I would hang out with a crowd of girls.

One Saturday evening I had a date with a girl; we were going to the pictures. I was waiting on the Mile End Road outside an underground station where we would catch the tube up West to one of the big cinemas. I looked up to see my old nemesis Bobby Johnson approaching.

"Hello, Conner, what are you hanging around here for?"

"I'm waiting for someone."

"Well, I call it loitering, so move along." He was speaking in a deep tone of voice the British police use, especially the young ones to make themselves seem more mature.

"Fuck you, Johnson, I'm not breaking any laws. I'm not moving."

"I said move along." He punched me hard on the shoulder, which was exactly what he would do in school. I didn't see him as an officer of the law; to me he was still Bobby Johnson, the school bully, and a thorn in my side. I snapped.

I lashed out with a hard right cross to his jaw. It knocked him sideways and his helmet went flying. I grabbed him by the lapels of his police uniform and brought my knee up into his crotch. As he doubled over forward I hit him hard in the face with my head. He crumpled to the ground in a fetal position with his hands between his legs and rolled around moaning. I had opened up a good size cut over his eye.

It was all over in seconds. I looked up to see a small crowd of people standing around in stunned silence. The crowd parted as I ran up the street. I looked up to see my date approaching. I grabbed her arm and led her back the way she had just come. "Let's catch the bus up West."

"I thought we were going by tube."

"It's a nice evening; let's catch the bus."

We walked a hundred yards further up the street and waited for a bus. She could no doubt sense my apprehension as I looked back the way we had just come, hoping the bus would arrive before the cavalry in the form of the local police.

"Are you all right?" she asked.

"Yeah, I'm okay. I just had a spot of bother back there. Nothing to worry about."

But I knew I had plenty to worry about; I was in deep shit. I arrived home later that evening to find a police car and two very large policemen waiting for me. They handcuffed me and took me to the local police station. I was charged with assaulting a police officer and taken down to the cells. A short while later one of the officers who brought me in came back with Bobby Johnson. He'd had his eye stitched and had white strips of plaster over the stitches.

"That's gonna look good in the morning," I mused.

The one officer grabbed my arms and held them tight behind my back while Bobby Johnson punched me hard in the stomach three or four times. I had no defense although I did keep my legs tight together, aware that he might try to knee me in the bollocks as I had done to him. The officer holding me let go and I fell to the floor gasping for breath. I managed to mutter, "Fuck you, Bobby Johnson." But all that got me was a kick in the ribs.

"That's enough," I heard the other officer say and they left locking the cell door as they went.

The police cell was about six feet by eight feet, lined with brown glazed brick inside. The floor was matching brown tile. There was no window, just a vent near the ceiling. A wooden bench served as a bed. There was a wooden block at one end instead of a pillow and a two-inch thick horsehair mattress lay over the top. The only other thing in the cell was a piss pot and some hard nonabsorbent toilet paper.

I stayed in this cell all day Sunday. I was given three meals and let out to empty my piss pot and to wash, shave, and use the toilet. Monday morning around ten I was taken upstairs to appear before a magistrate.

Bobby Johnson was there and gave evidence. He left out the part where he punched me on the shoulder. His eye was completely closed now and was every shade of black, red, and purple. Looking at him I couldn't help but smile, which brought retribution from the magistrate.

"Edward Conner, you would do well to remember the seriousness of these proceedings," he said. "I'm going to remand you to police custody for a week and arrange for psychiatric reports."

I was led back down to the cells beneath the courtroom and as the cell door banged shut behind me, it began to sink in that I was in serious trouble this time. This was not a trip to the headmaster's office for six strokes of the cane; this was more trouble than I had ever been in before. I had to spend another week in this damn place.

A short while later I was taken upstairs again; my mother had come to visit me. She started to cry the moment she saw me, which made me cry.

"Oh, Eddie, I knew this is where you would end up if you kept on fighting. Why do you let your father influence you this way?"

That was a good question. I knew my old man was an idiot, but deep inside I wanted his approval and my fighting brought that approval, but it was tearing me apart inside to see my mother cry. There was a glass screen between us and I couldn't even reach out to hold her hand.

"I'm sorry, Mum" was all I could find to say.

"Promise me you'll change your ways when this is over?"

"I will, Mum, I promise."

The visit was a short one and I was led back down to the cell. My mother had brought me a change of clothes, some clean shirts, and underwear. I was given a nightshirt to sleep in and a couple of blankets. Also I was given some books and magazines to read.

Two days later I was taken to an office upstairs in the court building to meet with the psychiatrist, or "trick cyclist" as we called them. He introduced himself as Dr. Paget. He sat me down in front of a large desk and began the interview.

"Your police report seems to indicate that you have a violent nature. What do you have to say about this?"

"What police report? I have never been arrested before; I have no criminal record."

"Nevertheless, I have information that indicates throughout your school years and since leaving school you have constantly engaged in fighting."

"So this police report you speak of is a statement by Constable Bobby Johnson someone who through his school years was a bully who constantly picked on kids smaller and weaker than himself? When I assaulted him I didn't see him as a police officer, but as that same tormentor from my old school days."

"Are you sorry for what you did?"

"I am sorry in the respect that I now have to pay for my actions and I am sorry I have hurt my mother, but sorry for Bobby Johnson? No, he had it coming."

"Do you agree that you have a problem with fighting?"

"No, I don't have a problem with it. But other people seem to."

These were probably not the right answers to be giving, but he was pissing me off with his line of questioning.

"What do think is the reason you get into fights?"

"Well, first let me make it clear that I rarely start a fight. If people like Bobby Johnson would leave me alone there would be no fight."

"Can't you simply back down?"

"No, if you back down the Bobby Johnson's of this world keep coming back to torment you over and over again."

The interview lasted forty-five minutes or so and afterward I was led back to my cell. I thought about the interview with the psychiatrist. I had not told him that one of the reasons I would fight was that I was good at it. My father had taught me well. The thing that stops most people fighting is the fear of getting hurt. I had become immune to the hurt. In all the fights I had been in, no one had hit me as hard as my old man, so I always went in unafraid.

The next day I had a surprise visitor. It was the girl I had taken to the pictures last Saturday evening right after I hit Bobby Johnson. Her name was Patricia, I called her Trisha. She was sixteen years old and lived in my neighborhood. I had arranged to meet her the day before but of course I was otherwise detained. She had asked around and found out where I was. It lifted my spirits to see her. After the visit I sat in my cell thinking maybe when I get out of here I should see Trisha on a regular basis, it would keep me out of trouble. It was not the same anymore since George and Roger left and none of my other friends had come to visit me.

The days passed and the following Monday I appeared in court again. My mother was there and so was Trisha. I pleaded guilty to assaulting a police officer. The magistrate said that I had a good work record. Dr. Paget gave his report and I was given two years probation with a proviso that I receive psychiatric counseling.

Chapter 13

IT WAS 1956; I HAD been dating Trisha for about six months now. She was about five feet three and had short blonde hair and hazel eyes. She was into high fashion as I was. The London kids at the time set the trends in fashion that the rest of the country followed. Trisha and I shared the same interests in music and the cinema. In many ways we were kindred spirits: her father was a heavy drinker and abusive to her and her mother just like my old man.

My probation officer had suggested that I look for some other interests so I had started running again and would run in a nearby park three or four times a week. The company I worked for had an athletic club, which I joined, and we competed against other companies in the area. I ran races at the mile and half-mile distance and after a while had some winning performances. My mother was happy and proud of the fact that I was doing something positive.

My father was indifferent. I wanted so much for him to come out and see me run these races but he never would. He also didn't like the fact that I was seeing a psychiatrist once a week. He said only lunatics saw psychiatrists and often referred to me as "his imbecile son," which hurt because after all it was his encouraging me to fight that had led to my seeing the psychiatrist in the first place. He and I still got into the occasional fistfight, but outside of home I was staying out of trouble. I even walked away from a few situations I never would have before.

If my life was changing then so was the scene around me. There was a buzz going around about a new film called *The Blackboard Jungle*. The buzz was not so much about the film but the soundtrack by *Bill Hayley and the Comets*. Trisha and I went to see it the first opportunity we had and were amazed. Kids were dancing in the aisles of the theater, which was something unheard of, and we were up there dancing with them. It was like nothing we had heard before. We went back to see the film maybe three or four times, just for the music.

Soon the jukebox at Steve's Café was playing records by Bill Hayley and later records by Elvis, Gene Vincent, Bo Diddly, and Chuck Berry. This was all I wanted to listen to now. I no longer went to the jazz clubs up West, but rather hung out at Steve's or went to the local youth center sponsored by the city. There they played rock-n-roll records.

The local dance hall, the Palais de Dance as it was called, had a resident big band that played the dance standards of the late 1940s and early 1950s. Now because of popular demand some were playing rock-n-roll covers. The Palais de Dance had a talent contest once a week and some of my friends urged me to get up and sing.

"Go on, Eddie," my friend Daisy said. "I remember how you used to sing at school. You have a great voice, get up there."

I got up onstage and did Elvis's *Heartbreak Hotel.* My performance got a good reaction from the crowd and I was urged to do another, so I did a Chuck Berry number. When I finished, the piano player asked me to stay and talk with him at the end of the evening.

His name was Ralph. He was older, probably in his forties as was most of the band, but a fine musician. He told me he had an idea that he wanted to put to the management of the dance hall. He wanted to do a show once a week that would be all rock-n-roll. There would be just him on piano with a bass player and a drummer.

"We need a singer. Would you be interested?" I was both flattered and elated. I jumped at the chance. I gave Ralph my address and the next evening he came 'round to see me. He said his idea had been accepted and arranged for me to go to his house to rehearse some songs.

We started out just doing a short set of songs in the middle of the evening while the main band took a break. I learned more songs and eventually we had our own show every Wednesday evening. We called ourselves *Eddie and the Eddie Sons,* which was kind of funny because the guys in the band were all old enough to be my father. A guitar and saxophone player later joined us and we started getting Sunday evening gigs at some local pubs. The dance hall was closed Sundays so the other guys in the band were free. We could have booked gigs for Friday and Saturday nights but the others didn't want to give up their secure job at the dance hall. No one knew if rock-n-roll was just a passing trend.

I loved performing onstage; I loved to hear the sound of my own voice through the speakers just as I had enjoyed hearing my voice as a kid singing in church. I loved the attention I was getting; everyone wanted to be my friend. As I walked around my neighborhood strangers would stop and tell me that they had heard me sing at the Palais de Dance or the local pubs.

Things were not getting any easier at home. I was letting my hair grow longer after the style of Elvis and my old man was giving me a hard time about it. Ralph shared a house with two other musicians and said I could move in with them. I ran the idea past my probation officer but he was against it. One Saturday evening I was shaving in the kitchen when my father came and stood behind me.

"Am I hurting you, son?" he asked

"No, why?"

"I should be, I'm standing on yer fucking hair. Get it cut." I said nothing knowing what the outcome would be. I finished shaving and turned to face him.

"Get yer hair cut, you look like a woman."

I knew what my answer was and I knew what he would do, so I looked him in the eye and said, "Fuck you." Before he could react I hit him in the face as hard as I could. I managed to get two or three more good punches in before he recovered. Then he came back as he always did and hit me even harder. I went down and stayed down.

"Get yer hair cut." I said nothing. I got cleaned up and went out.

I came home late that evening and walked in the front door. I could hear my mother and father arguing in the next room. I almost went straight upstairs but sensed something was wrong. I walked into the living room. My mother was sitting in an armchair; she had a bloody nose.

"You bastard. You hit my mother again." I moved toward my father, who was standing in the middle of the room. I hit him hard in the face with my head. There was a stupefied look on his face because I had never done that before. I hit him again with my head, then punched him right, left, and another right to the jaw. He sank to his knees and I pulled his head toward me and brought my knee up into his face. I just wanted to punish him for hitting my mother. For all the beatings he had given me, I was through fighting fair. He tried to get up.

"Stay down or I'll kill you." He reached for the edge of the table to pull himself up, he got to his knees and I kicked him in the face. "I said stay down." He rolled over on his back. His face was a mask of blood.

"Eddie, stop! Didn't I always teach you to fight fair?" he pleaded.

"Fight fair. Where was the fairness when I was eight years old and you punched me and knocked me down—was that a fair fight? Where was the fairness when you stubbed a cigarette on the back of my hand? Is it a fair fight when you punch my mother in the face? Don't even talk to me about a fair fight and don't you ever hit my mother again."

Only after I got all the words out and my anger spent did I become aware of my mother tugging at my arm and saying, "Eddie, stop, please stop." She was trembling. I led her into the kitchen and bathed her face.

"Please leave, Eddie, please go now." She was crying and still trembling.

"Will you be okay?" I asked.

"Yes, please just leave."

I walked back through the living room; my father was still lying on the floor. He spoke as I passed through on my way out. "You couldn't beat me in a fair fight; you had to use your head and your boot."

I said nothing and walked out of the front door and into the street. It was late, close to midnight; I turned my collar against the cold night air. I felt cool and calm as I walked. It was not that I felt good or elated over what I had just done, but I felt at peace.

"Where to now?" I wondered.

I considered going over to Ralph's house; he was sure to be up. Instead I walked to the nearest underground station and caught the tube over to the Circle Line. The Circle Line is a large loop that goes all around London and I could ride all night round and round.

I spent some of the time dozing, some of the time studying the other passengers, wondering if their lives were any less complicated than mine right now. I had forced my own hand; I could not go back home to live after this. I decided that I would go to Ralph and see if his offer to live with him still stood. I would have to talk to my probation officer and hope that he understood.

Sunday morning came and I got off the tube and bought myself breakfast. I was pretty hungry. I knew it was no use going over to Ralph's place yet, he was not an early riser. I remembered we were playing at a pub that night. I would need a change of clothes and maybe I could go home later when my old man was sure to be at the pub.

I finished breakfast and walked over to Trisha's house; she came to the door surprised to see me this early. She got her coat and we walked down to Steve's Café and we sat and talked over a cup of tea. I explained what had happened the night before. "I have to leave home, I can't live there anymore." I told her.

"God, I wish I could leave home" was her response.

I was unaccustomed to seeing her without makeup; she looked so pale, so young. She looked up. "Couldn't we get a place together? I mean we don't have to get married or nothing, we could just say we were married."

I knew this was not an option, I reached out to hold her hand. "Trisha, we can't do that. You're only sixteen and even if you were eighteen we couldn't afford it."

"Couldn't we leave London and go somewhere where it is cheaper to live?"

"We can't do that either. I have to finish my apprenticeship, and don't forget I'm on probation."

She agreed that her idea was not possible.

I took Trisha home and caught a bus over to Ralph's house. Ralph said I could stay with him and drove me back home in his car to pick up my clothes. My old man was at the pub as I had predicted. My mother said that my father was all right, he was cut and bruised but this was no worse than beatings he had suffered before. I was concerned for my mother. Who would protect her now I was gone?

Ralph and I and the other band members performed at a local pub that evening and the events of the night before seemed like the distant past. However, they were brought back to the forefront the following week when I had to talk to my probation officer and the psychiatrist.

My probation officer was okay. He knew what my relationship with my father was like and when I explained that I had arrived home to find my father beating my mother, he was somewhat sympathetic. Dr. Paget, the psychiatrist, took a different view. He suggested that I had a serious problem and I might consider voluntarily checking into a mental hospital for some treatment. This seemed a little drastic to me and I explained I had been keeping out of trouble recently, and now that I was away from my father things would be better.

Things did get better for the rest of 1956 and into 1957. Johnny, the guitar player who also lived at the house with Ralph, and was teaching me how to play guitar. Johnny was not in the dance band with Ralph so we did a few weekday evening gigs as a duo. There were not too many rock-n-roll bands around at that time and we were in great demand. We were even making money, which was great because I loved performing and would have done it for nothing.

More rock-n-roll records were coming out, so there were more songs to add to our repertoire. Johnny and I had even started to write our own songs. I wrote the lyrics and Johnny wrote the music. Our reputation was spreading and we were doing gigs further and further afield. I was staying out of trouble and had less than a year of my probation to do.

Chapter 14

AS I WALKED HOME LATE on a cold December evening after taking Trisha home, a car pulled up alongside me and a voice called out, "Hey, Conner."

I turned to see Bobby Johnson in the passenger seat; another man I recognized as a police officer was driving. They were not in uniform and I could tell Johnson had been drinking. I tried to ignore them. Bobby Johnson got out of the car and approached me. "Hey, Conner, didn't you once tell me that if I ever wanted to meet you out of uniform…? Well, guess what? Here I am, out of uniform and off duty. Why don't you get in the car and we'll drive to a quiet little place where we can have it out, just you and me."

"Do you think I'm fucking stupid enough to get in a car with two of you?"

"No, c'mon; he's just the driver. It'll be just you and me."

"Forget it, Johnson." I started to walk away. The next thing I knew, Johnson grabbed me from behind, his arm around my neck in a chokehold and wrestled me to the ground. He and the other officer held me down and handcuffed my hands behind my back. They carried me to the car and drove down to the dock area, which was pretty deserted at that time of night.

In an alleyway behind a warehouse they dragged me from the car and with my hands still cuffed behind my back, the one officer held me while Johnson punched me in the stomach and in the face. He went back to the car and got a truncheon, which is a nightstick that the British police carry, and proceeded to beat me with it. After a few blows to my arms and legs he hit me on the side of my head. I saw a flash of light before being engulfed by a pool of blackness.

I woke up in a hospital bed; a nurse ran to get a doctor. He looked into my eyes and asked me my name. "Do you remember what happened to you?"

"Yes, I was beaten up by two police officers. One of them was named Bobby Johnson."

"No, these were the officers who brought you in, they found you down by the docks. You're a little confused, which is not surprising. Did you know you have been unconscious for almost three days?"

"What day is it?"

"It's Tuesday." I remembered this had happened Saturday evening.

"I tell you, it was Bobby Johnson that did this."

The doctor shook his head. "No, I believe they have already arrested someone for doing this. I'll let the detective know that you are conscious; he will want to talk to you."

The next day I got a visit from Dr. Paget and a detective. The detective asked me what had happened. I told the story exactly as it had happened. The detective asked, "Do you know Charlie Ryan?"

"Never heard of him."

"He has confessed to beating you up with an iron pipe, he goes before the magistrate on Friday. He's pleading guilty so you won't have to be there."

"It was Bobby Johnson and another police officer. I don't know his name but I've seen him at the station."

"Constable Johnson brought you to the hospital; he may have saved your life. I know you've had problems with Constable Johnson in the past but you should realize he helped you this time."

"How did you come to arrest this Charlie Ryan?"

"Constable Johnson saw you and Ryan walking toward the docks. They had gone back to see what you were up to. That's when they found you unconscious. Ryan was picked up later and he confessed."

I shook my head. "No, that's not what happened."

The detective and Dr. Paget got up from the bedside and walked a short distance away. They spoke briefly in soft voices but I did pick up the words "suffering from delusions." The detective left and Dr. Paget came back to my bedside.

"Eddie, why won't you accept that you and this Charlie Ryan got into a fight and he got the better of you?" he asked.

I knew it was hopeless to argue. The police obviously had something far more serious on Charlie Ryan and he had agreed to plead guilty to this instead. The maximum sentence a magistrate could give out was six months. Charlie Ryan was ready to accept that rather than face a far more serious charge.

Dr. Paget continued, "Eddie, do you remember we talked about your going voluntarily into a mental hospital? I really think this could help you. Why don't you think about it?"

Later the medical doctor came back to check on me. He was in his twenties, not much older than myself. I liked him and trusted him. I told how the police had set up this Charlie Ryan to take the fall for Bobby Johnson. I think he may have believed me. He said, "I understand that Dr. Paget wants you to check into a mental hospital."

"He wants me to think about it. I don't feel I need to. What do you think?"

"Did you know that all it takes is a doctor and a magistrate to certify someone insane?" I could see that he was genuinely concerned.

"What are you saying?"

"I know Dr. Paget and I know he has had quite a few patients certified insane when I didn't think they were all that bad. Now I'm not a psychiatrist and I probably shouldn't be talking to you this way, but you seem like a bright young man and I would hate to see you spend years or maybe your whole life in a mental institution."

I was shocked. "Could this happen?"

"Oh yes, very easily. My advice would be to go in as a voluntary patient for a short while, finish out your probation, and then get as far away from Dr. Paget as you can."

I spent the rest of that week in the hospital and on discharge agreed with Dr. Paget to sign in for six weeks as a voluntary patient in a psychiatric hospital. I was driven by car to a rural area some thirty miles north of London to a place called Arlesey. Seeing the countryside again reminded me of my childhood and I was thinking maybe this experience wouldn't be so bad after all. Chance to relax, get myself together, and figure out what to do with my life.

The place I was taken to was an annex of the main hospital and was a large red brick Victorian house with acreage around it. As we pulled in through the huge iron gates and up the driveway the driver pointed out the main hospital off in the distance. It looked a foreboding place on this cold, gray December morning, almost like a prison, and I was glad I was not going there.

Soon after arriving, I had an interview with a Dr. Phillips who was the head psychiatrist at this annex. After the interview my clothes were taken away and I was given pajamas, a robe, and slippers to wear. All the patients at this place were dressed the same; we all looked as though we had just got out of bed or were just going to bed. I didn't care for this part; I was not used to sitting around in pajamas all day. I felt uncomfortable. The other patients were all men of varying ages. There were a few my age but mostly they seemed to be in the forty to sixty age group.

The next day I was taken to a room and given some bitter-tasting medicine in a cup. I drank it down and was told to lie on a bed. Within a few minutes I became semiconscious and was aware of several people around me, strapping me to the bed, placing something on my head, and pushing a rubber plug in my mouth.

Next there was a high pitched sound "wheeeeeeeeeee" accompanied by pain and zigzag lines of light rather like interference on a TV screen going left to right somewhere at the back of my eyes. This lasted for maybe a second, then nothing.

I awoke after what seemed only moments later. The room was empty. The first thing I noticed was that I had pissed in the bed. I was lying in a pool of urine that soaked my whole back and the ammonia was burning the insides of my thighs. My head felt like my brain was twice its normal size and was trying to get out through my eye sockets.

A male nurse came into the room.

"What the hell did you just do to me?" I asked.

"You had ECT—electroconvulsive therapy. Do you have a headache?"

"Yes, I've got a headache to end all bleedin' headaches." The nurse laughed. "I'm glad you find it funny." I said as he led me to the shower and I was given clean pajamas. I went to lie on my bed, slept for most of the day, and my headache finally went away.

The next day I saw Dr. Phillips in his office. "What is this ECT you're giving me?" I asked.

"Electroconvulsive therapy. It's part of your treatment."

"You didn't explain this to me when I arrived. What does it do?"

"It erases the memories of your past. The problems you have today are caused by memories of your past. Wipe out the memories and you wipe out the problem."

"But I don't want my memories wiped out, memories make me who I am. Without memories I have no personality; I am no longer a person. I am nothing but a fucking zombie. You can't do this to me, this is not what I signed up for. I want to leave."

"You can't leave."

"But I came here as a voluntary patient."

"You agreed to a course of treatment and you can't leave until that course is complete."

"I will fight you bastards; you can't do this to me."

I was standing in front of Dr. Phillips' desk with my fingers under the top edge. I lifted the desk up and turned it over on top of him. There was a loud crash and the phone bell gave a "ding" as it hit the floor. Dr. Phillips was on his back with the desk across his chest. The next thing I knew there were men in white coats everywhere, punching me, pummeling me, kneeling on me, and picking me up and carrying me from the room. They put me in a straightjacket, threw me in a padded room, and locked the door. I lay there wondering what the hell I had got myself into now.

That evening Dr. Phillips accompanied by two male nurses came to see me. He said, "I had a phone call from your girlfriend this afternoon, she wants to come and see you. If you behave yourself and have your treatment you can see her tomorrow afternoon."

"And if I don't I suppose I won't see her."

"That's right and what's more we'll give you an injection and carry you unconscious into the treatment room for your ECT."

"Then I guess you have me by the short and curlies. Okay, I'll behave myself."

The two nurses loosened the straps on my straightjacket and I was allowed to join the other patients for the evening meal.

The next morning I reluctantly went in for my second ECT session. It wasn't any easier. I had the same headache when it was over although I didn't piss the bed this time.

Trisha came to see me in the afternoon; she came by train from London. The train station was within walking distance of the hospital annex. It was a beautiful warm sunny day, more like spring than mid-December. We walked on the grounds of the house.

"Trisha, do you remember when you said we should move out of London and find a place together? Do you still want to do that?"

"Oh yes, Eddie, I do."

I told Trisha about the ECT treatment and what it did. "I've got to get out of here as soon as I can. Can you come back here tomorrow night? Go see Ralph and get my clothes. I have a savings bank book in the top drawer of my dresser. Bring that; we'll need money."

We walked around the side of the house and I could see an open barn with straw bails in it maybe half a mile up the road. There were no other buildings between the barn, and us. I told Trisha, "Get here as late as you can. It'll be midnight before I can get out of here. Wait for me in that barn up the road. Find the earliest train leaving Arlesey Station to anywhere—I don't care. Hopefully we can be gone before they find I'm missing." We agreed on the plan.

"What if you don't make it?" Trisha asked anxiously.

"I'll be there, don't worry; just make sure you're there."

I was fortunate not to have ECT the next day. I guess their plan was to give it every other day. It was warm sunny day again; I walked on the grounds of the house and planned my escape. There was a rainwater spout alongside my bedroom window, it was solid cast iron as were most of the gutters and rain spouts on these old Victorian houses. I casually strolled up to the side of the house and leaned on the rain spout. It seemed pretty solid, no one was around so I grasped the spout and gave it a shake. It didn't move so I felt that it would bear my weight.

The time seemed to drag that day and I stayed up as long as I could, watching television until 10 P.M. when we were told to go to bed. I had checked the casement window in my room earlier in the day, it gave a loud squeak when opened so I opened it when I went to bed, just wide enough for me to get through. It was a clear night with a heavy frost. It was freezing in the room with the window open but I figured I might as well get used to it; I would be out in it soon.

My bedside clock showed midnight; I put my head out of the window. All was quiet and dark on my side of the building. Fortunately the staff slept on the other side of the house and the rooms below mine were offices or treatment rooms. I put on my robe and slippers and squeezed my upper body through the window. I lay on the windowsill and reached out for the rain spout. Gently I eased my body out of the window, the rain spout held and I slipped easily down to the ground.

I tiptoed across the lawn and climbed over the low brick perimeter wall and on to the road. The moon was almost full and I could see clearly; I just hoped that no one would see me. I ran up the road toward the barn. My carpet slippers kept coming off and eventually I removed them and ran barefoot on the grass at the side of the road. I got to the barn and called out softly.

"Trisha, Trisha." She stepped out of the shadows and ran to my arms.

"Oh, Eddie, I thought you were never going to get here. I was so scared."

We hugged and kissed, then I asked, "Where's my clothes? I'm freezing." Trisha led me to a suitcase and we took it to the rear of the barn away from the road. I opened up the case and quickly dressed. I was about to dump my pajamas and robe but decided to take them with me. If they found the pajamas and robe they would know that I had help and a change of clothes.

"Did you find out the time of a train out of here?" I asked.

"Yes, there is a milk train to Luton at 5 A.M."

"That's perfect; hopefully they won't discover I'm gone until six."

Luton was a large industrial town north of London. General Motors and Chrysler had car plants there. It would be the ideal place to go; there would be plenty of jobs.

"Let's get over to the station now. There will be a waiting room there and it will be warmer than waiting here."

We walked the mile up the road to the tiny station and bought two tickets to Luton. There was a waiting room that had a potbelly coal stove inside; it was really warm, even a little too warm. We sat on the hard wooden benches and waited. We had only been there a short while when we heard voices and looked through the waiting room window to see a policeman talking to the ticket clerk. Trisha nudged me.

"What if he comes in here?" There was panic in her voice.

"Just stay calm, pretend to be asleep. Let me do the talking."

The policeman looked in through the window and then came into the waiting room. He was an older man with an ample stomach.

"Evening, all," he said in typical British bobby fashion. "What brings you young people to this neck of the woods?"

I had already thought of my story before he even entered the room. "We were going to Luton last night from London and we got on the wrong train and ended up here, so now we're waiting for the five o'clock milk train."

"Well, at least you have a warm place to wait; it's damn cold out there tonight."

"You can say that again, but the weather's been beautiful the last couple of days, more like spring," I said trying to make casual conversation. He stood with his back to the stove then turned and held his hands over the heat and rubbed them together.

"Well, I mustn't get too warm or I won't want to get back out there." He turned and walked to the door. "You youngsters take care now."

Trisha gave a big sigh of relief as he closed the door. "I don't know how you can be so calm. I was peeing my pants."

"You've got to be calm when it comes to Old Bill; they can smell the slightest hint of nervousness."

The rest of the night was uneventful. Trisha lay on the bench with her head on my lap and slept. When it got near to five o'clock, three or four more people came in to wait for the train.

The train arrived on time; it had only two passenger cars. The rest of the train was made up of special boxcars to carry the milk churns from the local farms to the city. It seemed like forever until all the milk was loaded and we were on our way. The trip to Luton was not far but took almost two hours, as the train stopped and there was a long wait at every little station while more milk churns were picked up.

Chapter 15

I NEEDED TO FIND A job, and soon. We had only been in Luton one day and already the money I had drawn from my savings was gone. We found a tiny furnished room and had paid a month's rent in advance. The biggest expense had been buying clothes for Trisha. She had been unable to bring any of her own clothes because she had essentially run away from home and as her mother was there when she left, she could not walk out with a suitcase.

The problem was it was a week before Christmas and most companies would delay hiring new people until after the holidays. My best bet was to find a temporary Christmas job. I found one such opening in the local newspaper for help in a butcher's shop preparing turkeys for the oven. I'd remembered my mother cleaning the insides from chickens and I figured turkeys would be much the same. The butcher's shop was about two miles from the boarding house so I walked over there and applied for the job, saying that I had experience in this kind of thing.

The butcher's name was Edwards; he spoke with a Welsh accent and called me Boyo. He was a small man a little over five feet, fiftyish, not too heavy but with a little round belly. His thinning dark hair was slicked down and parted in the middle. He wore a white coat and blood-stained white apron that came almost down to his ankles. I was hired and asked to start the next day; I would be paid three pounds for the week, not a lot of money but I was in no position to turn it down. My next stop was the local library where I found a book on preparing poultry for the table. I spent an hour or more studying and memorizing the procedure so I could at least look like I knew what I was doing the next day.

I arrived at the butcher's shop bright and early the next morning. Edwards gave me a white coat and apron to wear. Then he slapped a large turkey on a bench and handed me a knife. "Okay, Boyo, let's see you perform."

Thankfully, the turkey was already dead. All its feathers had been removed but it still had a head, complete with eyes and a beak, and some very big feet still attached. My mind was racing going back over the photos and text I had studied at the library the day before. I turned the bird on its back and cut its head off. Next I removed the bone from inside the neck remembering to leave the skin long enough to tuck inside, to avoid a large gaping wound where the neck used to be. I was working very slowly and methodically; if I cut something off that shouldn't be cut off I could hardly sew it back on. Edwards became impatient and snatched the knife from my hand.

"Now, look you, it's dead and it doesn't have a mother. Don't be afraid to cut the bloody thing." And with expert strokes of the knife blade he demonstrated the art of preparing turkeys giving a commentary in his thick Welsh accent as he did so.

"Now, look y'ere, Boyo, I'll show you just once. You cut it y'ere, you pull everything out from inside. You save this, this, and this; these are the giblets, wrap them in wax paper and put them back inside. You cut 'round the leg joint y'ere, give it a twist to break the joint, and pull the sinews out with the leg, because you don't want to be chewing on sinew when biting into a turkey leg, do you? You tie the legs up with string like this and there you 'ave it. Put the finished turkey over y'ere and grab another one."

The turkeys were hung on a rail at the back of the shop suspended by their feet with their necks dangling down. I went to get another and Edwards left. I was glad; I didn't care for him and I could certainly work better without him standing over me. This was not brain surgery; I could handle it.

There were two other men who worked in the shop, both in their forties and friendly enough although Edwards was not a man to allow his workers stand around talking so I never got to know them very well.

During the week there were deliveries of meat. A van would pull up in the alleyway at the back of the shop and we would all have to go out and help unload it. This was not a pleasant job. There were sides of beef and whole pigs, frozen stiff, heavy and difficult to hold on to.

There were some frozen turkeys on the van and these were left to thaw out. They were already dressed and oven ready so I didn't expect to have to work on them; I was wrong. The next day I was told to remove the giblets from inside the turkeys, rewrap in wax paper, and put them back. There was an aluminum tag on a wing of each bird, stamped "Produce of Argentina." I had to remove the tag with a pair of pliers and they were put on display in the shop window with a sign that read "Prime English Turkeys."

"How come these Argentinean turkeys end up as prime English?" I asked.

"I think they flew over here during a storm," was the answer I got.

I did other work around the shop. Each night I had to sweep the floor and scrub the benches. In the morning I would put fresh sawdust on the floor. I also made sausages. All the leftover pieces of meat went into sausages; even meat that had been dropped on the floor was washed off and went into the meat grinder. I ground up the meat, mixed it with cereal fillers, and seasoning, then put it in the sausage machine that extruded the meat into the skins.

Christmas Eve was my last day at the butcher's shop. The shop was staying open until nine o'clock so customers could pick up their orders. It was close to seven and I asked if I could leave. Edwards said no because he wanted me to sweep the shop floor after closing. One of the other men offered to sweep the floor, so Edwards reluctantly gave in to my request.

"I suppose you want paying now," he said, moving over to the cash register.

"That would be nice, thank you."

Edwards open the drawer and handed me a one-pound note.

"What's this?" I smiled thinking he was fooling with me.

"I didn't have such a good week, this is all I'm paying you."

I realized he wasn't fooling. "Oh no, I agreed to work for three quid."

"You're not worth three quid."

I stepped behind the counter. "You fucking little git." I didn't hit him, maybe because he was smaller than I was. I grabbed him by the throat with my right hand and pushed him backward toward the other two men standing at the far end of the counter. One of them grabbed him under the armpits and prevented him from falling on his ass. I snatched up a large butcher knife lying on the counter.

"Stay back there, all of you." I moved back to the cash register, still open. The three moved toward me but stopped when I looked back at them. "I'm taking three quid. No more, no less."

I held up the three one-pound notes for them to see. I closed the drawer, threw the knife down on the counter, and ran out through the door.

I ran for about half a mile then stopped and looked back. No one was following and I walked the two miles back to the boarding house at a fast pace. I went straight up the stairs; Trisha was waiting in our room. I told her what had happened.

"Eddie, why do you do these things?"

"Don't you bleedin' start, you sound like my mother. We have to leave, the police will be here."

"Where will we go? It's Christmas Eve and we've got no money."

She was right.

"Damn, I should have grabbed a handful of money, I'm gonna get nicked whether I'd taken three quid or three hundred."

"Maybe they won't call the police," Trisha reasoned. "You did only take the three quid he owed you."

I thought over that possibility for two seconds. "No, I can't take that chance; let's pack."

It didn't take long to throw the few things we had back into the suitcase and we headed down the stairs. We walked through the front door and met two very large men coming up the steps. I knew immediately they were the police even though they were in plain clothes. The wide-brimmed hats and the big overcoats were a giveaway. No one wore hats like that anymore, only the police; they might as well be in uniform.

"We're looking for Eddie Conner."

"Sorry I don't know him. Ask the landlady inside."

I tried to walk around them but they were not going to allow that; they marched up the steps forcing me back into the hallway. Once inside again I knew it was no use resisting or lying. I didn't even consider running, they would probably have a man on the back door and I couldn't leave Trisha behind.

"Okay, I'm Eddie Conner."

"I'm Inspector Manning and this is Detective Platt. I have to ask you to accompany me to the police station."

I looked at Trisha. "Well at least we don't have to pack; we're ready to go."

Detective Platt led Trisha out first and I followed. Manning had one huge hand around my wrist and the other on my coat collar. I knew that if I even attempted to get away, my arm would be up my back faster that a ferret up a trouser leg.

They had an unmarked car parked in the street outside. It was a two door; Platt opened the door and folded the front passenger seat forward, Trisha climbed in the backseat and I followed. Manning put the seat down and sat sideways in it with the door still open. Platt walked around the back of the house and came back with a uniformed officer. I muttered "huh" under my breath, smiled, and shook my head as I realized I had been right about someone 'round the back.

"What?" Trisha asked.

"Nothing." I was not feeling too proud of myself and being right about something so trivial was not going to make me feel any better. The uniformed officer removed his helmet and got in the backseat with us; he took up half the seat and Trisha and I shared the other half. I put my arm around her shoulder.

"This is cozy," I remarked; no one responded.

Inspector Manning got back in the passenger seat and Platt drove. On the way to the police station, the three officers talked amongst themselves about their Christmas plans, ignoring Trisha and me as if we weren't even there.

We arrived at the Police Station; Trisha and I were separated. Trisha was led away by a woman police officer and I was taken to an interview room. Manning and Platt were both in the room with me. Manning spoke first.

"Where are you from?" he asked; I told him.

"London, Stepney."

"Things are fairly quiet around here and we don't take too kindly to young tearaways from 'the Smoke' coming here and causing problems. Now tell me what happened at Edwards the Butchers."

"He took a liberty wiv' me. I worked all week an' he said he'd pay me three quid, then he give's me a quid. Would you work all week for a quid?

"You took money from the till."

"I took what he owed me, three quid."

"And threatened him with a knife."

"Well, there were three of them, I only put the fright'ners on 'em. I wouldn't have done nothin'."

"That's armed robbery."

"Armed robbery, you make it sound like I went in there wiv' a bleedin' shooter, I just took the three quid he owed me. I could have took the lot but I'm not a thief."

"Well, what are you? Have you been in trouble before?"

It was no use lying. "Yes, I'm on probation."

"For what?"

I was thinking, Oh shit, he's not gonna like this. "Assaulting a police officer."

"Ooooooh, Detective Platt, are you scared? I am. We've got a tearaway here from London who likes to mix it with police officers." He reached across the table and grabbed the front of my shirt lifting me from the chair. "You're in big trouble, m'lad, and don't even think you can fuck with me."

He threw me back into my seat and left the room. Detective Platt spoke for the first time. "Don't worry about him, his bark's worse than his bite. Would you like a cup of tea?"

I gave a little smile. This was the old "good cop, bad cop" routine. "Yes, thanks, I would like a cup of tea, and something to eat if you have it, I'm bleedin' starving."

Platt left the room and came back with a cup of tea and a sandwich. "This is a sandwich I had left over from lunch; it's a little stale but you're welcome to it." I thanked him and he sat at the table with me.

"Would you like to make a statement?"

"I've already told you what happened."

"Yes, but we need to get it down on paper."

I told the story again and Platt wrote it down. I read it through and signed it.

"What's going to happen to Trisha?" I asked.

"She is not charged with anything but I understand she's under eighteen so she'll be sent home."

"Can I see her?"

"Let me check."

Platt left the room and was back in less than a minute. "I'm sorry, I've been told she's already left. A policewoman is taking her back to London by train."

"Damn, you could've let me see her before she left."

"I'm sorry. If it was up to me I would have but I didn't know she had gone."

His concern was little consolation to me as I was led down to the holding cells.

When that cell door slams reality hits like a slap on the back of the head. It was Christmas Eve, I was stuck in a police cell, and my girl was on her way back to London. I lay on the hard bed; my hands behind my head, fingers laced, I stared at the ceiling. I thought over the events of the day.

Is it my fault that I'm here? It's gotta be my fault. I could have took the quid that Edwards gave me and said nothing. But you can't let people fuck with you like that. Damn that little turd, why did he have to fuck with me? Why do people do that?

Chapter 16

CHRISTMAS DAY CAME AND WENT. The highlight of the day was when they brought Christmas Dinner with turkey, mashed potatoes, and gravy, followed by the traditional plum pudding and custard. Someone was on duty cooking for the police officers working that day; as I was the only prisoner there in the cells they decided to share the dinner with me. And so the spirit of Christmas was alive and well even in "the nick."

The day after the holidays I was taken to the magistrate court, which was in the same building. I had been charged with armed robbery. Edwards was there to give evidence; he told the court how he had given me one pound.

"How long did this young man work for you?" the magistrate asked.

"A week, your honor."

"A week. He worked a whole week for a pound?" I sensed the Magistrate might be on my side. When it came time for me to speak I explained how Edwards had promised me three pounds and then paid me only one. The magistrate turned to the police chief.

"Couldn't this armed robbery charge be reduced so that I can deal with this now?"

The police chief refused his request and approached the Magistrate; the two talked in muffled tones. I couldn't hear what was said but I imagined the police chief was filling him in on my past record and the fact that I was on probation for assaulting a police officer. The magistrate spoke to me. "Edward Conner, I can sympathize with your feeling that you were cheated, but you took the law into your own hands and you cannot do that."

Bail was refused and I was remanded in custody to appear at the next Bedford quarter sessions to be held in mid-February. Luton is in the county of Bedfordshire and the criminal court for the county is in the town of

Bedford some twenty miles north of Luton. Bedford also had a prison, which is where I would be for the next six weeks awaiting trial.

That afternoon the door of the police cell opened; a uniformed officer came in and introduced himself as Constable Mott. He was a big man about six feet six inches and with his helmet he appeared even taller. Probably in his forties, he was a jovial man with a big smile. "Okay, Eddie m'lad, you an' me are going on a train ride up to Bedford." He was holding a pair of handcuffs in his hand. "Now because I don't want to hold yer hand all the way there, we're gonna put these on."

He put one side of the cuffs on his own huge left wrist and the other side to my right wrist. "There, that's better. I would hate for us to get separated in a crowd and you get lost."

He made a good point; I was unlikely to escape with a six foot six, 250-pound bobby attached to my wrist. He took me upstairs and I signed for my suitcase and other personal effects. Constable Mott took the suitcase and we went outside where a police car was waiting.

"It's just like we're off on our holidays," Mott quipped as he put my case in the front seat. I was glad I had someone cheerful for the trip to Bedford.

We climbed in the backseat and were on our way. As before, the driver and Mott talked back and forth. The driver called him Charlie. "Charlie Mott," I was thinking. "He looks like a Charlie Mott." He was okay; I liked him.

We arrived at the train station and the driver went to buy two tickets. Charlie Mott got my suitcase and we walked inside. The driver handed over the tickets and the two officers said their goodbyes. We stood on the platform and waited for the train. Charlie's arms hung by his side, his hand was about level with my elbow so I had to bend my arm. I felt like a little boy holding his mummy's hand, it was embarrassing. There were a lot of people waiting for the train, they all gave us a wide berth as they walked by and stood their distance from us. Charlie could no doubt sense I was feeling uncomfortable, so he tried to make conversation. He looked down at my shoes. They were Italian style, which was popular in the late 1950s. They had very long pointed toes.

"Tell me something, do your feet go all the way to the end of those pointy toes?"

I looked down at my feet. "No, they don't. Can I ask you a question?"

"Yes, what?"

"Does your head go all the way to the top of that helmet?"

"You cheeky young bastard." Charlie burst out laughing. "I set myself up for that one."

We both laughed aloud and people on the platform were staring at us.

The train came and we had a compartment to ourselves. One lady did come in briefly but when she saw the handcuffs she got up and left. The train pulled out of the station and we were on our way to Bedford.

"How old are you, Eddie?" Charlie asked.

"I'll be twenty-one in February."

"I've got a boy just a few months younger than you."

"He's lucky to have a father like you. My ol' man's a bastard."

I went on to explain what my father was like. Charlie listened then said, "Eddie, we don't get to choose our parents, your father sounds very much like my father was. I made up my mind I would never treat my son like that. You can break the cycle, you know."

I nodded in agreement. "What does your boy do?"

"He's in the air force."

"I had a brother in the air force; he was killed in the war. Damn, I just realized he was younger than me when he was killed."

"I was in the air force during the war; we were shot down over Germany and I bailed out and spent the rest of the war in a prisoner of war camp." Charlie continued, "You know, Eddie, I was very much like you at your age. I was always getting into trouble but the war came along and I grew up very fast. You don't have a war so you're fighting your own bloody war on the streets and with society. It's a war you can't win."

We arrived at Bedford Station and were met by another police car to take us on the last leg of our journey. After a short drive, we pulled up in front of the prison gate, which was more like huge double doors than a gate, solid wood reinforced with steel and big enough for a bus to pass through. Painted black and alongside on the wall was a sign also black with gold lettering, proclaiming "H. M. Prison, Bedford." Her Majesty's Prison. Now I could officially say I was a guest of the Queen.

We got out of the car. Charlie took my suitcase and we walked up to the gate. Cut into one side of the big gate was a small man-door just big enough for one person to pass through and in it was a peephole with a hinged flap. Charlie rang a doorbell; we waited.

"There's nobody home, let's go back," I said.

Charlie chuckled. "You're a funny lad, Eddie, but let me tell you something, you can joke around with me, but I wouldn't advise it when you get inside. You may find they don't have my sense of humor."

We waited and then heard footsteps; the flap in the door opened and a face checked us out.

"I've got a warm body for you," Charlie said. There was no smile on the face. There was the sound of a key turning in the lock and the man-door swung open. We were still handcuffed together so we had to go through sideways. My suitcase went first, then Charlie, then me.

Inside the main gate we were in a large solid brick archway with another iron barred gate at the other end. If a vehicle drove in or out, one gate would be locked before the other opened. This I soon found out was how it was in prison. Every time I passed through a door or gate there would be another a few steps away. I had to wait while one was locked behind me before going through the next.

Charlie removed the handcuff from his own wrist and then from mine. The prison guard opened a small gate off to one side and locked me behind it. I watched through the bars as he signed Charlie's paperwork and opened the man-door to let him out. Charlie turned to me as he stepped outside.

"Bye, Eddie, good luck to you." My goodbye was lost in the slamming of the door.

The prison guard unlocked the gate; his orders were brief and impersonal. "Pick up your suitcase. Walk straight ahead. Stand there."

I was taken to the reception area, which adjoined the gatehouse. My suitcase was opened and its contents logged. A guard described each item starting with, "One suitcase, brown, imitation leather."

An older man wrote down each item. He had gray hair and a gray uniform and it didn't occur to me immediately that he was a prisoner. My stuff was put back in the suitcase. I signed the bottom of the list and the case was labeled and taken away. I was allowed to wear my own clothes as I was not convicted yet, but took the option of wearing a prison shirt, socks, and underwear.

I was ordered to strip, take a shower, and then see a doctor for a medical exam. I stood naked in front of the doctor as he sat at a table, he said, "Cough."

I coughed and then he said, "Okay, get dressed." He wrote something down on a report card. This was the standard prison medical exam.

I got dressed and was told to go to a window in a wire cage where another prisoner issued me with blankets, sheets, and pillowcase, and a piss pot with a lid. I was ordered to stand to one side and wait with some other prisoners, some on remand like me, others convicted and in gray uniforms. After about half an hour my arms grew tired holding the blankets and sheets, I let them droop. The lid fell off my piss pot and rolled in a circle across the floor making a loud clatter.

"Hang on to that bloody thing!" a guard yelled out. And as I went to retrieve it, he said, "Get back in line."

"That screw is a bastard," said the prisoner standing next to me.

The guard approached me. "What did you say?"

"Nothing."

"You say 'sir' when addressing an officer." He picked up the lid I had dropped. "What's your name?"

"Conner." I hesitated then quickly added, "Sir."

"Here, you drop this once more and you'll lose it, then you'll be charged with losing it when you have your next inspection." He handed me the lid and added, "I'm watching you, Conner."

This was a new experience and I did not like it one bit. The guard turned to a prisoner still getting dressed. "Come on, we haven't got all bloody night." The prisoner scrambled to finish dressing and rushed over to get his bedding and pot. He fell into line with his shoelaces undone, his shirt open, and his tie hung around his neck.

"Everyone right turn, keep in single file and stop when I say stop." The guard unlocked the door and we stepped out into the prison yard. It was dark by now, a clear night, almost a full moon; the temperature was near freezing.

"All right, stop there." The guard barked out his orders after we covered the few yards to the main cellblock. Another gate and another door to pass through and we were inside.

This was an old building at least 100, maybe 150 years old. Four floors high open in the center, forty or fifty feet to the roof, with huge windows at the ends looking not unlike the nave of a cathedral. However, there was not the peace and tranquility of a cathedral here. Voices called out from behind closed doors, not saying anything in particular but rather just to make noise, as if to give the perpetrators some small satisfaction of hearing their own voices echoing around this huge hall. It was difficult to figure exactly where the sounds were coming from. One close by, maybe on the second floor, would be answered by another way off in the distance somewhere in the far top corner. If this place wasn't foreboding enough for a newcomer like me, there was this constant noise. Like being in the jungle not knowing if the sounds were from something harmless or dangerous.

"All right stand here, face the front, and no talking." The guard left us for a moment.

The walls of the cellblock were whitewashed brick except for the bottom part which was gloss paint, a light shade of brown to a height of about five feet. A dark brown stripe about an inch and a half finished off the transition between gloss paint and whitewash. This drab color scheme was repeated on each floor. Each cell had a solid steel-faced door painted with the same gloss paint as the walls.

On each floor was a landing or walkway about four feet wide constructed of iron supports with stone walkway. These landings went the length of the cellblock on each side. They had iron safety railings, and two bridges on each floor went from one side to the other. Iron staircases connected each bridge with the one above and gave access to the other floors. Anything made of iron was painted dark green. This seemed to be the color scheme rule as I studied the railings, stairs, and ornate cast iron landing supports.

Just above my head, stretched across from the first landing to the opposite side, was a net made from chain-link fence material. Maybe it was a little more forgiving than the stone floor below it, for anyone jumping or being pushed from the floors above. But its main purpose, I think, was to stop heavy objects being dropped on someone's head.

The guard who had brought us from reception was a good candidate for getting something dropped on his head, I was thinking as I watched him talking to another guard further down the hall. Two prisoners were sweeping floors, one on the ground floor not far from us, one on the third-floor landing.

The two guards came back and we were handed over to the second guard who seemed to be a little more human than the previous. He unlocked a cell and turned to me. "This is yours." He placed a card with my name and court date on it in a rack outside the door. "Put your bedding down and get yourself some water."

"From where?" I asked.

"Is this your first time?" I answered that it was. "Take your water jug." He pointed to a large aluminum jug standing in a washbowl on a triangular corner table.

"Just follow the others; you'll soon figure it out."

I did just that and walked about a third of the way down the cellblock to where there was an open area about the width of two cells. I later learned that this was called a recess. There were four recesses on each floor, two each side. The recess was deeper than the cells so there were windows in the back corners to the left and right. On the right was a cubicle with a low door that housed a toilet. Someone was sitting on the toilet, his head showing above the door carrying on a conversation with someone on the other side.

Next to the toilet on the left was a large sink with a faucet for emptying piss pots. In the left wall of the recess were two faucets, one hot, one cold water. I had just showered so didn't need to wash. I took cold water to drink.

As I walked back to my cell, the prisoner sweeping asked me, "Got any snout?" He indicated cigarettes with two fingers pressed to his lips.

"No, sorry, I don't smoke." I would soon learn that tobacco was currency in jail and even if I didn't smoke it would behoove me to carry some.

I went back to my cell and the guard closed the door. It locked automatically; there was no handle on the inside. Flat steel faced with a little round glass peephole with a flap on the outside to cover it. The cell was painted the same drab brown gloss and whitewash scheme as the hall outside. The brickwork that was the walls formed an arch that became the ceiling; the floor was stone. Solid brick and stone surrounded me in this eight-by-ten-foot cell.

An iron bed frame with a horsehair mattress stood against the wall. I laid it down and began to make my bed. As I unfolded the sheets and blankets I started to sob, tears rolling down my face. What did I do to deserve this? I knew I would be here for the next six weeks but what came after that? What if I was given a jail term and I had to spend more time here? This was without a doubt the worst situation I had ever been in. I finished making my bed and still on my knees I closed my eyes and prayed out loud.

"Please, God, deliver me from this and I will never fight or get into trouble again."

Chapter 17

I SOON FOUND OUT BEING on remand meant being locked up for most of the day. We were on the ground floor and kept separate from the convicted prisoners. For the midday meal we lined up in front of a serving hatch opening into the kitchen. Food was served on a tray and we carried it back to our cells to eat. All other meals were brought to us.

The only other time we got out was for forty-five minutes of exercise each morning and afternoon. Exercise consisted of walking around in circles in a small yard outside. We had to keep moving but we were allowed to talk and socialize. My first day on exercise a young black man about my own age approached me. He asked.

"Do I know you? Your face seems so familiar." I looked at him, I could tell he was from London by his accent and the cut of his stylish brown, pinstripe double-breasted suit, but I didn't recognize him.

"I'm from Stepney. Where are you from?"

"Walthamstow."

"We're practically neighbors. As a matter of fact I'm in a band and we played over there six weeks ago, in a pub off the Forest Road. My name's Eddie Conner."

"Eddie and the Eddie Sons—I was there that night. I knew I'd seen you somewhere before. I'm Colin Bates; my friends call me Snowball."

I looked at him. "That's appropriate. Were you born in Walthamstow?"

"Yeah, my mum and dad are from Jamaica. My dad's a stevedore."

"My old man is too. A stevedore, I mean, not from Jamaica."

"Yeah, I can tell by yer complexion he's not from Jamaica." He reached over and shook my hand. It felt good to meet someone from close to my old neighborhood and here was someone who almost knew me.

"You were good that night I saw you play. How did you end up here?"

"It's a very long story, trust me. But I got nicked in Luton."

"Me too, we were shop-breaking. I was the only one to get me collar felt; all the others got away. It's my first time; maybe I'll get probation. The only thing not helping me is my color and the fact that I won't grass on the others."

"Did Old Bill give you a kicking?"

"Yeah, but I wouldn't grass."

I looked over at his face. "You don't look too bad for it."

"You should've seen me when I came in. This was the first week in December, I've been in here over five weeks now."

"That's funny, I got a kicking from the police about that same time."

"In Luton?"

"No, in Stepney." Walking around in circles, I filled in the details of my encounter with Bobby Johnson, and how it eventually led to my being where I was. Snowball listened then asked, "What do you think you'll get?"

"I don't know. The problem is I'm already on probation."

Just then a guard blew a whistle to indicate that exercise was over. Snowball's cell was on the other side of the cellblock, not too far from mine.

That night in my cell I was thinking about Snowball and then my mind went back to the first time I saw a black man, the American soldiers during World War II. Those poor bastards put their life on the line like everyone else and they were treated like shit. The injustice of it all made me angry. I thought of my old man and what a bigot he was, how he had beat up my friend Running Horse.

I wondered whatever happened to Running Horse. Did he survive the war? Was he even alive? What was that story he told me once? Something about a man seeing a wild beast in the distance and as he got closer he saw it was his brother.

I got up and sat at the table with pen and paper. I began to write.

As a child I was afraid of things I didn't understand,
Of darkness and of shadows, I'd run and take my father's hand.
He taught me how to be a man; I listened to the words he said.
And bigotry a different fear he placed inside my head.

I saw the Devil in the distance; my heart was filled with fear.
I looked again and saw it was a man but still afraid as he drew near.
I looked again as he came closer; it was then that I discovered
This man I'd been afraid of, I saw it was my brother.

The words flowed and as they did the melody came too. I stood up and sang the completed song.

Damn, where did that come from? I remembered what Running Horse had told me that all creativity comes from the Spirit. That's it. I didn't write this, it was already there; I just picked it up.

Late that evening I was in the recess standing in line to get water before being locked up for the night. Snowball was in an argument with someone; I couldn't hear what it was about but I was watching closely. All of a sudden someone else stepped in and grabbed Snowball by the shirt. I heard the words, "You black bastard."

I was over there in about three steps and hit the man holding Snowball on the side of the head with my empty water jug. The lightweight aluminum jug gave a loud "doink" as it connected and probably had the stunning effect of a percussion grenade rather than inflict actual injury. I let the water jug fall to the floor, where it made a loud clatter amplified by the glazed brick walls of the recess. I grabbed his shirt and hit him with my head; as he sank to the floor I stepped over him and hit the other one who was first arguing with Snowball. He backed off and I turned around to meet with a big fist in my face. The next thing I knew I was being hit from all directions. Whistles were blowing and I was on the floor; a guard was kneeling on me with a nightstick across my neck.

The next morning I was brought before the prison governor. "Conner, you are not convicted yet, but while you are on remand here you will abide by the prison rules. This will go on your report and it will not help you when you come up for trial."

I was given what is called "chokey" for three days—put in a cell with no furniture. I was allowed a bed at night but had to take it out the next morning. I still got forty-five minutes of exercise morning and afternoon but alone at a different time than the others. The other part of this punishment was a diet of bread and water for three days.

On the second day I had to see a psychiatrist appointed by the court to do a report on me. I had a bruise under my left eye and a cut on my lip. The doctor was a man in his fifties with brown wavy hair and matching bushy eyebrows. He had a red face with tiny blue veins in his nose. He wore tortoiseshell-framed reading glasses with semicircular lenses, and read over some papers before looking up at me. "I see by your report you have a history of violence and looking at your face I see that has continued in here. Tell me, why do you fight?"

"That's a good question and I've never really analyzed it. I've been doing it for so long now it's second nature. My old man started me with his boxing lessons when I was eight years old."

"It says here that you beat your father up." The doctor peered at me over his glasses.

"Does it say in that report that he was beating my mother?"

"No it says here that he was trying to discipline you and you beat him up."

"That's a bleedin' lie and it's not fair that it should say that in a report. I was never brought to a court and given the chance to defend myself. Where did this report come from?"

"It's a probation report, a probation officer interviewed your father and this is what he told the officer."

"And that's it. Everyone takes my father's word for what happened?"

"It was up to the probation officer to make a judgment. Your mother was there, she didn't refute it."

"My mother is terrified of my father." I felt like I had a volcano inside my chest and it was about to erupt through the top of my head. I wanted to reach out and snatch those stupid glasses from his ugly blue veined nose. I gripped the side of my chair. I knew I could not and must not act on my feelings; I was in enough trouble.

"What would you do if you were let out of here?"

"I have had some success recently as a singer and songwriter; I perform with a band."

"Really? What type of music?"

"Rock-n-roll, sir."

He smiled. "Yes, I understand that's very popular with the young people." He wrote something in the report and then spoke without looking up. "I will make a note here that you dispute your father's statement and give your version of what happened. You may go now."

"Thank you, sir," I stood and left the room.

I served out my three days of chokey and returned to the normal routine. I caught up with Snowball in the exercise yard.

"Eddie, I appreciate you helping me out, but you didn't have to do that, I can look after myself. My father taught me how to deal with that crap."

"Well, my father taught me how to fight. So I helped you out, say no more."

"Thanks, Eddie, you're a good sort." Snowball shook my hand.

"Who was I fighting with? I didn't even get a look at 'em."

"Those two over there." He indicated two men who were looking our way. They turned away as I looked over and I knew there would be no more trouble.

I showed Snowball the song I had written and after reading it through he said, "Eddie, you're so bleedin' talented, you can't be wasting yer time in here. You gotta get out and start performing again."

"I know but it doesn't look all that promising. I went to see the trick cyclist yesterday and the probation report he had did not sound good."

That night in my cell I thought about my prospects at my upcoming trial and what could I do. There were not a lot of options open to me. I thought about my days in the church choir. I decided praying couldn't hurt. I rolled up my trousers and knelt with my bare knees on the stone floor. I felt that if I made it uncomfortable my prayer might have more of a chance. After all I had done wrong I needed to punish myself. I prayed.

"Please, God, deliver me from this and I will try my best to be a better person."

I kept up this ritual every night and morning until my trial date.

That day came and after the usual breakfast in my cell, a plate of oatmeal and a mug of tea, we were taken down to reception and turned in our bedding and other prison gear. I hoped this was an omen that I was not coming back.

The courthouse was attached to the prison so we were marched to the opposite side of the prison complex and down some steps to a basement under the courts. There we sat in a holding cell with bench seating around three walls and bars and a gate on the other wall. Snowball was with me and after about an hour he was called up. I watched as he climbed an iron spiral staircase in the center of the next room.

"Good luck, Snowball." I don't know if he heard me as he disappeared from sight. After about twenty minutes he was down all smiles.

"Got probation." He mouthed the words to me.

"Good one, Snowball. Stay in touch." And he was led away.

Sometime later a barrister came down complete with black robe and gray wig. I was taken to another room with a table and chairs. He introduced himself; I didn't really catch his name. "I've been assigned by the court to defend you. I assume you're pleading guilty?"

"Er—well, I think the armed robbery charge is a bit strong. Can't that be reduced?"

"You've admitted arming yourself with a knife. That's armed robbery. I suggest you plead guilty and let me make a plea for leniency. What can you tell me that might help your case?"

He had a copy of the probation report. I told him my version of what happened and how my father had punched me around since I was eight years old. I was taken back to the holding cell and spoke to one of the other prisoners. "Some defense. He comes and talks to me for five minutes just before I go up there."

"I know they don't get paid much as a public defender so they don't bloody care," I was told.

It was late in the afternoon before I was taken from the holding cell to climb the spiral staircase. At the top I found myself in the center of the court in the dock, which was like a box enclosed on four sides. The only way in or out was via the spiral stairs. A prison guard followed me up and sat behind me. I looked around the court at the judge and the barristers in their gowns and wigs. I had witnessed this familiar scene so many times in films and on TV, but now it was real, not a movie.

The prosecution read the charge and the judge asked, "How do you plead?"

I responded, "Guilty, your honor."

The prosecution handed the judge a copy of the probation report and he read through it. He looked up and asked, "It says here the defendant is a rock-n-roll singer. What's rock-n-roll?" There was snickering around the court from the barristers.

"It's a type of music peculiar to the African American, m'lud. It's very popular with the younger generation."

The judge did not respond but kept reading then turned to the defense counsel and asked if he would speak on my behalf. The defense barrister stood. "If it please, my lord, the defendant wishes it to be known that he regrets the incident that led to his being here today. It came about when he felt that his employer had cheated him. He agreed to work a week for the sum of three pounds and was paid only one pound. He took three pounds from the cash drawer. The drawer contained several hundred pounds and he could have taken more, but he only wanted the amount he felt he was owed.

"I would also like to bring to the attention of the court that over the years this young man has been brutalized by his father. Is it any wonder that he should have predisposition to violence when this is all he has known? Since the age of eight years a punch on the jaw has been an everyday occurrence. The attack on his father mentioned in the report was only in defense of his mother. He has a good work record and would like the opportunity to finish up his five-year apprenticeship in engineering."

The judge listened and then asked if there were any prior convictions. The prosecution spoke. "There is one prior conviction for assault on a police officer for which he is on probation and he is in breach of that probation."

The judge looked directly at me as he passed sentence. "Edward Conner, you have pleaded guilty to the serious offense of armed robbery. It seems to me that you are of a violent nature and I consider you to be a dangerous young man. You will go to prison for one year and for the breach of your probation a term of six months. The sentences to run concurrently."

The prison guard behind me touched my shoulder. "That's it. Down the stairs." I turned and started down the iron staircase, the judge's words still ringing in my ears.

Damn a year and a half—I don't deserve that. And what did he mean dangerous? I'm not bleedin' dangerous. It's not like I beat up some old lady or something. I reached the holding cell and one of the other prisoners asked, "What did you get?"

"Eighteen months."

The guard was locking the gate when he said, "You didn't get eighteen months; you got a year. The judge said the sentences run concurrently, which means they run together. While you're doing the twelve months you're also doing the six months. You will only serve a year and with time off for good behavior you will only do eight months."

That felt better, I had gone from thinking I had a year and a half at the top of the stairs to only eight months by the time I was in the holding cell.

The other prisoner explained further, "If the judge had said 'consecutively instead of concurrently' it would have been eighteen months."

I counted eight months on my fingers. "I'll be out by the middle of October, that's not too bad."

"Nah, you can do that standing on yer head," the other prisoner commented.

Chapter 18

TWO DAYS AFTER I WAS sentenced I celebrated my twenty-first birthday, although "celebrated" was hardly the word. I didn't get the key to the door or a cake with twenty-one candles. I did get a card and a letter from Trisha, the first time I had heard from her since my arrest. She was very unhappy; things were now far worse since her return home.

There was physical and mental abuse from her father. She indicated that on her eighteenth birthday coming soon she would leave home and move out of London. She said she didn't know how she would survive financially but she would do whatever it took. This disturbed me but there was little I could do under my present circumstances. She asked me to be careful what I said in a letter back as she feared her father might intercept it. I wrote back not mentioning her leaving but indicated I would be out in October and the time would soon pass.

My sharp tailored suit and Italian shoes were now replaced with drab prison gray and my haircut looked like the barber had caught me screwing his wife. My uniform had a red star sewn on each sleeve indicating that this was my first time in prison. "Star" prisoners as we were called were kept separate from the recidivists and I was told I would soon be transferred to another prison exclusively for first time offenders. Bedford was a local prison and only held local prisoners serving short sentences and people like me, passing through.

After two weeks I was told I was to be transferred to Wormwood Scrubs, the largest prison in London. I felt I was going home. This was West London near Shepherd's Bush and not the East End but it would only be a short trip by bus or the underground for people to visit me. The transfer was by bus and the trip would be about fifty-five or sixty miles.

The morning of our departure was bright and sunny but bitter cold. It was the first week in March, and we stood shivering in the prison yard waiting to be let into the reception building. Once inside we turned in our bedding and prison clothes and got to wear our own clothes again just for the trip. There were sixteen of us to be transferred, which was convenient because we were handcuffed in pairs for the journey. The bus was waiting between the inner and outer gates. It was a small twenty-seat bus chartered from a local tour company.

We filed on board and took our seats; two prison guards, or "screws" as we called them, accompanied us. One sat at the rear of the bus, one at the front. The big main gate opened and for the next two hours we would get a glimpse of the world outside. I quickly realized I had not seen a female for two months, and as we drove through the town of Bedford, I found my head swiveling around at the sight of every pretty young leg. I had led my shackled partner on the bus and grabbed a window seat and was glad of it.

Twenty miles south and we drove through Luton. More pretty legs in spike heel shoes. We drove past Edwards Butcher shop and I turned to see if I could catch a glimpse of the little Welshman, but the bus went by too quickly. On into the countryside with open fields, a few more small towns, and we were on the outskirts of London, or "the Smoke" as those from outside called it.

We pulled up in front of the main gate.

"Wormwood Scrubs," the screw at the front of the bus called out.

"Du Cane Road, East Acton. This will be your new address." He stepped off the bus and walked to the gate to ring the bell; the driver closed the door behind him. The prison looked like some medieval fortress, there were towers on either side of the gate with castle-like ramparts. The prison wall seemed to stretch the entire length of the street; in actuality, the frontage was about a quarter of a mile.

The gate opened and the bus pulled inside. As soon as the gate closed we disembarked and walked through to reception where our handcuffs were removed. Then we went through the now familiar ritual of check in personal property, undress, shower, stand naked before the doctor, cough, and get dressed in prison clothes.

I stood by a gate in reception looking out across the prison yard, there were neatly manicured lawns and a huge church just inside the main gate. The church was at least as big as St. Clement's Church. There were four big cellblocks, or wings as they were called. When all sixteen of us were ready we marched across the yard and entered C wing, right next to the church.

Once inside I could see the layout was exactly the same as Bedford Prison except that it was at least three times longer. My cell was on the second floor next to a recess. Everything about this place was bigger including the exercise yard, which was huge.

The next morning I was walking around the exercise yard with several hundred other prisoners when someone grabbed me from behind around the waist and lifted me bodily off the ground. I didn't know what was going on at first but soon realized it was a playful gesture. After being carried for several steps I was put down and turned to see a face I never expected to see.

"George, what the hell are you doing here? I thought you were in Borstal."

"I was. I escaped and got involved in some more thievery and got two years. What are you doing here?"

"Twelve months."

"For what?"

"Armed robbery."

"Armed robbery? You were never a thief, Eddie."

"I know, it's a diabolical liberty what they done me for." I started to fill George in on the details that led to my arrest.

George listened then said, "So it was that bastard Bobby Johnson that started all this. Don't you remember I told you to leave him alone? 'He's not worth it,' I remember saying it. See what happens when I'm not there to look after you?"

I looked at George; he was huge with a broad chest and shoulders.

"You've put on some weight."

"I know, I got into lifting weights in Borstal. They don't have weights here but I use two buckets of sand and do bench presses with my bed frame. Feel that."

He flexed his biceps and it looked as though the seams of his prison jacket would burst. No wonder he had just lifted me from the ground like I was a six-year-old child.

"Where are you working?" George asked.

"I haven't been assigned yet. I only got here yesterday."

"You'll probably get in the brush shop; that's where I am."

After exercise I went to see the governor, as did all new inmates, and I was assigned to the brush shop as I had hoped. In the brush shop they made scrubbing brushes, nail brushes, brooms, just about every kind of brush that would be used in prisons all over the country. George was sitting on the opposite side of the shop but after lunch he said, "Come and sit with me." He spoke to an older prisoner in the seat next to him. "Do me a favor, go sit over there."

"I don't want to sit over there."

George opened a tobacco tin and placed a thin hand-rolled cigarette on the bench in front of the man. "Now, do you want a smoke or a punch in the ear?" The man took the cigarette and moved. I sat next to George.

"Ain't this grand? Just like we're back in school." He was right—it warmed my heart to be with my old friend again and we had not had the opportunity to spend this much time together since school. We were together practically all day except for the time we were locked in our cells.

The next Sunday we went to church. Church was mandatory for those listed as Church of England. We filed into our seats; there was a huge pipe organ that took up the whole back wall of the church. I recognized the music playing as a piece by Bach I had heard played in St. Paul's Cathedral. It was being played extremely well. Later I turned around and saw the organist coming down the steps from his elevated seat. To my surprise he was a prisoner, an older man, and his face seemed familiar.

I nudged George. "That geezer playing organ. Where do I know him from?"

George looked around. "He's from D wing, a turd burglar in for fucking little choir boys."

"That's it. He was the organist at St. Paul's when I was in the choir there. I don't believe it, that dirty old bastard."

I got a chance to say a few words to him as I filed out after the service.

"You were the organist at St. Paul's. I was in the choir there when I was twelve; I don't suppose you remember me. I remember you."

He shook his head. "I'm sorry, we had a lot of boys pass through over the years."

"And I understand you passed through a few of them yourself."

He smiled. "Yes, unfortunately, it's a weakness I have."

"Well, I don't agree with what you did but I'll say this: Some of those kids in that choir—they needed fucking. One kid in particular named Nigel."

His face lit up as the lightbulb went on in his head. "Wait now, I remember you. You were the boy who punched another boy on the nose at the Easter service. I was playing the organ that night. I remember it well. It's a small world. Whoever would have thought we would meet again under these circumstances?"

George had moved on and the last few prisoners were filing past. I caught up with George in back in the cellblock.

"So, did he go after your little bum when you were in the choir?"

"Nah, I'd have punched his lights out if he had." George started reciting, "Twinkle, twinkle little rectum, get big pricks when least expect 'em."

A week later I got a visit from Ralph the piano player and Johnny the guitarist. I was very happy to see them and they seemed pleased to see me.

I told them, "I am so sorry about this. I really screwed things up, didn't I?"

Ralph spoke. "Eddie, when will you be out of here?"

"Mid-October."

"That's not too far off. We found another singer but he's not as good as you. We played last week and the crowd started chanting 'We want Eddie, we want Eddie.' It was unbelievable. We're prepared to wait until you get out."

I felt a lump in my throat and my eyes began to tear up. "You have been so good to me, I don't know what to say."

Johnny picked up a guitar case by his side. "I've brought your guitar, would they let you have it?"

"I don't know."

I got up and asked the guard in the visiting room. He told me it could be left at the gate to be put with my other property and I would have to ask the governor for permission to have it in my cell. I went back to the table and relayed what I had been told.

Johnny said, "If you can get it, play as much as you can. You know the basics—you just need practice."

I was excited. "Yeah, and I can write more songs. Here's one I just wrote." I pulled the words to "Devil in the Distance" from my pocket. Johnny read it over and passed it to Ralph.

"That's good, Eddie, keep it up."

Ralph finished reading and looked up. "We'll keep playing just to keep the band tight, but I'm not doing too many gigs with this singer or we'll lose the following we have."

The visit ended and I shook hands and hugged them both. "I must have done something right to have friends like you."

"You have a lot of talent, Eddie, and we like you. We miss having you around. We'll come see you again. Keep writing those songs."

I was taken back to the brush shop and took my seat next to George. I told him about the visit I had just had. "Hey, you've never heard me sing, have you?"

"Yeah, at school."

"No, I mean rock-n-roll with a band. Damn, I wish you could've heard me."

The next morning I put in my request to see the governor and after exercise instead of going to the brush shop I went back to the cellblock to wait outside the governor's office. I was one of the first to be called in. The governor was a tall man with a reddish face and graying hair, wearing a brown tweed suit. He looked up as I entered and without much expression asked my request.

"Sir, I have an acoustic guitar in my personal property and I would like permission to have it in my cell."

The governor said nothing and I felt a little intimidated. I continued talking. "I am a songwriter and it would make my time here productive if I could practice and continue to write songs."

The governor pondered my request. "Tell me more about your songwriting."

"I have the words to a song I wrote that I would like to show you." I pulled a sheet of paper from my pocket and held it out for him to take.

"Why don't you read it to me?" I nervously read over the words. Afterward there was a pause that seemed like an eternity.

"That's very good. I will grant your request but let me add this: I see by your record you have a history of violence including an assault on a police officer. Any hint of that kind of behavior here and this privilege will be taken away. Do you understand?"

"I do, sir, and thank you."

It was hard to keep a huge grin from spreading all over my face as I left the governor's office and was taken over to the brush shop. Later that morning a screw came for me and together we walked to reception to pick up my guitar. I signed and dated an amendment to my personal property sheet and we went over to the cellblock.

The screw told me as I put the guitar case in my cell, "I'd advise you to keep your door locked when you're not in your cell, 'cos believe it or not we do have thieves in this place."

I closed the door and it locked automatically. Now I would have to wait for a screw to open it whenever I needed in, but this was a small inconvenience. I couldn't wait for the workday to end so I could get back to my cell. That evening I didn't wait to be locked up, I closed my own door locking myself in and opened up the guitar case. There was the guitar with a shoulder strap together with a dozen picks, two packets of spare strings, and a tuning fork.

I put the guitar strap over my head and played a few chords. I was out of practice. My fingers fumbled for the right strings and the sound coming from the instrument was awful. Supper came and food was eaten while standing, a mouthful at a time without putting the guitar down. Gradually my fingers moved a little easier, and the sound became better. I quit only when my fingertips became raw and the pain was too much to bear.

Chapter 19

AFTER MY CONVICTION I GAVE up my twice-daily routine of kneeling and praying. What was the point? It obviously hadn't worked; I felt let down and told myself there was no God. And if there was, He wasn't looking out for me. From now on, I was on my own.

I was experiencing a roller coaster of emotions. There was the high of the visit from Ralph and Johnny and my playing guitar and making music again. Then there was the low of my letters to Trisha going unanswered and my pleas for her to come visit seemingly ignored. Was she even getting my letters or was her father intercepting them? I knew that if she wasn't receiving my letters she would still contact me if she wanted to. It seemed she didn't want to.

It had been six months since I had seen her and I had only received one letter from her on my birthday back in February. I was beginning to accept it was over between us and I needed to move on, when out of the blue on a sunny June day I was taken from work and told I had a visitor. It was Trisha.

Since it was a warm day, visits were outside on the lawn by the church just inside the main gate. Roses blooming in flowerbeds with neatly manicured edges made a nice setting. I hugged and kissed her and a guard warned we had to keep physical contact to a minimum. We sat on two folding chairs facing each other. She looked tired, worn. It seemed she had aged several years in only six months. Even the heavier than usual makeup couldn't hide the dark circles under her eyes.

"I've come to say goodbye. I couldn't leave without seeing you again."

"So you're going then. Where?"

"I have an aunt and uncle who live in Nottinghamshire in a little town called Mansfield. I'm going to stay with them. They say it's beautiful there, in Sherwood Forest. You know, Robin Hood and his Merry Men."

"Watch out for those merry men."

Trisha smiled. "I see you haven't lost your sense of humor. How are they treating you in here?"

"I'm doing good. Hey, guess who's in here? George. Oh, I forgot you never met George but you heard me talk about him. We went to school together, he's one of my best friends."

"That's good."

"And Ralph and Johnny came to see me. They're keeping the band going 'til I get out and I have a guitar and I'm practicing and writing songs."

"That's wonderful, Eddie, it looks like everything is going to be all right."

"Trisha, I owe you a lot. I couldn't have got out of that mental hospital without your help and God knows where I would be if I'd stayed there. My brain would be fried by now from that ECT treatment and I would probably not be able to write songs anymore. I shudder to think."

We sat and talked about this and that, reminiscing about old times, talking of the future.

"Eddie, we had some good times. You were good to me, but now it's time to move on. You have to stay in London for your music and I have to get as far away from here as I can."

She was right and I knew it. I didn't blame her for wanting to get away from her abusive family situation and I didn't want to leave London. But knowing she was right didn't make this goodbye any easier. I felt a tear roll down my cheek. Trisha wiped it away with her thumb.

"Don't, Eddie, please."

We stood; she kissed me lightly on the lips, turned, and walked quickly toward the gate. I stood and watched her go; she didn't look back.

That night in my cell I felt the emotions of earlier that day and put those feelings into words and music. I imagined a situation where it was me who was leaving but the feelings were the same.

> *I just came by to tell you I was leavin',*
> *It's been a year, I must be movin' on.*
> *When I came to this ol' town I was just passin' through.*
> *You're the only reason why I stayed this long.*
>
> *I'm trav'lin' light and carrying a load,*
> *Strings that tied me here tug at my heart along the road.*
> *All I've got is my old guitar and a change of clothes.*
> *I'm trav'lin' light, carrying a load.*

I picked up the guitar, found the chord changes and wrote them in over the lyrics. I played and sang it over, then sat down to write a second verse and a bridge.

> *Please don't be askin' me for reasons,*
> *They're as hard to find as ways to say good bye.*
> *I had my words all planned that I would say to you*
> *But lost them all the moment I saw you cry.*

> *It was denial that always told you that promises were made*
> *When the truth is we both know there were none,*
> *But the truth don't make the leavin' any easier to bear*
> *And neither does the knowing that you've done nothing wrong.*

> *I'm trav'lin' light and carrying a load,*
> *Strings that tied me here tug at my heart along the road.*
> *All I've got is my old guitar and a change of clothes.*
> *I'm trav'lin' light, carrying a load.*

That night I had a hard time sleeping. My new song was playing over and over in my head. Emotions were still running high from the visit with Trisha earlier but at the same time I was pumped up and excited about the future.

"Now don't fuck it up this time," I told myself. "Remember what the governor said—any hint of trouble and you'll lose the privilege of having a guitar to play."

The next morning I talked to George in the exercise yard. "I have a golden opportunity here to practice and become a better guitar player and also to write more songs but I'm worried. The governor said if I get into any fights I lose the guitar and you know me, George. I never backed down from a fight in my life."

"Well, now might be a good time to start. You've got nothing to prove, Eddie, least of all to me. Most people here know your reputation so they'll leave you alone and those who don't, I'll take care of them."

"Thanks, George, you're a good friend to have."

"There's something else you can do," George suggested. "You don't smoke but you could buy yourself half an ounce of tobacco and some papers and hand some snout around. It'll buy you a lot of friends."

I took George's advice. We were paid a small amount for our work in the brush shop, not in cash but credit in the prison canteen where we could buy tobacco, candy, soap, and other personal items. Because I didn't smoke I had not spent my earnings; there was nothing I needed. I bought an ounce of tobacco and some papers and rolled some thin cigarettes otherwise known as snout.

A couple of snout could buy a lot of favors in prison, a good haircut for example, because the barber was a prisoner. I was trying to let my hair grow again and when a screw would order me to get a haircut, I would sit in the chair and the barber would be going "snip, snip" with the scissors behind my head but cutting nothing off.

Each evening after our meal we had what was called "association." We got to hang out together in the main hall downstairs. We had a record player and could listen to music. Ralph was sending me records so I could learn more songs, so these benefitted everyone.

I would bring my guitar down and there would be quite a large group sitting around while I played. One evening a young kid showed up with a pair of drumsticks and an empty plastic bucket.

"Do ya' mind if I sit in?" I told him that was okay and he proceeded to play. Sitting on a chair he held the upturned bucket with his feet and lifted it up and down making a "clop clop" sound on the floor, keeping a steady rhythm going while doing drum fills with the sticks. He got different tones by striking the center, the rim, and the sides of the bucket. I was impressed and he got a good reaction from the others listening. I held out my hand.

"What's your name?"

"Danny. Danny Christmas."

"Are you pulling my plonker?"

"No, that really is my name." His name was as unusual as his playing style. He was a skinny kid, wiry. He had the most unusual steel blue eyes. He and I performed together from that time on. His playing definitely added to the music and made it more fun for me.

A few more weeks went by and I had another visit from Ralph and Johnny.

"We have a little problem," Ralph said. "You remember I said we didn't want to do any more gigs with this new singer? Well the others didn't like that idea and they've gone off on their own, so it's just Johnny and me right now."

"So what now?" I asked.

"I don't see this as a real problem." Ralph continued. "We need a younger band anyway. Johnny here is okay, he's only twenty-seven but the rest of us are all over forty. We're playing to a young audience and I think we'd do better if the whole band was about your age, Eddie."

"So what do you suggest?"

"You still have a few months to do so we'll look 'round for a replacement drummer and bass player. Johnny can switch to bass if we need to. That just leaves a drummer." I immediately thought of Danny.

"Hey, there's a kid in here that plays drums. He plays on a plastic bucket now but he says he has a drum kit at home. He's pretty good. He gets out next month and he's from Islington, not too far away."

"How old is he?"

"About my age."

"Perfect, talk to him and have him come an' see us when he gets out."

"What about you, Ralph? You're not going to quit, are you?" I asked.

"Johnny and I were discussing this on the way here. If we have you playing and singing and another guitar, we don't really need the piano. I might just leave the band and become full-time manager."

"Do you think we need a full-time manager?"

"I do, Eddie. I think these small rock-n-roll bands are the wave of the future. We could get a lot of work."

I thought over the prospects. "So I don't see this as a problem; it's probably for the better."

"That's our sentiments exactly." It was Johnny who spoke and he turned to Ralph, who nodded his agreement.

I showed them my latest song; Ralph read it first and handed it to Johnny.

"That's excellent, Eddie, you definitely have a flare for writing good lyrics."

Johnny agreed but added. "I see this as a ballad. Can you write some rhythmic lyrics that would lend themselves to a more upbeat number? I can come up with the riffs if you can write some words." I said I would try to come up with something.

That night in my cell I tried to think about an upbeat song. I really liked Chuck Berry's lyrics, the words had a rhythmic feel to them. But what to write about? I thought of Trisha moving North to Nottinghamshire to a small town.

"She'll really knock 'em dead with her high fashion, she's a real City Girl." I started to write.

The day was hot and hazy,
A young boy feeling lazy,
When I saw her out the corner of my eye.
Like something out of Hollywood
She turned my head, she looked so good
And I could only stare as she walked by.
She wore high heels with an ankle strap
And stockings with the seams at back,
Around her neck she wore a string of pearls.
She would be eighteen I guessed
And I could tell the way she dressed
She was every inch a City Girl.

City Girl, where are you?
You broke my heart in two.
I was just a small town boy
And a big time fool over you.

The next morning I caught up with Danny on the exercise yard.

"Hey, Danny, how d'ya feel about playing drums in a band with me when I get out?"

"Well, what do you think? Of course I would, I'd jump at it."

I gave Danny Ralph's address. "Now you get out next month, right?" Danny indicated that was correct. "Go see Ralph 'cos he's putting the band together now so that it will be ready to go when I get out in October."

Danny asked, "Do you need a guitar player?"

"Yes, it just so happens we do. Why?"

"I've got a younger brother, he's only nineteen but he's damn good, he's been playing since he was eleven years old. He was the reason I started playing drums. His name is Harry."

"Harry Christmas. What is it with your parents and their choice of names."

"Well, my father's name is Dwight and my mother is Mary, I guess they thought they'd keep it going."

The weeks passed. Danny wrote to his brother Harry and he went 'round to see Ralph and Johnny. Johnny wrote to me and said he was very impressed with the young guitar player. So much so that he would switch over to playing bass. Everything was falling into place.

Chapter 20

IT WAS A GRAY OCTOBER morning when I stepped out from the gate of H. M. Prison Wormwood Scrubs a free man, my debt to society paid. More free than when I went in at the beginning of the year. No more probation, no mental hospitals, and no more trick cyclists. I had earned full remission on my one-year sentence and served only eight months. I had not been in one single fight during my sentence and it was not that difficult.

I was carrying my suitcase in one hand and my guitar case in the other. Ralph was going to meet me in his car but was not there waiting. I was not worried, he would be along, maybe delayed in traffic or he set out late. He was not an early riser. I sat my cases down by the curbside and looked up and down the street. I was not sure which direction Ralph would come from.

People driving by turned their heads to stare as they passed. A man standing curbside outside a prison gate early in the morning with a suitcase is obviously someone just released. By contrast people walking did not make eye contact but rather kept their heads down and hurried by.

"Amazing how much braver people are in a car going by at forty miles per hour," I observed.

A double-decker bus stopped on the opposite side of the street; almost every passenger was staring at me. I smiled and waved; all heads turned back to see who I was waving to, then back to stare at me again.

I muttered to myself under my breath. "You poor bastards, your lives are so bleedin' boring that someone standing at the curb is entertainment. Come on, Ralph, where the hell are you?"

As if to answer my call Ralph pulled up at that moment, he got out to put my cases in the backseat. "Sorry I'm late, been waiting long?"

"Nah, ten minutes maybe, I knew you'd be here."

"I overslept. Johnny's gonna cook breakfast and the others are coming over. We're going to get you working right away, I hope you're ready."

"I've been ready for the last eight months."

As Ralph drove he filled me in on his plans. "We can do a gig this Saturday if we're ready. It's at a local pub; I haven't publicized it so if we don't do it that's okay. The place is always packed at the weekends so there will be an audience."

My head was spinning trying to take in all that Ralph was telling me, plus the excitement of being a free man and driving through London again. Unfamiliar streets at first but as we drew near to the East End, recognizing places I knew. It was almost a year since I left and there had been changes. Buildings demolished and new ones being built. Old businesses closed while others were opening up.

We pulled up outside the house and Ralph rang the doorbell then returned to the car to get my cases. Johnny answered the door in a cook's apron, held out his hand to shake mine pulling me up the steps and into the house as he did so. He hugged me and slapped me hard on the back.

"Welcome home, Eddie. Ya hungry? It's all ready. I just have to throw it in the pan."

Ralph dropped my cases inside and closed the door. I followed Johnny through to the kitchen. Seated at the table were Danny and his brother Harry. Danny stood and came around the table to shake my hand. I had not seen him since his release in July and it seemed strange to see him out of prison gray.

"Eddie, this is my baby brother Harry. Harry, this is Eddie." Harry stood and reached over the table to shake my hand. He seemed a little shy. He greatly resembled his brother Danny but his hair was a little longer and his eyes were a different color. I told him.

"Pleased to meet you. I've heard great things about your guitar playing."

Johnny returned to cooking breakfast while Ralph continued to fill me in.

"Harry's been singing vocals during practice. He doesn't have your pipes, Eddie, but he's not bad, maybe we can work out some harmonies for him to sing."

We sat down to a typical English breakfast of eggs, bacon, and mushrooms along with fried bread, washed down with large mugs of tea. After breakfast Harry cleared the table and helped Johnny wash dishes while Ralph started going over song arrangements with me. I asked for a pen and pad to make notes.

The dishes done, we moved to the front room, where Danny's drum kit and the bass and guitar amps were already set up.

"We've been playing nearly every day," Ralph told me. "We leave this stuff here. It saves setting up each time."

We started out playing a few familiar cover songs first. The band sounded good, very tight. Johnny on bass and Danny's drumming held a rock-solid rhythm while young Harry on lead guitar just blew me away. I had never heard anything like it. The many hours they had spent playing together were obvious and it was easy for me to fit right in with my vocals.

Ralph did not play piano even though there was one in the room. He just adjusted the sound on the mixing board and added input in between songs. It was clear he was the leader and musical director, and that was fine with me.

We worked on the new songs I had written. While writing them I had an idea of what they would sound like with the band. But what Ralph and the others had done was way beyond my expectations. This was exciting.

It seemed we had only played a short while when Ralph said, "Hey, it's past one o'clock, let's break for lunch."

We walked down the street to a corner pub, the Coach & Horses.

"This is where we will be playing at the weekend." Ralph told me. Once inside he said, "Let me introduce you to the landlord. Eddie, this is Cliff." Cliff was a big man with a broken nose and scars over both eyes. He held out his hand, his big arm covered with fading tattoos.

"Pleased to meet'cher, Eddie. I understand you just finished up some porridge."

Time in a British jail is referred to as "porridge," after the plate of oatmeal served for breakfast each day. It was obvious Cliff had himself done some "porridge" if he was familiar with this term.

"Hey, yer first drink's on me. What'll y'have?" Cliff asked.

"Oh, a pint of shandy will be fine."

"A shandy? What kind of drinking man are you?"

"I'm not a drinking man. My father does enough for the whole bleedin' family."

Cliff laughed as he poured my glass of shandy made up of half beer and half soda pop. We took our drinks and sat at a large table in the corner where we ordered lunch and talked while we waited.

"I'm still with the big band a the local dance hall," Ralph told me, "but I'll probably give that up once we get going. You can live at the house rent-free for now; you might want to get a part-time job for some spending money."

Danny spoke up. "Me an' Harry clean windows part-time; you can join us if you like. We work our own hours." The idea sounded good.

Ralph continued. "I'm putting my own money into this project now because I see the potential to make a lot of money once the word gets around. Then the band will be our full-time job."

We finished lunch and I told the others, "I have to go see my mother. I want to get over there before my ol' man gets home from work."

"Do you want me to drive you?" Ralph asked.

"Nah, you've taxied me around enough. I'll catch the tube. I'll be all right."

I walked to the nearest underground station and caught the tube to Stepney. I knocked on the door of my old home. My mother answered the door.

"Eddie, oh do come in. I wondered when I would see you."

She hugged and kissed me. It had been nearly a year since I had seen her, and I was amazed at how old she looked. Maybe I just hadn't noticed before. She was sixty now and her hair was white rather than gray. It was as if I was looking at my grandmother not my mother.

"Would you like a cup of tea?" she asked.

"No thanks, I've just had lunch." She ignored me completely and emerged from the kitchen with two cups of tea and chocolate biscuits. We sat at the table.

"Is dad treating you all right?" I asked. "He's not punching you around is he?"

"No, he's really slowed down his drinking. We have a TV now so he stays home more. Your sister Elizabeth joined the Air Force; she's in Lincolnshire."

"So it's just the two of you now."

"That's right. What are you going to do, Eddie, are you going back to the crane works?"

"No, I'm singing with the band. I'll get a part-time job but soon the band will be full-time."

"Oh, Eddie, that's not a proper job. You do worry me so. Promise me you won't get into any more trouble."

"I promise, Mum. I'm through with all that."

"Why don't you go back to the crane works? Singing in a band is all right as a hobby, but it's not a proper job."

I wished I had not told her about the music. It was hard for her generation to see the potential of a rock-n-roll band. "Mum, do you remember how you used to be so proud of me when I sang in church? Well, one day I'll make you proud again. Singing is the one thing I do really well and it's what makes me happy."

"All right, Eddie, as long as you're happy. That's all any mother wants."

The next day Ralph said he wanted to work with Harry and me on harmonies.

"Now you'll both have to use the same mike, so, Eddie you step slightly to the right and turn slightly to the left. Harry you turn to the right and step up to the side of the mike." We practiced our moves then Ralph continued.

"Let's do Eddie's song *Trav'lin' Light.* When you get to the chorus, Eddie will be singing this." He sat at the piano and played the melody. "Now, Harry, you sing this." He played different notes. "This is the harmony part." He played it again and Harry sang it through. Harry rehearsed his part a few times.

"Okay, now both together." Ralph played the chords on the piano and we both sang our parts in harmony. It sounded wonderful and I remembered singing in the church choir how all the harmony parts blended together.

"Now, let's do the next line. This is Eddie's part and this is Harry's." Ralph played the different parts on the piano and I realized what an asset it was to have Ralph with his knowledge of music. Johnny and Danny came in from the other room.

"That sounds fuckin' great," Johnny said.

"Okay, let's try it all together." Ralph got up from the piano and Johnny and Danny took their places. We did it through from the top and when it came to the harmony parts Harry and I looked at each other and couldn't help smiling; it sounded good and it felt good.

When we finished Ralph said, "Do it exactly like that onstage. The crowd loves to see people having a good time up onstage. It's infectious."

That Saturday we carried our equipment down the street to the Coach & Horses and set up in the lounge. We were in the same corner where we had lunch earlier in the week. The big table was moved out and a small portable stage brought in. It was triangular in shape to fit in the corner, about a foot high, and just big enough for the four of us.

"Good thing we decided to do without the piano," Ralph quipped.

"Oh, you just quit playing 'cos it interfered with yer drinkin'," Johnny said.

"Damn right. I'll be here on this corner barstool where I can watch. Cliff, you just keep the beers coming, Eddie an' young Harry don't drink much so I'll drink theirs."

We started to play around eight o'clock; there was a good-sized crowd. The young people were up in front of the stage dancing in the somewhat limited space. By nine o'clock the place was so packed dancing was no longer possible.

It was a cold and damp evening but in spite of the cool temperature outside, it got very hot inside because of the number of people packed so tightly together. All the doors and windows had been opened up and the sound of the music carrying down the street only served to bring more people in. Eventually when the room could hold no more the crowd spilled out into the street.

We had originally planned to play for an hour and a half and then take a break. But nine-thirty came and it was obvious we could not get off the stage. We were literally painted into a corner, not by wet paint but by a sea of happy faces standing shoulder to shoulder, bouncing and swaying to the beat of the music.

We kept on playing and by about ten-thirty I could see through the open doors and windows that police were moving people off the sidewalk. I knew we had a problem. A policeman came to an open window next to the stage and beckoned me over. I had to lean out of the window as he spoke directly into my ear.

"You have way too many people in there. You're going to have to stop playing now or the landlord will face a heavy fine."

I was having a great time but I was ready to quit; I was exhausted. My voice was shot, my throat hurt, and my eyes burned from the sweat that was running into them. The police officer turned his head so I could speak into his ear. "Can we just do one more? Then we'll quit."

He nodded agreement and held up one finger to reinforce 'Just one more.'

I returned to the microphone and addressed the crowd.

"We've had a great time tonight and we want to thank you, you've been a wonderful audience. Old Bill is here an' says we have to wrap it up."

There were boos from the crowd.

"But we're gonna do one more." The boos turned to cheers.

"This is for the local constabulary—"Jailhouse Rock," which is where we'll be if we don't stop now."

I started to sing and the band jumped in with me. After we finished the song, I stepped off the stage and was immediately mobbed by the crowd. I looked behind me and could see that the rest of the band was getting the same treatment. All I wanted to do was to get outside to cool off. I fought my way to the door; the crowd followed me into the street. I was being hugged, slapped on the back, and kissed by young girls. I was bombarded with questions.

The crowd eventually thinned as people left and I made my way back inside to find the others. I found Ralph at the bar talking to Cliff.

"Good job, Eddie. Bloody fantastic." Ralph put his arm around my shoulder, giving me a one-arm hug. Cliff pulled a pint of beer and sat in front of me.

"Here drink up. You've earned it."

I drank it straight down. "Fill it up again, Cliff, this time with water."

"Water? Are you serious?"

"Yeah, my throat feels like I've done a forced march across the bleedin' Gobi Desert."

Cliff filled the glass with water and I emptied it.

"More?" he asked.

"Please, more."

He filled it again. "Damn, I'd be in the fucking poor house if all my customers were like you." He winked at Ralph as he said it, then added, "You can leave yer stuff here tonight. Come an' pick it up in the morning."

"Good idea," Ralph agreed.

As exhausted as I was that night, I had a hard time sleeping. The music was still ringing in my ears, and the excitement of the evening was still fresh in my mind. It was hard to believe that just a few days earlier I was in a prison cell.

The next morning we went to get our gear from the Coach & Horses. Cliff was still talking about the night before.

"Do you know people were buying drinks at the pub down the road and bringing them here. I know this for a fact because after all the breakages we still ended up with more glasses than we started out with."

"People couldn't get to the bar," Ralph commented.

"Maybe we should look for a bigger venue. You could do the catering and profit from that. We could charge at the door to cover our costs."

"Good idea," Cliff agreed. "Let's look into that."

Chapter 21

SIX MONTHS HAD PASSED SINCE we first played at the Coach & Horses; it was spring 1959. We became victims of our own success. A lot of pubs would not let us play because too many people would show up; near riots and fighting would break out. Cliff would always let us play at the Coach & Horses but we would not publicize it and he had to put people on the door to regulate the numbers coming in. The word would get out that we were playing and the pub would be packed an hour before the show started as people came early to ensure a place.

We had tried to find a larger venue without success. There were several church halls in the area but they didn't allow drinking. We did use these sometimes and put on a show for the teenagers selling soft drinks only.

Our break came when a furniture shop next door to the pub went out of business. It was Ralph who first saw the potential and spoke to Cliff one morning. "Hey, Cliff, I see the shop next door is vacant. I got a key from the agent and took a look in there. It's got a basement with a hardwood floor just perfect for dancing."

"What would you do with the upstairs?" Cliff asked.

"You could put tables and chairs in there, extend the bar through from in here. People could drink upstairs and dance downstairs."

"I dunno," Cliff didn't seem too thrilled with the idea.

"Do you still have the key?" I asked. "Can we take a look?"

Ralph led the way and Cliff and I followed. The door to the shop opened from the street into a large room about twenty feet wide by sixty feet long. A few feet inside the door was a staircase leading down to a basement. We walked down and Ralph flipped on the lights. It had a well-maintained hardwood floor that had been used to showcase furniture.

"There's nothing to do down here, just build a stage at one end. Perfect."

"But what about upstairs?" Cliff asked again. We climbed back up the stairs.

"Why don't you cut a hole in the floor so people can watch the dancing and listen to the music." I suggested.

Cliff stopped his mouth open and his eyes got big and round. "That's fucking brilliant, Eddie. Why didn't I think of that? Cut the center of the floor out, put a safety rail around, and people can sit up here and have a drink and still see the entertainment."

Ralph thought about it.

"It's gonna cost a bit to do that."

"It's the only expense," Cliff pointed out. "You said yourself, there's nothing needs to be done downstairs." Ralph thought it over.

"Yeah, and if we don't serve drinks downstairs, the kids can go down there. We can get the teenage crowd and the drinking crowd."

"That's right," Cliff added. "We could make an opening through into the pub and extend the bar along that wall." He indicated the wall to the right that adjoined his pub next door."

And so that day a partnership began between Ralph and Cliff to open a nightclub. Ralph put up most of the money and Cliff got his liquor license extended to include the club. Permits were obtained from the local council and work began. The biggest job was getting the hole cut in the floor. Steel beams were inserted to support the floor after the opening had been made. Ralph bought an antique cast iron spiral staircase and installed it toward the rear of the dance floor as an additional access to the bar upstairs.

Carpenters built a long bar and an opening led through behind the bar in the pub. They put oak paneling inside the storefront window about three feet back from the glass, reaching floor to ceiling. On this paneling was a large neon sign with the name "Ralph's." Pictures of the band were displayed. Above the stairs leading down to the dance floor was a smaller neon sign that said, "Rock-n-roll." The band members, including myself, did much of the painting and decorating. We also built the stage and Ralph put in the sound system.

It took three months to complete the work and during this time we talked about it constantly during our weekend gigs at the Coach & Horses. The opening of Ralph's in the summer of 1959 was met with great anticipation. The place was packed; it drew people from miles around.

The band became known as the Eddie Sons. We played four nights a week, Thursday through Sunday. The club was closed on Monday. A DJ played records on Tuesday and Wednesday and teenagers got in free as a service to the community.

"It keeps 'em off the streets," Ralph said.

On my evenings off I would often go alone up to the West End jazz clubs. The music scene had changed since the early fifties when I used to go there. The young people who hung out at these clubs were students and middle-class kids and the music they listened to was traditional jazz, Dixieland, and New Orleans style that had been popular in America in the 1920s and 1930s.

I enjoyed the company of the middle-class girls. They could hold a conversation about any interesting topic; they had more self-confidence. There was no shortage of girlfriends where I lived but somehow their admiration seemed false, only because I was a singer in a rock-n-roll band. In the West End clubs no one knew me so meeting girls was more of a challenge.

I met a girl one evening named Sally Benitto; she was a student at the London School of Economics. Sally had black hair, a dark complexion, and dark brown eyes. Her grandfather had come from Italy some years before and founded an ice cream and chocolate manufacturing company that her family still owned. We somehow got into a conversation about Italian art and she mentioned a painting in the Tate Gallery. I told her I had never been there.

"You've never been to the Tate Gallery? I should take you there."

"I would like that. When?"

"I'm out of school for the summer so anytime is fine."

We arranged to meet the next morning in a coffeehouse near the Tate. She was waiting when I got there. She smiled as I arrived, a waitress came, and I ordered coffee.

"You're not working today?" she asked.

"I work evenings and I get Monday, Tuesday, Wednesday off."

I didn't volunteer that I played in a band. I noticed she was wearing an engagement ring. I reached out and took her left hand touching the ring with my thumb. "You're engaged?"

"Yes, my fiancé lives in Cambridge with his parents."

"What would he say if he knew you were out with me today?"

"We're just two friends spending the day together, nothing more. Did you expect more?"

"I expect nothing; I take what life brings me."

"That's a good philosophy." We finished our coffee and she said, "Let's go look at some paintings."

We walked around the gallery; she knew all the paintings, the artists, and the dates when they lived.

"You know a great deal about art," I commented.

"I do, except for the most important thing—how to create it. I wish I could paint."

"You can, just go to the spirit within you. It's the source of all creation whether it is music, poetry, or painting. A teacher once told me that and it's always worked for me."

"I wish I'd had a teacher like that; all I was ever taught was facts and figures."

"This was not a school teacher; it was someone I met during the war. An American GI."

This is what I liked about a girl like Sally; I could reveal my innermost thoughts and feelings. My other friends would think I was crazy if I talked like this. The feelings I had were difficult to put into words, so it was refreshing to have someone at least try to understand. Sally questioned me further.

"You talked about music, poetry, and painting. Where's the connection between the different art forms?"

"Well, take this painting, for example. It has rhythm, it has melody, it is the same as a piece of music, only it's in a different form."

"That is so deep, Eddie. I believe you know far more about art than I'll ever know. All I know is names and dates."

That year—1959—was one of those rare British summers. The sun shone every day and Sally and I were constant companions. We walked in parks; we went swimming at public pools; and went to museums and art galleries. I cared for her deeply as I had never cared for anyone before. But I never let my feelings be known because I was afraid I would lose a friendship that meant more to me than anything. The summer ended and Sally went back to the School of Economics. I still saw her occasionally although not as often as during the summer.

George was released from prison and came 'round to see me. I introduced him to Ralph and Cliff.

"Can we give George a job here? He'd be useful on the door, he's a strong lad."

Cliff agreed and George started part-time as a doorman. During the day he helped his father with his bookmaking business. It was soon after that, I was performing one night when a young person came up to the edge of the stage and was shouting at the top of his voice, "Conner, you're fucking shit. You can't sing worth a damn."

I didn't know what his problem was but he was distracting me. Harry was playing a solo and I was trying to concentrate on the music to know when to come back in with the vocal. That moment came, I picked up the mike stand to sing, and clipped the loudmouth under the chin with its heavy cast iron base, making it look like an accident. The next thing I knew I was being dragged off the stage by my feet and my head hit the corner of the stage as I fell. I staggered to my feet slightly dazed to see my assailant being set upon by a dozen or so screaming girls. I saw George come into the fray, grab this person around the neck, and drag him toward the door. Someone else was punching George and I rushed over hitting the second person with my head laying him out cold. Cliff came on the scene and carried the unconscious body out.

After the show I was still pumped up from the fight. "Damn, that felt good, just like old times. 'Aye, George?"

Ralph looked serious. "Eddie, I don't want you fighting. One, you could get hurt, and two, you have a police record and you could get arrested for hurting someone else. I've got too much invested in you, so no more fighting."

Cliff spoke up. "We have a another problem. Two local twin brothers, who shall be nameless, came over today and talked about buying the club. When we said we weren't interested, they talked about paying them for protection. I showed 'em the door. What happened tonight was the result; the two we threw out of here were their cronies."

George spoke up. "Let me talk to my dad; he's got connections."

And so George talked to his dad and he talked to Big Arthur, who controlled all the illegal gambling in the East End. Arthur came to see us the next morning. I hadn't seen him in years. Maybe his black hair came from a dye bottle now but apart from that he looked exactly the same.

I reached out to shake his hand. "Big Arthur, do you remember me? I used to come to your office as a kid. Eddie Conner."

"Yeah, of course. Eddie, how the fuck are ya?"

Cliff and Ralph talked with Big Arthur. They had a few drinks, a phone call was made, and the twins came over. I don't know what transpired at the meeting but I was told after that we would play over at the twins' club in Bethnal Green on alternate weekends. The band that played at their club would switch and play at Ralph's.

I knew of the twins' reputation; they were people you did not mess with if you valued your life. I was a little apprehensive about playing for them but felt I had no choice. The first night we played there, the twins met us at the door. One of them introduced me as I entered.

"Eddie Conner, this boy cannot only sing he can march on a bit. Put the nut on Bruce here and laid him spark out."

He stepped aside and there stood the young man I was in the fight with a few days earlier. He held out his hand and with a smile and a wink said, "There'll be no further problem, Eddie, we're all working for the same firm now."

I was still seeing Sally whenever I got the chance. I had never told her that I played in a band. It was the working-class versus middle-class thing; she and I were from different worlds. She had once asked me what I did and I replied that I worked in a club but didn't volunteer any more information. The summer of 1960 was coming up and I was looking forward to seeing more of her as I had done the previous summer.

She lived in Richmond and one day asked me, "I want you to come over to where I live to see Chris Barber. They're a trad band."

I went with her. The band was good and we spent most of the evening dancing. During the break she asked me, "Do you like traditional jazz?"

"I like all forms of music. To me there are only two kinds, good and bad."

"I agree completely."

"So do you like rock-n-roll?"

"I love it, especially Elvis."

After the show I asked her if she would come and see a band that I liked. She said she would and I gave her the address of Ralph's. "Bring a crowd of your friends. They'll like it."

That Friday I was onstage and looked down to see Sally standing there smiling, her mouth open exaggerating her amazement. She had three other girls with her. During the break I joined her and her friends and we found a table upstairs.

"Eddie, why didn't you tell me? How long have you been playing?"

"For two years now."

Sally introduced me to her friends.

"You wrote those songs you were doing. I'm impressed. There's a whole side to you I never knew about."

After that Sally became a regular at Ralph's and she went to the twins' club a few times, bringing more of her friends. I think these middle-class girls liked to think they were slumming.

One Friday after the show Ralph called all the band members together. The twins were there and they introduced us to a man in his mid-thirties wearing a smart business suit and tie.

"This is Adrian Becket; he is an agent and we've asked him to help in the promotion of the band."

After shaking hands all around, Adrian spoke. "I've watched you play tonight and I like what I see. You are as good if not better than any London band, so we need to get you exposure outside of the East End. The problem is that no one from outside this area comes here to listen to music. We need to take you to them. I've got you booked at the Shepherd's Bush Empire, which is owned by the BBC. They've given us a Monday night, which will be a slow night but they say if we can build a following and fill the place they will put the show on television."

The Shepherd's Bush Empire was the one of the biggest venues in London. I had been there many times to see the big American bands when they toured. The first night we played there was to a small but enthusiastic crowd. Each week more and more people showed as the word got around. Adrian got us good reviews in some of the UK music papers.

I came into the club one morning and Ralph, who was there with Adrian, was all smiles.

"Eddie, we've got two Friday nights booked at the Shepherd's Bush Empire. I'm going to try my best to get the BBC executives there," Adrian told me.

"What about this place?" I asked Ralph.

"We're going to charter buses and take everyone from here over there."

Later that week I saw Sally and told her the good news. "Try to be there, it's an important night. Bring all your friends."

She said she would.

Friday night just before the show I peeked out between the stage curtains. The huge auditorium was packed. Ralph had chartered three buses and filled them with our fans from the East End. I could see many familiar faces out there.

The curtain went up and we played like we had never played before. Harry and I found that singing harmonies was second nature to us now, we had done it for so long. We were confident. Harry strutted up to the edge of the stage as he did his solos, then casually dropped back again as I stepped up to sing. We brought the house down.

After the show I talked to Adrian. "Were the BBC people here?" I asked.

"Yes, and they are impressed. They are going to record next week's show and there's a good possibility it will be on television."

I peeked out through the curtains again, looking for Sally. I could see her but knew if I stepped out there the fans would not let me get to her. I called George over.

"You remember Sally, you met her at the club. Go get her and bring her back here."

He did so, and we walked down a passageway behind the stage. She seemed very subdued.

"What's wrong?" I asked

"Eddie, I'm not going to see you for a while. I've finished school and I'm moving to Cambridge to be with my fiancé. I've known this all week but I didn't want to tell you before the show."

I felt as if the world had been ripped out from under my feet and I was floating in space.

"We'll still be friends, Eddie. I'll write to you, I promise, and I'll see you whenever I come back to London."

I gave her a hug and told her, "Thanks for coming and thank your friends too."

"I have to go, someone's driving us."

I watched her walk away then went to find the others. I helped load our gear into a van we'd rented. Johnny turned to me. "Come on, Eddie, we're going to get something to eat. Celebrate a bit."

"You go on. I don't feel so good. I'm going home," I told them.

"Do you want me to go with you?" George asked.

"No, I'll be okay. You go with the others. I'll catch the tube."

I stepped out of a side exit and into the street. I crossed the road and walked up an alleyway. I just wanted to get as far away as I could, away from the crowds, away from people who wanted to talk to me. I wasn't sure of the area or where the nearest underground station was.

"I'll just keep walking 'til I find one," I told myself. "I'm in no hurry, in fact I've got all night. I can walk all the bleedin' way to Stepney for that matter."

I was aware of four young kids walking the same direction as me on the opposite side of the street. They were rowdy, probably drunk, and were calling out to me. I ignored them.

"Couple of shandys and a smell of the barman's apron and they're drunk," I muttered to myself.

The four crossed over and stood in front of me blocking the sidewalk.

"Fuckin' leave it out," I said as I tried push past.

"*Leave it out*," one of them said, mocking my accent. "Ya Cockney git."

I could tell by their accents they were from the north of England probably football supporters down for tomorrow's game. I was getting pretty mad. They were all young, maybe seventeen, eighteen years old.

I knew I could take all four of these young bastards. Two of them were right in my face. I punched one in the face with a right cross and hit the second one with my head. They both went down. The other two jumped back. I heard a metallic click and saw a glint of light reflected on polished steel. A switchblade knife.

"Fuckin' great. What else did yer get for Christmas?" I said as he danced around me. The others dropped back.

"Come on." I reasoned. "There's four of you and you can't take me without a bleedin' knife."

He slashed at my face and my hand instinctively went up for protection. I felt the knife cut into the palm of my left hand. It cut into the fleshy part at the base of my thumb. It hurt like hell. I kicked out with the sole of my shoe and caught him on the knee then ran as hard as I could up the street. I could hear them close behind me.

Up ahead I could see a portable sign standing outside a tobacconist shop. It had a heavy round cast iron base, a short piece of one-inch pipe and an enameled metal sign on top advertising some brand of cigarettes. Usually these signs are taken in a night but this one had been left out. I was praying that it wasn't chained up to something.

I reached the sign and picked it up; it wasn't chained. I held it out in front of me and tried to catch my breath. They must have been doing the same because they just stood there. The one with the knife stepped forward; I poked him in the chest with the base of the sign.

"Now put the bleedin' knife away and go home." I told them.

They gave no ground. I had to disarm the one with the knife. I thought if I hit him on the arm he would drop the knife or at least not be able to use it. The sign was heavy and my hand was hurting. I didn't know if I could swing this thing. I mustered all my strength and swung aiming at his right elbow. As it connected he threw his arm upward deflecting the base of the sign. It bounced off his shoulder and hit him on the side of the head. He cartwheeled over, hitting his head on the wall as he landed in a crumpled heap like an old overcoat thrown in a corner. I didn't see where the knife had gone but I stepped forward to make sure no one else picked it up.

Out of the corner of me eye I thought I saw the crumpled heap move. I spun around and hit him hard on the leg with the base of the sign. I just wanted to make sure he didn't get up again. The other three took off running down the street. I was not sure if the one on the ground had moved or not, but he certainly wasn't moving now. I threw the sign down and it spun around like a top. For a moment it looked as if it would stay upright but then fell over with a loud clatter.

I staggered up the street, wrapping a handkerchief tightly around my hand to stop the bleeding. I stopped in a pub and asked directions to the nearest underground station; there was one on the next street. I didn't go home but went instead to my local hospital. The cut on my hand needed attention.

I walked into the emergency room. "Can you look at my hand? I've had an accident." I told a nurse.

"How did you do that?" she asked.

"I was opening a can of beer with a knife and it slipped." Beer cans back then had solid tops and a special opener was needed to punch a hole. After my hand was stitched the nurse filled out a report. I signed it and left to walk home.

Chapter 22

THE NEXT MORNING RALPH SAW my bandaged hand. "What happened to you?"

"I got in a fight."

"What did I tell you?"

"I couldn't avoid it. I tried to."

"How are you going to play guitar now?"

"I'll just have to sing tonight. I'll be all right by next weekend."

"You'd better be. Here we are with a chance to be on National Television and you go get in a fight."

"Leave it out, Ralph ,please. All right?"

"So what happened?" It was Johnny who spoke this time. I told the story of the night before.

"We should call the police."

"No, don't do that. I hurt this kid pretty bad."

"How bad?"

"Bad, trust me, it was bad."

"Jesus fucking Christ, Eddie." Ralph shook his head. I tried to reason with him.

"What could I do? Tell me what could I do? He was going to cut me; he did fuckin' cut me. Look at me bleedin' hand."

I thought about the situation. "Look they were football supporters from Yorkshire or somewhere. This happened all the way over in Shepherd's Bush. No one's gonna know it's me."

"I fuckin' hope not," Ralph said.

"D'you want breakfast?" Johnny asked.

"No, I'm not hungry." I walked out slamming the front door behind me. Why is it when you need the comfort and support of those around you, you never get it?

I walked around the corner and hopped on a bus over to George's house, I knew he wouldn't be critical of me. His mother answered the door; George was still in bed. She invited me in.

"What did you do to yer hand?" she asked.

"Oh, a little accident opening a can of beer."

"I didn't think you drank, Eddie."

She was right; I would never open a can of beer at home. That was the problem with lying—you had to come up with one story that was believable to everyone.

George came downstairs, yawning and scratching his head. "What'd ya do to yer hand?"

"He cut it opening a can of beer," George's mother spoke through the open kitchen door.

"You? Opening a can of beer? I knew you were down last night but I didn't think you were that desperate. It must be serious love to drive Eddie Conner to drink."

"Do leave off, please, George." Then I whispered. "I'll tell yer later."

"Would you like something to eat, Eddie?" George's mother asked.

"Yes, thank you. That would be nice."

A few minutes later we were eating bacon and eggs with toast and drinking mugs of tea. After breakfast we left the house and I told George what had happened.

"Damn, I knew I should have gone with you last night. I fucking knew it."

"Do you think Old Bill can tie me in?"

"Did you leave yer prints on the Tobacconist's Sign?"

"Oh shit, I didn't even think of that."

"It's the first thing ya' think of. What's the matter with you, Eddie?"

"I don't have your experience, I don't think like a thief. Do you think they can find me with my prints?"

"Well—yes, that's why they take prints."

"But they must have millions of prints down at Scotland Yard. They can't look at 'em all, can they?"

"I dunno, but if they even suss that it's you, then they'll check."

"I can't see how I could get sussed, I mean I was in Shepherd's Bush; they don't know me over there. It's not like I'm on me own manor. I'm sure they'll check the prints of the local villains but they won't check mine."

I was putting this argument forward for my own benefit more than trying to convince George.

Later that week I took the bandage off my hand. My left thumb was a little stiff but my fingers were okay. I played my guitar. It was uncomfortable at first but got easier as I played. I practiced for a couple of hours Thursday morning and performed at the club that night.

"How's yer hand?" Ralph asked.

"It's fine. I'll be okay tomorrow night."

Friday night we followed exactly the same plan as the previous week. We chartered buses and brought in our East End fans. We arrived at the Empire and the BBC were setting up their cameras. Before the show Adrian introduced a Mr. Collins who was a BBC producer.

"I've heard great things about you and your band; I'm looking forward to the show." He shook hands all 'round and then said, "I'll talk to you later."

The curtain went up and the reaction to our first number was even better than the previous week. We did a flawless first set. Backstage during the break Adrian told us that Mr. Collins was blown away.

"It's in the bag, Eddie." He gave double thumbs-up.

I went back onstage feeling great. The events of the previous week seemed light years away. Toward the end of the final set I looked across to the left and saw two very large men standing in the wings. They were not BBC executives, they were not smiling, and they were not tapping their feet to the music. I finished the song and turned to the right and saw a uniformed bobby on the opposite side.

My suspicions were founded. I turned my back to the audience and mouthed the word. "Fuck." Beating my head against an imaginary brick wall as I did so. I took a deep breath and turned to face the audience with a smile. I remembered feeling this way before, singing in St. Paul's Cathedral as a kid just after I'd punched Nigel on the nose. Only this was way more serious, this was deep, deep shit but the task at hand was the same. I concentrated on the music and sang as I had never sung before.

We finished the final set and the band filed off stage. I remained center stage, my head hung as the crowd chanted, "Ed-die, Ed-die."

Standing alone I picked up my acoustic guitar and started to play and sing.

> I just came by to tell you I was leavin',
> It's been a year, I must be movin' on,
> When I came to this ol' town I was just passin' through.
> You're the only reason why I stayed this long.

There was not a sound in the house, I could even hear myself breathe. Tears were streaming down my face and some of the audience was crying with me. Although they had no idea what was going on they obviously felt my pain. I continued with the chorus.

> *I'm trav'lin' light but carryin' a load,*
> *Strings that tied me here tug at my heart along the road.*
> *All I've got is my old guitar and a change of clothes.*
> *I'm trav'lin' light, carryin' a load.*

I finished the song to a wild frenzy of applause as I set my guitar on its stand and walked off the stage. The two policemen each grabbed an arm and one told me above the noise of the crowd. "We must ask you to accompany us to the police station."

I tried to put on a brave face. "Wait, I'll go get me banjo?" Then added, "I always wanted to say that." As they handcuffed me I thought, "No bleedin' sense of humor."

I was led out and saw Mr. Wilson coming toward me, a big smile on his face and his hand outstretched. His face changed to a hurt puzzled look, as I did not return his handshake. We pushed on by and probably then he realized my hands were cuffed behind me. Out through a side exit and into a waiting police car.

Down at the police station a police detective questioned me about the incident the week before. I refused to tell him anything. "He's in serious condition you know, brain damage. He might even die."

I did not respond. "How did you get this cut on yer hand?"

I didn't answer. He pressed his thumb into the still tender wound.

"Ow, you bastard." I snatched my hand away.

"Make a statement, just tell your side of what happened." A pen and note pad was placed in front of me.

"No. I'm not making a statement. The last time I did that I was charged with armed robbery for takin' me own bleedin' money. Talk to my solicitor."

"Oh, Mr. Big Shot Rock-n-Roll Star has a solicitor."

"Fuck you." That got me a slap across the face, as I knew it would. I jumped to my feet and tried to put the nut on him. I received two hard punches to the stomach for my effort.

"We don't need your statement, we've got witnesses and we'll probably find that those prints all over the tobacconist sign are yours."

So they hadn't tied the prints to me yet. How the hell did they finger me then?

The next morning I was taken outside to the station yard for a police identification parade. There were other young men about my age and build in the lineup. They brought out two teenage boys one at a time. I recognized them both as being among those I had confronted the week before. They both walked straight to me without hesitation and touched me on the shoulder. I was taken inside and formally charged with causing grievous bodily harm (GBH) to one Andrew James Strickland, aged seventeen.

I thought to myself, "Seventeen. What's a seventeen-year-old doing on the London streets with a flick-knife acting like Jack the lad. Why didn't he just quit when I picked up the tobacconist sign? I would have only threatened him with it. I didn't want to do him serious harm. I wouldn't have wished this on a seventeen-year-old kid."

They read me my rights and then asked, "Do you have anything to say?"

"No—hey let me see you write that down. N-o. I know what you bastards are with yer verbals." I didn't see anyone writing anything. A "verbal" is when they read you your rights, then make something up you allegedly said afterwards. Something incriminating and you can never disprove you said it, because it's their word against yours.

A young detective led me down to the cells. I spoke to him as he opened the door. "I'm curious, can I ask you a question?"

"What's that?"

"How did the police finger me?" He gave a little half smile.

"The two youths who just picked you out in the ID parade. They are brother and cousin to the one in hospital. They decided to stay here in Shepherd's Bush when young Andrew was hurt, so as to be near him. Quite by chance they went to your show at the Empire. They had no idea they would see you until the curtain went up and there you were. They called the police and now you're here. Ironic, isn't it?"

"Yep, shopped by me own fans, so to speak."

"Ain't life a bastard," he said as he slammed the door.

"Yeah, and so are you." He never heard it, he was gone; I was talking to myself.

Monday morning I appeared in court. I looked around for any familiar faces as I was led in; George was the only one I saw. He waved to me from the public benches. My hands were cuffed in front of me so I could not wave back. I raised my eyebrows and gave my head a little upward bob to indicate I had seen him.

For someone who didn't see himself as a career criminal, these proceedings were becoming way too familiar. The charge was read. I was refused bail and remanded in custody to appear at the Old Bailey for trial some three months down the road in October. I was led from the courtroom and tried to signal to George as best I could with my hands shackled. I pointed toward the floor and mouthed the words. "Come down and see me."

About twenty minutes later George came in for a visit.

"Thanks for coming," I told him. "Where's the others? I was hoping Ralph would be here."

"Ralph's pretty pissed off; he's not saying much."

"Talk to him for me please, George, I need to see him. I need legal representation, a mouthpiece."

"Are you pleading self-defense?"

"Yeah, it's my only chance, but I need a good solicitor."

"I'll talk to him."

"Thanks, George. Can you go an' tell my mother. Tell her it wasn't my fault. God, this is gonna kill her."

"So you'll be in Brixton for the next three months."

"Yeah, unless I can get bail. This is another reason why I need a solicitor."

"I'll talk to Ralph," George said as he got up to leave.

That afternoon I was driven in a police van to Brixton Prison, just a short distance across the river from my home in Stepney. Brixton was used as a remand center to hold people awaiting trial.

It would be a week before Ralph came to visit. He was looking pretty serious when he arrived; he didn't return my smile. I told him, "Ralph, I'm sorry about this. I told you before what happened. I feel I have a good case for self-defense but I need a good solicitor."

"And who's gonna pay for that, Eddie?"

"I'll pay you back, you know I will."

"But what if you get jail time? How will you pay me then?"

"If I have a good lawyer I might not get jail time."

"Don't count on it, that kid's in a pretty bad way."

Ralph was silent for a moment then said, "Eddie, I've had it with you, I've invested three years of my life and a whole lot of money and for what? Sweet fuck all. We were all in a position to start having some success and you threw it all away." He stood to leave and added, "I have to decide what I'm gonna do now, and you have to do the same. I wish you well, Eddie, but I'm sorry I can't help you anymore. You'll have to go it alone."

I was taken back to my cell. I didn't blame Ralph. He was right, he had been good to me. But it was me who was facing jail time. In my cell was some information about the Legal Aid Society, the public defenders. I wrote them a letter asking if someone could come visit me before my trial date.

About a month before my trial date I had a visit from a young man who introduced himself as Peter Hollingsworth. He seemed to be about my own age and was probably fresh out of law school. He was wearing a blue pinstriped hand-tailored suit not unlike the style I would wear. He said he had been appointed as my solicitor, but that someone else would be defending me in court. In British law a solicitor prepares the case and a barrister is the one who stands in court.

He asked if I would consider pleading guilty and throwing myself on the mercy of the court.

"Why would I do that?" I asked.

"Well, if they bring the victim into the court it could invoke a lot of sympathy from the jury. He's still in a wheelchair, his right leg broken. Plus he has brain damage and some speech problems."

I was shocked. "Damn, I had no idea he was injured so bad."

"Yes you really did a number on him and this is the problem. In self-defense you are allowed to retaliate with an amount of force equal to that which you are being attacked."

"That's all very well in theory but he had a knife and the only thing available to me was the tobacconist's sign. I tried to hit him on the arm. He deflected it up to his head."

"But then you broke his leg after he was lying there unconscious. That's not going to look good."

I told Peter exactly what had happened. He took notes and said he would prepare a defense. I thanked him; we shook hands, and he left.

Chapter 23

STANDING IN THE DOCK AT the Old Bailey was surreal. I couldn't help but feel detached from the whole proceedings, as if it was happening to someone else, with me in the role of observer.

I looked at the players in this bizarre theater with their robes and gray wigs. I wondered who decided two centuries ago when this was the accepted fashion of that day and said, "Hey, this look's cool; let's hang on to this style." And as the rest of the world moved on, the British courts and judicial system stayed frozen in time.

I looked at the jurors seated off to one side. They weren't ordinary working-class men and women. No, these were middle-class folks bussed in from the suburbs, as far removed from my world as caviar from fish-n-chips.

The charge against me was read and I was asked,. "How do you plead?"

I replied, "Not guilty." The proceedings began.

The prosecution gave its account of what happened but no mention of a knife was made. I was not surprised at this omission as it was me accused of assaulting someone, not the other way around.

The first witness was the arresting officer. He told the story of how after a call to the station he and another officer had gone to the Shepherd's Bush Empire and brought me in for questioning. He continued to read from a small black notebook. "The accused was uncooperative and refused to answer any of our questions. Two witnesses subsequently picked him out on an Identity parade as being the assailant. He was formally charged and after being warned of his rights was asked if he had anything to say to which he replied, 'That young bastard had it coming.'"

I shook my head in disbelief. Didn't he just say that I was uncooperative and had refused to say anything? Then at the precise moment after being told that anything I say could be used against me, I allegedly said,

"That young bastard had it coming," thus incriminating myself. To challenge the verbal was always a waste of time because the average citizen—in other words, the jury—held the British police in such high esteem that not only were they incapable of lying but they would never use a word like "bastard."

The prosecution asked for the tobacconist sign to be brought in. It was still covered in blood, mostly mine. There were clear bloody handprints and fingerprints all over it. The officer testified that the prints matched mine.

The first of the four youths was brought in. He told how they were walking home when I attacked two of them and ran up the street. They all four chased me and I picked up the tobacconist sign and beat Andrew Strickland unconscious. Then as he lay on the ground I hit him again breaking his leg.

My defense council spoke for the first time. "Did your friend Andrew have a knife?"

"No, sir."

"No further questions."

No further questions? I wanted to scream out, "You lying bastard." But I restrained myself.

The next two youths took the stand with an identical story. What had happened to the knife? Obviously, they had returned to the scene after I left and removed it.

To admit there was a knife was to admit they were at least partly responsible for the injury to their friend, and that would bring down the wrath of their parents and families. This was the difference between these young kids and those from my neighborhood. If we attempted to use a knife and were injured as a result, we would accept responsibility for our actions. So who was moral in this case? To use a knife and not accept the consequences, then to deny the existence of that knife to me was immoral.

The prosecution brought in Andrew Strickland. His appearance was for one purpose only: to shock and influence the jury, because as a witness he would be clearly useless. He hardly knew if it was day or night let alone something that happened three months ago. His appearance made the bile churn up from my stomach, to think that I did this.

He was in a wheelchair, his right leg still in a cast. His head rolled over to the left and he drooled from the corner of his mouth. He could not take to the stand so was allowed to stay in his chair. His hand had to be placed on the bible and when asked to give the oath he spoke in unintelligible grunts and moans. The prosecution asked that he be excused and the defense council did not object.

My council called me to the stand. I walked down the steps and out through a door into the well of the court. I climbed the steps into the witness box and took the oath. I told my version of the events of that night.

Then I was cross-examined by the prosecution. "Edward Conner, you say you were attacked and your hand was cut with a knife. Why did you not go to the police?"

His question caught me off guard. Apart from the fact that I had a criminal record it was not my nature to go running to the police if I was hurt in a fight. But I could not reveal that here. "I didn't want to get these young boys into trouble." My excuse seemed very lame.

"At the hospital where you had your hand treated you said you cut it opening a can of beer."

"Yes."

"So you were lying. How do we know you are not lying now?"

"Because I am under oath."

"Might I suggest that you really did cut your hand opening a can of beer and that Andrew had no knife?"

"No, because I had just played guitar at the Shepherd's Bush Empire and could not have done so with a cut hand."

"Maybe you did it right after the show?"

"But my friends would have driven me directly to the hospital. I would not have walked out from there with my hand untreated and pouring blood."

Had I known I would be up against this line of questioning I could have brought forward witnesses to prove my hand was not cut when I left the Empire.

"Maybe you cut your hand on the tobacconist sign."

"It has no sharp edges, none that would cause a wound for me to lose that much blood."

"Show the jury the scar on your hand."

I held up my hand; the problem was that my local hospital had done such a fine job stitching my hand, now three months later there was hardly any scar that could be seen clear across the court.

The judge spoke. "Let me see your hand."

I held out my left hand and the judge leaned over to inspect it. He said, "It is my opinion that this wound was made with a sharp knife. As to who had the knife and at what time the wound was inflicted is up to the jury to decide."

I felt this was a small victory, but then the prosecutor took a different line. "Why did you hit Andrew again breaking his leg when he was already unconscious and therefore no threat to you?"

"I thought he moved. I was afraid he would get up and attack me again with the knife."

"But he could not have moved; he was unconscious."

"I know that now." This was not a good note to end on. I went back to the dock and council for the prosecution started his closing speech.

Again, he did not mention the knife but played heavily on the fact that I had hit Andrew Strickland, breaking his leg as he lay helpless on the ground. He finished by stating that I had gone way beyond what was reasonable in self-defense.

My defense council stood to give his closing argument. "What is reasonable in self-defense? It is true that the defendant sustained a cut hand while Andrew Strickland has brain damage and a broken leg but that was not my client's intention. He did not get to choose his weapon but used what was available. What if the tobacconist sign had not been there? He could have been stabbed through the heart and be dead now; so what is reasonable in self-defense?

"My client tried everything possible to avoid this confrontation. He ran away but was followed. He was outnumbered four to one and confronted by one armed with a knife. After he picked up the tobacconist sign to defend himself, he did not immediately attack but told his adversaries 'Put the knife away and go home.' Had they responded to this request there would have been no further injuries. The four continued to threaten my client and it was then he tried to disarm Andrew Strickland by hitting him across the arm. It was the victim himself who threw up his arm deflecting the tobacconist sign causing the head injuries. This was a tragic accident; my client only wanted to knock the knife from his hand and did not intend to inflict such serious injury.

"Much has been made of the fact that the defendant broke the victim's leg after he lay unconscious on the ground. Try, if you can, to put yourself in my client's position that night. He had been attacked with a knife and his hand had been slashed. He was probably in shock and certainly had lost a great deal of blood. He had just knocked down his adversary but did not know where the knife was. He could not look for the knife because he was still being threatened by the other three. Out of the corner of his eye he sees Andrew Strickland move and he fears that he is about to be attacked again. As far as he knows, Strickland still has the knife. He had no time to think over his actions; he reacted rather than acted. He didn't hit the victim in the head but in the leg. He only wanted to disable him to prevent further attack. This was a tragic chain of events brought on not by my client but by the victim himself and his colleagues. I ask that you weigh all the evidence and bring back a verdict of not guilty on the grounds of self-defense."

The jury retired and I was led back down to the holding cells to await their verdict. I felt that my council had put forward a good closing speech but seeing Andrew Strickland in court had disturbed me and I was sure it would affect the jury. It was six hours later that I was led back up to the dock and the jury filed in to take their seats.

The judge asked the jury foreman, "Have you reached a verdict?"

"Yes, your honor."

There was a pause that to me seemed an eternity, then, "We find the defendant guilty."

Strangely I was not surprised at the verdict. Not that I felt I was guilty or that I had acted unreasonably under the circumstances, but I knew how the system worked. Someone had been badly hurt and someone had to pay for it. That someone was me, Eddie Conner. It had always been that way even at school. If there was trouble someone had to pay. Invariably that would be me or someone like me.

The judge asked if there were any prior convictions, and my previous record of assault on a police officer and armed robbery were read out. I was thinking how bad the record sounded. To say armed robbery without filling in the details conjures up a picture of robbing a bank with a gun.

The judge spoke to me. "Edward Conner, you have been found guilty of a very serious crime. I can appreciate that this offense was committed under extreme provocation and if I did not feel this way the sentence I am about to give you would have been much longer. You have a history of violence and you must be made aware that this behavior is unacceptable in our society. You will go to prison for five years."

I turned and walked down the steps, feeling that it could have been a lot worse. And I was still better off than that poor bastard in the wheelchair. I quickly figured out that with time off for good behavior I would do only two thirds of five years, which would be three years and four months. Still a long time but I could do it. I had to do it. I had no choice.

That evening I was driven in a police van along with other prisoners convicted that day to Wandsworth Prison in southwest London, not far from Richmond where Sally lived. I wondered how she was and whether I would hear from her again.

Wandsworth Prison had been built in the mid-1800s like so many other London prisons. The floor plan of this one was like a wheel with a center hall at the hub and the six prison wings radiating off like spokes from the center. Like a six-pointed star or an asterisk on a map marking where I would be for the next few years.

Chapter 24

AFTER INTERROGATION BY POLICE AND interrogation by the court, there is the self-interrogation brought on by spending hours alone behind a locked door. Questions like "What am I doing here?" and "Where did I go wrong?" Questions that never get answered.

You can blame the system, but you can't beat the system. You can blame things that happened in the past, but you can't change the past. You can blame God, but if God won't answer prayers, He's not going to take blame either.

While on remand in Brixton awaiting trial I had considered praying again for a fleeting moment. I had dismissed the thought immediately— one, because it hadn't worked before and two, because if there was a God, He had to be pretty damn smart and would see through me. I was only praying because I was in trouble. But the question "What am I doing here?" didn't just apply to what was I doing in prison, but what was I doing on this earth. I questioned my very existence.

I picked up the Bible partly because it was the only thing to read and partly because I wanted to make some sense of it. I opened it at the beginning, Genesis, Chapter 1, and read.

In the beginning God created the heaven and the earth. And the earth was without form, a void.

If there was a void, there was nothing, right? So out of what did God create the heaven and earth? I read on.

And the Spirit of God moved.

The Spirit had to be conscious of Itself in order to move and start creating. Was this the same as the Spirit of Creation that is inside me? I knew this spirit existed because it was there every time I wrote a song. It was as if the song already existed and I simply wrote it down. The feeling was so strong that often after writing a song I would wonder, "Now did I just write that, or did I hear it before on the radio or somewhere?"

Were God and the Spirit the same thing? If in the beginning there was a void, nothing but Spirit, then Spirit plus nothing equals Spirit; it didn't take a mathematical genius to work that out. So Spirit created everything, including me, out of Itself. I read some more.

And God said let there be light, and there was light.

I closed the Bible and set it down. I wanted to believe in something, but what? The spirit was inside me. It was the truth because I experienced it. It was one thing when I read or was told something, but when I actually experienced it, *that* was the truth. No one could take it from me.

That was the answer; from now on I would only accept truths, things I experienced. I didn't believe in a God that answered prayers and looked out for individuals like me, but I did believe in the Spirit, the Source of All Creation.

This Spirit that created everything, including me, also creates through me and all humankind. When cities and roads are built is this any different from an ant building an anthill? Are we nothing more than super-destructive termites?

"Now don't tell anyone about this," I told myself. "Don't go around the nick preaching 'the truth' or they will think you are some kind of nutter or something. Eddie Conner, you *are* a bleedin' nutter."

I got pencil and paper and began to write.

I've always been a thinking man,
Shit runs through my brain,
Since I read a book on philosophy
Things'll never be the same.
My friends are growing tired of me,
They all think I'm insane,
'Cos all I do is sit an' think
And shit runs through my brain.

I couldn't sleep the other night,
I lay awake in bed,
With thoughts about the meaning of life
Running through my head.
I went over to the window
And looked into the night,
I saw a million twinkling stars,
It was an awesome sight.

Now I became excited
And I began to shout,
"What are we all doing here
And what's it all about?"
A voice came back with an answer
And this is what it said,
"It's none of yer fuckin' business
Now get back into bed."

It felt good to write, even if it was a nonsensical piece like this. I always got high on creativity and the time just flew. I had lifted my spirits, made myself laugh—if only at myself.

The next day I went to see the governor and asked if I could have my guitar. Permission was refused and he told me, "You are in prison as a punishment and part of that punishment is being deprived of things you had on the outside."

I was about to leave when he added, "At some point you may be transferred from here. If you go to another prison they may allow you to have your guitar."

This was a blow but I decided not to let it get me down. There were other ways to create. I had access to paper and pencil, so I could draw and write.

One thing that surprised me was the number of people I knew in Wormwood Scrubs two years ago who were here now. A short time ago being back in prison was the furthest thing from my mind. I had been in Wandsworth about two weeks and had decided to keep myself to myself. I would be friendly toward everyone but a friend of no one.

I was on exercise one day and saw someone I knew up ahead walking alone. He was a man in his fifties, gray hair thinning on top. He was tall, slender, and walked with a slight stoop. I don't know why I felt the urge to talk to him; I broke into a trot and caught up to his side.

"Remember me? I was in the Scrubs two years ago." He leaned forward to look at my face.

"Oh yes, you're the young kid who used to play guitar and sing. How are you?"

"I'm fine. The name's Eddie, Eddie Conner."

He held out a large bony hand. "Norman."

"Pleased to meet'cher, Norman." We shook hands.

"I used to enjoy your singing. I remember you wrote some of the songs. You're pretty talented."

"Thanks. I went to see the governor to see if I could have my guitar but he said no."

"That's too bad. Can you still write songs without the guitar?"

"Oh yes and I have a melody too, but it's just in my head."

"It's good to have a talent for something in prison, it gives you status. People respect you for it and they leave you alone. I paint myself."

"What, pictures?"

"Yeah, oil paint, portraits mostly. I copy photos that people bring me, y'know their wives or kids. It gives me pleasure and makes me a few smokes."

"So where do you get yer paint?"

"There's an art class, meets once a week. They'll give you paint and canvas if you have any talent. They usually start you out doing pencil sketches."

"I've got a bunch of drawings I've done already."

"I'd like to see those, Eddie."

After exercise Norman followed me to my cell and I showed him my drawings.

"Oh yes," he said. "These are good. The art teacher will give you paint, no problem. Would you like to see my stuff? I'm on the threes."

I followed him up to the third landing to his cell. There were paintings everywhere.

"Here's one I'm working on now." He showed me a portrait of a child copied from a small snapshot.

"It's hard to do kids, they don't have any character in their face; they haven't lived yet."

He showed me another. "Here's a self-portrait."

Now here was character. The deep lines of living permanently etched into every part of his face like an old wooden fence post ravaged by the sun and rain. Here lines caused by the sunshine of laughter and others worn by the storms of misfortune and pain. And like the wooden post the smooth bark of its youth long since shed to reveal the sinewy grain, cracks, and imperfections that make it unique.

I was inspired, fired up. I wanted to paint. "So how do I get into the art class?" I asked.

"Go see the governor, put yer name down, and if there's room you'll get in."

I applied to attend the art class and some three weeks later when I least expected it my cell door was unlocked one evening and a voice called out, "Art class."

I peeked out of my door to see prisoners from the various levels all heading downstairs carrying art materials. A screw with a list of names on a clipboard was unlocking cells further down the landing. My name was obviously on the list so I gathered up my pencil sketches and followed the others down to the ground floor of the main hall.

I found a group of twenty-five or thirty men sitting at trestle tables on folding chairs, the same ones we used for our meals. I spotted Norman and took a seat next to him. The teacher was there; he was a young man in his early thirties with dark hair on the long side. He wore rimless glasses and had on a checkered shirt.

He asked newcomers to show hands; there were four of us. He introduced himself as Roger Browning and said he taught art at one of the local high schools. This was an additional part-time job he had been doing for two years. He said the best work from the class was shown in exhibitions outside the prison from time to time. Money from any artwork that sold went into a fund to buy paint and materials for the class.

During the evening Roger Browning looked at my pencil sketches and said that my work showed promise. He gave me a large pad of art paper and a small box of watercolors. During the following week I created a picture of the London docks, featuring the big cranes I had worked on as an apprentice. After about a month I got my first canvas and oil paints. I painted a night club scene as I remembered it from Ralph's. I composed the picture from memory but took faces from magazines as a guide. I loved the medium of oil paint, its texture, and the way paint could be put over more paint until the desired effect was achieved. Mistakes could be painted over; rather like life I thought.

> *I'll paint the picture with no clouds of gray,*
> *I'll paint bright tomorrows, no regrets for today,*
> *I'll paint over sad memories so they won't show through,*
> *I'll paint the picture and I'll leave out the Blue.*

I received a letter from Sally. It had been sent to the house and either Ralph or Johnny had redirected it to me. I wrote back to her; she had no idea what had happened to me and was shocked to find I was in prison. She replied to my letter almost immediately and we corresponded once a week after that. I was only allowed to write one letter a week so occasionally I would have to miss a letter and write to my mother. Sally would always write me every week. Her letters were a great comfort and a continuation of the conversations we used to have.

George wrote occasionally; he was never a great letter writer. He was not allowed to visit me because of his own prison record. Ralph, Johnny, and the others in the band had not been in contact; it seemed they had disowned me. I had one visit from my mother but it upset her to see me under these circumstances and she cried most of the visit. I didn't ask her back again. Sally wrote on a regular basis for about a year; I never got to see her because she didn't return to London. Then she wrote to say she was getting married. The letters got fewer and fewer, and eventually stopped.

I buried myself in my painting. Roger Browning sold almost everything I painted, so the canvases got bigger and the paint supply was unlimited. I would do paintings that took me a month or more to complete. I would paint every opportunity I had. I would paint until the lights were turned out around ten o'clock, put my brushes in oil so they wouldn't dry out, and continue at first light in the morning. Some of the screws would leave the light on and I would paint until midnight or later.

When I was painting I was lost; I had no thoughts. No thoughts of Sally or of being in prison or even thoughts about the painting. I drew from something deep inside and the brush in my hand followed. Sometimes I would start painting with no clear idea of where I was going and after several hours a picture and an idea would emerge. Some of my best work was created this way.

Chapter 25

ABOUT A YEAR AND A half into my sentence I was told I would be transferred to Wakefield Prison in Yorkshire. My first question to the governor was, "Will I be able to continue painting?"

"Oh, I'm sure you will, most prisons have an art class. In fact I will put something in your report recommending that you be allowed to continue."

I thanked him and left his office feeling pretty good about the move. A change of scenery would be good. Later I found that Norman was going also, so I felt even better. Norman was not so thrilled; he was married and his wife would have a long journey up to Yorkshire to visit. For once I felt good about having no ties with anyone on the outside.

Roger the art teacher gave me some small canvases and a supply of oil paint to keep me going when I got to Wakefield. He also gave me a letter of introduction for the art teacher there.

The transfer was by bus and we were handcuffed in pairs for the trip. Norman and I were cuffed together and we talked as we drove northward.

"Y'know, Eddie, I'm fifty now and I'm doing twelve years; I'll only do eight but I'll still be almost sixty when I get out. I can do it but it's killing my missus; we've been married almost thirty years. Do you have anyone on the outside?"

"No, thank God."

"My advice to you—give it up now, while you're still young. I've been a thief since I was your age and I've done all right over the years. Had some nice little tickles; I was never caught until four years ago. When I was in The Scrubs that was my first time inside. I should have quit then but I got involved with a bunch of tear-aways and we planned to do one more big one. I broke my own rule. I always worked alone and in thirty years I was only caught once. But when a bunch of people are involved there's always one who can't keep his mouth shut."

"So what did you do?"

"We tunneled into Lloyd's Bank on the Mile End Road."

"That was you? I remember that."

"Yeah, we dug a hole in the road outside. We put cones around it and a little tent over it. Everyone thought we were the telephone company or something. We worked for a whole week getting under the vault then we broke through over the holiday weekend when the bank was closed for three days. We got out with over forty grand."

"Split how many ways?" I asked.

"Five, eight grand a piece. Of course it's not worth it, doing twelve for eight grand but at least they never found my share. As a matter of fact, that was the verbal they got me with. When they arrested me I allegedly said, 'You'll never find my share.' They knew I was there because of the anonymous tip but had no other evidence. I was convicted solely on that verbal."

"Yeah, it's a diabolical liberty what the Filth can get away with."

"But like I say, it's me own bleedin' fault. If you can't do the time, then don't do the crime, I always say. What about you, Eddie, what are you in for?"

"GBH."

"Now that is stupid. So you didn't make anything, you're doing time for nothing."

"You're absolutely right, Norman, I'm not even a good thief. This has to be my last time."

We headed north on the M1 Motorway built just a few years before. This was the first time I had traveled it. Norman and I continued our conversation. I asked him, "You said you always worked alone. What did you do?"

"I was a Peter man." I knew he meant safecracking.

"How?" I asked.

"Explosives, gelignite. I learned how to use the stuff in the army during the war."

"Something's always puzzled me. When you blow the door off a safe, don't you destroy everything inside?"

"That's it, you don't blow the whole door off like in the pictures. You just blow the outer skin off the door exposing the lock mechanism, so you can lift the lock levers manually to open the door."

I was seeing a whole side to Norman I never knew existed. He was obviously a very clever man. Highly intelligent. I wondered what he might have achieved if he hadn't embarked on a life of crime.

We reached the city of Leicester roughly the halfway point of our journey. We pulled into the prison there. Our handcuffs were removed; we got to walk around the exercise yard for half an hour and then had lunch.

On the second leg of our journey, Norman and I swapped stories. He told of his experiences during the war, blowing up bridges and railway lines. I told of my childhood during the war—meeting Running Horse and how he had brought out my creativity. I talked about my father; Norman was about his age and I wished my old man could have been more like him.

If the floor plan of Wandsworth was like a six-spoke wheel, then Wakefield Prison was laid out like a half wheel. Four wings—A, B, C, and D—pointed south, southwest, northwest and north. We entered on the east side into a central hall that was half an irregular dodecagon in plan, with a cupola top that gave light. Each wing was four floors high with open galleries. A staircase to the upper floors was situated in an alcove between B and C wings. The wings had barrel vaulted ceilings with ribs carried on corbels and roof lights. The prison was constructed of brick and built around the mid-1800s, the same time as Wandsworth.

I quickly settled into my new surroundings and resumed my painting. Wakefield had a good art program run by the owner of a local art gallery; his name was Richard Waugh. He showed great interest in my work and I was soon working on large canvases again. I recreated some of the work I had done earlier in Wandsworth.

Some six months later both Norman and myself were given trustee status. We wore red armbands and were allowed to walk unescorted within the prison grounds. I worked in the store that supplied bedding and clothing and was responsible for getting clean items from the prison laundry and redistributing them to the inmates. Norman was in charge of records of cells where prisoners were housed. A cell on A wing near the center hall was used as an office where Norman worked, and he occupied the adjacent cell. Being in charge of cell allocation, Norman was able to get me relocated to a cell just three doors from his.

We were left unlocked in the evening until lights out around ten so Norman and I could socialize. I would often be in my cell painting with the door unlocked, and Norman would sit and watch, offering input. There were prison visitors that came in the evening, local businessmen who gave their time to visit prisoners in their cells. They would stop by and talk to Norman as he could tell them the location of prisoners.

One such visitor was looking for Norman one night and found him in my cell. He became interested in a large painting I was working on and stayed quite sometime talking about the work and asking questions about myself. He introduced himself as Ian Fisher; he became a regular visitor stopping by to see how the picture was progressing.

Mr. Fisher expressed interest in purchasing one of my paintings. I told him the work became the property of Mr. Waugh, as he supplied the art materials. I did, however, give him a small picture done on a canvas brought from Wandsworth. He later bought a larger piece I had done.

There were prisoners in Wakefield who had musical instruments, including two with guitars. One was playing on association one evening and I stopped to listen. I spoke with him and told him that I used to write songs. He offered his guitar. "Here play something."

I took the guitar and started to play. I was amazed that I played quite well in spite of not holding a guitar in almost three years. I sang one of my songs.

"That was damn good," he said, as I handed back the guitar, and joked, "Not bad for a cockney."

"Oh, there's good music comes out of London," I told him.

"I'm from Liverpool," he told me. "You should hear what's coming out of there. A band called the Beatles; they're getting played on the radio."

A few days later I heard a Beatles record. I had to stop what I was doing and listen. It was like a breath of fresh air. I thought of the harmonies Harry and I used to do with the band. Now here was someone else doing and doing it extremely well. Later I talked to Norman about the Beatles.

"Why don't you get a guitar and start playing again?" he asked.

"Nah, I'll be twenty-seven when I get out of here and by the time I get anywhere again I'll be thirty, too bleedin' old. I had my chance an' fucked up. Besides, how much longer can rock-n-roll last before something else comes along?"

It had felt good to play again but there had been no contact with Ralph or Johnny since I was sentenced. How could I write now and ask if they would send my guitar?

The year 1963 was drawing to a close; this would be my last Christmas and New Year's in prison. Not just my last time this sentence but my last time. Period. I was determined never to come back to prison again. I had changed; I had not been involved in one single fight during this term. I told myself, "If I can stay out of trouble in a place like this, surely I can do it on the outside."

I had decided not to go back to London, or if I did it would not be to the East End. Living in that shadowy zone where crime is all around, you turn a blind eye but constantly risk being dragged in. The corrupt police there knew me.

I was working on a painting one night when Ian Fisher stopped by. He sat on a wooden chair and watched. "Are you going to continue painting when you get out?" he asked.

"I'd like to but I have to get a job and make some money first. I can't see making a living doing this right off the bat."

"Are you going back to London?"

"I don't think so. I'm considering staying here in the north."

"Sheffield's a good place, a lot of industry. My business is there."

"Oh, is it. What do you do?" I asked.

"We build overhead cranes for the steel industry."

I stopped painting; he had caught my interest. "That's a coincidence, I was apprentice with Anderson's, the crane builders in London."

"I know that company well."

"Of course, theirs were a different type of crane used on the docks. Yours are the overhead indoor type. We had those in the factory to move the heavy equipment. I'm familiar with overhead cranes."

"So you can weld?"

"Oh yes, welding, metal fabrication, all that stuff."

"When do you get out?"

"Next March."

He paused for a moment, then said, "I might have a job for you if you're interested."

"I would be interested, very interested. Thank you."

Mr. Fisher stood and reached out his hand. I picked up a rag and wiped the paint from my hands before shaking his.

"Merry Christmas, Eddie, I'll see you after the holidays and we'll talk some more."

Christmas and New Year's came and went. There were more and more Beatles records being played on the radio and then other groups from Liverpool followed. Norman was really into the music, which surprised me, him being from a different generation. I wandered into his cell one evening; he was reading a magazine.

"There's a band from London called the Rolling Stones; have you heard them?"

"Yes, I have. I didn't know they were from London."

"Yeah, it says here they got their start in Richmond."

I remembered Richmond was where Sally was from.

"Let me see that?" I asked. I read the article. "Damn, it says here they started in 1962—less than two years ago. We had been playing more than two years when I came in here."

I left and went back to my own cell. I lay on my bed staring at the ceiling. I wondered where I might have been now and what success I might have had but for that fateful night in Shepherd's Bush.

Chapter 26

ON MARCH 21, 1964, I LEFT Wakefield Prison. Warm and sunny on this first day of spring, it was a new season and a new start for me. I had the clothes I was wearing plus another set in an old paper grocery bag with string handles. The clothes in the bag were those I was arrested in. The suit I had on was the one I wore to my trial. Ralph had brought it with him on his last and only visit. All my other clothes and belongings had been left at Ralph's house. As there had been no contact for three and a half years I wasn't about to write now and ask for them.

Mr. Fisher had offered me a job and was waiting in his Jaguar when I stepped out into Love Lane, the street outside the prison. Ian Fisher had a demeanor that exuded success. About forty years old, five feet ten with a slim athletic build. He had black hair with flecks of gray and strong rugged features. He was always impeccably dressed, usually dark business suits, but today he had on a tweed sport jacket in a black-and-white Prince of Wales check.

We talked as we drove the thirty miles south to Sheffield. He told me about his company; his father, now retired, had started it thirty years earlier. The company, along with the steel-producing town of Sheffield, had seen a lot of growth in the years following World War II. They were a mid-size company employing about 150 people.

At about the halfway point we drove through the small town of Barnsley. Mr. Fisher told me, "This is where I live. Not here in the town but a few miles east of here on the outskirts."

"Do you have a family?" I asked him.

"Yes, I have a wife and two boys who are in school. Plus an assortment of dogs and horses. My wife rides, I don't."

I asked questions about the job. "Will anyone there know I've been in prison?"

"No, I haven't told anyone—not even my father who still hangs around the factory. You'll get to meet him, no doubt. The knowledge of your being in prison is strictly between you and me."

"I really appreciate what you are doing for me. Thank you again."

"That's all right, Eddie. Norman told me a lot about your background. He thinks very highly of you. It seems to me that you're not a bad person; you've had some tough breaks."

"I'm glad you see it that way because I've never been a thief and I have certain ethics. My father encouraged me to fight from a very young age and all my brushes with the law have stemmed from that. But I do accept responsibility for my actions and I am determined not to repeat these mistakes."

"Well, I'm glad to hear that. I notice you don't have much by way of clothes. I'll give you an advance on your wages because you'll need work clothes."

As we reached the outskirts of Sheffield Mr. Fisher said, "I hope you don't mind but I arranged for lodging with someone close to the factory. You don't have to stay there but it will be a place to start."

We pulled off the main road and onto side streets with row upon row of Victorian terraced houses, similar to the one where I grew up in the East End of London. We stopped outside one house made of red brick with a gray slate roof. The only differences between the houses were the doors and windows. Some were neglected with discolored and peeling paint; others looked freshly painted, which brightened up the otherwise drab surroundings. Others had the doors and windows completely replaced with modern double-glazing and doors with glass panels. This was one such house.

Mr. Fisher pressed the doorbell and somewhere deep within I heard ding-dong notes that had the musical ambiance of kitchenware being dropped from a great height. A woman came to the door and Mr. Fisher introduced her. "This is Mrs. Hardcastle."

She held out her hand. "Ee lad, I'm reet pleased to meet'cha."

If the paint on the outside of the house was an attempt to add color to the environment, then Mrs. Hardcastle's makeup was an extension of that theme. Bright red lips and cheeks against a white background. Eyes outlined in heavy black with blue shadow and thin-penciled eyebrows above. A mole on her cheek was highlighted with the same eyebrow pencil. Jet black hair with obvious gray roots. It was difficult to tell her age.

"Come in, lad, I'll sho'thee to tha' room."

I wondered which I would get used to first, her Yorkshire accent or her taste in decorating. The room was obviously squeaky clean but in chaos with every contrast one could imagine. The flowered wallpaper clashed with porcelain "ducks in flight" hung there. The furniture was every style and color imaginable, some antique, some ultramodern with tubular steel legs. Above the fireplace hung a picture of an Oriental woman with a blue face.

"Come on through, lad, I'm a widow tha' knows."

She led me through into the next room and up two flights of narrow stairs to an attic bedroom. "I've got one other lodger, Mr. Barns, he's been wi' me fifteen years. He works at 'factory. You'll get to meet him later; he's ever so nice."

The small room had a single bed, a dresser with a mirror, and a wardrobe. A small window looked out onto the slate roof. The houses opposite were all that could be seen of the street, hidden by the sloping roof. I put my paper grocery bag in the wardrobe.

"Is that all tha's got?" Mrs. Hardcastle asked.

"Yep, I'm trav'lin' light," I told her.

We headed back down the stairs and Mr. Fisher and I drove over to the factory, which was only two streets away. It had probably been built the same time as the houses in the neighborhood. The same red brick and gray slate roof. I was introduced to Charlie Barns, the other lodger with Mrs. Hardcastle; he was the welding shop foreman. Mr. Fisher left Charlie to show me around and told me, "Come see me in the office when you're done."

Charlie Barns was a big man, wearing a flat tweed cap and gray overall coat. He lit up a pipe before taking me 'round the factory.

"What dost tha' think of Mrs. Hardcastle?" And before I could answer, he continued. "She's a wonderful cook tha' knows. Tha's not tasted Yorkshire pudding until tha's tasted Mrs. Hardcastle's."

After showing me around Charlie took me back to Mr. Fisher's office. The room was paneled in dark oak and the large painting I had done a year or so earlier hung on the wall behind an oak desk. It was a picture of rooftops in an industrial city with smoke hanging in the air. A good choice I thought for the setting in which it was displayed now. Mr. Fisher was with his secretary, a pretty young girl a little younger than myself I guessed. We were introduced.

"Julie, this is Eddie Conner, he's going to be working here."

I shook Julie's hand and she left the room. Mr. Fisher opened his wallet and handed me fifty pounds. "Here, go get yourself some clothes. You can catch a bus right outside that will take you into the center of Sheffield. When you come back just look out for the factory so you'll know where to get off. You remember how to get to Mrs. Hardcastle's?"

I said that I did and thanked him again. As I walked out through the adjoining office someone called out.

"Bye, Eddie."

I turned to see Julie smile and give a little wave. I smiled back. "Bye, Julie."

"I'm going to enjoy working here," I thought as I walked out the door.

My first day at work I told Charlie of my experience with cranes but that I had not welded for five years.

"Do you have any scrap metal I could work with first?" I asked.

Charlie led me out back to a large heap of rusting scrap steel. "There you go, Eddie, have at it."

I picked out a few pieces of scrap and took them back inside; I'd remembered the approximate settings for the arc welder. I started to experiment. Charlie left me alone and by the middle of the afternoon I was laying down some pretty good welds. I went to find Charlie and told him I was ready to do some real work. He gave me a drawing and some small parts to weld. By the end of the day I was so stiff and sore my whole body ached. I was not used to doing a full day's work. Back home that evening I let Charlie clean up first and then went to soak in a hot bath.

Charlie was right about Mrs. Hardcastle's cooking. She would make a Yorkshire pudding that was the size of the dinner plate. At about one inch thick, this would have been a meal in itself but on this she piled meat, potatoes, and vegetables. This was enough food to feed two or three people and I had to eat it—to leave any would have offended her, I'm sure. She told me almost every day she was a widow and her husband had died some eight years earlier.

She nagged at Charlie constantly and he would snap back at her. I found this constant bickering embarrassing at first but then I could see the funny side of it. It was almost like they were married, but I supposed that's how it got after fifteen years.

After a while this constant arguing was no longer funny and started to get on my nerves. They were always respectful and kind toward me but not toward each other. I had grown up in a dysfunctional family situation and this was dysfunctional lodging.

Some evenings after dinner I would go into the front room and watch television. I would watch *Top of the Pops.* The Beatles and the Rolling Stones would be on and I often thought about playing again, more idle fantasy than serious consideration. But I did want to start painting again and that was impossible where I was.

After two months I paid Mr. Fisher the fifty pounds I had borrowed. I was working overtime at the factory making good money; I had started to save. I searched the ads in the paper and found a room to let some three miles north of where I was now. The room was in a large four-story Victorian house that was once home to a wealthy family and their many servants. The house was showing signs of neglect and was long past its former glory.

I was shown a room on the second floor. It was huge—about thirty foot wide by fifteen feet deep with a twelve-foot-high ceiling. There were two large bay windows facing north so there was plenty of light without direct sunlight. Perfect for painting. I took the room and paid the first month's rent. Then I went out and bought a secondhand bed. There was an alcove in the corner with a shelf and a rail underneath to hang clothes. This was all I needed to start out.

I would share a bathroom on the same floor with the other tenants. There was a large kitchen downstairs I could also share. There were two smaller rooms directly behind mine that were rented to a young married couple about my own age. To the rear of the second floor lived an older retired man.

At work I was becoming friendly with Julie, Mr. Fisher's secretary. If she was out in the factory she would always make a point of stopping by to chat with me. I found her very attractive but was reluctant at first to ask her out because I was not sure if a work-related romance was a good idea. I decided to approach her and my plan was to take things slow and cautiously.

The offices had high windows that looked out onto the factory floor. If people were standing in the office you could see their heads. I looked up one day to see that Julie was in Mr. Fisher's office. I knew he was out of town so I decided to make my move. I went up to the office; Julie smiled as I entered.

"Oh, I was looking for Mr. Fisher," I said knowing that he wasn't there.

"He's out of town and won't be back 'til Thursday."

My eyes wandered to the painting on the wall.

"Did you paint that?" Julie asked.

"Why would you think I painted it?"

"It has your name on it."

"Well, then that's a dead giveaway. Yes, I painted it."

"So you're a man of many talents. What others don't I know about?"

I hesitated then suggested, "Why don't we talk about that over lunch?"

Julie accepted and I met her at the front of the building at noon. She was a petite five feet tall and just came up to my shoulder as we walked a short distance to a little café she knew. We ordered lunch and I looked across at her as we engaged in small talk. Her shoulder length brown hair was straight and shone with reddish highlights in the sunlight. Her pretty face and hazel eyes had only the slightest hint of makeup.

Julie asked me questions about my background and where I was from. I felt uncomfortable and wondered if this was such a good idea after all. I didn't want to lie but at the same time I did not want to reveal that I had just been released from prison. I told her I had moved here from London, which was not a lie; I just didn't say when I moved. I needed to change the subject. "That's enough about me. How long have you lived in Sheffield?"

"All my life."

"Which is how long?"

"Well that's a crafty way to ask a lady her age. Twenty-three years, and how old are you?"

"I'm twenty-seven."

"Most men are married or at least engaged by twenty-seven. How come you're not? Nice-looking young man like you, I'll bet all the lasses in London were after you. How come you got away?"

"Do leave off, please, Julie." I could feel my face getting bright red.

"You didn't get someone in't puddin' club, did you?"

"You're terrible, of course I didn't."

"Well, a girl has to know what she's getting into."

"Oh, and you think you're getting into something?"

"Well, I don't have lunch with any old Tom, Dick, or Harry y'know."

I reached across and squeezed the back of her hand. "I'm very flattered you had lunch with me."

That afternoon I thought about my lunch date with Julie.

"She's too much woman for you, you'd be better off with some little scrubber that works in a factory or something," I told myself. Or maybe I didn't want to get involved with anyone just yet.

The end of that week, I got paid so I found an art supply shop and bought a large canvas, brushes, and paint. I spent the whole weekend painting. It was the middle of the following week I was at work and heard a voice behind me. "Are you avoiding me?"

I turned; it was Julie.

"No, of course not. What makes you think that?"

"You haven't been to see me."

"Well, you haven't been to see me either. The path between here and the office runs both ways."

"I'm here now."

She looked a little hurt so I smiled and said, "So you are; it's nice to see you."

"Would you like to have lunch again?" she asked. "I'll buy this time."

"Well, there's a offer I can't refuse. Okay, I'll see you up front at noon."

By being cautious I had inadvertently caused Julie to show a great deal of interest in me. After our lunch date we later went out to dinner, dancing, and to the cinema. I decided to stay cautious and move slowly. I had the same feelings toward her I once had for Sally and I did not want to get hurt.

Chapter 27

I HAD BEEN IN SHEFFIELD six months; summer was ending. At work I was sometimes part of an installation crew that would go out and remove an old overhead crane and install a new one. It would mean working high up in the roof of a steel foundry with dust and soot that had accumulated for years. Or I would do repairs on cranes in foundries that were operating. The heat above the steel smelting furnaces was intense along with smoke and sulfur fumes. I knew I could not do this for the rest of my life but I earned good money and I felt an obligation to Mr. Fisher to stay there for a while.

I had bought myself an old van to transport paint canvases; it was difficult to carry them on a bus. I had never driven a car before; there was always public transport in London. I took driving lessons and passed my test on the first attempt. I tried to sell my paintings at local art galleries without success. Some offered to take paintings and sell them on consignment but I decided I would keep them in my room until I had enough to rent a hall and put on an exhibition.

Julie and I were still going out and I had a dilemma. I had grown extremely fond of her, but before our relationship could go to the next level I had to tell her I had been in prison. I could not hide this from her forever and it would not be fair to have her make a commitment and then tell her much later. She came by the house one evening to watch me paint as she sometimes did. She was very quiet.

"Is something wrong?" I asked.

"No."

She was quiet for another minute then said, "Where are we going, Eddie?"

"Oh, you wanna go out?"

"No, I mean us—our relationship."

172

"Why do you ask? I mean now at this time."

"Someone else asked me out. What should I do, Eddie?"

My heart sank. I thought, "My God, she's gonna dump me." I set the brush down and wiped my hands. "I care for you a lot, Julie, but I don't own you. You're free to do whatever you want."

She started to cry. "You daft bat, I luv ya', can't you see that? I don't want to go out with anyone else, but I don't know how you feel, Eddie, you never tell me."

I held her tight and she sobbed uncontrollably, her face buried in my chest. I patted her lightly on the back and told her, "You don't know me, there's things I haven't told you and I don't know if I'm ready to tell you yet."

"I know you've been in prison."

Her voice was muffled against my chest so I was not sure if I heard her right. I pushed her away and held her at arm's length, my hands on her shoulders. I looked into her face; tears had washed mascara down her cheeks.

"What did you say?"

"I know you've been in prison. If that's what's bothering you, I've known since the start."

"How do you know? Did Mr. Fisher tell you?"

"No, not directly. When he brought that painting to his office over a year and a half ago, long before you came to work there, he said that a prisoner in Wakefield had done it. So that first time we went to lunch when I asked if you painted the picture, I knew then."

"Does anyone else know? I mean at work."

"I don't think so. I never told anyone and I never mentioned it to Mr. Fisher."

"Oh Julie, Julie." I hugged her to me. "I was afraid to tell you, I was afraid you'd leave, but I knew I'd have to tell you soon. You don't know what it's been like for me caring for you the way I do but not being able to tell you."

"You daft bat, Eddie Conner."

Her lips found mine. For six months I had never kissed her. When we broke off for air she immediately pressed her lips back again, she was making little noises deep within her throat. When we finally stopped I said.

"Let's go out and celebrate."

"No, Eddie, just stay where you are, just hold me."

Summer ended and autumn came and went. Julie and I decided to get engaged at Christmas and married sometime the following year. I gave Mr. Fisher the news and told him the story about the painting in his office.

"Eddie, I'm sorry, when I bought that painting I had no idea that I would be offering you a job later. I told Julie in all innocence, never thinking you would meet her let alone marry her."

"That's all right, everything worked out for the best. Julie knew right from the start and obviously accepted me in spite of my past."

"Well, I'm happy for both of you but I hope she's not going to leave. I don't want to be looking for another secretary."

"No, we both plan to keep working and saving. But I need to ask you a favor. Can Julie and I have the week off after Christmas? I want to go down to London to see my mother. I haven't seen her in four years."

"Of course you can. I'll give you both the week off with pay; it'll be my engagement present to you."

A week before Christmas we picked out an engagement ring and on Christmas Eve I pulled up outside Julie's house in my old van. The van was a "Commer," built by the British Chrysler Company; we referred to it as our "Commer-cal" van. The engine was inside between the driver and passenger seats, and was so noisy when running that conversation was impossible. I opened the sliding passenger door and helped Julie into her seat. Before we drove away I slipped the ring on her finger and she slid across to sit on the engine cover so she could hold onto my arm and lay her head on my shoulder. We drove to a restaurant for a celebration dinner.

Christmas Day I went to Julie's house. Her mother was a tiny woman, even smaller than Julie; her father was about my own height with a barrel chest and strong arms. A steelworker with scars from burns and cuts on his hands, arms, and face to prove the many years in this punishing profession.

"I hope you've brought your appetite," Julie's mother said as I walked in.

"Yes, I'm starving." I told her.

Julie's father said, "Well, sit thee down here, lad, by'fire."

Julie no doubt saw the puzzled look on my face. "No, Dad, he means he's hungry." She went on to explain to me that "starved" in Yorkshire meant that you were cold. I wondered if I would ever get used to this Yorkshire dialect.

Two days after Christmas we caught a train for London. As we pulled out of the station Julie said, "I'm so excited, I've never been to London before and I'm so looking forward to meeting your mum and dad."

"I don't know how my father is going to be," I warned her.

I had told Julie about my relationship with my father. I had written to my mother and told her we were coming to see them and asked what my father's reaction would be. My mother had written back saying how pleased she would be to see us but said nothing about my father, which led me to believe that things were not good. I was prepared to apologize to him and try to patch things up, but whether he would respond was a different matter.

I dozed on and off during the long train ride to London. Julie would keep waking me to point out things on the way, then on arrival in London she was sound asleep and I had to wake her. From the station it was a short ride on the underground and we were in Stepney. The street looked exactly as it did over four years earlier, when I was last there. I stood in front of my old home.

"This is it," I told Julie. I reached for the doorknocker and knocked three times. The door opened and my father stood there. He stared at me for a second then without a word stepped back and closed the door. I turned to Julie. "I don't believe he just did that."

As I reached for the knocker again the door opened and my mother stood there. "Come on in," she said, smiling and turning to my father. "Ted, what's the matter with you?"

My father mumbled something incoherent and walked upstairs. I stepped aside to allow Julie to enter first and I followed with our suitcase, closing the door behind me.

"Mum, this is Julie." My mother took Julie's right hand with both of hers and held her at arm's length, smiling as they studied each other. Then almost in unison they both said, "I'm pleased to meet you. Eddie's told me so much about you."

My mother turned and hugged me. "Eddie I'm so happy for you; I've prayed for this day." She started to cry and I felt my own eyes start to water.

"Now stop that, Mum, this is a happy occasion."

"You're right. Now come on through and I'll make a cup of tea."

We followed her through to the living room. I heard my father come downstairs followed by the sound of the front door slamming. I rushed out after him and ran to catch up to his side. He just kept walking.

"Dad, after all this time can't you forgive and forget? I'm sorry for what I did, I truly am." He stopped and we faced each other.

"What you did almost killed your mother."

"Don't give me that load of old bollocks. When were you ever concerned about anyone's feelings other than yer own? This has nothing to do with Mum; it's about you and me."

"Fuck you," he said and walked on. I didn't follow.

"Fuck you too." I mumbled to myself as I walked back to the house. Inside I spoke to Julie.

"I'm sorry about my dad." I stood silent for a moment then said, "No, damn it, why should I apologize for him? He's just an ignorant stubborn old bastard."

Julie stood and put her arm around me. My mother spoke. "Your dad's the way he is and we can't change that."

"God, how many times have I heard that over the years? Y'know in spite of everything he's still my father and deep down inside I love the old git." I started to sob uncontrollably. "I just want him to be a friend, I don't expect him to love me."

My mother stood and she and Julie hugged me.

"He loves you, Eddie, I know that," my mother told me.

"He's got a damn funny way of showing it."

"Tea's getting cold," Julie said. I walked into the kitchen to rinse my face.

Over tea my mother said, "You can have your old room, Julie can sleep in Elizabeth's old room."

"No, Mum, we can't stay here. It'll be too much stress for you, us, and for dad the way things are. We'll get a room somewhere, we'll come and see you every day when dad's not here."

My mother didn't argue, I think she knew it was for the best. Later we took a taxi over to the Coach & Horses; I knew Cliff had rooms to let. We pulled up outside and I paid the taxi driver. The first thing I noticed was that Ralph's club was gone; it was now a dance studio. We walked into the Coach & Horses; I didn't see anyone I knew. I asked a man behind the bar.

"Is Cliff around?"

He looked surprised. "I'm sorry. Cliff died almost two years ago. I'm the landlord, the name's Bob Thompson."

He held out his hand across the bar and I shook it.

"Were you a friend of Cliff's?" he asked.

"Well, yes, I used to work in the club next door. That was over four years ago."

I noticed the opening in the wall behind the bar that went through to the club had been closed up again. Bob Thomson looked back as if he knew what I was looking at.

"Yes, when Cliff died the club closed down. Ralph moved out to Dagenham, I believe."

There was a moment's silence as I thought over the situation.

"My name's Eddie and this is my—er—wife Julie and we were hoping to stay here until the end of the week. Do you still have rooms?"

"Yes, certainly, just follow me." He came out from behind the bar and led us down a passageway and up some stairs.

"Was Cliff ill for any length of time?" I asked.

"No it was very sudden, heart attack. He just dropped down one morning."

Bob took us to a room at the rear of the building.

"Come on down when you're ready; if you want to eat later you can order at the bar."

I thanked him and he left.

"What is this place?" Julie asked. "And you said something about you worked next door?"

I had never told Julie about my singing in a band. I never wanted to talk about it and every time I saw the Rolling Stones or some other band on TV I secretly wished I was up there. That evening we sat in the bar eating dinner and I looked over to the corner where we had set up our stage and played to a packed house over six years ago in 1958. It seemed a lifetime away.

The next morning we took a bus over to George's house. His mother came to the door.

"Eddie. Oh my God, how are you? Come on in." We followed her through to the living room.

"George is doing a three stretch; he's in Wandsworth. You didn't know?"

"No, I live in Sheffield now and I'm completely out of touch. This is Julie, my fiancée."

"I wish George would find a nice girl and settle down."

"I just found out yesterday that Cliff died and the club shut down."

"Yes, Ralph moved to Dagenham. I heard he's managing a dance hall or something."

"What about the others?" I asked. "Where are they?"

"Well, the two brothers—what was their name? The Christmas boys."

"Danny and Harry."

"Yeah, that's them. I heard they opened a music shop not far from where the club used to be. Wait, I'll get the phone book." She left the room and was back moments later.

"Here it is, Christmas Music. Funny name, that."

I wrote down the address and phone number.

"Call them if you like." George's mother pointed to the phone.

I dialed the number and someone picked up after the first ring.

"Danny?"

"No, it's Harry."

"This is, Eddie, Eddie Conner."

There was a one-second silence. "Eddie, how the bleedin' hell are you? Where are you calling from?"

"I'm over at George's house."

"Is he out?"

"No, I'm with his mum. Can I come over?"

"Of course, do you know where we are?"

"Yes, I have the address."

"Well, come on over. Danny's just stepped out but he'll be back by the time you get here."

We said goodbye to George's mother and hopped on a bus back the way we had just come. We found the music store. Guitars hung from the walls and ceiling and various other musical instruments were on display. As we entered the shop Danny and Harry stood there just grinning ear to ear. I was doing the same—in fact, my face hurt I was grinning so wide.

I shook hands and hugged them both, then stepped back to introduce Julie.

"Julie, these are two old friends of mine, Danny and Harry."

"So how long y'been out?" Harry asked then hesitated giving Julie an apprehensive look.

"It's okay, she knows. Almost a year now, I'm living in Sheffield."

"Sheffield, that's a bleedin' long way off. Are you still playing?"

"Nah, I haven't touched a guitar in four years. How about you?"

"I'm doing a lot of studio work. Sound tracks for film and TV, some commercials. Making pretty good money."

Danny took an acoustic guitar off the wall and handed it to me. "Let's see if you've still got it."

Harry picked up an electric guitar and plugged into a small amp. Danny got a snare drum and a pair of brushes. "Let's do *Trav'lin' Light*. Do you remember the words?

I played the opening chords; Harry played along with me adjusting the amp as he did, hardly missing a beat. I started to sing. Julie was staring at me, not knowing what to make of this impromptu performance. We finished the song and Julie said, "Eddie, you never told me you could do that."

Danny looked at her. "He never told you? He wrote that song. One of the best songwriters I ever knew. Let's do another."

We played several more. A slim, dark-haired girl entered the shop and stood watching us. When we finished the song, Danny stood and introduced her.

"This is my wife, Gloria." She shook hands all 'round and Danny said, "Say, we should all go out tonight. Celebrate. What d'ya say, Eddie?"

Julie and I agreed and Danny turned to his brother. "Is Marge free tonight?"

Harry went to call his girlfriend and the evening out was arranged.

"We'll pick you up at the Coach & Horses," Harry said as we left the music shop.

Back in our room I sat on the bed and Julie spoke about the music. "Why did you not tell me, Eddie?"

"I dunno, I don't like to talk about it. If I hadn't gone to the nick we'd have been on the telly by now along with the Rolling Stones and the others. Not just me but Danny and Harry too. I screwed it up for them also and you notice they don't hold that against me; that's because they're good people, damn good people.

Julie sat on the bed beside me and put her arm around me. I turned to her. "You know what, my love, if I hadn't gone to the nick I wouldn't have gone to Wakefield and met Mr. Fisher. I wouldn't have met you, so you see it's not all bad."

Later we met the others in the bar downstairs. Harry introduced his girlfriend Marge; she was an attractive redhead. The three girls seemed to hit it off immediately.

Danny told us, "I've booked a table at a little Italian restaurant up west. How about we get a taxi up there?"

We all agreed and I ordered a round of drinks while Danny called for a taxi.

In the restaurant we ordered dinner and sat talking while waiting for the food to come.

"I hear Ralph moved to Dagenham," I commented.

Harry responded, "Yeah, he's managing the local Palais there."

"What happened to Johnny?" I asked.

"I dunno; he just disappeared. I did hear he got married."

"One thing's for sure," I said. "We should stay in touch from now on."

"I'll second that," said Danny.

"I want you all to come up to Sheffield next summer for our wedding," I added.

Chapter 28

IT WAS THE EVE OF our wedding in June 1965. Danny and his wife Gloria together with his brother Harry and his girlfriend Marge had driven up from London. There were the traditional hen and stag parties. Gloria and Marge were with Julie and her friends; Danny and Harry stopped by my place to pick me up. I showed the two brothers my paintings that were now hung all over the walls of my room; others were leaned against the wall.

"I know sod all about art, but I can see these are good," Harry said after looking at a few canvases.

Then Danny spoke. "It's like you carried on with the painting right where you left off with the songwriting."

Harry looked at his brother. "That's a bit deep coming from you."

"No, I mean in terms of talent; he was a talented songwriter and now he's an equally talented painter."

"Well, it's all creativity," I told them. "It all comes from the same place, in here." I patted myself over the heart with my hand.

"That's for bleedin' sure," said Danny.

I brought out a canvas I had kept hidden. "This one's for you to hang in your music shop."

I had done a painting of the Eddie Sons performing onstage.

"Thanks, Eddie, that's great. I know just where we'll hang this," Harry said, then Danny spoke.

"You know, Ralph blamed you for what happened but we didn't. I couldn't see how you could have avoided what happened. It wasn't your fault; it was fate."

I told them, "Water under the bridge now, life goes on, all that old bollocks. Let's go meet the others."

We drove to a local pub where I had arranged to meet some of my young coworkers.

The following day Julie and I were married at a civil ceremony held at the Sheffield registry office and after there was a reception at a local Steelworkers Union Hall. My mother came by train from London; my father stayed away as I had expected. My sister Elizabeth, who I hadn't seen in years, was there with her new husband she had met in the Air Force.

That was it for my side of the family; we were greatly outnumbered by Julie's uncles, aunts, and cousins from all over Yorkshire and the north of England. Later that evening Julie and I left for a four-day honeymoon in Blackpool, a resort on the northeast coast.

After our short honeymoon we returned to the house I had been living in. The young married couple who lived in the two rooms next to mine had moved out and we took over that space. There was a living room with a kitchenette and a bedroom. I continued to rent the room I had been living in to use as a studio. Julie and I spent the first month in our new home decorating and furnishing.

At work I was becoming an accomplished welder and I wanted to try my hand at building a metal sculpture. I asked Mr. Fisher if I could use the scrap metal at the factory, doing the work on my own time. I decided to present my first project to Mr. Fisher.

I remembered as a child seeing my friend Running Horse carve an eagle from a piece of wood. I would construct the form of an eagle, wings outspread holding a fish in its talons. This would imply "Fisher," the name of the company, and the eagle lifting the fish would imply the product the company made, which was cranes. Its tail feathers on a base, giving the impression that the bird was in flight, would support the whole piece.

I did some preliminary sketches and thought over the method of construction. At first I thought of making a wire frame or skeleton, to which I would weld feathers cut from sheet steel. Then I decided I would use the wire frame only as a form to build the bird over. I would construct the body in two halves and then remove it from the wire frame and weld the two halves together making a hollow self-supporting structure. This was not intended to be an exact lifelike replica but rather an abstract piece that implied an eagle in flight.

The finished piece stood three feet tall with about the same wingspan, it took me several weeks to complete. I presented it to Mr. Fisher and he was impressed, as was his father Henry Fisher who was there at the time. The older man wanted me to build one for him. Ian Fisher asked, "Could you make a bigger one?"

"How big?" I asked.

"Let me show you what I have in mind."

He led me outside the front of the building to the lawn with small shrubs; he stopped in the middle of the lawn.

"Here." He said. "I would like to see one here only it would have to be bigger."

I looked at the area and the building behind it. "It would have to be really big or it will just be insignificant against the building and would look no better than a garden ornament."

"I agree." The older Mr. Fisher said.

"It needs to be about eighteen feet tall," I told them.

"Could you do that?" Ian asked.

"Why not? You have all the equipment here. I would have to make it from steel plate instead of sheet metal but you have the machines to cut and bend the material right here in the factory."

Ian Fisher thought for a moment then said, "Let's do it. Order the material you need and you can work on company time. I can't expect you to work on a project this big on your own time."

"Can I have the one you just made?" Henry Fisher asked..

"Yes, but before you take it away I need to measure and make drawings for all the parts scaling them up six times bigger."

I couldn't wait to get home and tell Julie the news. She had seen the sculpture I had just made. I told her of my conversation with Ian Fisher.

"Can you do that?" she asked.

"Do what?"

"Build an eagle that big."

"Yes, it won't be a problem, I'm used to working on large projects at the factory."

"I have something to tell you," Julie said.

"Oh, what's that?"

"I'm pregnant. I went to see the doctor today."

"Oops."

"Is that all you have to say? Aren't you pleased?"

I gave her a hug. "Of course I'm pleased; it's just that we didn't plan it this soon. I think it will be wonderful to have a little sprog of our own."

"Little sprog! How dare you call our baby a little sprog."

"Well, we don't know if it's a boy or girl, so until we do it's a sprog."

Julie smiled and shook her head. "Eddie Conner, I sometimes think you're one egg short of a Yorkshire pudding."

The following week I began work on the giant eagle. There was always a feeling of euphoria when I embarked on a new art form. I found it refreshing to work on a project where I didn't have to follow precise measurements as I did when building cranes. I could use my eye and my senses to see and feel what was right. As before, it was as if the giant eagle was already there; I simply had to bring it into being. This was not work for me—it was fun and satisfying.

Given the size and weight of the finished sculpture, moving it after it was built would be a problem. The ceiling height in the factory was enough to build and move the finished piece, as were the doors at the rear of the factory. But exiting through the rear of the building would mean moving this huge structure along the busy street outside to get to the front of the building. There was a roll-up door at the front of the building but the ceiling height was lower there. Making the eagle in two pieces solved the problem; the wings could be removed and bolted on once the sculpture was in place.

I got a great deal of ribbing from my coworkers.

"What's tha' makin', Eddie?" I was asked over and over again.

"Looks like a bloody gre't chickin," was another comment. "Careful tha' don't lay a big egg."

But the jibes ceased when the sculpture started to take form and they could see what it was. Mr. Fisher came out daily from his office to watch the progress. It was nearing completion when he said, "I should probably check to see if we need a permit to put this outside the factory."

He made a phone call and a few days later an inspector from the town council came by to look at the sculpture. The inspector took measurements and went to the front of the building to see the proposed site for the eagle. It was three weeks later before the answer came back: "Permission refused on the grounds the sculpture is not in keeping with the factory building and the surrounding area." Also it was stated the eagle would be a distraction to motorists driving by and might become a potential traffic hazard.

Ian Fisher was furious. "You would think with the amount of taxes I pay and the number of local people I employ, I would be allowed to put whatever I like outside my own bloody factory. They haven't heard the last of this."

Mr. Fisher called the local newspaper and that afternoon a reporter and a photographer came around. They interviewed both of us and took pictures of the sculpture with Mr. Fisher and myself standing by it. The headline in the paper the next day read, "Is this art or an eyesore?" The article intimated the local council had labeled the work as such, which was not strictly true, but it stirred up a lot of controversy.

When the newspaper article came out Mr. Fisher got a call from a local television station. They brought their cameras and filmed me welding in the factory and interviewed Mr. Fisher and me. They also took pictures of my painting hanging in Mr. Fisher's office. We were featured on the TV news that evening.

I started getting calls from the local art dealers who had originally turned down my work; now they wanted to buy. I talked to Ian Fisher and asked for advice.

"Just sit tight and do nothing yet. I have had offers for the eagle sculpture."

He contacted the BBC in London and within the week we were on national television. I got a call from Danny in London saying he had seen me on TV. After the BBC broadcast, Mr. Fisher asked me, "How many paintings do you have?"

"I dunno, twenty-five or thirty. Why?"

"I think we should hold an auction to sell the eagle sculpture and your paintings."

"Where would we hold the auction?" I asked.

"In the canteen at the factory. We can move the eagle sculpture outside and display your paintings inside."

"Twenty-five or so paintings wont be much of a display. I wish I had more."

"Do you remember Richard Waugh, the art teacher at Wakefield Prison? He has a lot of your paintings I'm sure he'd like to sell. I can contact him and he can pay us a commission on his sales.

"I'm going to let my father organize the whole thing. He's expressed an interest in doing it. He has a huge circle of friends and business associates; he could generate a lot of interest."

The auction was held some ten days later on a Saturday afternoon. On Friday after lunch, tables and chairs in the factory canteen were moved and the paintings put on display. Richard Waugh came down from Wakefield with another twenty paintings. Henry Fisher placed ads in the local papers as well as a small one in the *London Times*. The paintings were on display for viewing Friday evening and Saturday morning before the auction. The local TV station brought their cameras along and we were on the late news broadcast Friday evening.

There was a good crowd on Friday evening but the number of people doubled by Saturday. We hired the services of a professional auctioneer and bidding started at two o'clock in the afternoon. I did not put minimum prices on any of the paintings so everything sold. Some of the larger canvases went for over a hundred pounds. I was writing down the amount of each sale as the auction progressed and by the end the total was over two thousand pounds, more money than I had ever had in my life at one time.

Finally the "big eagle," as everyone affectionately called it, went on sale. The auctioneer announced that bidding would be in one-hundred-pound increments and the buyer would pay for transportation from the factory to its destination. The first bid was five hundred pounds; there were initially three people bidding. One dropped out when the price went over two thousand pounds. The bidding went on and the hammer dropped at 3,100 pounds.

After the auction people were all around me, congratulating me, wanting to shake my hand. I had not experienced anything like this since the time I was performing music. But this was different—people wanted to talk to me about my painting or sculptures. There were art dealers and others who wanted to talk business; I was totally unprepared and not sure how to handle this. I sent them over to talk with Henry Fisher.

Things eventually quieted down as people left. I got to talk to Julie again; the crowd had separated us.

"I'm so proud of you," she said hugging my arm.

Henry Fisher came over.

"A highly successful event, wouldn't you agree?"

"I'm overwhelmed," I told him. "I can't thank you enough for all you've done."

"It's been my pleasure. The money we got for the eagle—we decided we should give you half after deducting expenses."

"I wasn't expecting anything from the eagle—that was yours, you paid me to build it and paid for the material. I don't know what to say. Thank you, thank you both."

"You're welcome, Eddie, and I want to take you and Julie to dinner tonight. How about I pick you up at your place at seven?"

After he left I turned to Julie. "Somewhere in my life I must have done something right to have people like the Fishers be so good to me."

Mr. Henry Fisher and his wife picked us up and took us to a restaurant in the center of Sheffield. It was a place that was way beyond my price range. After being seated, Mr. Fisher handed me an unsealed envelope. I lifted the flap. Inside was a check for three thousand, five hundred pounds. This was more money than I made in a whole year. My jaw dropped and before I could speak, Mr. Fisher said, "That's the money we took for the sale of your paintings plus your share of the proceeds from the eagle."

I pulled the check partway from the envelope so the amount could be read and showed it to Julie, then slipped it inside my jacket breast pocket.

"What are you kids going to do with all that money?" Henry asked.

"Well, I'd like to put a down payment on a house. We have a baby on the way and where we are now is hardly suitable for raising a family."

"Congratulations." It was Mrs. Fisher who spoke this time. "When is the baby due?"

"The end of May," Julie told her.

The waiter came and we ordered; Mr. Fisher ordered wine. The wine arrived and Henry talked as we waited for dinner.

"Eddie, I have a proposition for you. I had serious inquiries today for two large sculptures and several for the smaller ones. I've been retired now for a year and a half and it's driving me crazy. I need something to do. How would you like to go into partnership with me and build these sculptures?"

"Where would I work?" I asked.

"At the factory initially; I've talked to Ian about this. There is space not being used and we can use their equipment. After we produce the first two sculptures we will have enough money to get our own studio. What do you think?"

"I think this is a dream come true; this is what I love to do."

Mr. Fisher continued, "I will handle the business side and all the sales, we would be equal partners, and when I do eventually retire the business will be yours."

Dinner arrived and we talked more about the venture. Mrs. Fisher spoke. "This will be good for you, Henry. You don't know what to do with yourself around the house and Ian doesn't want you hanging around the factory."

"No, he likes to do things his way and that's okay. Eddie, you've made an old man very happy."

"And you have made two young people very happy, Mr. Fisher."

"Please, if we're going to be partners, call me Henry."

Chapter 29

I TOOK A THOUSAND POUNDS of the money from the art auction and made a down payment on a small Victorian terrace house. It was in the neighborhood near the Fisher factory and only two streets from Mrs. Hardcastle's house where I had lived a short time following my release from Wakefield Prison.

The floor plan was similar to the house in London where I had grown up. The only difference was there was a small room above the kitchen that had been converted to a bathroom. Julie and I moved in and waited the arrival of our first child.

The business venture Mr. Henry Fisher and I had begun was running smoothly. Our overhead was low, we were not paying rent at the factory, and I had agreed to work without salary for the first six months. This was my part of the investment into the business. I still had money left from the art auction that I could live on. Our goal was to move out of the Fisher factory by the end of our first year and be self-sufficient in our own studio, owning our own equipment.

Most of the commissions for my large sculptures came from architects' designing offices and industrial buildings. Orders were coming from all over the United Kingdom. I had stumbled on a unique niche market, as there were few artists who had the equipment and the know-how to construct these large pieces. A project usually started with the architect sending me drawings of the building. Sometimes they would give clear indication of what they wanted. Other times I had complete control over the design.

One thing I would always take into consideration was the transportation of the finished sculpture. Would it pass under bridges en route to its destination? Would it be a "wide load" and incur extra cost in moving? I had learned valuable lessons from my first piece and would design some of the larger sculptures in two or more pieces, to be bolted or welded together onsite.

A new project would start by submitting sketches, then I would make a smaller-scale model first for approval. Often I traveled to the site to meet with the architect. With all this traveling and the long hours working, I was not at home as often as I should and Julie was not happy. She knew I was working for our future and did not complain as she might have.

I was impervious to the long hours. When the creative process was flowing the time would just fly by and I would often look at the clock to find it was ten or eleven o'clock at night, sometimes midnight. It was one such night when the phone rang. It was Julie's mother calling from my house. There were complications with Julie's pregnancy.

I jumped in my old van and drove home. An ambulance was at the door when I arrived and they were loading Julie in. As I parked, the ambulance pulled away.

"How is she?" I asked her mother.

"Eddie, why weren't you here with her? You knew she was close to her time."

"She's not due for another week and she could've phoned me, I was only a short distance from the house."

"She didn't want to disturb you; she called me instead. When I got here I knew there was a problem so I called for an ambulance."

"Do you want to come with me in the van?" I asked her.

"No, you go ahead. I'll go home and get Julie's dad."

I drove to the hospital and rushed into the waiting room. I asked the nurse at the reception desk how Julie was and if I could see her.

"You'll have to wait. The doctors are with her now and as soon as we know something we'll let you know."

She handed me a clipboard. "Would you fill out this information for us?"

I took the clipboard and sat down. My hands were still dirty from work and I had put a large black thumbprint on the edge of the form. I set the clipboard down and went to find a washroom.

I was filling out the form when Julie's mother and father came in.

"How is she?" Her mother asked.

"She's with the doctors; they won't let me see her."

Julie's mother went to the reception desk.

"Tha' looks like tha's been workin' overtime," Julie's father said.

"Yes, I should have been with her."

"There's nowt wrong wi' workin', lad, we all have to do it." He placed his large hand on my shoulder, "Don't thee worry, lad. She'll be fine."

I found his soft Yorkshire dialect and his quiet reassurance comforting. Here was a good man, working class, the same as I had grown up with in the East End of London.

It was almost two hours before a doctor came to speak with us.

"You have a daughter," he told me. "Mother and baby are fine. We had to do a cesarean delivery and the mother is still sleeping, but you can see the baby."

A nurse led me to a room where there were several babies in cribs. "This is your little girl."

There lay the tiniest baby, just perfect in every way. I put my hand inside the crib and she held on to my little finger with a grip that was unbelievable.

"Hello, Alison, I'm your daddy."

I don't know where the name Alison came from. We had not thought of names beforehand, but I knew this was Alison. A tear rolled down my cheek. Here was life no more than a few minutes old and it was life that was part of me. I stood for several more minutes; there was a love that flowed both ways through this tiny hand holding my finger. I tried to pull my finger away but Alison just hung on. I reached in with my other hand and gently pried away the little fingers.

"I've gotta go, Alison, let yer grandma and grandpa come an' see you."

I walked back to the waiting room and the nurse took Julie's parents through to see the baby.

"Isn't she wonderful?" I said when Julie's mother and father returned.

"Why don't tha' go home, lad, get some rest," my father-in-law suggested.

Ten minutes before when the doctor came out I couldn't keep my eyes open. Now I was wide awake. "I think I will go home and clean up, then I'll come back."

"Take tha' time, lad, we'll be on't phone if owt happens," Julie's father called out as I left.

I drove home, took a shower, shaved, and put on clean clothes. I went downstairs, made a pot of tea, and cooked up some bacon and eggs. After eating I sat in the armchair and I must have dozed off because the phone ringing woke me with a start. It was my mother in-law calling to say Julie was awake.

"I'm on my way," I told her.

Back at the hospital I asked the receptionist where Julie was. I was directed down a long hallway and found Julie sitting up in bed holding baby Alison. I gave Julie a kiss.

"Can I hold her?" I asked.

Julie handed me the little bundle. Julie's parents stood and her mother said, "We'll be going now, leave you two alone. We'll be back later."

"I was hoping you'd be here when I woke up," Julie said as her parents closed the door behind them. Her tone was argumentative.

"I was here most of the night. If they'd have let me sit with you I would have stayed. I went home to clean up; I was still in my work clothes. I wanted to hold the baby last night but couldn't because my clothes were so dirty."

Little Alison started to cry; I passed her back to Julie.

"What do you think of our little girl?" she asked.

"She's beautiful."

"What shall we call her?"

"How about Alison?"

"Oh yes, that's perfect. She looks like an Alison."

I was glad Julie agreed with me because our daughter would always be Alison to me, even if her official name were different.

Julie and Alison stayed at the hospital for another week. I visited them both each day, and each night worked into the early hours of the following morning. With Julie away from home there was no guilt about not being there. But on her return I resolved to be home more and tried to leave work by six o'clock each evening. I talked to Henry about this.

"I have a daughter now; it's not fair to work late into the evening and leave Julie and the baby home alone. At the same time, we have so much work I don't want to get behind with the orders."

"Maybe we should consider getting help, employing another person."

"That would help but I still have to be involved with the design and main assembly, people are paying for a sculpture by Eddie Conner."

We took on a young man named Steve. He was able to cut and prepare the steel plate, and after I had assembled the piece Steve was able to finish the welding and final clean-up process. This increased our production and gave me a little more time at home. It also meant that work continued when I was away visiting new job sites.

A few weeks after Alison was born I had to go look at a job in Nottingham, a large city south of Sheffield. I traveled down by train in the late afternoon and found a hotel room in the city center. I had to be at the job site early the next morning. I decided to spend the evening at a cinema within walking distance of the hotel.

Leaving the theater a little after ten o'clock it was a weeknight and the streets were fairly quiet. Several women of the night were plying their trade as I walked back to the hotel. A small Chinese girl asked me, "Would you like to take me home?"

"What all the way to Hong Kong? No thank you." I kept on walking.

Fifty yards further on was another girl and I looked away as I passed trying not to invoke a solicitation. I heard my name spoken in the form of a question.

"Eddie Conner?"

I turned and looked. I kind of recognized the woman who spoke but was not sure. She spoke again.

"I thought it was you. Don't you recognize me? It's Trisha."

"Trisha, what are you doing here?"

"I was just about to ask you the same thing."

"I'm here on business, I live in Sheffield."

"Sheffield—that's a long way from the East End of London."

"Well, it's a long story. Are you on the game?" I asked. She nodded yes. "I'm sorry—" my voice trailed off. I felt kind of stupid and didn't know what to say.

"Don't be sorry for me, Eddie, I'm doing all right. Making a lot of money, I'm even buying my own house. I have a little girl now."

"Yes, me too."

"Let's not stand around here, we might get picked up by the fuzz. Do you fancy a drink?"

I agreed and we walked a few yards to a nearby pub. I got a beer at the bar and a gin and tonic for Trisha and carried them over to a quiet corner table. She lit a cigarette and turned her head to blow the smoke away from me.

"You haven't changed, Eddie."

"Neither have you."

I was lying; I wanted to be kinder to her than the years had been. The pretty young face I once knew now heavy with makeup had that hard-as-nails look. I was thinking that she must be in her mid-twenties but she looked ten years older. We sat and talked. I told her how I came to be in Sheffield.

"How did you end up on the game?" I asked her.

"You remember I went to live with my aunt and uncle in Mansfield, which is about twenty miles north of here? I wasn't there long when my uncle started climbing in bed with me."

"The bastard."

"Yes, I moved away from one form of abuse and into another. He was my father's brother, I should have known he would be no better than my ol' man."

"So you moved out?"

"Yes, I figured if my uncle had me laying on my back for nothing, I might as well do it for money. I never realized I was sitting on a gold mine."

"And you have a little girl now. Is there a man in your life?"

"No, I've no time for men unless it's professionally. My daughter's five now; I have no idea who the father is but she's the best thing that ever happened to me."

"What's her name? I asked.

"Cilla, short for Pricilla. I have an older woman who lives with me and looks after her when I'm working. Speaking of working, I should get back out there. I've got a mortgage to pay."

Outside the pub Trisha and I hugged. "It's been great seeing you again, Eddie."

"Likewise, take care of yourself, Trisha."

Standing for a moment I watched her walk away. My mind went back to the last time I watched her leave, as she walked toward the prison gate at Wormwood Scrubs. I turned and walked in the opposite direction. I had mixed emotions about our meeting. Here was someone who had once been a part of my life, and it hurt me to see her lifestyle now even though I had no right to judge her. It was her choice and she appeared to be happy. I wondered how different her life might be but for my actions, and the turn of events in my own life some eight years before.

Chapter 30

IT WAS 1970 AND MY daughter Alison, the love of my life, was four years old. Her hair once blonde as a baby had darkened to become the same rich chestnut brown color her mother had. The years since her birth slipped by so fast, but on looking back I had achieved more in this short time than I had ever done. For the first time in my life I had financial success and owned a brand new car.

The business had grown not only beyond my expectations but had surprised my partner. Henry Fisher had originally taken on this project as a hobby to fill his retirement years only to find he was at the head of a prosperous and growing company. My creativity and the experience and business savvy of Henry Fisher were a winning combination.

We now had ten employees. I was still making the large welded steel sculptures but our business had expanded and we were now also making structural steel components for buildings. In particular any steelwork that would remain exposed and therefore needed to be decorative and pleasing to the eye, for example, the steel framework to support a domed roof.

We had moved out of the Fisher factory after our first year and now occupied a brand new building on an industrial estate on the outskirts of Sheffield. I was also in the process of building my own custom home near the business. I designed the house with the help of a local architect and business associate. The home featured a forty-foot square living room with an abstract steel sculpture centerpiece that was fireplace, chimney, and roof support all in one.

That summer Henry went to a machine tool exhibition in London to check out the latest equipment. I stayed behind to take care of the business. He called me the night before his return to say he had met an American businessman from Los Angeles who was in the structural steel business and wanted to come and see our operation. The next day I drove to the train station to pick them up.

Henry introduced me to his traveling companion as they got off the train.

"Eddie, this is Chuck Pollard. Chuck, this is my partner Eddie Conner."

"Good to meet you, Eddie, I've heard a lot about you. I understand you're the creative side of the business."

Chuck Pollard was a tall man with a slender build, about fifty years old, I guessed. His smile showed teeth that seemed extra white against his deeply suntanned face, hollow cheeks, and graying hair cropped short in a crew cut. He was wearing a dark blue blazer and light colored trousers, a plain white shirt, and no tie. I could tell immediately before he spoke that he was American, even though his dress was conservative compared to others I had seen.

We drove back to our studio. We always referred to it as a studio even though it was really an industrial plant. This reference gave the impression to our employees and customers that our work was art and we were artists.

After looking at what we did Chuck said, "We're in the structural steel business but ours is the basic steel beam, nuts-and-bolts type of work. None of the beautiful-looking stuff I see here. But I would like to get into this type of work; there's a big demand for it particularly in California where we are."

"You're in Los Angeles?" I asked him.

"Actually, Anaheim, which is Orange County, but to you Los Angeles is close enough."

We stepped into the office and Chuck continued. "Henry's been telling me about this fireplace you built in your new house. I'd like to see it."

"Yes, I can drive you over there. Are you coming, Henry?"

"No, I'll stay here, you go ahead."

We drove to my new house, which was nearing completion. I took Chuck through to the living room. He walked all around the central fireplace looking up and down from every angle.

"Pretty impressive," he commented.

I started to explain some of the features.

"It has an internal chimney and an air space between it and the outer sculpture that you see. This is so the outside doesn't get hot, which would be a hazard to children as well as a fire risk. An electric fan inside circulates the hot air from around the chimney back into the room or it could be directed to another room."

"Are you going to produce these?"

"Yes, that's the plan. This is the prototype; as soon as I get the design standardized we'll go into production."

Chuck was quiet for a moment then said, "What would you say if we produced and sold these in the U.S. under license to you? You would get a percentage of everything we made."

"I would be interested but we would have to talk to Henry. I leave all of these type of decisions to him."

We drove back to the studio and Chuck put forward his proposal to Henry. "Why don't we all three discuss it over dinner tonight?" Henry suggested.

That evening Henry stopped by my house with Chuck and picked me up. We drove into the center of Sheffield to the same restaurant Henry had taken Julie and me almost five years before, the night we started this business venture.

Seated at the dinner table Henry opened the conversation. "I've been thinking about your proposal, Chuck, and I figure we would want fifteen percent of each piece that you sell. This could go down if you sell above a certain number in a year. How does that sound?"

Chuck thought it over. "It's a place to start. I would have to figure out our costs to see if the market would stand the added fifteen percent. Also I would need you, Eddie, to come over and help us get the project started."

"For how long?" I asked.

"About three months, I would say."

"I don't know, I've been trying to spend more time at home recently. Three months away is not going to go down too well with Julie and I'm not sure I want to be away from my daughter for that long."

"Is your daughter at school?" Chuck asked.

"No, she's four."

"Well, bring them with you. I'll pay all the expenses and you can make it a vacation."

I thought about it. "I've always wanted to go to America; let me talk it over with Julie."

Later that evening I discussed Chuck's proposal with Julie.

"I don't know, Eddie. We don't even know this person."

"I trust Henry's judgment and Chuck's paying all expenses, so we have nothing to lose."

"When's this going to happen?"

"Not for another two or three months."

"But that's about the time the new house will be ready."

"We can delay moving in; the house will still be here when we get back."

"I don't want to delay the move, I've been looking forward to it. Why don't you go on your own."

"I don't want to be away from you and Alison for three months. Do you want that?"

"No, not really."

"Well, think about it, it will be wonderful. Sunshine, beaches, we can take Alison to Disneyland."

"I wouldn't mind going to Disneyland. I'm sorry, Eddie, I should be more supportive of you and the business but lately it seems we're drifting apart. You have the business and I have the home. We're living separate lives."

We both stood and hugged. I said, "Do you remember when we stood like this the first time we said we loved each other? You called me a 'daft bat.' I am a daft bat for neglecting you and Alison and I'll try to do better because you're both the most important thing in my life."

Chuck Pollard went back to Los Angeles. I worked on the fireplace design and sent drawings over to America. There were phone calls and correspondence back and forth, negotiations over the license agreement. By the time we reached agreement I delayed going to the United States, because it was getting near to Christmas and I did not want to be away from home over the holidays. Julie was an only child so Alison was her parents' only grandchild, making Christmas a big occasion for them.

We agreed to go to California in January and so got to move into our new house after all. This was a time when Julie and I moved closer in our relationship as together we chose furniture and decorations. Alison was at an age when she was a joy to be with. There is no other love a man can experience like the love of his little girl. That Christmas was probably one of the best I had ever experienced and the future looked promising.

I was growing excited about our upcoming trip to America. Alison talked continuously about Disneyland and Mickey Mouse. Even Julie who was apprehensive at first was warming to the idea, although I knew it would be hard for her to be away from her parents for that length of time. She had never been separated from them before. Julie's father was retired now and had offered to put in a lawn at our new house and work on the landscaping while we were away.

On the day of our departure we drove over to Julie's parents'. There were tearful goodbyes between Julie and her mother and this started Alison crying. Julie's dad drove us to the train station in my car. I told him, "Use the car whenever you want, there's no point in letting it sit in the garage."

"Oh, I will, don't tha' worry, lad and I'll have t' landscaping done by the time tha' gets back."

At the station Julie's dad helped me with the suitcases and on the platform hugged Julie and picked up Alison and held her in his arms.

"Say hello to Mickey Mouse for me."

"I will, Granddad."

As the train came in he shook my hand.

"Look after lass an't' young'un."

"I will. We'll call you when we get there," I told him.

This was Alison's first train ride and her excitement reminded me of my first trip by train to see my grandmother after World War II. Her tongue was going the entire trip with comments and questions; I remembered doing the same.

On arrival in London we took a taxi to Heathrow Airport. We could have used the underground but I didn't want to deal with the heavy suitcases. The airport was a whole new experience for me; I had never flown before.

If the train ride had been fun for Alison, the flight was anything but. There was nothing to see through the windows but clouds, and she soon became bored. We were flying through the night so Alison slept on my knee most of the trip. But, however you look at it, almost twelve hours on an airplane is a long time for anyone; for a four-year-old it's an eternity.

The long flight did eventually end and we landed in Los Angeles. After collecting our suitcases and clearing customs, we walked in sheep-like procession toward the exit. We reached a point where others stood, watching the sheep spilling out from the terminal. I realized this must be the place where we meet Chuck and I looked around for him. I heard my name and turned to see Chuck fighting his way through the crowd toward us.

"This way," he said as he grabbed a suitcase from me and a smaller bag from Julie. The crowd thinned as people dispersed in different directions. We stopped when we met with a slender woman in her forties with bleach blonde hair.

"This is my wife, Thelma."

I set the suitcase down and shook her hand. "This is Julie and my daughter Alison."

The introductions over we walked outside to the parking lot. The first thing I noticed was the heat. We were dressed for northern England winter weather and here it was eighty degrees under clear skies. We reached Chuck's car, a Cadillac convertible with the top down—probably the biggest car I had ever seen. Had it not had wheels and been on dry land I would have taken it for a yacht. It was about double the length of the car I had just left in England.

We stowed our suitcases in the ample trunk and shed our coats and sweaters. Julie and I sat in the backseat with Alison between us; there was room for another two people back there. Chuck drove and Thelma sat in the front passenger seat. We cruised along, the warm wind blowing in our face. Palm trees stood like sentinels at the roadside. The surroundings familiar to us, seen so many times on film and television, seemed unreal now that we were actually here.

We arrived in Anaheim and pulled into the parking lot of a two-story apartment complex.

"I've rented a two bedroom apartment for you," Chuck said. "I think you'll like it."

We carried our suitcases along a cement pathway between two buildings with white stucco walls and red Spanish tile roof. The grounds were laid out with neatly manicured lawns, shrubs, and trees. Chuck stopped at the door of a ground floor apartment and took some keys from his pocket. He unlocked the door and handed the keys to me. I opened the door and stepped aside to let Julie and Alison enter first.

"Oh, look—it's got a big television," Alison said and climbed on the sofa to face the TV. Chuck turned the set on and switched through the channels to find some cartoons.

"Look, Mummy, it's colored." Our TV set in England was black and white.

The apartment was simply but adequately furnished. A long living room had a kitchen at one end. There was a small dining table and four chairs. The two bedrooms each had a bed, a dresser, and a built-in closet. A small bathroom had a tub with a shower.

"I hope you'll be comfortable here," Chuck said. "We'd like you to come over to our place for dinner tonight. I'll pick you up around six."

That evening at the Pollard house was a social blur. We were tired from the trip and there were so many introductions to friends and family. Everyone wanted to talk about England; my mind became blank after a while. I did remember that Chuck had a married daughter who was there with her family. After dinner, in a rare moment alone, I found myself looking at a photograph of a young man in army uniform. Chuck walked over and stood beside me.

"Is this you?" I asked.

"No, this is my son Robert; he was killed in Vietnam."

"I'm sorry." My words seemed futile.

"He was only nineteen, a good son. I miss him."

I could sense he was choking up, I reached up and touched his elbow.

"I had a brother who died at nineteen in World War II. There's an old cliché, 'Only the good die young,' and it's true. My father who is a total bastard lived through it all and my brother had to die."

I think Chuck was shocked at my comments about my father and I wouldn't have said it if I had been thinking straight, but it just came out. But it did have the effect of distracting him from thoughts about his son.

"You shouldn't talk that way about your father. You should try and make your peace with him before it's too late."

"Oh, I've tried, believe me I've tried. He's got that stubborn Protestant Irish mind-set, I don't know who he hates the most me or the Pope."

Soon after, we made our excuses and Chuck drove us home early. It was two or three days before we adjusted to time change.

Chuck gave me the use of a company car. Driving on the other side of the road was a challenge but I got used to it. Julie had never learned to drive a car. Back in Sheffield there was a good bus service and a car was not a necessity but this was southern California and was a different matter since distances were far greater.

It was four miles to the grocery store, eight miles there and back if you tried to walk it. In England if you went four miles from the center of most big cities you were out of town. So Julie's inability to drive was a problem we had not anticipated. When I was at work she was housebound at the apartment. There was a swimming pool and Julie and Alison made good use of it, but after a while even that got old and was not fun anymore.

Chuck's wife Thelma came over and took Julie and Alison shopping, but it seemed that Thelma and Julie did not get along, for whatever reason.

"She's always telling me how to raise Alison. Even my own mother doesn't do that," Julie complained one night.

"Oh, she means well, it's a different culture here. Don't take it so personal," I tried to reason.

Weekends Julie just wanted to get away from the apartment and do things like go to the beach or to Disneyland. Chuck and Thelma wanted us to spend time with them. They had a boat and offered to take us on the ocean, but Julie was not keen.

Julie and I fought over this problem and after six weeks she announced, "I want to go home."

Two days later I drove Julie and Alison to the airport. Alison cried because I was not going with them.

"It won't be long, sweetheart," I told her.

I left the airport sad that my little girl was gone but at the same time feeling relief that my conflict between work and family was over.

I threw myself into my work—the new fireplace project plus other design work that Chuck gave me, and I was happy to take on. There was no point in staying in the apartment, I moved in with the Pollards. The weekends we took a boat trips down to Mexico and up to Santa Barbara.

When my three months were up and I was ready to get back to Julie and Alison, I was missing them. The night before I was to leave Chuck spoke to me at dinner. "What would it take for you to come and work for me? You can name your own job and your own salary."

"I can't, Chuck. I love it here and I love you both, you've been wonderful to me. But Julie will never move here, I know it, and I'm not about to leave my wife and little girl."

"No we wouldn't expect you to," Thelma said.

"I promise you this—I will come back, maybe next year."

Chuck raised his wineglass. "To next year."

Chapter 31

BY 1976 MY LIFE HAD became somewhat routine, with an annual trip to southern California every January through March. It meant I could spend Christmas with my family and I would get away from the cold English winter and return in the spring. Julie never went back with me again, even though she had since learned to drive. Alison was at school now and I could not take her away for three months each year.

I always looked forward to my yearly trip; I loved southern California. I enjoyed being with Chuck and Thelma; we became more than just business associates we became very close friends, almost family. Chuck was the father I wished I had, and maybe I was the son he lost.

We were always working on some new project; he would get an idea and I would develop it and bring it to life. Chuck paid me well while I was in California, as well as royalties throughout the year on everything I designed. Money I made in the United States I invested there. My business in England was doing well and to bring in money from America only meant more UK taxes, which were higher than the States.

I bought a house in Newport Beach on the coast not far from Anaheim. It was a little cottage on the edge of a harbor. It had a private boat mooring and Chuck kept his boat there. I figured it was a good investment; I had a very nice place to stay each year and I let Chuck and Thelma use it whenever they wanted.

Every year when I went to California I thought about not coming back, and every March when it was time to return I couldn't wait to get home to Alison. I could never leave my little girl. Julie and I got along; we did not fight. But we lived separate lives. I loved her as the mother of my child but it was no longer a passionate love; it was more a deep friendship.

In the early 1970s my business grew at a steady rate. There was a tremendous amount of new building, but by the middle of that decade there was over-construction. New buildings stood empty and the bubble burst. We had to scale back the business and lay off a few workers, something I hated doing. We survived by aggressively going after business not connected with the building industry. But this type of work was no longer a creative challenge to me; it was just work to keep the business going and the employees working.

Henry Fisher, now in his seventies, let me know it was time he stepped down. As promised he turned the business over to me. He told me, "I made very little initial investment and I've drawn a paycheck each month. Why take money from you to give to the tax man?"

I had been blessed in my life to have people like Henry Fisher there at the right time. He had taught me so much about running a successful business that I knew I could carry on.

As time went on, my daily routine of going to my business became drudgery. I had long since stopped any hands-on or design work. My day consisted of sales calls, ordering materials, and estimating costs; I was miserable. The only light in my life and the thing that kept me going was Alison, who was now ten years old.

I looked forward to my annual trips to California even more now and would have stayed longer than three months. But without Henry back home to run things, three months was as long as I could afford to be away.

I talked to Julie about divorce.

"How can you think about leaving Alison? You know she dotes on you."

I was feeling bad enough; the last thing I needed was a guilt trip. "Should I talk to her?"

"No, you'll break her heart. If you're going I think it's best you leave in January as you usually do. Let her get used to you being gone before we tell her."

I called Chuck on the phone the next day and told him of my plans. He said, "Your timing couldn't be better. I've been thinking seriously about retiring and I was wondering whether to sell the business. How would you like to come and take over from me?"

"I'll accept that offer, thank you. I'll sell this business here. I can't run both."

That week I put the business up for sale. It was late September and I would be leaving in January. The economic climate was not good and I wondered if I would find a buyer.

There was only one serious bid for the business and I took less than I thought it was worth but I was glad to get out from under it. I put the money in a bank account under Julie's name. This would be enough for her to live on comfortably for a while, after which I had agreed to continue support for her and Alison. I also signed the house over to Julie.

I wondered how much Alison knew. I think she had an idea that I had sold the business because I was not going to the office each day. I wanted to tell her but Julie insisted we do things her way. I spent time visiting people; I went to see Henry and his son Ian Fisher. I went down to London to see my mother; she did not understand my decision to leave. My father would still not speak to me. In my mind I had forgiven him and bore him no grudge and that was all I could do. I went to see my friends Danny and Harry Christmas; they now ran a successful recording studio.

The time came for me to leave and Julie drove me to the station. When Alison was small this was always a tearful experience but in recent years she had not cried when I left. But this time just as the train pulled in she threw her arms around me and held on tight. She started to cry. "Please, Daddy, promise me you'll come back."

I couldn't bring myself to say those words knowing I could not keep such a promise, I simply said, "Bye, Alison. Remember your daddy loves you."

Then I pulled myself away from her, gave Julie a quick kiss, and stepped on the train. I took my seat and looked at Alison and Julie standing on the platform; they were both crying. I waved as the train pulled away; I was crying openly and people stared at me. I left my seat and went to the washroom to clean up. Alison was on my mind for the whole trip.

Chuck picked me up at the airport and for the next week my thoughts were distracted as we went over every detail of the business. Chuck continued to come to work part-time for a couple of months before handing over to me completely. With more than a hundred employees, this business was much larger than the one I had in England. Construction was still booming in California, especially the building of shopping malls, so there was a lot of steelwork.

The house I had bought in Newport Beach had doubled in value. I borrowed against the equity and went out and bought some new furniture and a Porsche sports car—something I had wanted for some time.

As before, I spent weekends with Chuck and Thelma. Apart from that I had little time for a social life since I spent long hours at the plant. I was determined to expand the business and bid on jobs outside California, as far away as Chicago and Cleveland.

March rolled around and I knew I would have to talk to Alison. I spoke with Julie one evening.

"Have you said anything yet?" I asked.

"Well, I've hinted enough but she's in denial; you're going to have to tell her."

"Okay, put her on."

I waited wondering what the hell I was going to say to her. She came on the line.

"Hello, Daddy, are you coming home soon? I can't wait to see you."

"Alison, I'm not coming home. I have to run Chuck's factory here in America."

I could hear Alison sobbing.

"Alison, are you there?"

There was a crash as she dropped the phone.

"Alison?"

Julie came on the phone. "Well, you handled that real well. She's run upstairs, I'm going to have to talk to her."

"Should I call back?"

"Call back tomorrow, I have to calm her down. You're a bastard, Eddie."

She hung up the phone. Never in all the years I had known Julie, had she ever spoken to me like that. I put the phone down and immediately picked it up again. I did not know if I should call back or call the airport and book the next flight to England. I realized neither was a good idea and hung up again.

"Eddie Conner, you are a bastard," I told myself. But I was past the point of no return, I could not justify giving up everything I had in California and going back to England where I didn't even have a business anymore.

I called back the following evening and asked Julie if I could speak to Alison.

"Not a good idea, Eddie. I've only just managed to get her to stop crying; I do not want her starting all over again. Be patient, leave it to me, and when she's ready I'll have her call you."

It would be two weeks before my phone rang and it was Alison calling. "Hello, Daddy."

"Hello, sweetheart. How are you?"

"I'm fine, I miss you though." She started to cry.

"Now don't start crying or you'll make me cry and then my mascara will run."

I heard a little chuckle. "Daddy, you're so silly."

"It will soon be your long summer holidays, would you like to come and see me."

"Can Mummy come too?"

"I don't think your Mummy likes America too much. No, I'll fly over and come and get you. It'll be just you and me, we can go to Disneyland again."

"Yes I went there when I was four, I don't remember much about it."

Early July I flew into Heathrow Airport. Julie brought Alison down by train and I met them at the station. I did not want to fly straight back so I got in a few days early. I took Alison around the London tourist spots, the Tower Of London, the Houses of Parliament, and to St. Paul's Cathedral.

"I used to sing in the choir here when I was twelve years old," I told her.

"I didn't know you could sing."

"Yes, I even sang solo. That's where I used to sit." I pointed out where my seat was. The vestry door was open and I peeked inside, I remembered the time I punched Nigel on the nose. I smiled to myself and wondered where Nigel was now.

We went to see Danny and Harry at their studio. At some point, as always when I saw them, guitars were brought out for an impromptu session. After the first song I turned to Alison.

"See I told you I could sing."

"Yes, you can—and play guitar too."

"Actually I'm always amazed that I can still play and sing. Not as good as at one time but I can still do it.

"It's like riding a bicycle," Danny said.

We played for half an hour or so. Harry had a tape running and he played it back. I was surprised. "Hey, that doesn't sound half bad."

Harry said, "Sounds pretty good to me, you should really think about playing again."

"If I could ever find the time."

"You should make time," Harry said.

The next morning I took Alison to see my mother. My father was there but he left the house soon after we arrived. My mother had not seen Alison often as she grew up and it saddened me, but it was mainly due to my father's attitude toward me. It just made everyone feel uncomfortable and took the pleasure out of visiting.

That afternoon we left for Heathrow Airport and took an evening flight to Los Angeles. Alison and I talked on the plane.

"Are you and Mummy going to get a divorce?"

"Yes we are."

"Don't you love Mummy anymore?"

"Of course, I still love her, your mother is a wonderful person. But people get married when they're twenty-something and as they get older they change and want different things. For example, I wanted to live in America and your mother is happy in England. So it's probably best that we go our separate ways so we can both be where we want to be."

"But what about me and the things I want?"

"So what do you want?"

"I want to have both of you living with me."

"As you grow older, you'll find you can't always have all the things you want in life. You have to compromise."

"What does compromise mean?"

"It means you can choose most of things that make you happy but not all of them. It would be like having a cake and you want to eat it all. A compromise would be to share it with your friends. That way you still get cake and your friends get some too. So everyone is happy."

"So compromise means sharing?"

"Yes, in a way. It's sharing the things that make the most people happy but in doing so we have to give up some things. Our whole life is a compromise, and all the problems in this world are caused by people who won't compromise."

Chapter 32

I FIRST MET DAWN IN 1981. She was a cocktail waitress in a little bar and restaurant called Bernardo's on the Pacific Coast Highway just outside Newport Beach. I often stopped in there for something to eat and a cold brew on my way home after working late. She was always friendly but I didn't fool myself that she was interested in me. It was part of her job to be friendly and a smart waitress will make more in tips if she gets to know the customers by name.

I was seated alone one night, having just finished eating, when Dawn came into the bar. She smiled and walked over to my table. "Hi, Eddie, do you mind if I join you?"

"Not at all, please do." I pulled out a chair.

"You're not working tonight?" I asked as she seated herself.

"No."

"You love this place so much you can't stay away even on your night off?"

"Not exactly. I've been on a photo shoot and I was passing by on my way home. I wasn't ready to go home so I stopped in."

"What was the photo shoot about?"

"I'm a part-time model and actress; I was getting some promotional photos done."

"So a model and actress is what you want to be?"

"Acting would be my first choice, but I have to live and pay the rent so that's why I wait tables and do the occasional modeling job."

The waitress came and Dawn ordered a drink. "Do ya want another beer, Eddie?"

"No, I've had my two-beer quota for tonight. I'll have a cup of coffee though."

We continued our conversation and the topic of relationships came up.

"Any man in your life?" I asked.

"No, my career is my number-one focus right now and men can get so possessive. You know, the reason I sat with you tonight is because you never hit on me like everyone else does."

"Like you, my work is my main focus." My social life had been practically nonexistent since I came to California five years before. I was considering asking her out before she commented on her attitude toward men.

That night as I drove home I told myself, "Don't be stupid, Eddie, you're twice her age." But she was extremely easy on the eye.

Later that week I stopped by Bernardo's on my way home. Dawn was working and came over and chatted intermittently between serving customers. At the end of the evening she asked me, "Do you have any plans this weekend?"

"Nothing concrete, why?"

"I have a modeling job out in the desert and I've never worked with this photographer before. I'd feel a lot more comfortable if I had an escort."

"I'd be happy to. Shall we take my car?"

"Well, yes, that was my other concern, I don't think my old car would make it that far. I'll pay for gas and I'll buy you dinner."

"It's a deal."

Dawn gave me her address and phone number.

Early Saturday morning I picked her up at her apartment in Huntington Beach, the next town north of where I lived. She was wearing a simple cotton summer dress and sandals and carried a large makeup case. I opened the car door for her.

"I didn't know you had a Porsche," she said as she got in. "Can we ride with the top down?"

"Of course."

I reached inside to release the top.

"Wait, let me get something for my hair."

She ran back to the apartment and returned minutes later with her hair in a ponytail.

We drove to Barstow, a town in the Mojave Desert about halfway between Los Angeles and Las Vegas. We were to meet the photographer at a Bob's Big Boy Restaurant. As we pulled into the parking lot Dawn said, "He'll be driving a brand new bright red Jeep. That's what we're doing the photo shoot with."

"Should be easy to spot."

I drove around the restaurant parking lot.

"I don't see him."

"I don't know about you but I could eat breakfast," I suggested.

We went inside and a waitress brought coffee and took our order. The food came and we ate, watching through the window as we did so.

"I hope I haven't brought you on a wild goose chase," Dawn said as she looked at her watch.

"That's okay; it's a nice day for a drive in the desert."

I turned to see a red open top Jeep pull into the parking lot. "Here he is."

A slightly overweight and flabby young man got out and came into the restaurant. Dawn waved to him as he looked around. He walked to our table.

"Are you Dawn?" he asked.

He and Dawn shook hands and she introduced me. "This is my friend, Eddie."

"Hi, I'm Bob." His handshake felt like a wet fish had been placed in my hand.

"Hi, Bob, is this your restaurant?"

My remark went completely over his head but got a smile from Dawn.

"Where are we going?" I asked.

"About five miles east of here; we're going to turn off on a dirt road."

Bob led the way and we followed. As we pulled off the main road Dawn said, "I'm glad you're with me, Eddie, this guy gives me the creeps."

We drove on the dirt road for about three miles. Bob got out and looked at the terrain. "This is a good spot," he said.

He turned the Jeep around to position it against a backdrop of some rocks and large cactus. He unloaded and set up his camera equipment as Dawn applied her makeup. Bob indicated that he was ready and Dawn stepped from the car and took off her dress. She was wearing a bikini underneath.

"Hold this for me." She handed me the dress.

She had a body that most women would kill for, and most men would die for. Her smooth skin, evenly suntanned, shone in the sunlight and feminine muscles rippled beneath the flesh. A picture of health and beauty. I was conscious that I was staring at her and was embarrassed.

I walked away and stood watching from a distance as Dawn crawled all over the red jeep. She sat on the hood, she lay on the hood, and she knelt on the hood with her arms resting on the top edge of the windshield. She sat in the driver's seat; she stood in the driver's seat with the hot desert breeze blowing her long blonde hair.

In between takes as Bob moved his camera, I walked back and offered Dawn her dress but she declined and seemed to be completely comfortable with her lack of clothing. When I was close to her not only could I not keep my eyes off her, but also I had to suppress a strong urge to touch and stroke her beautiful skin.

The photo shoot over, Dawn put her dress on and we stood by the car as Bob packed his equipment. He finished and came over to speak with Dawn. "I don't have cash, will a check be all right?"

"No, it won't. I told you on the phone, bring cash. I don't know you."

"I'm sorry, I don't have enough cash on me."

I picked up the camera case that was lying nearby and dropped it behind the passenger seat of the Porsche. Then I opened my wallet and took out a business card and handed it to the astonished Bob.

"I'll just keep your equipment as collateral and you can stop by my office with the cash at your convenience."

I opened the door for Dawn to get in, then walked around the driver's side.

"Wait, let me see how much cash I have." Bob opened his wallet and counted out bills on the hood of the car and handed them to Dawn.

"I'm ten dollars short."

"I'll take a check for the ten dollars." She counted the money as Bob wrote the check.

"I don't think I have enough gas to get back to LA," Bob whined

"Have you got coins for the phone?" I asked as I handed back his camera case.

"Yes, I think so."

"That's okay then. I wouldn't want to see you stranded."

Bob got in the Jeep and drove off in a cloud of dust. Dawn put her hand on the back of my neck and gently kissed me on the lips.

"Thank you, Eddie, you're a sweetheart. Now where do you want to have dinner tonight?"

"How about Las Vegas?"

"Are you serious?"

"Why not, we're halfway there. We can drive back late tonight or we can get a hotel—I'll get separate rooms."

She thought for a moment. "Can I drive?"

I handed her the keys. We reached Vegas by mid-afternoon.

"Let's get a hotel room," Dawn said. "I need to take a shower."

As we walked into the hotel lobby she said, "Get one room. It'll be okay."

I wasn't about to argue. After we cleaned up Dawn handed me a wad of rolled-up bills. "I'm going to gamble half my money; hold the other half for me."

We went down to the casino, she bought some chips, and we headed for the roulette tables. For the first hour she was a little better than even but after that gained steadily until she had tripled her money.

"Come on, let's quit while you're ahead.," I told her.

"No, I wanna keep going."

"But I'm getting hungry."

"Okay, but let's go shopping first. I want to buy a dress for tonight."

Dawn cashed in her chips and we walked down the Strip. After going in and out three different shops she found something she liked. It was a little black sequined dress with spaghetti shoulder straps.

"Now I need shoes."

Two more shoe shops and she found a pair she liked. I told her, "If you're going to look as good as I think you are, I'd better get a new shirt."

"Yes, come on, I'll buy you one."

In a men's clothing store I picked out a shirt. Dawn chose a tie for me and paid for both items.

Back at the hotel room I waited while Dawn got herself ready in the bathroom. She emerged and did a pirouette in the center of the room.

"What do you think?" she asked.

"Absolutely stunning." Words could not do justice to the way she looked. The little black dress accentuated every curve of her body and long slender legs.

"Let's go eat," she said as she led the way to the door.

We went downstairs to a restaurant within the hotel serving fine French cuisine. As we were shown to our table it seemed that conversation stopped and all eyes were upon us. I could not help feeling self-conscious, but at the same time pride to be escort to such beauty.

A waiter came and I ordered wine. Dawn studied the menu and I couldn't help but study her. Shoulder length blonde hair, blue eyes, and perfect features.

"How old are you?" I asked.

"Twenty two, and you?"

"Twice your age—old enough to be your father."

"But you're not my father. I've dated men my own age and I get tired of the macho thing. For example, the way you handled Bob the photographer today. A younger man would have used physical threats but you didn't do that."

She was right. As a young man I probably would have knocked him out cold and taken his money. Leaving myself open to prosecution for assault and robbery. The years had mellowed me.

I asked about her aspirations in acting and shared with her my past experiences. "When I was in my twenties I was an artist, a painter, and a sculptor. Certain people became my mentors and helped me. In fact, I am where I stand today because of these people. If there's any way I can help you, let me know."

"I need someone to give me advice now and then. Like today, for instance, I probably shouldn't have taken on that job."

"But it turned out to be a fun weekend," I added.

"Yes and the weekend's not over yet."

Back at the hotel room that night I unlocked the door and reached inside for the light switch. As we entered and I closed the door, Dawn reached past me to turn the light off again. She embraced me with a long and passionate kiss.

"Just because I don't have a man in my life doesn't mean I don't sometimes want a man. Right now I want you." She slipped the thin straps of her dress off her shoulders and let it slide to the floor.

"I was wondering if there was anything under that dress," I said.

"And now you know. Just me."

Chapter 33

IF I HAD TO DESCRIBE my relationship with Dawn, I would say she was my companion and lover. My marriage to Julie had been love without passion; with Dawn it was all passion and little else. I cared for her but I was trying to be realistic about the situation. Initially I did not expect the affair to last more than a couple of months and I guarded against becoming emotionally attached to her for fear of being hurt later.

I asked myself would she have stayed around if I didn't own a Porsche and a harbor-front cottage in Newport Beach. But that was okay, I enjoyed being with her. Before Dawn came along my life revolved around my work. Now at least I had a social life, and I will admit it stroked my ego to be seen with her.

Following our weekend in Las Vegas, Dawn spent most weekends at my house. We used Chuck's boat for trips to Catalina Island and up and down the coast. Chuck was not using the boat as often now since his wife Thelma was not in good health. Evenings would find us in the restaurants and nightspots of LA.

After about six months, Dawn was spending more time at my place than her own and I suggested she move in permanently. She kept her job as a cocktail waitress but cut back the hours to devote more time to modeling and acting. She got involved in an Actors Studio and Workshop in Hollywood and was also taking dance lessons. She needed reliable transport to get to these activities so she took the Porsche and I used one of the company vehicles.

Dawn was into physical fitness; she ran on the beach every morning and belonged to a nearby gym. She encouraged me to exercise again. I had been into running as a kid and had exercised a little since coming to California but nothing serious. I was a little overweight but not too bad.

After struggling for the first few weeks I started to whip my body into shape and began to enjoy exercise.

During the week I often found myself alone in the evenings; Dawn would be working at Bernardo's or at her actors' workshop. I was becoming bored with TV and decided to buy a guitar and start playing again. I found playing and singing relaxing.

I came home from the office one evening after a very stressful day. A client was disputing the price on a large job I had bid for. There had been a handshake on the agreed price but after the contract was drawn up the customer said we had agreed on a much lower price. To make matters worse a check we received to start the job had bounced.

I thought about the time when I was twenty years old and worked all week for a butcher who paid me less than we agreed on. The same feelings came up. Back then I settled my disputes with physical violence and it got me in a lot of trouble. I knew I could not do that now but it didn't stop me from wishing I could. An idea came to me for a song; I got pen and paper and wrote a few words. I picked up my guitar and started to sing.

> *Spent all week workin' for the man,*
> *Got the paycheck Friday, took it to the bank.*
> *The check bounced so high it ain't come down,*
> *Went looking for the man all over town.*
> *Found him drinking in a downtown bar,*
> *I knew he was there, I recognized his car.*
> *I went inside, took him by the throat,*
> *Said, "Come on, man, this ain't no joke.*
>
> *"I want the cash up front, the dollars and cents,*
> *I want the greenback pictures of the dead presidents.*
> *Don't give me the line about the check's on the way,*
> *Gimme cold, hard, currency USA."*

I had turned my anger into humor in a song. It felt good to write again.

"It's not earth-shattering, but it's a start," I told myself.

Dawn was finding success in her career; she landed some parts in TV commercials and was dancing in an amateur production in LA. She gave up her cocktail waitress job. I enjoyed sharing in her success and her enthusiasm. Life was good right now.

Life was not so good for my friend and colleague Chuck. His wife Thelma had been diagnosed with cancer. She and Chuck had been life-long smokers; Chuck had been able to kick the habit some years earlier but Thelma had not. As is often the case, she had been diagnosed too late and died within three months.

Chuck's daughter had moved to Colorado and after the funeral went back. I made a point of spending a lot of time with Chuck, as I knew the loss was hard on him. He spoke to me one day. "I need to put my affairs in order, it might not be long for me."

"I wish you wouldn't talk like that, you're in good health," I told him.

"Nevertheless I want to sign the boat over to you now and when I go, I intend to leave the business to you."

"What about your daughter?"

"She will get everything else—I have a lot of other assets. You have worked hard over the years and I feel it's only right that you should get the business."

I stood to give him a hug. "Chuck, I'm very grateful, but more than anything I want you around for many more years."

I arrived back home and Dawn ran to meet me as I walked in. "I have some wonderful news."

"I need some wonderful news. I've just been with Chuck. I'm afraid he's giving up on life. What's the news?"

"I've got a part in a pilot for a TV sitcom."

"That is wonderful, congratulations. When do you start?"

"Next week. The story line is about a bunch of kids hanging out on the beach, I play an eighteen-year-old. Do you think I can pull it off?"

"Of course, you can. See, all your hard work is paying off."

"I couldn't have done it without your help and support." She gave me a hug and a kiss. When she was excited and filled with so much en-thusiasm I had feelings for her that went beyond the physical attraction.

In the weeks that followed I saw less of Dawn as she worked long hours on the filming of the TV pilot. I tried to see Chuck every day and was concerned because he seemed to be sinking into depression. I told myself there was nothing more I could do, but give him time to mourn. After a few more weeks I did see an improvement.

Dawn finished filming and I told her, "Let's go somewhere this week-end and celebrate."

"Do you know what this weekend is?" she asked.

"No, what?"

"It's the anniversary of our weekend in Vegas. Can we go back?"

"What a good idea. We can set out early and have breakfast again at the Bob's Big Boy in Barstow."

"Yes, let's do it."

That Saturday we set out in the Porsche with the top down as we had done a year earlier. This time we took a small suitcase with a change of clothes. As I drove I reflected on the past year. Dawn and I had got along well; I did not recall a single argument or disagreement.

"This time last year did you expect us to still be together by now?" I asked her.

"Of course—didn't you?"

"I don't know, we kind of drifted into this without ever making a commitment or anything. I think we've done very well."

She leaned over and laid her head on my shoulder hugging my arm. "Yes, I think so too."

After stopping for breakfast as planned we arrived in Las Vegas around lunchtime. We checked into the same hotel and after cleaning up went down to the casino. We played the roulette tables and Dawn's luck seemed to continue where it had left off a year earlier. She played for several hours, winning steadily. Then after a short losing streak I said, "Let's quit. We can come back later."

We stepped outside in the hot Nevada sun and walked along the Strip. Dawn asked, "What shall we do now?"

"Let's get married."

If ever in my whole life, words had come from my mouth and I wished I could take them back, this was it. Dawn started to jump up and down dancing around me and squealing like an excited child.

"Oh, yes, Eddie, yes. Do you really mean it?"

People turned staring at us, smiling and shaking their heads as they walked on. There was no way out of this. I could not turn now and say, "Just kidding." I had spoken without thinking, caught up in the emotion and euphoria brought on by the occasion and the place we had come to.

"Yes, of course I mean it."

From now on I was along for the ride and what a crazy whirlwind ride it was. A short distance along the street we found a jeweler and bought a ring. The jeweler recommended a wedding chapel and we drove over there. We paid for a license and that evening we were married. Two chapel employees were witnesses.

After the wedding we had dinner in a quiet little restaurant. I looked across at my beautiful young bride. I was feeling better about the events of the day.

"I'm a very lucky man," was all I could find to say.

In September, three months after our wedding, the TV pilot that Dawn had starred in was aired on network television. We decided to throw a party the evening of the show; we invited friends and some of the other cast members. Chuck was there and I spent most of the evening talking with him.

The program came on and the room went quiet as everyone found a seat and settled down to watch. I stood toward the back of the room with Chuck. As the show unfolded I was thinking, "This is not good; in fact, it stinks."

The pilot ran for a half hour and as it ended those who worked on it stood and cheered and gave each other high fives. Dawn came back to me. "What did you think?"

"You did great, I'm proud of you," I said giving her a hug.

I was not lying; she and the other cast members had all done a decent job. But the material, the writing, and the story line were pathetic. I drove Chuck home later and asked him, "Was it me, or did that show suck the big one?"

"It didn't appeal to me, but I guess it was aimed at the young crowd."

"I feel sorry for Dawn and the others in the cast; they put so much effort into this and they all think it's great. But they're too close to see it as it really is."

It was about three weeks later I came home from work one evening to find Dawn sitting on the living room sofa. A box of tissues and a half-empty bottle of vodka were on the coffee table in front of her.

"What's wrong?" I asked.

"I got a call today. The network is not picking up the show. After all the work we put into it they're not even going to give it a chance."

I sat beside her and put my arm around her shoulder. "Well, one thing's for sure—this is not going to make it any better." I picked up the vodka bottle and tipped it to one side to show the level of the liquid. "Let's try and get a perspective on this. First of all you were great in this. It was not your fault the material you had to work with was bad."

Dawn reached for a tissue and blew her nose. "I've been watching the video again and it's not very good," she admitted

"So can you blame the network for not picking this up? It's like in music. It doesn't matter how good the band is—if you don't have a good song, you don't have shit."

"But all that work we put into it…"

"I know, but at least you were in it. Look at all those who got rejected. You got the experience, now it's time to move on."

"You're right, Eddie."

"This business is tough but that's what makes it more rewarding. If it were easy everyone would do it. If you're an artist and you can't take disappointment and rejection, don't be an artist."

"What should I do now?"

"How about I take a more active roll in your career? Become your manager?"

"I would like that."

"First thing I think we should do is get you a better agent. Someone who will get you more exposure."

The next day I called my attorney, who was also a good friend. "Do you know any attorneys in LA who have show-biz connections? What I'm looking for is the name of a good agent."

That afternoon my friend called back. "I have a name here. Craig Southerland."

He also gave me an address and phone number. Then added, "You're on your own on this one. My associate who gave me this doesn't know you so he's not going to recommend you. This Southerland may not even talk to you or return your call."

"I understand, thank you."

I put down the phone and looked at the address, it looked familiar. I went to some old job files. I was right, ten years before when this building was under construction, I had made a large sculpture for outside the building.

I drove up there to make sure the sculpture was still there and that it was indeed the same address. The sculpture was there and apart from the pigeon shit, it looked the same. This would be my calling card, my way in. The next day I called; an operator answered.

"Can I speak to Craig Southerland?" I asked.

"Mr. Southerland is in a meeting. Can I take a message?"

"Yes, I'm calling about a possible new client for Mr. Southerland. And would you mention I'm the artist who did the sculpture outside your building?"

There was a brief silence, then, "Please hold."

I sat listening to the hold music for thirty seconds or so.

"This is Craig Southerland, I've just been told you're the artist who did the sculpture outside. I've admired that work for years. What's your name?"

"Thank you, I'm Eddie Conner. I did that piece ten years ago."

"What can I do for you today, Eddie?"

"I was calling on behalf of my wife. She's an actress who has done some TV commercials and a pilot for a show recently. I was hoping we could meet to discuss your representing her."

"Yes, let's do lunch on Thursday. I look forward to meeting you both."

That Thursday Dawn and I stood outside the office building looking at my sculpture. "I built that."

"You mean, your company."

"No, I mean I actually built it with my own hands. That's how I got started in this business, as an artist."

Dawn looked at the piece, walking around it. "You see this type of thing outside buildings and you never really look at it let alone think of the person who built it."

"That's for sure. I have my work in several major cities in the U.S. and all over the UK. And who really gives a shit?"

I was wrong. We went to lunch with Craig Southerland and all he did was talk about my work. It was embarrassing as we were there to discuss Dawn's career. He did, however, take her on as a client.

When we got home there was a message from Chuck's daughter in Colorado.

"This doesn't sound good," I said as I dialed the number.

I got the news that Chuck had suffered a massive heart attack and had died that morning.

Chapter 34

THE BUSINESS I INHERITED FROM Chuck continued to prosper in the years following his passing. I had built a first-class team of employees at the plant and I could leave at any time, either on business or pleasure, knowing that the company would run without me.

Dawn's career progressed in the hands of Craig Southerland. Along with the successes she still had a few disappointments and failures, like the time she had a small part in a major movie only to have it end up on the cutting room floor instead of in the final version that went on general release.

One thing that troubled me was with each setback, Dawn turned to drink.

"I have a low tolerance for drinking," I told her one day. "Not because I'm being self-righteous but because of my father and my upbringing. It's just a huge turnoff for me."

It was 1986 and my daughter Alison, now twenty, was to be married that year to her fiancé, Dean, who was twenty-one. I felt this was much too young but was not about to interfere with her plans. To do so would drive a wedge between us.

When the time came for the wedding, Dawn was working so I went back to Sheffield alone. My mother and sister were there. My mother was now in her eighties and very frail. She complained to me about my father; he was still abusive toward her, not physically but verbally abusive.

"For God's sake, why don't you leave him?" I asked her.

I talked to my sister about it and she said she had offered to have my mother live with her.

"Who would look after your father if I left?" my mother said when I talked to her again.

"I will pay for him to go into a retirement home," I told her.

What is it with her generation? Love, devotion, stubbornness, or codependency? Or do they take the vow, "For better or worse seriously and stick with one mistake"? Unlike our generation who make the same mistakes over and over with different partners.

Brand new girlfriend, same ol' fight,
Brand new heartache, same ol' sleepless night.
Same ol' problems running through my brain,
Same ol' same ol' same.

Same hard time she puts me through,
Just won't see my point of view.
It's the same old heat from a different flame,
Same ol' same ol' same.

Same ol', same old déja vu,
Isn't this the scene I just went through
With another girl with a different name?
Apart from that, nothing's changed.
It's like some bad recurring dream,
Same ol' movie on the same ol' screen,
Here comes the part where I get blamed,
Same ol' same ol' same.

At Julie's house I looked at the fireplace I designed back in 1970. It had been so chic when I built it, the height of fashion. But now it looked horribly outdated.

"What the hell was I thinking of when I built that?" I commented to Julie. "Why don't you get rid of it?"

"How can I? It's part of the building."

"You could build over it with brick or stone."

"I've been wanting to do that for years but was afraid I would offend you."

I put my arm around her shoulder and gave her a hug. "You're a sweetheart to still care about my feelings."

"Are you happy, Eddie?"

"You know that's a damn good question and one I ask myself often. I still love California, I have a beautiful home, a beautiful wife, and the business is doing well, but there's something missing."

There was an awkward silence.

"What do you think of Dean the bridegroom?" I asked, changing the subject.

"He's a good boy, a steelworker like my dad."

Dean reminded me too much of myself at that age for me to care for him. But I was not about to tell Julie or Alison.

The wedding was at a local church and Alison looked so beautiful as I led her down the aisle. I was amazed at how much she looked like Julie when we first met. After the wedding a reception was held at the same Steelworkers Union Hall Julie and I had used for our wedding.

The next day I took the train down to London and went to see my old friends Danny and Harry.

"I'm playing again, even writing a few songs," I told them.

Guitars were brought out for an impromptu session.

"I can tell you've been playing; you're getting your chops back," Harry said.

"We play down at a local pub this weekend. Why don't you join us?"

I called the airline and switched my flight to Monday, then I called Dawn. She was not home so I left a message. Danny and Harry went over my new songs with me. I wrote down the chord progressions for them to follow. They brought in a bass player; a young black guy named Dennis. We played at the pub on Saturday evening. There was a mixed crowd of people of all ages.

We started to play and I stepped up to the microphone to sing. I heard my voice coming through the monitor speakers. It was like I had never been away; it was the most natural thing in the world. I reached the chorus and Harry stepped up to sing harmony. He grinned at me. I could tell he was having fun also. Some young couples got up to dance. We finished the song and went straight into the next.

Halfway through the evening, my throat hurt and my voice was shot—I was not used to this. Harry sang a few songs to give me a break. We did songs from the old days that we had forgotten earlier and so had not rehearsed. But we got through and I surprised myself by remembering the words.

After the show I talked with Danny and Harry. "I've decided, this is what I want to do. When I get back I'm going to knuckle down and write more songs and get out and play them. Maybe even get a band together."

"I'd like to record an album of your songs," Harry said.

"When I have enough quality songs to fill an album, I'll take you up on that."

On the night flight back to Los Angeles I had a hard time sleeping. I was still pumped up from playing again and my head was filled with plans for the future. I reclined the seat and closed my eyes. I thought of the wedding and how beautiful Alison had looked. I thought of Julie. When she had dropped me off at the train station in Sheffield a few days earlier, it had made me think of the time I left for the United States, her and Alison crying on the platform. I started to write a song in my head.

I'm lying here listening to a train,
Movin' slowly along a distant track,
My mind goes back in time, you're standin' at the station,
When did I decide I was never coming back?

A train of thought takes me back to you,
On a single-track wheels turn in my head.
The train runs right on time each night as I lie here and go over
The broken ties and the lines I left unsaid.

There was a time when we were both in love,
At some point we took different lines,
But you became the mother of our baby,
That's why you're still here in the quiet times.

A train of thought takes me back to you,
On a single-track wheels turn in my head.
The train runs right on time each night as I lie here and go over
The broken ties and the lines I left unsaid.

When I got to LAX, Dawn was not there to meet me. I was concerned because she had not returned my call after I left the message the previous week. I had called from Heathrow before I left and got the answering machine once more. I tried again and reached my own recorded voice. I placed a call to the factory and had someone drive over to pick me up. I arrived home, unlocked the door, and saw a note standing by the phone. It was short, to the point, and pretty hostile.

"Fuck you, Eddie, I'm leaving. Don't try to find me."

I set my travel case down, closed the door and walked into the bedroom. Dawn's closet was empty. I walked through to the garage; the Porsche was gone. I lifted the lid of the trash can and saw several empty liquor bottles. Back in the living room I fell back into the center of the sofa and spread my arms out along its low back. I thought about the situation. A feeling of relief came over me; I didn't have to deal with her drinking anymore.

I went to get my guitar, I was anxious to play the new song I had written on the plane. I opened the case; the guitar was in two pieces, the neck broken off just above the body.

"Damn, she didn't have to do that."

In the days that followed I bought another guitar, and I bought an old 1975 Ford pickup in good running order. I had decided to do this even before I found myself car-less. I intended to go out and play music and I wanted people to accept me for the quality of my songs, not because I drove a Porsche. I had a Lincoln company car that I could use for business trips. As I had done before when there had been a drastic change in my life, I buried myself in my work, and this time in my music.

Late one evening some six weeks later, I had just gone to bed when I got a call from the North Hollywood police. Dawn had been in an accident. She was not hurt but the Porsche was damaged. She was charged with driving under the influence of alcohol. After giving me the details of the amount of bail and the location where she was, the officer asked, "Do you want to talk to her?"

"Yes, put her on."

"Hello, Eddie." She was crying. "I'm sorry, I screwed up."

"Well that's a bleedin' understatement."

"Can you come and bail me out?"

"It's after eleven o'clock, it'll be almost 1 A.M. by the time I get up there."

"Oh please, Eddie, don't leave me here all night. It's awful, you don't know what it's like."

I knew all too well what it was like. "I can't do it. I have clients flying in from Seattle tomorrow morning. The earliest I can get there is tomorrow afternoon."

"Please, Eddie, please."

"I'm sorry, I can't do it. Not tonight."

I hung up the phone. I sat on the edge of the bed and thought about what she was going through right now. I thought about the time when I found myself in a police cell and had no one to turn to. I mumbled to myself, "What the hell, I'm wide awake now and I probably won't sleep."

I stood and reached for my clothes. "Goddamn it, Dawn, what did I do to deserve this?"

The company car was at the factory so I got in my old pickup truck and drove to North Hollywood. Traffic was fairly heavy as it is in LA anytime of the day or night. I rolled down the windows and let the cool evening air blow in my face. I could hear the tires on the road; they seemed to beat out a steady rhythm that sounded like per-dum, per-dum, per-dum. Before long I had a tune in my head.

If you're leavin' in the morning don't wake me if I'm sleeping,
Tiptoe softly 'cross the room, and close the door.
Let your car roll down the driveway before you start the engine,
I've lost enough sleep over you; I ain't losin' any more.

So goodbye my love, I wish you well, (Per-dum, per-dum)
I hope you find what you're lookin' for. (Per-dum, per-dum)
I hope you find happiness, wherever it may be
But when you leave, (Per-dum, per-dum) don't slam the door.

If you're leavin' use the back door,
the screen door at the front's inclined to squeak,
Be careful not to wake up the sleeping dog next door.
If you need to call somebody use the pay phone down the street.
I've lost enough sleep over you; I ain't losin' any more.

At the North Hollywood Police Station I spoke with the officer on duty. He went to get Dawn. When she saw me she ran to throw her arms around my neck.

"Eddie, you changed your mind. Thank you."

I was still pretty mad at her and was not in the mood to show a lot of affection. But at the same time I didn't feel I should push her away. I patted her lightly on the back and said, "Let's finish up this paperwork and get out of here."

In the parking lot outside, Dawn asked, "Whose truck is this?"

"It's mine, it's what I'm driving by choice. I'm through with the fancy cars. When the Porsche is fixed I'm selling it."

She did not respond and I added, "The way I see it, you won't be driving for a while anyway."

"I know you're mad at me and I don't blame you."

"Of course, I'm mad at you. What do you expect? You took my car, you broke my guitar, and you left me a note that implied I could go fuck myself. Do you expect me to welcome you back with open arms? I want a divorce; you can stay until we get this mess sorted out. But at some point I want you out of my life."

"I'm sorry about the guitar."

"That was pretty juvenile."

"I know. I got mad at you. I was so looking forward to your coming home; I was going to cook you a special meal. I was out grocery shopping when you called. I came home with all this stuff and got your message that you weren't coming until Monday. I just lost it. After I broke your guitar I felt bad so I left."

I said nothing in response. She had turned things around and somehow I now felt I was partly to blame. She continued. "I've been a fool; I've been miserable since I left and I've been drinking nonstop to hide the pain. I know I need help and I'm going to get it. Please give me another chance. I'll make it up to you, I promise."

"Let's talk about it tomorrow; all I want now is to get home and get some sleep."

The next afternoon we drove back to North Hollywood to get Dawn's clothes. She had been staying with an actress friend of hers. While I was there I made arrangements for the Porsche to be repaired. On the way home we talked.

"All right, let's give it another try," I said, "but if I see any signs of drinking again or I find liquor in the house, it's over. I just can't handle it."

I hired the best attorney I could for Dawn's trial. His services did not come cheap but he did get her probation along with a heavy fine. He was also able to get a concession that she could drive to and from work.

After the trial she told me, "I'm going to pay you back every penny that you've spent."

I believed she would; we had always had separate bank accounts and kept our respective earnings apart. She went right back to work; I didn't sell the Porsche but let her use it for the commute to LA. She worked long hours and I was often gone in the evenings.

I was starting to play music in the clubs and coffeehouses in LA and Orange County. I was meeting new people and making new friends. These were people like myself, musicians and songwriters. There were certain venues throughout Los Angeles and the surrounding area where I would always run into the same people. We were like a community of artists within this huge city. We were supportive of each other; we inspired and fed off each other.

Chapter 35

AS THE YEAR CAME TO a close I got a call from my sister Elizabeth to say my mother had died. She fell and broke her hip and her heart failed during the operation that followed. My sister asked if I would be coming over for the funeral. I asked what my father's reaction would be. If he was going to be hostile toward me, I felt it would best for everyone if I stayed away. As I put the phone down I thought to myself, "My mother has finally left my father."

Only a week before I had a conversation with a young girl who worked for me. She was in an abusive marriage and had tried to leave her husband but he followed her and continued the abuse. She was moving to somewhere in the Northwest—Washington or Oregon, I presumed, as she would not even tell me exactly where she was going. I got pen and paper and started to write a song. The story was about my young employee but the sentiments and the feelings I had were all for my mother.

> *She stands and she looks in the mirror*
> *At the dark circles under her eyes,*
> *After too many nights without sleeping*
> *She's finally realized*
> *That the man in her life won't ever change,*
> *His ways are written in stone,*
> *She can follow a road going nowhere*
> *Or she can start a new life of her own.*

She's leaving him,
She's packing up her things,
She had to use a little soap
To remove her wedding ring.
There's a mark on her finger
Where the ring used to be,
And she knows that it will fade
Long before the memory.

She knew the dreams her man had wouldn't happen,
They were just so much pie in the sky,
And he'd always blame her for his failures,
But she could never understand why.
I spite of all this she didn't hate him,
But she hated what she had become,
Just something to take all the anger he spilled
And soak it all up like a sponge.

She's leaving him,
She looks 'round the house once more,
She hears the taxi waiting,
She's walking out the door.
She's got a ticket for the Northwest,
She tries to block the fear,
So she thinks of where she's going,
They say it's nice this time of year.

In the spring Dawn gave me a large check for almost half of what I had spent on her trial. It made me feel good that she was working hard and seemed to be in control her drinking habit.

"I'm proud of you," I told her.

The following week she came home one evening very excited. "I've just been offered a part in an independent movie to be made for cable TV. I have a favor to ask you, though."

"What's that?" I asked

"They're on a very low budget and the producer wants to borrow your boat for a few days."

"Does your part in the movie depend on my lending them the boat?"

"No, but you would be doing them a big favor. They want to do some filming here in Newport Beach and then take the boat to San Diego for some shots down there."

"Yes, of course, I'm only too pleased to be able to help out."

The next day Dawn introduced me to the producer, Jason Lazaro; I was somewhat taken aback by his appearance. He was in his early thirties; he wore jeans and an old tee shirt. He was unshaven and had long greasy hair.

"He's probably some rich kid with nothing better to do," I told myself.

I agreed to lend him the boat providing he would insure it for the period he would be using it. He agreed and filming was to start the following week; Dawn would be in San Diego for a couple of days.

On the day of the shoot I said my goodbyes to Dawn and left for work. That evening the boat was gone as expected and I spent the evening playing my guitar.

Two days later I was at work in my office with two of my design staff, going over some plans, when three police cars pulled up outside.

"What the hell do they want?" I asked and walked out to the reception area to meet them. There were three uniformed officers and one dark-haired young man in a gray suit.

"We're looking for Eddie Conner." It was the gray suit who spoke.

"I'm Eddie Conner. What's the problem?"

The gray suit pulled a badge and ID from his pocket.

"I'm Tony Garcia with the DEA."

"And what can I do for the Drug Enforcement Agency?" I asked.

"We'd like to ask you a few questions."

"Why don't you come into my office."

Tony Garcia and the three policemen followed me through and I closed the door. Garcia held out a Polaroid photo.

"Do you recognize this?"

"Yes, it's my boat."

He held out another Polaroid.

"Do you recognize this man?"

"Yes that's Jason Lazaro; I lent him my boat. What's this all about?"

"I have a warrant for your arrest."

"For what?"

"For conspiracy to transport cocaine from Mexico to the USA."

He began to read me my rights and one of the uniformed officers asked me to place my hands on my desk and spread my legs. He patted me down then placed a handcuff on my right wrist.

"Now wait a minute," I protested. "I'll cooperate with you in any way I can; you do not need to handcuff me."

"I'm sorry, sir, but we do this for your safety and ours."

The officer pulled my hands behind my back and closed the cuff on my other wrist.

"Where are you taking me?" I asked.

"To the Long Beach Police Headquarters," Garcia said.

As I was led out through the outer office I spoke to one of my staff. "Call my attorney and tell him what's happened and have him come to the Long Beach Police Headquarters."

I was led outside and placed in the back of one of the police cars. I looked back as we drove off; it seemed my entire staff was standing staring through the window, no doubt in utter disbelief. I couldn't believe what was happening myself.

In the interview room at the police headquarters Tony Garcia took off his jacket, hung it on the back of his chair, and loosened his tie. He was a short muscular build, probably lifted weights. Obviously Hispanic, as his name suggested, but with no trace of an accent; second generation I guessed. He sat in a chair facing me across a table and asked, "What's your relationship with Jason Lazaro?"

"There is no relationship; I only met the man once."

"You only met him once and you let him use your boat?"

"I'll tell you what. Let's stop right now and wait until my attorney gets here."

"Why do you think you need an attorney if you have nothing to hide?"

"I am simply exercising my right to have an attorney."

Garcia left the room; another DEA officer in uniform took his place. I wanted to tell my story, protest my innocence. But my experience and common sense told me to say nothing. Anything I might say could be misunderstood or turned around and used against me.

It was over an hour later when Tony Garcia returned with an attorney I had not met before. He was a tall man, six feet four inches, about my own age, his dark hair showing a few strands of gray. He handed me a business card and introduced himself.

"I'm Evan Proudfoot. Your attorney Mr. Skerritt is out of town and his office called me to come down here to be with you. I came as soon as I could."

He turned to Tony Garcia. "Could I have a word with my client alone, please?"

The two officers left the room and closed the door. Evan Proudfoot spoke first. "Now fill me in with what's going on here."

I told the whole story as Evan took notes.

"What do you think?" I asked him as I finished.

"They have to prove conspiracy and I don't see much evidence apart from the fact that you loaned Lazaro the boat."

"Can you get me out of here?"

"I can't do much tonight. But you're due to be arraigned tomorrow morning, I'll push for bail then."

Later that night I lay on my cell bed and thought back to the last time I found myself in this position many years before.

What did I do wrong this time? I could think of nothing apart from taking Dawn back and giving her another chance. I had no idea she was involved with drugs. I remembered recently she often had a hard time sleeping and was up during the night but I had not connected this with drug use. I had only looked for signs of drinking.

The next morning at our hearing I appeared in court with Dawn and Jason Lazaro. Charged along with them were two other men I had not met before. I sat next to Evan Proudfoot, my attorney, and was separate from the others, who had their own attorney. Bail was set for Dawn and myself at 250,000 dollars each. The others were refused bail. I put up my own bail but declined to do the same for Dawn. She had deceived me once and I felt I could no longer trust her.

I arrived home to find that the DEA had searched my house. They had broken the lock on the front door and the house was a mess, after they had gone through everything. I called a locksmith and straightened the place up while I waited for him to come.

I put in a call to Dawn's agent Craig Southerland; I wanted to know more about this Jason Lazaro. Craig was out for the day so I made an appointment to see him the following day. The locksmith arrived and I had him change all the locks on the house.

I went to my business and called a meeting of my staff to explain to them what had happened. I also found the insurance document Lazaro had faxed me before he took the boat. It clearly stated that the boat was to be used for a film shoot. I called Evan Proudfoot and he asked that I come in and see him.

I arrived and he spoke to me in his office. "I've been thinking. Your wife has a public defender now. If you were to pay for her defense and our company handled it we might be able to work out some plea bargain deal for her."

"Why should I do that?" I asked.

"Part of that deal would be for all charges against you to be dropped."

"Would she stay where she is? I don't want her living with me."

"It might look better if you stood her bail. Make it look like you're trying to help her and not just yourself."

I thought it over for a moment. "I'll agree, if she goes into drug reha-bilitation."

"I'm sure she'll agree and rehab would look better to the DA."

"What the hell," I agreed. "It's only money and I'm past caring about that. Let's do it."

The next day I drove up to LA to see Craig Southerland. He told me he knew nothing of Jason Lazaro.

"I haven't seen Dawn in several months," he told me.

"She was working, I assumed it was for you."

I went on to tell him the whole story and of the position I now found myself in. He listened then said, "I heard through the grapevine that Dawn was working in a strip club in the San Fernando Valley."

"I wish you had told me."

"It was not my place to interfere; besides it was only hearsay."

"You're right. I should have called you about this Jason Lazaro but I trusted Dawn and I was anxious to help her out."

"I'm sorry about this; if there's anything I can do...," he said as we shook hands and parted.

A few days later I received a letter from Dawn. She admitted she had been working as a stripper and said she did it so she could pay me back the money she owed me. She also gave this as the reason she got in-volved with Lazaro. I did not respond to the letter.

I had to mortgage the house to make the bail payments and to pay the attorney fees. I decided to sell the house. I was tired of the lifestyle. If I didn't go to jail, I decided to simplify my life. Why did I need all these material things?

I put the Porsche up for sale and advertised my furniture in the clas-sified section of the local paper. I called a meeting of my top employees and asked if they would be interested in buying into my business and running it as a cooperative venture, sharing the ownership. They agreed and I had my business attorney draw up a contract. They would pay me a lump sum every six months; I would keep controlling interest in the busi-ness and would draw a modest salary. This would be an income I could live on.

The case dragged on; months passed and I finally got a call from Evan Proudfoot. The district attorney was ready to talk. I met with Evan and we drove in his car to the meeting. Dawn was there with her attor-ney. On the other side were the district attorney and Tony Garcia. The DA spoke to Dawn first.

"If you will agree to be a witness for the prosecution and will plead guilty to a lesser charge of being an accessory, we will recommend that you receive a sentence of no more than two years. You'll be out in less than a year."

Dawn's attorney spoke. "My client will agree to that providing all charges against her husband are dropped."

"We agree, but we may call on Mr. Conner as a witness."

I agreed and as we stood to leave, Tony Garcia said, "We are going to confiscate your boat."

I was about to protest but looked at Evan Proudfoot. He clamped his lips tight and shook his head as if to say, "Don't push your luck."

Outside I asked him, "Can they take my boat?"

"Yes, they can take boats, houses, cars if they have been used during a crime. They have dropped charges against you but this is their way of saying they still think you're guilty."

"So just like in England, you can't beat Old Bill."

"I'm sorry, I don't understand."

"Forget it. I was just thinking out loud."

"We can fight it later but quite honestly it might be cheaper to wait 'til the boat comes up for auction and buy it back."

"Fuck it. I'm not going to pay money to buy my own boat back to turn around and sell it again."

I lay in my bed that night thinking over the events of the past year. It had been a nightmare but now it was over.

"I am so lucky," I told myself. I could so easily have gone back to jail for a very long time.

From now on I would be careful who I associated with and I would stay away from relationships for a while. I wanted to work full-time on my music; to hone in on the craft of songwriting.

Chapter 36

IT WAS 1991. I WAS driving across the California desert in my old Ford pickup truck heading toward Flagstaff, Arizona. More than three years had passed since the trial of Dawn and the others. Dawn was given a two-year sentence, she had since been released but I had not heard from her. Jason Lazaro and his cohorts each got a fifteen-year sentence.

Dawn and I were divorced; I had sold my house in Newport Beach and my business. I had some money in the bank, my old truck, and a few other personal belongings. I was debt free and I was doing what I wanted to do, play my music. After selling my house I had moved in with some musician friends in LA but found too many distractions to engage in serious songwriting. I had some good songs but I wanted to write more.

I needed to be alone for a while, and what better place to do that than the desert? I had once stopped off in Flagstaff after a trip to the Grand Canyon and was attracted to this smaller high-desert town. Situated in the mountains to the north, it was a little cooler than southern Arizona.

I arrived in Flagstaff by late afternoon and checked into the first low-price motel I came across. The following day I scanned the rental ads in the local paper. I found one that interested me and went to check it out. It was an old trailer home on the outskirts of town, down a dirt road back from the main road. There was not another house within half a mile. I could play music without fear of disturbing anyone. I decided to take it.

The trailer despite being old was dry and spotless. It was sparsely furnished but had all I would need. There was a bed with a clean mattress. In the kitchen was a refrigerator, a table with two chairs, and a few utensils. The living room had an old sofa and a coffee table. There was no TV and I had decided I would do without that for a while. There was a working swamp cooler on the roof to keep the trailer cool when the weather got hot.

I had a phone installed and one of the first things I did was call my daughter Alison. I had always made a point of calling her at least once a month. This time I sensed there was something wrong. "Are you crying?" I asked.

"Daddy, it's Dean. We had a big fight and he walked out and I don't know if he's coming back."

It tore me apart to hear her cry. I wished I could be there to hold her and make the hurt go away. But there were six thousand miles between us. I tried to reassure her as best I could. I hung up the phone and thought back to the time I left when she was ten years old. The memory ripped the scab from an old wound I thought had healed long ago. I blamed myself for the problems Alison was having now. If I had just stayed until she was a little older maybe things might have been different.

I remember the first time I held you,
A little baby new to the world,
A love without end began way back then
Between a daddy and his little girl.
I remember the time I left you
And you were only ten years old.
How you clung to me as we said our goodbyes,
Your tears like a knife turned in my soul.

Take all of the pain and the heartaches,
There's one that cuts me deep inside,
And will always bring me down to my knees
When I hear my little girl cry.

Time has passed and now we're older,
We've been there for each other through the years,
Marriages ended, lovers passed on by,
We shared the good times and the tears.
The miles there are between us
Disappear with a telephone call,
But if I hear you cry and I'm not there to hold you,
It's the toughest call of them all.

Take all of the pain and the heartaches,
There's one that cuts me deep inside,
And will always bring me down to my knees
When I hear my little girl cry.

I've loved others but you're the only one
I can say I will love until the end,
But I would give anything if I could create
A world in which you'd never cry again.

Take all of the pain and the heartaches,
There's one that cuts me deep inside,
And will always bring me down to my knees
When I hear my little girl cry.

I settled into my new home. I spent my days and evenings playing guitar, writing new songs, and rewriting old ones. I found a little bar in town called Moon Doggie's. They had live music and on Tuesday evening there was an open mike. Open mikes are great for trying out new songs and getting to meet the local musicians. I went there the following Tuesday.

There were not many participants on this particular evening so I got to play for over an hour. There was a small but appreciative crowd and after my set I went to sit at the bar. The man behind the bar was an old hippie in his fifties, with long hair pulled back in a ponytail and a full-length untrimmed beard. He was a tall man with an ample beer belly.

"Hi, I'm Jay. I'm the owner," he introduced himself.

"Eddie Conner. I've just moved here from LA."

"I moved here from the Bay Area twelve years ago. What'll you have?"

I ordered a beer and as I reached for my wallet Jay said. "That's okay. This is on me. You sounded good up there."

I thanked him and took a drink. He continued. "You're not originally from LA?"

"Well, who is? No, I'm English."

"Would you like to play here next Friday? We have the tourist season coming up and I like to have live music as often as I can."

"I would love to. In fact, that's why I came here—to play music."

"I can't pay you much. But you can play for tips and I'll give you free food and beer."

"It's a deal. I'd rather play here than sit at home and play to myself."

I became a regular performer at Moon Doggie's and Jay, always on the lookout for publicity for his bar, contacted the local newspaper. A young female reporter spoke to me one evening during a break in one of my shows. She took notes and also took some photos during my second set. A good length article appeared in the paper that weekend, and the following week there was a noticeable increase in the size of the audience. During the break and at the end of the evening I spoke with people who mentioned they had read the article.

There was one person in particular who stood out from the rest. He was an older man with shoulder-length gray hair and was unmistakably Native American. His features were craggy; deep lines were etched into the dark skin of his face. Apart from that and his gray hair he looked remarkably fit and muscular; his posture was straight and erect. He wore jeans and a heavy, checkered flannel shirt. Around his neck were several black leather thongs, some threaded with turquoise and silver beads. He approached me at the end of the evening as I packed up my equipment.

"Hi, my name is Tom Waters."

I shook his hand. "Eddie Conner, thank you for coming."

"I read the article in the paper. I understand you're English."

"Yes, that's right."

"I was in England during the war."

"Where in England?"

"I don't know exactly; they wouldn't tell us for security reasons."

I stopped what I was doing and told him, "I met a young Native American during the war when I was a child. His name was Running Horse."

He stood for a moment staring at me intently, then said, "Tell me what you remember of him."

"Well, I remember he was Navajo Indian. He was twenty years old. He would be in his sixties now. Would you know him by any chance?"

"Well, I'm Navajo Indian."

"Let me finish packing here. I want to talk some more. Can I buy you a beer?"

"I have a beer at my table over there. Can I get you one?"

"That's okay, my beer is free."

I called to Jay at the bar to pour me one, finished my packing, and joined Tom Waters at his table. He spoke first. "Tell me about the time you first met Running Horse."

"I remember it well. He was sitting under a tree carving an eagle from a piece of wood."

"Go on."

"We used to go fishing. He was just a wonderful friend and things he told me are with me to this day."

"Did he ever meet your parents?"

"Yes, my mother and my father, who, I'm sorry to say, beat him up."

"I want to show you something." He pulled a small black leather pouch that was hanging around his neck out from under his shirt.

"Do you know what this is?" he asked.

"Yes, it's a medicine bag."

"How much do you know about the medicine bag?"

"Not very much, I'm afraid; I've seen them for sale in the gift shops."

"A person puts inside the bag any item or number of items he chooses. It may be a stone or an animal bone for example. The medicine bag protects the wearer from illness and danger."

He began to open the bag. "Normally, you never show anyone what you have in the bag, but I have good reason to show you."

The dry leather began to tear and crumble as he opened it. "I need a new one; I've had this one for so many years."

"Are you sure you want to do this?" I asked.

"Yes. Do you remember this?"

He placed a small object on the table in front of me. I stared at it for about five seconds then picked it up. It was the lead toy I had given Running Horse all those years ago. I didn't believe it at first but there were the rider's legs either side of the horse where the rider had broken off. The paint that was once on it had worn away over the years and it was now plain gray lead. But there was no mistake this was the same item.

"Where—where did you get this?" I stammered.

"You gave it to me."

"I—but you're not Running Horse."

"Yes, I am. Running Horse was a nickname. When I joined the army during basic training I could run faster and further than anyone in my unit so they called me Running Horse. The name stuck; my real name is Tom Waters."

I reached out to shake his hand, then held his right hand with both mine. We were both grinning from ear to ear but at the same time choking back the tears.

"I remembered your name," he told me, "so when I read in the paper about an 'Eddie Conner from England' I just had to come down here and check it out."

"I'm so glad you did. You had such a profound influence on my life. I have been an artist, a painter, and a sculptor; and now I'm a songwriter. You once told me about the Spirit of Creation being inside me. That has always been the source of my creativity."

"I'm glad to have been an influence on your life but let me tell you this, you saved my life."

"How?" I asked.

"With this little lead horse." He picked it up and held it between his thumb and forefinger then placed it in his shirt pocket.

"The army took away my medicine bag and said I could only wear dog tags. On the night before the Normandy invasion we were all pretty scared. I took the little horse, wrapped it in a piece of rag, and hung it around my neck with a piece of string. This was my medicine bag. I prayed to the Great Spirit for protection."

Tom took a drink of his beer then continued. "One time in northern France a German shell landed right in the middle of a group of us. A man standing next to me was killed, as were three others, and four more were seriously wounded. Apart from being blown off my feet I was unhurt."

"That's amazing. You believe your escape was due to your medicine bag?"

"Well, I was the only one in the group uninjured and the only one wearing a medicine bag."

I called Jay over and shared with him the details of this amazing reunion.

"It's a small world," was all he could find to say.

I turned to Tom. "A small world, indeed. I have thought of you so many times over the years. Wondering if you survived the war and where you were now. But when I came to this town it did not occur to me that you might be in this area."

Jay indicated that he wanted to close for the night and Tom helped carry my equipment to my truck.

"Can we meet again? " I asked him. "I have so much I want to talk about."

"Are you free tomorrow morning? How about we meet for breakfast?"

We decided to meet at ten at a restaurant just down the street.

Chapter 37

THE FOLLOWING MORNING AS I pulled into the restaurant parking lot, I saw Tom sitting in a brown Chevy truck. I parked next to him and he got out to meet me. We shook hands and I followed him inside. We were seated in a booth next to a window; a waitress brought us coffee.

"Where do you live?" I asked Tom.

"About sixty miles east on Navajo Reservation land. I stayed here in town last night."

"I had no idea you came so far. Are you married?"

"My wife died five years ago. I have two sons; one is married, the other lives with me."

"Do you work?"

"I still do wood carving, believe it or not. That was what I was doing the first time we met. You will see some of my work in the gift shops around town."

"Do you still make eagles?" I asked.

"Oh, yes, I've made a lot of eagles over the years."

"I made eagles out of steel at one time, some eighteen-feet high. They were all inspired by you."

A waitress came and we ordered breakfast.

"What made you come to Flagstaff?" Tom asked.

"I came here to be alone and work on my music. I just went through a divorce, and I'm at a point where I wonder where my life is going. Why am I not as happy as I could be? And what can I do to change that?"

"What are your spiritual beliefs?"

"That's part of the problem, I don't have any. As a child I went to church and I believed in God, but as a child you tend to believe whatever adults tell you. When I became an adult it seemed to me I needed a 'tooth fairy' mentality to continue with that belief."

"I presume you are talking about the Christian church."

"Yes, but are any of the other religions any better? I look at all the turmoil and unrest in the world, people killing each other in the name of religion. I look at the poverty, disease, and suffering in third-world countries where religion has its stronghold. Religion has failed the people."

"I agree. The problem I see with most religions is that they took a human, a man like you and I, and elevated him to God-like status."

"You mean Jesus, Buddha, and Mohammed?"

"Exactly. They can say they were born by immaculate conception or some other wonderful story but to a free-thinking person they were human and they walked this earth in the same way as you and I do. By placing so much emphasis on this human they have elevated to God, they lose sight of the real God."

"And who or what is the real God?"

"God is not a person or a thing; God is the Spirit that permeates the whole universe, everything we see, smell, taste, or touch, including you and me, is Spirit. The Great Spirit."

The waitress came with the food and Tom was quiet as we ate. The things he told me as a child had always had an influence on my life and here he was again giving answers to questions I had struggled with for years. Not only giving answers but raising more questions.

We finished eating and Tom said, "There is a special place I go to when I want to be alone and think over things. I'd like to show it to you if you have the time."

"Sure. I have no special plans for today. Where is this place?"

"It's about ten miles south of here."

We left the restaurant and I followed Tom in his truck for about ten miles, as he had indicated, then he left the main road and took a dirt road west. This bumpy trail slowed us down and we seemed to drive on forever. We finally stopped on a hill overlooking a valley. The first thing I noticed after I got out of the truck was the silence.

"It's so quiet here," I remarked. I noticed we were talking in whispers.

"There are certain places that are sacred to the Navajo people; this is one of them. I always come here if I want to be close to my God. The Great Spirit is everywhere, of course, and we are always connected but sometimes the distractions of everyday living are too much, so I come here."

"It certainly is a beautiful place," I said.

"Yes, it is hard to have a negative thought in an environment like this. But did you ever see anything in nature that is not beautiful? This is why when you create, if you connect with the Spirit you cannot help but create something good."

"So the Spirit of Creation that you told me about as a child, this is God?"

"Of course. Tell me, why did you believe in the Spirit of Creation and not God? Why did you not realize they were one and the same?"

"Because whenever I went deep inside myself to create something the result was always something good and wonderful. What I created was the proof that this Spirit existed. But a Spirit or God that answers prayers or looks out for me as an individual, I find hard to believe."

"Do you believe in the power of positive thought?"

"Yes, most people who are moderately successful do."

"What is a prayer but a positive thought?"

"I'd never thought of it that way."

"How do you think a positive thought works?"

"I suppose if you put a thought in your head then the subconscious causes you to do all the right things to make it happen."

"But sometimes a positive thought will cause other people to do the right thing. How do you think your thought can affect another?"

"I don't know. Telepathy?"

"What if this Spirit is intelligence? Let's say a universal Intelligence. And what if this intelligence is our intelligence? Then a thought we put out there maybe is picked up by another."

"Yes, I have experienced thinking of someone and the phone will ring and it will be this person calling me. Or I'll be talking to someone about a third person and the third person shows up. This is so common we have the saying, 'Speak of the devil and he's sure to appear.'"

"There is intelligence all around us in nature. The swallow and the salmon returning to the place of their birth. How do they do it?"

"Instinct," I suggested.

"Instinct makes them want to return, but what actually guides them on their journey? Not their tiny bird or fish brain, but some other intelligence."

"I've often wondered about that. We have a brain, which is an organ, and we have a mind. Where is the mind? Is it part of the brain or is it separate?"

"Why not consider that the mind is a universal mind we all use. If I misplace something I always tell myself the universal mind knows where it is. And I go on quietly looking and find the item I was looking for."

"The positive thought again."

"It only works if you believe it will. This is where the faith comes in. It is not a blind faith of believing everything you read or are told but as you experience things you know it is the truth."

"Exactly, I believed in the Spirit of Creation because I experienced it."

"Thoughts are like seeds; whatever kind of seed you plant determines what will grow. Negative thoughts or a fear of something will bring to you the very thing you fear."

"So you are saying I don't have to belong to a religion or go to church to find God?"

"My relationship with God or the Great Spirit is personal, my own business. Between It and myself. If others find God through religion and that suits them, it is their business. Let's face it, God is still there whether we believe or not. Let me ask you this, what if humankind along with all the religions were to disappear from the face of the earth? Become extinct. Would God disappear also?"

I thought about that but did not give an immediate answer, so Tom continued. "Of course not. The sun would still rise in the east and set in the west. The rain would still fall and plants would grow. Animals would still live and flourish. In time, the cities humankind had built would decay and crumble. The desert would revert to desert and forest back to forest. The salmon would still swim upstream to spawn. The same Intelligence running things now would continue to run things."

"I have always felt that life and the universe are too complex to exist without some Higher Power running the whole show. But my problem has always been how to contact this Higher Power."

"Go within yourself to the same place you found your creativity. You know where that is, so you're halfway there. Do you remember the story of the prodigal son in the Bible?"

"Yes, I do."

"When the prodigal son returned and was nearing his father's home, his father came out to meet him. If you look inside yourself for the Spirit then the Spirit will come to meet you and show Itself."

"Did you have a Christian upbringing?" I asked Tom.

"No, I am basically a Shaman, but I do not ignore the words of the great teachers. I think it is a tragedy that these words have been turned around by religion sometimes to suit their own ends. Simple teachings have been turned into a mystery. The truth is we can learn from any source if we just keep an open mind."

"How do I sort out the truth from the bullshit?" I asked.

"I think you should come out here alone. Spend several days if necessary and think on the things we have touched on today. A word of warning, though, don't think too much. Intellectualizing about these things will get you nowhere; in fact, it will block you. Just sit quietly and go deep inside."

"As much as wanting to find God I want to find myself. I often wonder, who am I?"

"Some go in search of God and find themselves. Others search for themselves and find God. You can't find one without finding the other; the two are connected. Like looking for an apple tree and on finding it you discover the fruit. Or you look for the apple and then discover the tree it grows on. You cannot find one without discovering the other."

Tom pointed further down the trail we were on. "If you follow this trail around the hill you see up ahead, there's a mountain stream with the purest water you've ever tasted. Bring some dry food and hang out down there for a few days."

I followed Tom back to the main road and before we went our separate ways, we exchanged phone numbers.

Driving back to Flagstaff I thought over the things we had talked about. I looked at my watch; it was close to five o'clock. I had spent the entire day with Tom. Suddenly I remembered I was out of cash and needed to get to the bank.

"Damn, the bank closes at five and I'm going to hit rush-hour traffic in town. I'll never make it," I mumbled to myself. Then I thought, "That's negative thinking, don't do that. I'll get there on time."

I drove into Flagstaff and the streets were deserted, there wasn't a car in sight.

"What the hell's going on?" I muttered. "Have I got my days screwed up, is it Sunday?"

I reached the bank and I could see people inside; it was open. As I pulled into the parking lot I leaned forward and looked up at the sky and said, "Thank you, God. I just needed to get to the bank on time. You didn't have to clear the whole fucking town."

I parked the truck and as I got out I noticed the normal heavy rush-hour traffic on the street I had just been on.

The power of positive thinking.

Chapter 38

THE NEXT DAY I DROVE back along the desert trail Tom had shown me. This time as I left the paved road I made a note of the mileage on my odometer. I drove past the spot where we had stopped the day before and followed the trail until I found the mountain stream Tom had mentioned.

I stopped, turned off the engine, and checked the odometer; I was twelve miles from the main road. I stepped from the truck and the first thing I noticed again was the silence. Then as my ears adjusted I realized there was the constant sound of water running over the red rock. I looked around; the whole landscape was red—red rock and red dirt. Sparse bushes grew here and there along with a few stunted trees and cactus.

To the right of the trail was a hill rising several hundred feet. A gradual slope, easy walking, then near the top the rocks more vertical, and finally flat on top. In the distance ahead, huge vertical rocks rose from the desert floor like cathedrals.

I took a pen and notepad from my truck along with a jug of water, walked a short distance, and found a shade tree to sit under. I looked out at the desert and thought over the events of the day before, particularly driving into Flagstaff at five o'clock to find the town deserted. I asked myself, "How could this happen? In any good size town in the USA at 5 P.M. there's going to be traffic as people leave work, go shopping, and take care of other business."

I looked for an explanation.

Didn't Einstein say that time was an illusion? Maybe traffic was moving along as normal but in my mind I pushed the time back. My positive thought cleared the streets for me at that moment because a few minutes later when I got to the bank, traffic was flowing as normal. Was this the

Father coming to meet the prodigal son as Tom had suggested? How much control do I have over my life? Probably more than I realized.

I thought about my childhood, how, in spite of the problems caused by my father and schoolteachers, I was happy then. Especially when I was alone as I was now, alone with nature. I started to write on my notepad.

I used to lie in the long grass
And watch the world go by,
As a child my world was happy
Only people made me cry.
And if the sun had never set
I wouldn't have gone home,
The moments I remember
Were the times I spent alone.

And I owned castles in the sky
And horses that could fly,
They'd take me there on golden wings
To a place where no one cried.
I go back there for a while
And always know that I'll
Be welcome there,
A Prodigal Child.

When I grew up they told me
There were no castles in the sky,
And I should not imagine things,
It was wrong to tell a lie.
If I worked and studied hard,
Climbed the ladder of success,
Then money and its power
Would ensure my happiness.

So busy counting what I'd made
I didn't count the cost,
And things I thought I needed
Weren't missed when they were lost.

With all the knowledge I had gained,
After all the things I did,
I realized I had it all
When I was just a kid.

And I owned castles in the sky
And horses that could fly,
They'd take me there on golden wings
To a place where no one cried.
I go back there for a while
And always know that I'll
Be welcome there,
A Prodigal Child.

I realized the reason I was happy as a child was that I lived in the moment. As a child I didn't think more than ten minutes into the past or future. I told myself I should do more of that and if time is an illusion as I believe it is, then the only thing I can be sure of is the moment. The past is only a memory and no matter how bad or good the past was it is never going to change. So why even dwell on it, other than to learn from it?

Likewise with the future, it is only imagined and to imagine a bad future is to think negatively. So from now on I will only think of good things for the future and if the future turns out any differently, I will deal with it at that time.

That night I slept in my truck bed. I had brought a sleeping bag and some blankets with me. I also had a tarpaulin to cover the truck should it rain but this particular evening was clear. I lay on my back looking at the millions of stars that are not visible in the city because of the lights.

I began to reason. There are millions of stars and perhaps millions of galaxies but only one universe. It has no outer limits; it is Infinity. There can only be one Supreme Being or God that created this universe so therefore that Being is Infinity. You can't have more than one Infinity therefore there can only be one God. But if God created the universe, who or what created God?

God is Infinity; therefore, not only is there no outer limit but also no beginning or end. So God was not created because God is infinite with no beginning or end. This is exactly why Tom told me not to think too much. With our concept of time, of birth and death, we cannot intellectualize or imagine something with no beginning or end.

My thoughts were broken by the sound of a coyote calling to its mate. Such things do not trouble the coyote, all he's concerned with is his next meal. Maybe I should learn from him. Just write and sing my songs and live my life the best I can. Spend less time worrying what life is all about and concentrate more on living a good life.

I remembered as a young man in Wandsworth Prison thinking on these things and writing a nonsense song about it. It had always stayed with me. "Maybe it is none of my business," I mumbled to myself. "The coyote doesn't make it his business."

I lay listening to the soothing sound of water running over the rocks. Somewhere between my thoughts I fell asleep.

In the morning I awoke very hungry. I had brought with me cereal, nuts, some apples and oranges, and chocolate. I had a bowl and spoon but no cooking utensils. I could only stay one more day as I was playing at Moon Doggie's that night. I figured I could do without coffee for one morning.

I poured some cereal in the bowl and moistened it with water. It was bland but fruit made it palatable. I washed the bowl and spoon in the stream and also washed my face. For some unknown reason I felt depressed.

"For Christ's sake, snap out of it," I told myself. "Maybe I should have brought coffee."

I sat on the tailgate of my truck and started to cry for no apparent reason. I tried to suppress it a first but then decided to let it out. It was like all the grief I had felt throughout my entire life was coming to the surface. I cried for my brother Alan who had died in the war. I cried over the ending of my first marriage and for my daughter Alison. I cried for the mother I had lost and the father I never found.

I cried like a child, I wailed, I sobbed, my shoulders heaving. I don't know how long I cried, maybe half an hour. It seemed a long time. When I was through I got up and washed my face in the stream again. I went back to the truck for a towel and stood with my head buried in it for a moment wondering what the hell had just happened.

As I pulled the towel away from my face something caught my eye on the hillside ahead of me. It was a large white animal. At first I thought it was a large dog but as I watched it run I could see it was a cat. It had a long tail and it moved like a cat. It was a cougar, but strangely it was pure white. It was about three hundred yards away. I started to walk toward it; I wanted a closer look.

The cougar looked up and saw me coming; it started up the hill away from me. Not at any great speed but with a steady loping, undulating gait that is typical of a cat. Zigzagging between the rocks and scrub and every so often stopping to look back at me. It was as if it was waiting for me; I broke into a run.

Up ahead near the top of the hill the rocks were vertical and impossible to climb without equipment. But the cougar picked its way between the rocks to a place where the slope was gradual. It bounded from rock to rock climbing what seemed to be a natural staircase and disappeared over the top of the hill.

I followed and at the top of the trail was a large bush. I hesitated before going around it; for the first time I was afraid. This was a large wild animal I was dealing with. I wanted to get a closer look but not too close, and now it was on the other side of this bush but I did not know exactly where.

For a moment I thought I heard the sound of running feet. Then silence. I crept slowly around the bush; there was no sign of the cougar. The hill was perfectly flat on top. This had once been the desert floor maybe millions of years ago, before the wind carved away the soft soil around this rock leaving it standing as a hill. A few more million years and the gradual slope of the hillside I had just climbed would be gone leaving only the vertical rock.

I was no longer looking for the cougar; I stood and marveled at the scene around me. I could see 360 degrees and as I turned I saw desert in every direction as far as my eyes could see. The beauty of it took my breath away. I could not see one thing that was not natural, nothing created by humankind. Even my truck was out of sight below the rim of the flat-top hill. I told myself, "This is the Spirit of Creation in action. The Divine Mind Manifest."

I was seeing clearly for the first time, as clearly as I could see this beautiful desert landscape stretched out before me. I could understand the relationship between myself and Spirit. The Divine Mind, being the creative agency in the universe, finds in each individual a new and fresh starting point for Its action.

Every action, word, or thought I initiate affects someone somewhere at some time. This is why it is so important that I choose the right action, the right words, and good positive thoughts at all times. I could never understand why a loving God would place humankind on this earth and then deem that we suffer.

I now realized any suffering I may endure is brought on either by myself or some other person's wrong action, word, or thought. From now on, when I look at my environment and see things that are not desirable, I will try not to think of them as conditions fate has imposed on me. But I will recognize them as the orderly procession of the law of cause-and-effect moving in logical sequence to definite form.

My own thoughts in ignorance had bound me. That which bound me had now set me free.

I looked around the area I had parked, making sure I was leaving everything as I had found it. I climbed in my truck and started the engine. I looked back toward the hill and thought about the white cougar.

Did I really see that or did I imagine it?

I drove home and the first thing I did was call Tom Waters. He answered on the third ring. "Hi, this is Eddie."

"How are you, my friend?"

"I went to that place you showed me and I saw a white cougar. Is there such an animal? It was pure white."

"Maybe it was your Spirit Guide."

"Why do you say that?"

"Because the Native American believes that when a man reaches a certain age he is guided by a bird or animal to a place where he finds his true self."

"That's exactly what it was but did I really see it or did I imagine it?"

"What do any of us really see?"

"That's true. Some people see space ships and little green men. They can't all be crazy."

I put the phone down and it rang again immediately. It was my sister Elizabeth calling from England.

"Eddie, Dad had a massive stroke and he died in the hospital last night."

"I'm sorry to hear that. What time did he die?"

"It's morning here now, about six hours ago, I would say. Would you like to come to the funeral?"

"Would he want me there?"

"Probably not."

"Then I'll respect his wishes and stay away. But I would like to help out with the funeral expenses."

I put the phone down and realized he had died about the same moment I sat in the desert that morning and cried. At the time I thought it was for no reason; now there was a reason.

Chapter 39

I HAD BEEN IN FLAGSTAFF over two years. I was playing regularly at Moon Doggie's and also at some of the local hotels during the tourist season. I bought a small four-track recording machine to record my songs. I spent a lot of time recording, playing back the tapes, reworking, and fine-tuning. I called my friend Harry Christmas in London one evening.

"Harry, it's Eddie. Remember one time you said you would like to do an album of my songs. Does that offer still stand?"

"Of course, I'd be delighted."

"I've got a whole bunch of new songs and I've rewritten a lot of the old ones. I've got 'em all down on tape, I'd like you to have a listen."

"Yes, send them to me."

"How are we going to do this? Obviously, I need to come over there at some point."

There was silence for a moment as Harry thought over the logistics. "Tell yer what, send me the tapes along with the lyric sheets and chord progressions. I'll put down a scratch vocal track that we can later replace with your voice. That way I can record the whole thing and all you have to do is fly over and do the vocals at the end. Unless you want to be here to give input during the recording."

"No, I trust you, Harry. I'd like you to produce the whole thing."

"Good, then send the tapes. We're very busy, but I want to do this."

The next day I packaged the tapes and mailed them to England. A little over a week later the phone rang, it was Harry.

"Fantastic, Eddie, fan-fuckin'-tastic. That's all I can say. Here I've laid down some tracks already, listen."

The sound of a guitar, unmistakably Harry's style, came over the phone, followed by Harry's voice singing the lyrics so familiar to me.

"What do you think?" Harry asked as he faded out the tape.

"Sounds like you nailed it. I don't see as I even need to come over there."

"Of course you do, these are your songs. No one can sing them like you."

"Hey, I'm joking. I can't wait."

"I'll tell ya what, Eddie, I'm pumped and so is Danny. Here he wants to talk to you."

Danny came on the line and filled me in with the latest news. He told me, "We're getting a lot of work. We've been around a few years now and we've got a good reputation. Even the big record companies are sending work our way."

"Well, there's no rush on this project of mine."

"Are you kidding? I can't wait to get working on it. I'm getting tired of all this electronic, synthesized stuff the kids are doing now."

"So, what's your time frame?" I asked.

"Well, I can book you in for a week in eight weeks' time, if that will fit in with your plans."

"Suits me. Does that give you enough time?"

"We'll have the most of it done and if it's not finished we can lay down some more tracks later."

"Okay, I've marked it on my calendar. I'll go ahead and book a flight."

About six weeks later I got a package in the mail. It was a preliminary tape of all the songs. I listened to it; Danny and Harry had done a fine job. It had exceeded my expectations and this was not even the finished recording. I placed a call to the London studio; Harry answered.

"The more I get into this project the more I think we really have something," he told me. "I think we could pitch this to a major label. Would you be interested in staying here for a while and going on tour to promote the album?"

"Of course. I would love to do that."

"It would just be a little tour around the clubs and pubs. You know, try and get something going."

"Can you and Danny get away from the studio to go on tour? I thought you were busy."

"We are. I can come but Danny would have to stay here, but we know several other good drummers. We can put a band together, no problem."

"Would it just be a four-piece like the old days?"

"Probably, keep the cost down—you know, tour in a van."

"I can front the expenses for the tour, I've still got money coming in," I told him.

"The other thing we need you to do is come up with a name for the CD."

"I've already done that. *Prodigal Child*. That song will be the title track."

"I was thinking that would be a great name for the band."

"You're absolutely right, it sounds great. *Prodigal Child* can be the name of the band and the CD."

Two weeks later I flew out of Phoenix on an overnight flight for London. I was so excited I had a hard time sleeping the night before. But this was good because I was exhausted and slept almost the entire flight.

Harry met me at London's Heathrow Airport and as we drove to the studio we talked about promotion of the album.

"The way I see it," he said, "if we can create a buzz about this album and we can prove that there is an interest in it, it will be easier to pitch to one of the majors."

"What's your plan?" I asked.

"Start out in London. Danny and I already play most weekends, so we'll continue to do that with you fronting the band under the new name. We know a lot of venues all over London that would be happy to let us play."

It was always exciting for me to come back to London, even though I loved America and now considered it my home. I was taking in the sights around me but at the same time thinking about what Harry was telling me..

"I have some ideas too," I told him. "Newspapers will always give you coverage if there is a story in it. I have sculptures that I made in the late sixties and early seventies in various locations in London and the rest of the UK. I can see having my picture taken alongside some of these works and a story about leaving the UK as a sculptor and returning a songwriter."

"That's good and then there's the story of how you were on the way up before the Beatles and the Stones even got started. To me that's even more interesting."

"I'd rather stay quiet about that era," I told him.

"Why?" Harry glanced across at me, a puzzled look on his face.

"Remember I went to jail for wounding someone? He's probably still out there and maybe he's a bleedin' vegetable because of what I did to him."

"That wasn't all your fault."

"Maybe not, but I'm still not proud of it. I can see the press getting hold of that story and having a field day."

"You could be right. The press does love to build people up and then knock them down again."

We arrived at the studio; Danny was waiting for us. We went for lunch and continued our conversation about the project ahead of us. After lunch we went straight back to the studio and by the end of that day I had three vocal tracks completed.

"Your voice is better than it's ever been," Harry commented.

Danny agreed. In recent years I had been singing and performing every day; my voice was in great shape. By the end of that week the recording was complete. Danny and Harry did the final mix and the masters were sent out for production of the CDs.

We started playing weekends and some weeknights in all areas of London. Harry always played with us but Danny sometimes had to work at the studio and a substitute drummer would sit in. We talked continually about our upcoming album. During the day I went out on photo shoots. I had pictures taken in the old East End neighborhood I grew up in. I had others taken with the large steel sculptures I had made in the years before I left for the United States.

The CD came out and we had release parties in every venue we played at. We sold it at a bargain price so everyone attending could go home with a copy. We would sometimes move a hundred to two hundred CDs a night. When our sales were in the thousands, I approached one of the London evening newspapers and showed them the pictures of myself with the sculptures.

They ran a story with the headline "The Prodigal's Return." One of the newspaper's syndicated Sunday papers also ran with the story, which gave us national coverage. I wrote to the BBC, sent them a copy of the album and the newspaper articles. I followed up with a phone call. I mentioned that they had once filmed a piece about my sculptures in Sheffield back in the late sixties. I asked if they might still have this in their archives. I got a call back asking me to come in for a meeting.

At the BBC headquarters I was shown into an office. A young man in his early thirties greeted me. "Hello, I'm David Price. I'm one of the program directors here."

We shook hands and he invited me to sit. He told me, "I did as you suggested and looked in our archives for the video you mentioned. In recent years we computerized all our records and when we punched in your name another old black-and-white film from 1960 came up."

He went over to a VCR and put in a videotape. On the TV screen came images I had not seen before. It was the show we did at the Shepherd's Bush Empire the night I was arrested.

"This is you, right?" he asked.

I couldn't deny it. We were doing some of the songs that were on our new album. "Yes, the drummer and lead guitar are the same two who are with me now on the new album."

"Why did you not mention this?"

"I didn't know this tape existed."

"What I can't understand is why you were never discovered back then?"

"I guess we were ahead of our time."

I was looking for answers I could give without letting out the fact that I went to jail right after that show. "Are the people who produced this film still around?" I asked.

"No they've all retired long ago. Was this ever shown on TV?"

"Not to my knowledge, this is the first time I've seen it. The band broke up soon after this."

"That's a damn shame; you had so much talent. But you still do." David turned off the VCR and went back behind his desk.

"Here's what we would like to do. The BBC no longer owns the Shepherd's Bush Empire but we could talk to the current owners and see if you could play there again."

"What do you have in mind?" I asked.

"We want to do a one-hour special. We would show you performing at the Empire, cut between the old black and white and the new. Especially where you're singing the same song, that would be interesting. We would also feature interviews with you and show the sculptures you did in the late 1960s. What do you think?"

"I'm overwhelmed, but yes, I would be very interested."

I left the BBC in a daze and went back to meet with Danny and Harry. "I've got some not so good news and some very good news," I told them both. "The not so good news is they know about the old band we had in 1960." I told them about the old black-and-white video of the show at the Empire.

"And what's the good news?" Harry asked.

"They want to do a one-hour special on TV." I filled them in on the details of the proposed show at the Shepherd's Bush Empire.

"That great, Eddie. You deserve it," Danny said.

"So do you," I said. "We're going to get our moment of glory after all."

Harry spoke. "If we're gonna play at the Empire we need a bigger band. You know, a horn section and back-up singers, the lot."

"That's right," Danny agreed. "We should make this the start of a nationwide tour."

"You were concerned that it might come out about your being in prison. How do you feel now?" Harry asked.

"I'm going to think positive and not worry about it," I told him.

That same day Danny was on the phone calling musicians he knew, setting up auditions for the band.

That evening I called my daughter Alison in Sheffield. She told me she and her husband had parted. I was not surprised, I had known her marriage was in trouble. I suggested, "Why don't you come down here to spend a few weeks with me? When we start our tour we will be going to Sheffield at some point, so you can go home then."

"Daddy, that would be wonderful."

"I can put you to work. There is a lot to be done with organizing the tour and promotion."

About a week later I picked Alison up at the train station. I took her straight to the studio where we were about to start rehearsals with the new expanded band. We had put together a horn section made up of a trumpet, tenor sax, and trombone. We also had a keyboard player and there were two female backup singers who had performed on the album. One of the girls had sung two separate parts on the recording, something we could not repeat live. We needed a third singer.

"Can you sing?" Harry asked Alison as we walked into the studio.

"Who, me?" she responded in surprise.

"Yes, why don't you give it a try? You may have inherited yer dad's vocal chords." Harry told her.

"Go stand with the other girls; they'll show you what to do."

The rehearsal went well. We had the master tapes from the album, so we could isolate the various tracks for each player to learn. Harry did so with the female harmony tracks and made a separate tape for Alison to learn her part. She had a sweet-sounding voice, not too powerful but she could hold a tune. She seemed to enjoy what she was doing and it kept her mind off her marital problems.

We finally brought in a percussionist in addition to the drummer, making the full band twelve people. At some of the venues we played we could not fit that many people onto the small stage area and often had to do without the luxury of the percussionist. At more than one gig we played with the horn section standing precariously on a trestle table alongside the stage. The reception of the big band was good everywhere we played and sales of the CD increased.

During the day I went to the BBC Studios to record the interview that would be part of the special. We also went out on the street to film and talk about some of the large sculptures that were not far from the BBC

Headquarters. I talked about how I viewed all art forms to be the same. How a painting or sculpture could have rhythm and melody and a piece of music could have texture and form.

I went with David Price from the BBC to meet with the owners of the Shepherd's Bush Empire. They were anxious to accommodate us, as the TV broadcast would be good publicity for them. We would have to do the show early in the week on a Monday or Tuesday, as all other dates were booked. But as the BBC were paying for the venue I suggested giving away free tickets to ensure a capacity crowd.

We decided to distribute the free tickets through the London record stores. This encouraged them to stock our CD and brought the customers in to get the free tickets. We also advertised on radio, playing excerpts from the album in the ad, and gave free tickets to listeners who called in. This also got the radio station to play our CD and talk about the upcoming concert.

I was starting to get some income from sales of the CD, which was a good thing. My bank account was running low after all the money I had put out for this venture. But I was not too concerned; every detail was falling into place without a hitch.

Chapter 40

THE DAY OF THE CONCERT finally came. I was excited but not nervous. Danny and Harry had put together a band of fine musicians. We had rehearsed and had been playing together for a number of weeks. We were ready. We arrived at the Empire that afternoon to set up and do a sound check. We walked in the front of the building and through the auditorium to the stage area. The place had hardly changed since I was last there in 1960.

The BBC camera crew was already there, setting up their own equipment. A man with a hand-held camera followed us around backstage; this would be part of the final program. We started the long process of a sound check. First the drums, then the other individual instruments. Finally the vocal mikes for myself and the back-up singers. We played together and went through about four songs as the sound engineer made the final adjustments. The camera crew asked that we keep playing so they could check and adjust their equipment.

The sound check completed, it was back home to relax and get something to eat before getting ready for the big evening ahead. We arrived back at the Empire about an hour and a half before show time. There was already a small crowd waiting outside. The tickets were free but the best seats were on a first-come basis. I stopped to talk to the people waiting before entering the theater, thanking them for coming.

Just before the show started I peeked out through the stage curtains. The house was packed. We took our positions onstage and David Price stepped between the curtains to get the show started. He explained briefly what the BBC was doing and told the audience they were part of the show. He explained the cameras needed to move in front of the stage. He encouraged the audience to move forward toward the stage but to give way to the cameras as needed.

Then I heard him say, "Please welcome Prodigal Child."

There was applause as the curtains opened. I turned and nodded to Danny and his drumbeat started the first number. The horn section came in with the intro and I stepped up to the mike to sing. The lights were left on in the auditorium because the cameras were also filming the audience. I enjoyed this because I could see the faces and felt I could connect with the people. During the instrumental break I turned and looked back at Alison standing off to one side between the other two girl singers. I gave her a wink and a smile; she smiled back.

We finished the first song to thunderous applause and before it died I counted in the next number. During the long intro I walked over to Harry and spoke directly into his ear.

"Can you believe this is happening?" I asked him.

He smiled and shook his head. "No."

I moved back to the mike to sing the first verse.

The first set went off without a hitch and we took a short break. We filed off the stage and someone handed me a large glass of water.

"Great job, Eddie. Fantastic."

It was David Price who spoke. I told him, "With this band, anyone would sound good."

I made a point of speaking with all the band members to thank them for a great performance. I spoke with Alison.

"Daddy, I've never had so much fun," she said. "Thank you for letting me be a part of this. I'm so proud of you."

"I'm proud of you too, sweetheart," I told her.

About halfway through the second set I did the song that I had written for Alison "When I Hear My Little Girl Cry." Harry had given it an unusual, almost a reggae-type arrangement I really liked. I sang the first two verses and the chorus. The song went into an instrumental break. I looked over at Alison and I saw her wipe the corner of her eye. A lump came in my throat and as I stepped back to the mike, I lost it. With tears streaming down my cheeks I sang,

> *I've loved others but you're the only one*
> *I can say I will love until the end,*
> *But I would give anything if I could create*
> *A world in which you'd never cry again.*
>
> *Take all of the pain and the heartaches,*
> *There's one that cuts me deep inside,*

And will always bring me down to my knees
When I hear my little girl cry.

The audience was standing right up to the edge of the stage and I could see some of them were crying with me. I finished the song to great applause and I went along the edge of the stage touching the hands of those reaching up to me. I went back to the mike and told the audience, "I'm very proud to have my little girl here onstage with me."

I turned and beckoned to Alison to come down and join me. As she did so I introduced her. "My little girl, my daughter Alison."

We both took a bow at the front of the stage. I gave her a hug and a kiss and she went back to take her place. I took the opportunity to introduce the rest of the band. We finished the final set and during the last song I spoke to Harry again.

"I keep looking in the wings to see if Old Bill's waiting for me."

He laughed and shook his head.

We finished the show and were called back for an encore. We finished up with an impromptu rendition of Chuck Berry's "Johnny B. Goode" that turned into a wild fifteen-minute jam.

After the show David Price thanked me. I shook his hand and thanked him back. He told me that the show would be on television in about a month.

That month would turn out to be nonstop work. We wanted to start our tour right after the BBC show aired. Arranging the tour meant every day there were phone calls and meetings to attend. Danny, Harry, and I would often go off in different directions to various parts of the country, looking at venues and talking with owners and managers.

We talked to Virgin Records and asked the if they would distribute our album. We knew there would be a big demand for the CD after the TV show aired. We would supply the CDs they would distribute. If the album really took off I knew I would not have enough money to produce the quantities needed. But I also knew if the album did take off Virgin would want to pick it up anyway.

The tour was all set and we relaxed a little and waited for the TV special. The show aired prime time on a Saturday night. The whole band attended a party at Danny's house to watch. It started out with some shots of East End streets with kids playing and a voice-over saying:

"In 1960 before the Beatles, before the Rolling Stones, there was another young singer-songwriter named Eddie Conner who grew up on these streets and had a dream he would one day make it. For whatever reason, Eddie did not make it. Maybe he was ahead of his time, but as this old film from the BBC archives shows he and his band certainly had talent. This footage from 1960 has never been shown until now."

The old black-and-white film came on. Danny commented, "We *were* ahead of our time. Look at the way Eddie and Harry move about the stage. Bands didn't do that until the late 1960s."

The commentary continued. "Eddie Conner disappeared from the music scene to reemerge as a painter and a sculptor in the late 1960s. Samples of his work can still be seen in cities throughout the United Kingdom, including several here in London."

Images on screen were of the late 1960s news clip, this time in color with me being interviewed and showing the giant eagle sculpture and some of my paintings. Other shots were the ones I had recently done with interviews and pictures of myself with the London sculptures.

The program went on to tell the story of my emigrating to America in the mid-seventies and my eventual return to my first love, music, as well as my return home, the reforming of the band, and a new CD. The last part of the show was mostly from the new concert at the Shepherd's Bush Empire. The commentary at the end of the show was "Eddie Conner has an ability to reach out and touch his audience."

Film from the 1960 show of my final song standing alone with an acoustic guitar after the band had left the stage. My tearful performance with the camera panning in on some of the audience clearly crying with me. Not knowing, as I did, that the police were waiting for me in the wings. Following this, the image switched to the new show and an almost repeat performance during the song I had written for Alison, "When I Hear My Little Girl Cry."

"If that doesn't bring the people out to our shows, I don't know what will," I commented as the hour-long special closed. Everyone agreed and we were proved right when we started our nationwide tour the following week. At the first few shows there were reports of ticket sales being slow before the broadcast. But the day after the show aired there was a rush to buy tickets as people realized we were coming to their town.

The tour was like a journey through my past. The first stop north was Luton where the incident at the butcher's shop had led to my arrest. Then Bedford where I went to prison for the first time. From there it was on to Northampton, Leicester, and Nottingham, where I had last seen Trisha. I wondered if she had seen the TV show. Next stop Sheffield, where I had once lived. Alison's mother Julie would be in the audience.

Our album was getting air play and "When I Hear My Little Girl Cry" was the song everyone was talking about. We switched our set list to make this the final song each night. After which I would introduce Alison and the rest of the band. In two weeks "When I Hear My Little Girl Cry" reached number one on the British charts.

From Sheffield we traveled north to Leeds, the next big city. It was here after the show that one of my road crew came to me. "Eddie, there's a man outside who is insisting that he see you. I would have blown him off but he says if you can't see him at least call him."

My crewman handed me a note. There was a name and a phone number. I looked at it. "Andy Strickland. Why is that name familiar to me? Yes, I'll see him."

A few minutes later I met with a man about my own age, I guessed. I didn't recognize him.

"Have we met? I know your name from somewhere," I told him as I shook his hand.

"You went to prison for wounding me back in 1960."

"Andrew Strickland. Of course. I've wondered about you so many times and whether you suffered permanent damage."

"That's why I had to talk to you. I was never hurt as bad as was made out. I put on an act and it's been on my conscience ever since."

"Why did you do that? Did the police put you up to it?"

"No and I bore you no malice. If you can understand, I was seventeen at the time and up until that point I felt that my parents especially my father hated me. When I went into hospital and they thought I was seriously hurt they showered me with all kinds of love and affection. I milked it for all it was worth. I'm so sorry." He was genuinely shaken.

I suggested, "Here, let's go sit down." I led him to a dressing room and after offering him a chair asked, "So, at the Old Bailey trial you were not brain damaged?"

"I had a small skull fracture and a broken leg, but no, I was not brain damaged."

There was a moment's silence then he continued. "I put on an act of a slow recovery during which time my father would take me for walks in the wheelchair. We became close and have remained close ever since, the only good thing to come out of all this. But when I was in my twenties I went to prison myself and I realized what I had done to you."

I told him, "I can relate to your relationship with your father and believe me, if I could have faked brain damage when I was seventeen to get my father's love, I might have done the same."

"Can you forgive me?"

"Of course. The past is dead and gone and there's nothing we can do to change it. We can only move forward. Do you have a family?"

"Yes I have a wife and two sons."

"I trust you're a good father."

"I try my best." He stood and held out his hand. As we shook on it he told me, "Eddie, thank you for being so gracious about this. I've lived with this guilt for so many years and when I saw the show on television I felt I just had to see you."

"I'm glad you did. Could you do me one favor? I've been worried lately that the press might get hold of the old story about the trial. If they do, would you be prepared to set the record straight?"

"Of course, it's the least I could do."

I made a note of his address and I walked with him back to the door that led to the auditorium. We shook hands again and parted.

Later over dinner I told Danny and Harry of my meeting with Andy Strickland.

"You're amazing, Eddie, I would have wanted to kill him," Danny said after hearing the story.

"No, can't you see the good that came out of this? A father and son have a good relationship. As for me, have I really suffered? I have a very good life. Out of the seemingly bad things of life, some good comes to someone, somewhere."

"I admire you, Eddie. After all the misfortune and trouble you went through earlier in your life it hasn't affected you. What's your secret?"

"First of all I wouldn't say what happened did not affect me. I believe it made me stronger. To get your shit together it sometimes helps if you've spent some time standing in it. It all boils down to living by two simple rules. One, don't do anything to hurt anyone either by thought, word, or deed. And two, be responsible for your own happiness. If everyone lived by these simple rules, what a wonderful world this would be."

"You got that right," Danny said. "Especially the part about being responsible for your own happiness."

"I would go so far as to say that the greatest achievement a person can attain is his or her own happiness," I told them.

There was another two weeks of touring as we reached the far north of England, then returned south on the west side of the country. Then finally, along the south coast back to London. On our return, Virgin Records contacted us to say our album had gone platinum and we were now getting air play in America. My song "Trav'lin' Light" was being played on country stations as well as some soft rock stations. We had a rare crossover hit. We went for a meeting with the record company and talked about doing a U.S. tour. I arranged for meetings in New York with Virgin Records America.

Later that week I got a call from a Kevin Robinson with *Rolling Stone* magazine; he wanted to interview me. I told him I would be coming to New York and as soon as my flight and hotel were booked I would get back to him.

I spent the rest of the week relaxing and hanging out with Danny, Harry, and my daughter. In a quiet moment Alison told me, "I love you, Daddy."

I smiled. She was now a beautiful young woman in her twenties, and she still called me "Daddy." I guess she would always be my little girl.

When it was time to leave my two friends and Alison accompanied me to the airport.

"I'll see you all soon," I told them.

On the flight to New York I reflected on the past weeks and how everything had fallen into place. It was almost as if a script had been written. Then I realized, there was a script written. I wrote it with my positive thoughts.

> *Sometimes on life's highway I'd take a different turn*
> *And along with every detour was a lesson to be learned.*
> *The unknown road I travel on is of my own creation*
> *And the journey means more to me than my destination.*
>
> *There's a small change in perception between Heaven and Hell,*
> *I've found a God that I can trust, the one within myself.*
> *And if Jesus wears Levi's I know this much is true,*
> *He buttons up those 501s the same way that I do.*

I thought over my upcoming interview for *Rolling Stone* magazine. I decided there was no use talking about my career as a sculptor; I had only a few samples of my work in the States and they were mostly on the West Coast.

I wondered if I should come clean about my going to prison in 1960. There was no reason not to, now that Andrew Strickland had contacted me.

I arrived at Kennedy Airport and stood in line for the immigration check. At the counter I handed over my passport and green card. The agent checked his computer screen. "Mr. Conner, did you know the California Immigration and Naturalization Service have been looking for you?"

"No, I did not. For what?"

"It appears they wanted to talk to you about some drug charges brought against you and when they went to your house you had moved."

"The police dropped all charges, and yes I moved to Arizona, but I did give the post office a forwarding address and the phone company forwarded my calls. A simple letter or phone call would have found me."

He pressed a button on the edge of his desk and another agent came over and led me to an interview room. I had to go over the exact same story that I had just told the agent at the desk. The second agent looked at my green card.

"I see you were issued this card back in 1971. Who sponsored you?"

"Chuck Pollard."

"Is he still around?"

"No, he's deceased."

"Are you married to a U.S. citizen?"

"I was, but I divorced."

"I see." He stood and left the room. Another uniformed officer stayed with me. I tried to grasp what was happening to me.

"Just think positively; it will be all right," I told myself.

The agent returned about thirty minutes later and handed me my green card.

"All right, Mr. Conner, you're free to go. But you need to contact your local INS office within thirty days."

I went to get my bags and then took a cab to my hotel. I had a meeting scheduled for the *Rolling Stone* interview. I looked at the time as I checked in. I thought to myself, "Damn, now I'm going to be late." I took the elevator up to my room. Inside I set my bags down and thought about the interview.

Now what should I say? I didn't want to be talking about a previous criminal record for publication in *Rolling Stone* with this INS thing hanging over my head.

There was a knock at the door; I went to open it. A young man with reddish hair stood there.

"Hi, Mr. Conner, I'm Kevin Robinson. We spoke on the phone; it's nice to meet you."

I shook his hand and stepped back to allow him to enter. He asked, "How was your flight from London?"

Give the Gift of
Prodigal Child
to Your Friends and Colleagues

ORDER ONLINE AT **www.ProdigalChild.net**
OR FROM YOUR LEADING BOOKSTORE

❑ **YES**, I want _____ copies of *Prodigal Child* at $23.95 each, plus $4.95 shipping per book (South Carolina residents please add $1.44 sales tax per book). Canadian orders must be accompanied by a postal money order in U.S. funds. Allow 15 days for delivery.

❑ **YES**, I am interested in having E. David Moulton speak or give a seminar to my company, association, school, or organization. Please send information.

My check or money order for $_____ is enclosed.

Please charge my   ❑ Visa   ❑ MasterCard

Name _____

Organization _____

Address _____

City/State/Zip _____

Phone_____ E-mail _____

Card # _____

Exp. Date_____ Signature _____

Please make your check payable and return to:
Moomin Books
PO Box 81084
Charleston, SC 29416-1084

Call your credit card order to: (Toll Free) **866-488-3776**